From David
August 24th 1966.

# The Face of a Madonna

The Yorkshire in which Thomas Armstrong set *The Crowthers of Bankdam* and its sequels, *Pilling Always Pays* and *Sue Crowther's Marriage*, is the Yorkshire of steam and smoke, of mines and warehouses, of ports and mill-towns that came into existence nearly two hundred years ago. In this book he tells of another Yorkshire, further removed in time but still, as she has always been, the greatest of English counties. In the late middle ages her wealth and importance were attested by the number of abbeys— Fountains, Rievaulx, Kirkstall, Whitby and many more— whose ruins still enchant the eye and touch the imagination.

Ughtred, a monk of Rievaulx, who is a painter of rare quality, and Lazelle, a nun of the priory of Watton, thrown together by an accident of travel, discover a strong mutual attraction and sympathy. Both are repelled by the world-liness of their superiors and the harsh and narrow character of monastic discipline. Their very strength of character and honesty of mind make them, against every influence and every instinct, receptive to the Lollard teachings that are circulating everywhere in fifteenth-century England. Their defiance of the power of the Church leads after many unexpected turns to the dramatic scene with which the book opens.

Thomas Armstrong paints the high middle ages with the same colour and zest that he brings to his novels of modern life. In this strong and exciting novel the gay, glittering, corrupt and frightening world of the fifteenth century becomes as real to us as it was to Ughtred and Lazelle.

# The Face of a Madonna

*by*

THOMAS
ARMSTRONG

*Collins*
ST JAMES'S PLACE, LONDON
1964

# *The Immurement*

Within minutes, Ughtred of Monkseaton, a monk of the abbey of Rievaulx, and Lazelle, a former nun of the Double Order of Saint Gilbert at the priory of Watton, jointly convicted of heresy and condemned to death, would be walled into a prison cell when still alive.

Drawn up in front of the cell were contingents of the religious from the two convents: hooded monks of Rievaulx, canons regular of Watton, and, of the same house also, closely veiled nuns.

The court's amended sentence was being carried out in the cloister garth of an abandoned foundation belonging to the Abbot and Chapter of Rievaulx. At first thought destined to be a small daughter house, the property had been built in the exact form of a monastery, but in miniature; perhaps even then, so far back, the pioneer enthusiasm of the Cistercians for colonising was flagging, for the monks chosen for the task had not been at Riggs for many years when they started to report anxiously that the situation, high in the midst of barren moors and more immediately surrounded by the dense forest on the lower slopes of the valley, had been ill-selected. From then the little monastery of Riggs had declined: it became an out-grange managed by paid servants, to which monks sickly in mind from the monotony of the cloister might be sent for a change of scene, or monks who had erred could ponder over sins and omissions while pacing the narrow confines of their prison quarters in the western range of the quadrangle.

Finally, however, when the Chapter of Rievaulx had become wholly disillusioned about a possession which steadily drained resources—when wearied of replacing stock that had prematurely died, when patience had been lost about despatching grain to a place which should have contributed to *their* revenue—withdrawal was decided on.

7

Voices were seldom heard at this deserted spot nowadays. The abbey's shepherds, bringing their vast flocks down in snow-time, would use it occasionally as a refuge; and the community's post-messengers and rent-collectors would sometimes lay there overnight when the remaining miles homeward were too hazardous in darkness and bad weather. For these reasons a small stock of food was stored there and hay for foddering was always in the barn.

On this September day of solemn gathering the outlook everywhere could not have been more delightful, as clusters of fleecy white clouds sailed slowly across a blue sky. Nevertheless attention was concentrated exclusively on the monk Ughtred and the nun Lazelle, who were known to have had carnal associations within this very place, though it was not for this unforgivable offence, ecclesiastically-speaking only, that they were now to die.

The young man and the young woman, if in full health, might have made a most attractive pair, the one good-looking, with a sensitive face, his companion possibly quite lovely. But her eyes, as his, were inflamed; their cheeks feverishly flushed, their gait unsteady. A sheriff's man supported each of them as, in the final stage of their last earthly walk, they passed along the ranks of white-habited Cistercians and Gilbertines clad in black-and-white.

The prioress of Watton was standing near the refectory doorway. A leader of fashion, her cheeks were liberally whitened, and beneath her cloak could be glimpsed a wimple of saffron colour, not the official white upon which her Rule insisted. With her was the lord abbot of Rievaulx, a commanding figure in glittering mitre and embroidered vestments. His be-ringed hand rested on the jewelled crook of a staff only slightly less magnificent than the pastoral staff of his distinguished cousin.

She turned to him. " By the blood of Christ, I do not care for this," she said. " True, both seem too dazed to comprehend their fate, charitably plied with an abundant measure of potent liquor I have no doubt, but still it does not please me."

"Would you have it otherwise, Philippa, my sweet coz? " the abbot asked. " Grave as it may be for each of us to have harboured a Lollard in our respective communities, it would surely have been infinitely more serious could it have been held against us that we had failed to take the most vigorous steps to root out the putrid evil."

" Oh! I lack any regret on that score," Dame Philippa said decidedly. " Obviously the sternest example had to be made, but I would have preferred a sharper way."

" I suppose the original sentence would have been vastly quicker and certainly much more excruciating," Abbot Hugh mused. " However, the court in its clemency decided to vary it."

" You all changed your minds," the prioress remarked dryly, "because of the urgency of the representations of the archbishop and the lord abbot of Saint Mary's in York, and they clamoured for another course because of rising feeling. The populace everywhere is far from being happy about burning people for contrary religious opinions."

" Then I fail to understand your objection," the abbot said.

The Lady Philippa pointed to four masons in leather aprons who, the window of the death cell having been blocked earlier, were now standing by to seal the doorway. The mortar was already mixed, and an ample heap of freshly-cut stone had been prepared.

" If I have a sick hound or a hawk beyond hope I have 'em put down quickly," she said succinctly. " It would have been far better if that monkish painter of yours, and . . ." her lips thinned, " and that Devil-stiffened nun of mine had either been strangled in a dungeon or lost their heads to the axe."

The couple of whom she spoke were nearing the end of their slow progress, and their plight was even more sorry. The nun's head lolled, and her fellow victim, shivering convulsively, appeared to have lost his sight.

A monk sank to his knees before the abbot, and waited silently.

" As I live, they have hardly the bearing of martyrs prepared to die from scruples of conscience," Abbot Hugh was remarking when he noticed the prostrate figure. " Yes, my son? "

" My Lord, there is still a bell in the tower, and I have knotted together enough strands of rope."

The lord abbot nodded. " When I give the signal, my son."

The heretics, mercifully supported, had reached the door of the cell, close to which a tall Franciscan friar, with pointed hood, was standing. Now the last phase was here and the sheriff himself was turning towards the abbot, to notify him as the senior religious present. The friar, however, stayed him for a few moments, after which the sheriff nodded before crossing the garth to join the abbot and prioress, with whom he also had a short conversation. As a consequence all three went over to the doorway of the cell, so that the abbot could say a few words of benediction to the guilty couple before they passed forever from the sight of man.

In the event, this did not go off too well. Momentarily released by those holding them, the monk swayed forward against the prioress, whom he clutched, and the nun took a few erratic paces which left her with her forehead resting on the abbot's chest—none of which was to the liking of the two dignitaries, both of whom showed annoyance.

The proceedings were completed in a more seemly manner when—the Lollard sinners held upright again—the lord abbot gravely addressed them, a young man and young woman neither of whom was capable of comprehending that, despite their many wickednesses, it was the speaker's desire that they should pass in peace from the world of the living.

"*Vade in pace,*" Abbot Hugh said, his deep voice ringing in the garth. " And may God have mercy on you."

" *Vade in pace,*" the murmur arose. " God have mercy on you."

Immediately the condemned pair had been lodged in the cell, the masons began to work. The grey friar, beads of agonised sweat pinpointing his brow, prayed again for the salvation of two souls.

" Why have we a rapscallion friar here? " the prioress of Watton demanded. " By the spines of the crown of thorns, have not the mendicant Orders been for generations no better than the dregs of the towns? "

" It is but a small matter," the abbot said, shrugging. " I understand he volunteered to attend them when they awaited the stake in the city gaol, and I suppose he has made his way hither for the same purpose."

The passing bell began to sound, and after the first melancholy toll the cantor of the abbey of Rievaulx started to intone the Office of the Dead. It was taken up by nuns, canons regular, monks and, in parts, by as many of the sheriff's party as could remember them.

Steadily the courses of stone to block the doorway rose until the opening was filled almost to the lintel by walling two feet thick, as neat and secure a job as might be expected of skilled craftsmen working in front of an audience.

The massive seal was nearly completed when the Franciscan friar, his prayers abruptly ceasing, spoke urgently to the infirmarian of Rievaulx, an official high in the hierarchy of the monastery and well versed in physic. In response the infirmarian raised himself on tiptoe and stared into the gloom of the cell through the narrow gap remaining. When he turned his cheeks were ashen, and his lips perceptibly tremulous.

What he despairingly said in those first few moments was heard by all nearby; his frantic plea to the Almighty was sufficiently alarming to cause a mason to drop a trowelful of mortar on to the obedientiary's round-capped shoes, and caused others—men-at-arms, nuns, monks and canons—to quake. The solemn chanting ended, and only the regular peal of the bell continued.

Aware of the wave of unease, the abbot of Rievaulx frowningly watched the hurried and far from characteristic approach of the usually dignified infirmarian.

" What is it, my son? " he asked sharply.

The infirmarian had so far forgotten himself that he omitted to kneel.

" My Lord," he stuttered, " I have the most dire news. The . . . the condemned have all the signs of *Pestis Major*."

Appalled, his superior stared at him. " The Death! " he exclaimed. " Are you sure? "

The infirmarian's breathing was uneven. " The symptoms are identical with those familiar to me through my reading of the learned physicians, My Lord."

The prioress of Watton bit off a scream. " Dear God! " she gasped, " not the same terrible plague as the 'forty-nine? It was before my time but I know of the havoc it wrought."

The sheriff groaned. " Not more than one in two throughout the land was spared. They died as flies in a night of frost."

" That would be my diagnosis, My Lady," the infirmarian said miserably, wringing his hands. " We are in grievous plight."

" And they have been amongst us," the prioress wailed. " They have even touched some of us."

Panic was already widespread and the orderliness of the assembly was no more. Holy ladies dedicated to Jesus seemed indifferent to the disarray of their veils as, mixed in and amongst the men-at-arms, they backed from the western range of the cloister and soon formed part of a tightly-wedged crowd at the opposite side of the garth near the exit through the former chapter house.

The abbot licked lips suddenly dry, before speaking to the infirmarian. " The Death! " he repeated. " This is your business, my son, and you should be informed enough to advise us what is to be done."

The infirmarian made an effort. " My Lord," he admitted huskily, " I have no first-hand knowledge of these fearsome infections, and I suggest that a conference with the friar might not be unhelpful."

" With the friar! " the lord abbot said disdainfully. " Why so? "

" He has sojourned in the Levant and the Holy Land, and seen much of the plague, My Lord. More importantly, he has studied medicine and drugs at the famed University of Ravenna."

" Bring him," the Lady Philippa said, stamping her foot.

The gaunt, barefooted Franciscan was not at once helpful. His initial proposal was not well received—that as true Christians they might best serve their fellow creatures if, possibly sacrificing themselves as had the Son of Man, they limited the spread of any calamitous disease by remaining where they were.

" Why should we? " the abbot said harshly. " That is to invite contagion, and as yet it is by no means certain that we are impregnated."

The expression in the friar's deep-set eyes was unfathomable. " Or with precisely what, if anything," he observed. " Save that it may be the buboes called pestilential."

As though a lecturer before attentive students, he favoured them with a dissertation on the difference between bubonic and the oriental type of plague. Indifferent both to time and the harrowing effect of his observations, he also referred at length to *pestis indica*, which he explained, for the benefit of those who did not know, was to be found in India.

A senior canon of Watton, who had joined them, lost his nerve. " What is the difference to us, for all are fatal? " he shouted. " Is there any advantage in debating to which we have been exposed? "

The Franciscan rounded on him sternly. " In the interests of medicine and science it would be invaluable if an authentic and detailed study of what might follow could be recorded," he said. " The young man and the young woman in the cell—as you have witnessed, they are in a state of apathy. Will that turn into delirium? Will there be deep vomiting? When will the first onset of rigor be noticed? "

The Lady Philippa felt her forehead. " O dear God," she muttered.

" Take the tongue," the friar resumed relentlessly. " Was it initially furred with white, and will the white turn to darkish brown? Are there indications of a swelling of the tongue, until the tongue becomes as large as a monster toad, so slowly choking each palsied victim to death. How may the cruel end be expected? Will the fever rage so high that the eyes stand out as on stalks, or do they sink——"

" Cease your exposition," the lord abbot cried shrilly. " Let us have some practical outcome of your learning."

" Stay here, My Lord, as I have already advised you," the friar retorted. " By to-morrow night we might be a little along the path towards becoming sure. If by then no symptoms have developed we could go forth unafraid." He spread his hands meaningly. " If not, if signs were revealing themselves, then it would be of no matter, for we would soon be suffering such distress and agony that before long we would be unaware of ourselves."

" I knew it," the lord abbot said, his handsome face distorted. " As the Almighty is above, so I knew it."

The prioress tugged his arm. " Less of these riddles," she said. " Speak swiftly and tell me what you knew."

" The nun, your thrice damned nun with her fair face and depraved soul," Abbot Hugh said venomously. " But a few moments ago she fell on me so that she could thus blow her plague-laden breath on my face."

" In God's name, why should she have chosen you to vent her malice on? " the Lady Philippa asked angrily. " Why did she not seek to contaminate me, who has brought her to this sorry pass? "

The lord abbot shuddered. " Because she holds me responsible

13

for the fate of her lover," he said. " That is why, at the trial, she never ceased to stare at me unblinkingly . . . no, not even when her own life or death was under discussion."

The Lady Philippa eyed her cousin as though she wondered if he were sane, and had no qualms about inquiring.

" Are you out of your senses? " she demanded. " What would staring accomplish? "

" What you should perceive it has done," the abbot flared. " For she has the Evil Eye, and . . . and I knew it then and, Jesus preserve me, I do bitterly know it now."

The canon of Watton moaned. " May He deliver us safely," he muttered. " And would that these sinful creatures had expiated their crimes at the stake."

Such fire as was in any of them died from then, and the Lady Philippa probably expressed the general feeling after she had tottered to a stone bench against the refectory wall.

" Is there nothing we can do, good friar? " she called pitifully. " Surely, when the contact is so recent, there must be a means whereby we can be purified."

Fingering his chin, the eyes of everyone in the garth now on him, the Franciscan plainly gave the question much thought while pacing to and fro. Ultimately, turning gravely to the superiors, he tendered advice which, despite its humiliating and undoubtedly painful nature, was accepted without dissent.

A burst of activity ensued, followed by a long and miserable period of waiting. The first of these phases was begun by the sheriff's officer who, from the near side of the bridge, shouted to horse-keepers and cart drivers across the river, directing them to ride to the abbey of Rievaulx with all speed. From there they were to bring blankets and clothing of any description, sufficient to cover everyone within the precincts of Riggs.

At the same time a sheriff's party searched along the river bank for sand, and while doing so tried also to find two points, decently apart, one for the men and the other for the women, where crossings of the stream would furnish the appropriate conditions. The fords were to be such that in the middle they would be deep enough for total immersion, with a firm foothold. Meanwhile, an essential factor in the attempt at purification decided upon, a small body of nuns, canons, monks and men-at-arms was selected from those within the confines of the abandoned monastery. The qualification of each was brawniness.

"My nuns, the brides of Christ, naked under the sky," the Lady Philippa said faintly. "And myself . . ." she closed her fine eyes at the incredible thought, "to be rubbed down with sharp sand by my daughters Matilda and Maud, and thrice ducked by my daughters Hilda and Ealdgyth."

The sun's rim had sunk to the hills before the first of the riders, his beast's quivering flanks dark with sweat, and saddlebags bulging, arrived from Rievaulx. As soon as possible, piles of clothing, adequate in number if nothing else, were placed on the far side of the river bank opposite to the fording places; and those who had seen to this, where the holy maidens had to venture, were then peremptorily ordered to betake themselves behind a thick copse where, under penalty of instant excommunication should there be a failure to obey implicitly, they were to turn their backs and wait with heads bowed until instructions to the contrary were received.

Men and women, as naked as new-born babes, began to cross the river, figures strangely white against the flowing stream. Men-at-arms cursed fiercely, but submitted to the full terms of the ordeal, and several canons and monks uttered oaths inexcusable in the religious.

The women's passage was decidedly more noisy. Primarily ill-at-ease and embarrassed by the spectacle of their sisters' bodies, they shrieked piercingly as flesh was lustily scoured with sand, and even more shrill were the cries, three-times interrupted, when their heads were forced under water. This done, they floundered towards the bank, bedraggled hair hanging below their waists. Whimpering, tearfully murmuring prayers, or likening themselves to hogs at the spring fleece washing, they struggled into men's queer under-garments and donned cloaks and habits which more than enveloped them.

When a sorry-looking cavalcade began to move away from Riggs, the sky was rosy with the afterglow. Nuns of the Gilbertine priory of Watton, guarded at each side by horse-riding canons in ill-fitting clothing and blankets used as cloaks, were at the front, huddled miserably in jolting, hooded carts. Strung out behind them, almost as variously attired, monks of the Cistercian abbey of Rievaulx trudged unhappily, too stricken and apprehensive to raise more than token voice in humble plea.

The sheriff's officer and half a dozen of his men, an all-important duty theirs, were at the rear. On reaching the stone cross marking the final approach to Riggs they dismounted and, four of them heaving together, lifted the cross out of its oblong, stone socket. The cross was placed athwart the narrow track, and into the well of the socket ale from a leather bottle was poured. Abandoned clothing, with any money in it, had been left behind, but a few pennies had been commandeered from the horse-keepers, and these were dropped into the liquid.

" Soon no traveller, if travellers there ever be in this benighted place, will think it other than vinegar," the sheriff's officer remarked heavily. " With coins in it, it may be remembered that in some regions this was the sign of cleansing and warning, or so I think I was once told long ago."

One of his men pointed. " The cross of the Lord Jesus lying thus would be enough to cause me to suspect it would be wisdom not to pass beyond it, for whatever the reason might be."

Another man-at-arms joined in dismally. " By my faith, Sir Captain, let us hope that if there are to be warnings elsewhere, whether of this sort or otherwise, we shall live to see them removed. For me, I have had the full treatment. Those big bastards, Black Robin and Watty, nearly drowned me, and if I have a thumbnail size piece of skin that isn't red-raw I don't know where it is. But at that . . ." he sighed deeply, " well, of a truth, even the most learned doctors of physic can be wrong, and it need not do the trick."

The sheriff's officer crossed himself as he stared at the grange in the valley.

" Aye, God help us all, for we all may be dying before two cock-crows more," he muttered. " And God be merciful to the heretics, for they had the virtue of courage and could not have been wholly evil, I'll swear."

In silence, the party remounted and rode uphill again to where the track joined the rough highway. Another guide cross, directing wayfarers of former days to the abbey, stood at the junction. It was served in the same fashion as the other.

Night was fast approaching, and many miles to be feared were ahead of them; in places there were peat-bogs to each side which could quickly swallow man and beast, and, even more to be feared, the impenetrable gloom of the forest, which darkly harboured spectral, sinister things.

Hoarsely the sheriff's officer and his men began to sing the 51st Psalm. As regular church-goers, it was one of the two they had known by heart from boyhood.

*The Eleventh Month before Immurement*

# I

Ten abbots of the Cistercian Order in England, returning from a General Chapter of their community at the abbey of Cîteaux in Burgundy, were bidding farewell to a host who had entertained them sumptuously. This time it was the turn of the abbot of St. Mary the Virgin's abbey in Airedale to wish his friends godspeed. Hitherto, My Lord Abbot had been amongst those receiving lavish hospitality at great convents strewn throughout the length of the country, from Robertsbridge in Sussex to Roche in South Yorkshire, reached four days before. Now he was home again and, as with others who had earlier reached their own monastic foundations farther south, would travel forward no more.

Despite these hivings-off, the company which rode out of the inner courtyard at Kirkstall a little later was nevertheless still large, but would divide not long after passing beyond the massive gatehouse, when the abbots of Whalley, Sawley and Furness, in Lancashire, and Calder and Holm Cultram, in Cumberland, would turn their faces towards the west.

The other contingent, which would also diminish in stages, at the abbeys of Fountains, Jervaulx, Byland and Rievaulx, was last to leave, the abbot of Newminster, whose home was farther north, in the wastes of Northumberland, being with it. Headed by the superiors on fine blood horses, gilt bridles and embroidery on saddle cloths gleaming in the mellow October sun, this cavalcade also made an impressive sight—each ecclesiastical lord so sufficient a figure of authority and power as to strike with awe the usual Wednesday assembly of the poor, who were waiting outside the almonry for a dole of money and broken meat. Behind the abbots were their chaplains, secretaries and monks, cowled and hooded in black, while still farther to the rear were barbers, valets and servants in charge of the baggage mules.

For some miles the north-bound travellers' route was through richly-cultivated land farmed by the abbey's tenants, with now and then, farther up the densely-wooded valley of the sparkling river Aire, a glimpse of a snug manor house, usually with a fine dovecote around which corn-fed pigeons, fattening for the master's table, fluttered and wheeled. Occasionally there would be a short pause as a village in a clearing was reached, where peasants abandoned cottage looms to greet the distinguished passers-by, meantime church bells pealed joyously in honour of the event as handsome benedictions were gravely given.

Soon, when a bridge spanning a broad river had been crossed, and the forest grew nearer, less was seen of beasts feeding in the autumn stubble, and halts to observe the canonical hours were confined to an interval sufficient only for a *Pater* and a *Gloria* in the semi-gloom beneath an overhang of branches the sun failed to penetrate.

The afternoon was well advanced before the narrow track through the forest was left behind; but with Skelldale not far ahead and everywhere evidence that the riders had entered a great domain, spirits began to rise. In due course, quite unexpectedly, Fountains Abbey came into view, its church and the many buildings clustered about it contained within a lofty, battlemented wall studded with watch towers, of such defensive strength as might have caused raiding parties from Scotland, or moss-troopers from the Border country, to wonder how it could be penetrated.

The religious of Jervaulx, Byland, Rievaulx and Newminster stayed at Fountains for two full days, during which Abbot Robert justified a growing reputation for magnificence. His senior obedientiaries and younger sons, attendances at " the seven daily " Offices confined to token proportions, were no less obliging. Guests were taken on conducted tours by brethren proud of their house; they were shown priceless objects in church and treasury; the immense wool store—as with the visitors', the wealth of the community had been founded on the staple; and new buildings which in construction and adornment departed from the strict standards laid down by the early Cistercian statutes. From the stables, white horses bred at Fountains were brought out for critical inspection; and a short stroll along a lovely, fertile valley took the strangers to a clump of yews beneath which, existing on leaves and herbs boiled and seasoned with salt, the monkish pioneers of the abbey, agricultural-ists every one, had sheltered for a year from the start of their con-ception—the harshest of ordeals considering the locality was described by an ancient scribe as " covered with stones and briars, more suited for the haunts of wild beasts and reptiles than for the abode of man."

Stories were also told of flocks of sheep counted by the tens of thousands, and prime cattle in immense herds. If there was conceit it was scrupulously hidden—" To God only the glory " was con-stantly said, and as constantly was the reply: " *Soli Deo Gloria*," from the lips of those to whom these marvels were being revealed.

On the evening of the day before departure from Fountains, the lord abbot of Rievaulx summoned two of his sons, Roger and Ughtred. The former was a monk of the second class, of thirty-five years advancement, an auditor and, by inclination also, a man most passionately devoted to figures, correct balances and accounts; the latter was in the junior grade, of eight years profession, which meant that sixteen more years must pass before he attained the lowliest status of his companion's rank. Notwithstanding this, the young monk Ughtred had made a niche of his own, in that he was renowned, locally at least, as an artist. The vivid pictures and arresting frescoes which were gradually transforming the simple, Norman nave of the abbey church at Rievaulx were a testimony to his powers as a draughtsman and colourist.

The two monks awaited their lord's pleasure in the well-appointed, pillared hall of Abbot Robert's lodgings, and they became aware of their superior's approach when, at the far end of the long chamber, the throng of senior monks, officials and priests separated to form a passage, heads bent in obeisance. Shortly afterwards they themselves sank to their knees in readiness.

Abbot Hugh of Rievaulx was a tall, distinguished-looking man whose commanding appearance in gleaming vestments was enhanced by a towering, richly-ornamented, horned mitre of archiepiscopal pattern, to which some grumblers contended he was not entitled. He was in the best of humour, and part of that good humour was due to the compliments paid him on the Continent and nearer home upon his new pastoral staff, completed only a few days before departure for Citeaux. For that reason the monk Ughtred, who had designed staff and crook and watched over monkish craftsmen at Rievaulx making it—goldsmiths, enamellers, workers in precious stones, and expert wood carvers—was in high favour. It was a handsome staff, a series of exquisitely-patterned bosses hiding the several sections into which it could be divided for convenience in packing; the crook itself was the great glory—jewelled, coloured gorgeously with inserts of enamel, with leafy gold tendrils enclosing a compelling representation of the Lamb of God and tiny, amazingly-wrought figures of the saints.

Holding the crook of the tall staff in his left hand, the abbot of Rievaulx addressed the prostrate figures.

"You will listen carefully, my sons," he began.

His instructions were simple enough. Instead of attending service in the cathedral at Ripon the next day, and afterwards taking their places at the bishop's banquet, they were to proceed ahead and make a slight detour by way of Byland, to whose prior a letter from his superior was to be delivered. Similarly, on arrival home, a second letter was to be handed to their own prior. Both letters, the abbot intimated, contained orders regarding the nature of the hospitality to be prepared against the return of the respective abbots and their guests.

" Is that quite clear, my sons? " the abbot inquired.

" Wholly clear, My Lord," Brother Roger murmured.

Abbot Hugh condescended with an explanation: " It is our pleasure to do this service for the noble lord abbot of Byland, who is short of attendants since three of his sons passed into the arms of the Heavenly Father while in France, as you know. May they rest in peace."

" May they all rest in peace, *Domine*," Brother Roger echoed.

The abbot, about to raise his right hand to bless them before their journey, realised that the younger monk, who could not speak to him without permission, desired to do so.

" You have a petition to make, my son? " he inquired.

" My Lord, I ask and beseech God's mercy and yours," Brother Ughtred said urgently. " If it would please you to allow me to dally in Ripon a short while on the morrow I might obtain from the merchant Mawson a certain Mediterranean oil, to use as an ingredient in the new colour My Lord was gracious enough to allow me to speak to him about after we had visited the abbey of Clairvaux. My Lord may remember I told him that one of the monks there had been generous enough to confide in me what he used."

" It is well thought of," the abbot said with a nod of approval. " By all means, my son. Thereby," he smiled, " we shall lose less time in further beautifying our convent, so rendering tribute to God for his love of us."

" That is so, My Lord," Brother Ughtred said.

The abbot reflected momentarily before speaking. " As is usual after absences, my sons, you will both go into retreat for three days after your return, during which no soul will speak to you, nor you to any."

" As our Rule lays down, My Lord," said Brother Roger. " So enabling us, in divine peace, to shed the contamination contact with the outside world so surely brings upon those who adventure in it."

" That is so, my son," the abbot said. " As for you, my son Ughtred, there is no reason why, while denying yourself communication with your fellows, you may not proceed with the panel painting we have discussed in detail."

The monk Ughtred's sensitive face lighted up, and his eyes shone with delight.

" Gladly, My Lord," he said.

" Within the hours allotted to work and recreation," the abbot said with a touch of warning. " None other, my son."

St. Bernard the Blessed, in his directives, emphasised the necessity for absolute obedience. Ughtred of Monkseaton, monk of Rievaulx, bowed his head in humble acceptance.

Later, before Vespers, the abbot's chaplain sought out the two monks, to tell them they might start on their homeward journey a little in advance of the main party on the following day. And so it was.

The next morning was again bright as the monks Roger and Ughtred rode down the pleasant valley of the Skell. It was the time of the fall of the leaf and the changing shades of rowan, ash, sycamore and birch caused the hillside woods to flame into a tapestry of natural glory, whose hues of green ranged from deep to pale, with gold, coppers, and infinitely lovely russet browns contributing their striking but always harmonious effect.

As always when confronted with immense beauty, Ughtred's eyes pricked with tears. This was too much, after all he had seen abroad—the brilliance of southern skies and the wonders of a score of holy buildings: the superb magister in the abbey church of St. Bénigne at Dijon; the perfection of lace in the treasury of the cathedral at Troyes; the rose windows of Notre Dame; and the richly-stained glass of St. Pierre at Beauvais. Memory after memory; a feast never to be forgotten.

Quite unaware of his companion's inattention, Brother Roger, a practical and down-to-earth man, started to speak with a measure of acerbity.

" Our brothers of Fountains haven't been alone in possessing forerunners who by skill and ceaseless toil converted a wilderness into a valuable property," he said at one stage. " It is on record that the region of Byland was once described as strange and dismal, no more than a marsh hemmed in by forest. As for our own beloved Rievaulx, Brother Ughtred, I needn't remind you, need I, of what the Sieur William of Newburgh said of the terrain beforehand? A place ' *vastae solitudinis et horroris* '."

" Yes," said Ughtred.

" You know what it means, my son? " Roger snapped. " If, after all these years, your Latin is still insufficient to——"

" I understand quite well, Brother Roger," Ughtred said hurriedly. " Perfectly."

The auditor snorted. " I should think so," he said sardonically, although his mind was on another matter. " Nor should it be necessary for me to remind you that the wool of Byland and Rievaulx, though perhaps not Jervaulx, is as good as any the abbey of Fountains can produce, and has always been as much sought after for the Flemish and Italian looms."

Still irritated, he eyed the sanctuary cross on the approach to Ripon. Chafing, he scowled impartially at geese feeding in a harvested allotment and at various townsfolk who, with one eye watching for the first sign of the arrival of the notables, were either working on their strips of land in the town-field or deepening the town ditch.

" Count their flocks of sheep by the tens of thousands, do they? " he continued testily. " Possibly, possibly, Brother Ughtred, but so do we. And . . ." he growled, " I am the man who knows, eh? I say I'm the man who knows, my son."

Ughtred came into the present with a start, and from then decided it was only courteous to pay proper attention to the remarks of his senior. By now the cathedral stood out clearly on its eminence, and regularly about them were houses prettily situated in the midst of orchards, gardens and paddocks. From there the town soon closed in on them, with its workshops, smithies, shops and store-houses. About here, incredibly enough, Brother Roger nearly allowed himself to laugh, when they came across a stout matron in church-going, sky-blue mantle and wimple beneath a broad hat. She was taking haymaker swings at a lad whom her husband, a stocky figure wearing a scarlet frock-coat liberally furred at neck and sleeves, was energetically chastising. The luckless apprentice, so the amused passers gathered, had tried to sneak off to enjoy sights reserved for elders and betters, instead of obediently remain-- ing behind to watch over his master's property.

At the crown of the slope, the progress of the two monks was hampered on reaching the fringe of a large crowd who were listen-ing intently to an elderly, shabbily-dressed individual. It soon became evident that the speaker was fervently advocating the equality of man, which seemed to be acceptable enough to the majority of his audience. Trouble immediately loomed when, how-ever, all the more effectively because of his quietness of delivery, he began to talk about the scandal of priests who never visited their parishes and of soft-living monastic dignitaries who, largely with-drawn from the active world, saw little of the miseries of their fellow-men, and cared not at all.

" All of you, my friends, will have at least one of these gentlemen in mind," he went on. " The absent rector who draws his tithes and revenues, and out of them pays a mite to an ignorant clerk to stand in his place . . ."

" Silence, you foul-mouthed pest." The interrupter was an aged cleric, eyes bloodshot and full cheeks crimson to the point of apoplexy. " Would that God struck you dead, would that the spittle in your throat choked you, would that the worms be eating you before two more days have passed, would that——"

He, himself, was in danger of choking, and until a violent bout of coughing ended could neither damn his opponent further nor challenge the statements that continued to be made. But on recovering he furiously attempted to undo the harm that might have been done.

" You lie, you heretic dog," he bawled. " Never were there two Popes, nay, not for a day, and still less for nigh on a hundred years. His Holiness's seat was ever in Rome, and nowhere else."

The preacher, a man with an intelligent, careworn face, pulled a tattered university gown closer as he shook his head.

" Respected sir, you must know," he said, " that to the everlasting disgrace of our Church there was for many long years a schism dividing her, and during those years many devout men looked to a Pope in Rome and many others equally devout turned their heads towards a Pope in Avignon. Which of those were right, my friend? Who was there to say which were the heretics, though that was what each side, to the point of bloody conflict, accused the other of being? "

" I know who is the heretic now," the priest trumpeted. " You . . . you, with your rabble-rousing nonsense." He mimicked. " My friends," he went on, " when Adam delved and Eve span, who was then a gentleman? Equality! Bah! Oh yes, latterly we are encountering more of your glib-tongued, devil-inspired fraternity— penniless rascals who would despoil the——"

The monk Roger of Rievaulx leaned across to tug the monk Ughtred's arm. " Let us to our business, and enough of this malodorous Lollard," he said peremptorily. " While you trade with your merchant I will say a mass beneath the hallowed roof of St. Wilfred's, so that with the Lord's help I can cleanse my ears of the evil with which they have been wantonly assailed."

" A Lollard, Reverend Father? " the young man remarked inquiringly. " Who are they? "

He was sternly silenced. " Enough, I said," the auditor snapped.

They separated, after edging through the crowd and tethering the horses in a quiet place.

The monk Ughtred, quest successfully completed, was not delayed long by the merchant, who, although delighted to oblige an emissary of the great monastery of Rievaulx, was anxious not to miss anything stirring outside.

Clutching a small phial, thoughts strangely mixed, the young man walked slowly back. His resentment about the Lollard's attack on Holy Church and no-less Holy Monasticism had subsided, and he was thinking more about the preacher's tired, earnest face, the face of a seemingly God-fearing man to whom it was hard to attribute sinful persuasion.

Without conscious volition, his steps took him back to the crowd, now even larger. There was change there—five of the cathedral's canons had joined forces with the rector in an assault, partly theological, partly threatening, partly fish-wife, upon the heretical preacher, who did not appear to be yielding any ground.

" And what do you think of all this, Brother Monk? "

Startled, Ughtred turned, to discover he was being addressed by a friar habited in coarse brown serge girdled with a soiled length of rope, from which a rosary and a crucifix hung. The cloth of the pointed hood was as wear-worn as the Lollard's garments, and his feet were bare.

" What . . . what do I think? " Ughtred stammered.

Experiences abroad had given him a slight degree of confidence, but he was still largely unused either to contacts or intercourse with strangers.

What followed was brief and its nature odd, a conversation so strange and unconventional that Ughtred of Monkseaton was to ponder about it for some weeks to come—as he was to remember the Grey Friar, a man perhaps ten years older than himself, with mocking but kindly eyes, and cheeks sunken as if he had known many privations.

" I would take it that your business is to forward the Lord's purpose," the Franciscan remarked easily, wagging a finger. " Now that, to me, poses a question, which perhaps you would be agreeable enough to answer."

" I can but try," Ughtred muttered.

" It's this," the friar resumed encouragingly. " Has it ever occurred to you that an active and healthy young fellow might best serve humanity other than being boxed in by walls? "

Ughtred was recovering. " Perhaps I might remind you, Sir

Friar, that the Lord told Arsenius to flee and live a life of solitude and contemplation," he said stiffly.

"A fitting answer indeed," the Franciscan commented warmly. "Yes, I suppose a Cistercian who has the advantage of constant meditation always has an apt answer up his yard-wide and knee-length sleeves."

Never before had Ughtred experienced anything of this kind. "If that is a jest, Sir Friar," he said, "it . . . it is in the sorriest taste. A sneer about the habit of——"

"Tell me something else," the other interposed equably. "Are you truly happy in your vocation? Do you feel you are fully fulfilling yourself?"

"I am wholly happy," Ughtred said stoutly.

"It is not always so," the Franciscan friar said reflectively. "The restrictive life of the cloister, the long periods of prayers, the many hours of compulsory silence—do not always promote happiness, and often cause grim tragedy."

A few uneasy memories came to Ughtred. "That . . . that may indeed be, occasionally," he conceded. "But a few examples of weakness are as nothing, for weakness is man."

"Wonderful, O monk," the friar said admiringly. "There you are again, never at a loss. Would that I had the same devastating gift."

Losing shyness, Ughtred was also losing his temper, which was against all his years of training.

"Had the Almighty bestowed greater gifts on you, Sir Friar, you would be aware that the postulant is made fully aware, in *advance*, of the harshness of life in the cloister," he countered hotly. "He serves a novitiate of twelve months before acceptance can be considered, and even in the final moments no one would try to persuade him to remain if it were seen he had doubts or fears. He would be entirely free to withdraw from the convent, and if needs be would be adequately assisted on his way."

Once again the Franciscan uttered a baffling remark. "There may still be hope for you, Sir Monk," he said. "Yes, deep within you I perceive a lambent spark, a fragment of ember not as yet smothered."

"Who are you to be so saucy?" Ughtred demanded. "With

all respect, Sir Friar, would you dare deny that the followers of Saint Francis of Assisi have long ago departed from their once lofty ideals? "

The Franciscan shook his head. " It is true, my son," he admitted sorrowfully. " As with all the great Orders, we have grievously fallen from our former proud estate. It happened to the Benedictines, and so it has been with us."

Ughtred gasped. " The *Benedictines!* The Benedictines are as highly regarded as any religious in the land."

Once again he was reduced to a state of confusion by the other's incomprehensible switch.

" Some day, my brother, you must search through the learned doctors to discover why your own Order of Cistercians came into being," the Franciscan said mildly.

" My own Order? "

The friar's eye twinkled. " Such research may provide you with a morsel of stimulating food for thought in that sequestered cloister of yours," he said. " Well now," his tone changed to briskness, " I must be away. Vastly as I would be thrilled at witnessing My Lord Bishop receiving a number of great ecclesiastics at the west door of the Minster I have other affairs to attend to, and they are many miles away."

To Ughtred's amazement—as afterwards he recalled his feelings —he then found himself in the most friendly conversation with the gaunt Franciscan. He learnt that the friar had been convalescing at his Order's house in Richmond, after returning from far-distant Syria, where a malady affecting the intestines had first stricken him. Now, sound in health—an assertion contradicted by his looks—he was walking to York, where he was eager to take up work amongst the sick and needy.

" May God's blessing be on you, and on those you serve," Ughtred said just before they parted. " May His light ever shine on you, Sir Friar."

The Franciscan's face was transformed when he smiled. " On you also, my son," he said before turning away. " And do not worry yourself about anything I have said. Who am I, you asked me not so long ago, and with humility I now put to myself the same question. Believe me, my brother, there are many different ways whereby the Lord's purpose may be carried out, and who am I to decide that mine is superior to those of others."

When alone, Ughtred's thoughts were more chaotic than he had ever known them. Wandering away, he stared unseeingly first at the Lepers' Hospital and then at the episcopal palace before retracing his steps to the cathedral, which he entered. Still bemused, he barely noticed the multitude of candles burning at innumerable chantry altars, where kneeling priests, splendidly robed, were praying aloud for the souls of the honoured dead. But he became much more alive, the artist in him utterly repelled, while gazing upwards at the protruding heads of gargoyles, some quaint and others abhorrently grotesque, each an ancient craftsman's notion of a demon discomfited by the worship of God taking place below.

Beyond the main doorway again, he slipped past a resplendent line of the cathedral's most important dignitaries, with the bishop, in priceless vestments, at their centre.

It so happened that the abbots' procession from the abbey of Fountains had just arrived. Against all recognised precedent the proceedings were decidedly disorderly, with ladies shrieking and God-fearing men, tradesmen and gentry alike, cursing freely. The culprit was the abbot of Newminster, who, with scant regard for those in his path, had spurred his horse until he was close to the Lollard.

" So here we have another who would be the ruin of souls," he thundered. " Get you gone, spawn of hell; take yourself away, misbegotten snake crawling in the grass."

The preacher smiled at the throng, now gathering nearer after their fright.

" In his intemperance the lord abbot becomes irrational," he told them. " Far from hiding myself, I speak from the steps of this cross for all to see, as you all can see."

" Begone, I repeat," the abbot roared. " Lest far worse befall you, as by the holy saints I will ensure it shall if you persist in your contumacious conduct."

" You speak loudly from fear, My Lord Abbot," the Lollard replied boldly. " Fear of the inevitable sapping of your absolute power, fear of the abolition of the wealth that sustains your arrogance, fear that the lot of the landless labourer with his pitiful weekly pot of cabbage and bacon may be improved at the expense of your rich food, your foreign luxuries, your cellars filled with the choicest wines."

A few murmurs of agreement, although from persons whose appearance signified them as of small consequence, added fuel to the fire of the abbot of Newminster's wrath.

"Thrice scurvy dog," he bellowed. "Scourging your hide off would be insufficient to offset your insolence. But you shall endure more than that—you shall——"

"My Lord——"

"Silence, you heretic priest."

The Lollard's voice rang out. "I am on the Lord's errand, so why should I be silent at your command, My Lord Abbot? Are we not all, as the noble and illustrious Wycliffe so rightly wrote, tenants-in-chief under God, and hold from Him all that we are and possess, for the greater benefit of mankind? And to interfere between us and our divine suzerain is to grievously err."

"Do you dare to sermonise me?" the abbot stormed.

The preacher spread his hands. "All this heat, My Lord. Is it worthy either of you or your high office? Merely because I point out to these good people that the revenues of the Church and the monasteries, equal to one-third of the kingdom's entire revenue, might be more wisely applied for the benefit of our many starving countrymen? One third of the kingdom's, My Lord and friends— one-third, at the sole disposal of a handful of prelates."

Infuriated at the ruin of plans which would tellingly have taught the abbots how an ecclesiastic high in the councils of the state can stage elaborate ceremonial, the bishop bustled across. Puffing with annoyance, cheeks mottled, forgetful of dignity and of robes sweeping the dust, he brushed onlookers to one side.

"My Lord Abbot of Newminster," he snapped, "you make too much of this trivial affair."

"Trivial!" the abbot shouted.

"In the light of the much greater affairs we shall be discussing, yes," the bishop bawled. "I can vouchsafe that this matter will not be allowed to rest. I propose taking the immediate steps necessary for——"

"Trivial?" the abbot of Newminster demanded.

Not without effort, the bishop lowered his voice. " My Lord Abbot, might I suggest we continue elsewhere? It is not seemly that we, upon whom it is incumbent to set an example, should brawl in the public eye and within the hearing of a host of vulgar ears. As to this Lollard . . ."

The bishop was not the sole angry man in the vicinity. Brother Roger, finding the monk Ughtred, grabbed his arm and spun him about as if he were a newly-accepted novice.

" So this is where you are," he said sternly. " Why did you not repair immediately to the horses, where I have been waiting for you. In consequence of this I must warn you that I shall consider whether or not to cause you to answer in the chapter house for your behaviour."

He did not speak again until the day was almost spent, save when praying during each brief stoppage for a holy Hour. But his attitude passed completely over the monk Ughtred who, lost in his own thoughts, recalled again and again the strange sayings of the Franciscan, ever trying to find a clue to their significance. Nor could the young monk easily dismiss the Lollard's words—though fully realising how sinful it was to question in any manner—and he kept asking himself if the true virtue of the Church and the monasteries would stand out more clearly if both were less well endowed.

Ripon, with its ranging defensive mound, another sanctuary cross, and the bridge over the broad river, were soon left behind. For some way beyond the water, before the chill of the forest was met, there was much to interest a traveller not otherwise pre-occupied. The wastes were alive with game; here and there tenant-peasants and their families, making jollification of it, were building up stocks of winter fuel, taking by hook and by crook as many branches from their lord's trees as could be gained permissibly, which they defined as tip-toe reaching and stretching, with the pole at arm's length.

As the highway grew rougher and more narrow, with the danger from cut-throat robbers increasing, it was necessary to keep a careful lookout. There were moments of relief: once on meeting a solitary pedestrian who, short-sightedness causing him to fail to recognise the oncoming monks as of the religious, dived into a copse for safety; and again, the subsequent wryness of expression on the face of a clerk-in-orders who, surprised, hastily dropped and kicked aside a brace of hares and a pheasant he had illegally poached on the lord's estate.

In due course the unvarying monotony of the uneven, root-traversed road was broken by another river, bridged by a fine but decaying erection. Thirsk was not far along after that, and from there the two monks rode for a few miles on the stony highway leading to the distant city of York before turning eastwards towards the hills, where great herds of red deer, the most zealously preserved of all game, were frequently sighted.

The abbey church of Byland—of Saint Mary the Virgin, as all Cistercian foundations were named—was reached in the late afternoon. When the west front, with its three lancet windows, and an immense wheel window with stone tracery above them, came into view, Roger the auditor reined in his horse. As he gazed down at the abbey, which nestled so snugly in its immediate, fertile surroundings, he began to speak, very much out of temper.

" The Cistercians were always good farmers, Brother Ughtred. If our brethren of Fountains imagine their ancestors were more active than others in the clearance of land they are sadly mistaken. Indeed I would argue, and argue most strenuously, that the pioneer forefathers here, and our own at our house at Rievaulx, had more to cope with than was ever met with in the valley of the Skell."

Relieved by this outburst, he began to descend the steep hill, riding with caution to the bottom. The earlier promise of the day had gone—the clouds were low and sullen, and drops of rain were falling when Ughtred, at his senior's sign, bent from his mare to thump the knocker on the postern of the abbey gate-house. They were not alone in seeking refreshment and hospitality for the night, five more wayfarers joining them before the summons was answered: two villainous-looking vagabonds, a minstrel with harp in case, a ragged old ex-soldier of the French wars, and a merchant with a pack-horse.

The bolts were withdrawn and the porter surveyed them. " *Deo gratias,*" he said welcomingly, before asking names and speaking to subordinates.

The replies were uneven. " *Benedicite!* " all said, returning his bow.

In due course, after the newcomers' feet had been carefully washed by the sub-almoner, the guest master escorted them to the chapel in the guest house, where he remained with them for prayers. Then he provided his charges with soft, old shoes for their evening comfort.

As members of the same Order the monks Roger and Ughtred had special privileges. They ate in the second-best dining-hall in the guest house and had the exclusive use of the parlour, where the guest master fussed about to make sure the fire was not smoking, and glanced at cornices to be certain his hirelings had not left a single cobweb to mar his reputation.

When the dishes of steaming beans, spiced fish stew, and cheese cakes, with wine, had been nicely digested, it was time for Compline, which the guest master shared with the visitors. Then, when the triple prayer of the *Pater*, *Ave* and *Credo* had been recited at the conclusion, he took up a lantern and, the Great Silence having begun at half-past six, piloted them wordlessly to their beds.

When alone in his chamber, Ughtred exchanged his habit for an aged, much-mended habit used for night-wear, and re-girdled himself. Pulling the rough sheets and blankets back, he climbed into bed, snuffed the candle and, as the Rule required, drew his hood over his face. Shivering with the chill of the straw palliasse, he closed his eyes and waited patiently for a glow of warmth and for sleep.

*     *     *     *

The abbey of Jervaulx possessed lead mines and smelt-mills in Joredale; Rievaulx worked iron-mines in the Cleveland Hills, and, much nearer to hand, owned ironworks famed for their products; the Abbot and Chapter of Fountains, amongst other interests, were coal-owners; and Byland was renowned for champion tups whose services could be obtained for a fee for ewes elsewhere when the length of staple from a quality-declining breed of sheep required to be improved. Apart from considerable trading done generally by the four monasteries in these and many other ways they naturally " obliged " each other, but, as settlements were not always effected directly, accountantship could sometimes become complex.

The monk Roger had decided that while at Byland he must seize the opportunity of striking a correct balance in an involved series of transactions which, prior to his departure for Citeaux, had been filling the post-bags of the messengers of the various communities.

With the Cistercians the whole of the morning was devoted to religious exercises, and so it was past the second hour of the afternoon before the auditor and his companion were able to leave Byland. The wildest part of their journey was still before them, in weather which hardly could have been much worse.

Despite heavy rain and a strong wind, riding was at least tolerable along the valley and while ascending the lower part of a narrow lane—heavily fringed by trees and so running with water as to resemble a beck bottom. This tortuous track, higher up, climbed to the summit of an immensely high and precipitous scaur by means o many snake-like curves.

As the forest thinned conditions became much worse, and the two monks and their horses were in a sorry state long before reaching the barren, far-extending moors at the top, where a full gale was blowing. The highway beyond, a little better than poor even in summer, was hock-deep and more in clinging mud, deeply cut by peat-stained torrents racing tempestuously across it at scores o places.

Fiercely buffeted, hoods closed to a mere eye-slit, the two riders struggled on, leaving their horses to pick a path; to press would have invited disaster, although on such a leaden day night could fall much earlier than normal, and darkness there, miles from any habitation, was a scaring prospect.

The first slight indication of an improvement came when the moors, wildly-agitated seas of swirling, bending grasses, began to incline towards the great vale still so far ahead; the tearing gusts became a little less violent and the cloudy squalls, which had reduced visibility to a few yards, tended to become less charged with water.

Some time later, when the road dipped appreciably towards a swollen river, the auditor pulled up his animal abruptly to stare ahead, gazing incredulously in the failing light at a two-wheeled, hooded cart drawn by six horses. There were several riders with it, two of them clad in white cloaks; all were at a respectable distance from the lurching vehicle, either in front or to the rear.

" Canons regular of Watton, with servants! " he ejaculated.

" Surely none of their nuns can be abroad on a day like this . . .
though their prioress, the Dame Philippa, is of a strong and unconventional nature in many directions."

Aroused out of a reverie which had begun in Ripon, the eyes of
the monk Ughtred were nearly popping out of his head.

" Canons regular and holy nuns in company! " he gasped. " In
*company*."

Brother Roger scathingly rebuked him. " At Watton, there is
the strictest segregation, and never has a breath of scandal been
heard concerning the convent. And, as you would observe if we were
nearer, the guardians of the ladies, whom I judge to be present, are
chosen from those of mature years and sobriety—as we choose the
village pudding wives who come to make our pastries and black
puddings, or to wash our underlinen. These escorts, whether
canons regular or servants, ride discreetly apart from them, and the
driver, who is invariably aged, is under special instructions."

" It will be very necessary, Brother Roger," Ughtred said.

The auditor continued: " Nor may the blessed ladies, whose
carriage is so screened that they are out of the sight of man, ever be
approached . . . save when there is death, imminent danger, or other
affairs of grave consequence."

It was a long explanation, by one who had not spoken since
leaving the shelter of Byland. Furthermore, he also supplemented it,
with details of this Order, the only Order ever founded in England—
by Saint Gilbert, at Sempringham, in Lincolnshire. The priory
of Watton was a member house.

Amazed at the concept of canons regular living under the same
roof as the brides of Christ, the monk Ughtred revealed his astonishment.

" It is as though nuns of Rosedale or Wykeham were to take up
their abode with us," he exclaimed. " Never before have I heard,
of this strange Order of Gilbertines."

" Nor is it necessary for you to have knowledge that I myself
acquired in the course of my duties with the chequer," the auditor
said testily. " I chanced to learn it merely as the result of scrutinising
a transaction with the Gilbertines authorised by our lord abbot, the
signatory for the other party being the prioress of Watton, My
Lord's own blood cousin."

" My Lord's own cousin! "

The monk Roger's hood was nodded. " A lady of the same noble family who also shares My Lord's love of the chase."

" A prioress who delights in sport! " Brother Ughtred exclaimed. " Do you think she is in these desolate parts with deer uppermost in her mind? Or perhaps she had intended to rest overnight with My Lord."

The auditor made several pithy comments on that, pointing out to begin with that the Dame Philippa sat on many ecclesiastical councils graced by Abbot Hugh and would therefore know he had not as yet reached home from the Continent.

" Nor by reason of her high office and good name would the Lady Philippa ever consider staying at Rievaulx," he continued with less conviction. " True, she is a lady who pleases herself, but commonly the Rule of all nunneries prohibits nuns to lodge at monasteries, on account of malignant tongues. Moreover——"

He broke off abruptly, belatedly remembering that gossiping was a deadly sin listed high in the Rule. His lips tightened with annoyance at the realisation that he had been close to indulging in tittle-tattle unfit for monkish consideration.

" She must have had business to bring her to these parts, Brother Roger," the monk Ughtred remarked.

Incensed and uneasy, the auditor passed on his phlegm. " Whether so or not, you are not permitted to speculate about it," he shouted. " Deplorable as it is, it would seem that contact with the world outside must have sapped your resistance, and if that be proven so then disciplined you shall be until——"

A raging blast struck them, of such intensity that they were compelled to wait until it was easier to resume. As the gust began to die away, and the drenching mist lessened, both plainly heard, windborne to them, shrill screams of fear and anguish, and although the day was nearly over sufficient light remained to perceive what was happening below. At the point where the road reached a sharp curve in the river, the Gilbertine canons and servants were making desperate endeavours to save the hooded cart. It was tilted to a crazy angle, one wheel over the edge of a bank undercut by the swift flow of water.

" My . . . my son, if the traces break asunder may God in His mercy help those poor souls," Brother Roger was stammering as his young companion kicked his heels into his horse's flanks. " Or if He in his wisdom should decide——"

By then the monk Ughtred was flying down the slope, with rash regard for the dangerous state of the badly-eroded highway. He was quickly at the scene of the accident and was curbing his mare when, from the low side of the cart, one of the occupants fell into the foam-flecked flood below. At this, there was a piercing cry from a woman at the near side; her hands had been grasped by one of the canons and a servant who, if a precarious balance could be retained a few seconds longer, would be able to drag her to safety.

Sick at heart, Ughtred watched the leaping, tumultuous river take away its victim. It was only when he chanced to notice that the line of trees alongside the water curved back again towards the road, some distance farther down, that he appreciated there might be a slim chance after all. If he could cut across the base of the narrow loop quickly enough he might be in time.

Then followed a desperate race—the frantic gallop down the road until, at the side, flowing water glimmered between the trunks of trees; then the descent of a winding track as far as a level terrace, where there was a faint smell of wood smoke and baulks of newly-sawn timber in neat criss-cross piles.

The river was a few feet below, and the monk Ughtred quickly tethered his mare to a bark-covered post, one of the supports of a crude roof projecting over the entrance to a cave-like fissure in a rock face. Then, after throwing off his cloak, he slithered to the edge of the water where, eyes straining in the deepening gloom, he searched the oncoming stream, which there was almost three times as wide as where the mishap occurred.

In the fading light the river seemed to be surging past far more rapidly than probably was the case, and Ughtred had almost abandoned hope when he noticed an unidentifiable object, small and of whitish shade, moving on the darkening, wind-whipped surface. He entered the river, which was never deeper than a little over waist-high, but as he advanced towards the middle, from the lee of one great boulder to another, he was often desperately near to being swept off his feet. He fought for breath until his chest was a tight band of agonising pain, so intent on what he was striving to do that he hardly felt the stones and small rocks which, taken along the bed by the fierce flow, cut and bruised his feet and legs.

It was a struggle that did not end until, the woman in his arms, he reached the bank again, lower down where it shelved; and there, when with his last remnant of strength he had gently placed her down, he fell to the ground.

Night had fallen when, chilled and shaky, he became conscious again. Shivering, he tried to see the still shape near him, and sought for her wrist to find a pulse. After that, for some moments, he did nothing until, trembling as if with an ague, he fumbled in her clothes to feel her heart. She was living.

" O Lord Jesus, thank you for your goodness," he muttered. " Thank you, O My Lord, blessed redeemer of mankind."

A spatter of sleety rain stung his cheek. Suppressing a groan, he painfully and stiffly rose, stooped to lift the sodden burden and, his gait made erratic by holes and unseen obstacles, tried to find his way to the woodman's shelter. It was a quest which might have failed had not his mare whinnied.

In the peace of the small cave he noticed a faint glow from the embers of a fire, and thin kindling soon brought about leaping flames. In their light, as he chafed her wrists and hands, he was able to see the woman for the first time; saw that she was young and comely, saw she was neither a servant maid, a lay-sister, nor a girl sent to the convent to be educated. Horror-stricken, his glance remained rooted on a hood and veil that told him all.

" She is espoused to the Lord Christ," he muttered, awed and frightened. " Upon whom no man's glance may ever rest, save her confessor's, and probably not even his."

Her breathing was almost imperceptible but, shocked though he was, he knew he must do the unthinkable if she were not to slip out of life. Finding bracken in a corner he made a soft bed, and plied the fire with wood until flames were curling a yard high. Then he went outside.

" O Bess," he said tremulously as he led the mare to a place less exposed to wind and rain, " never have I been so terror-stricken in all my life. But . . . but if the lady is not to die she must be made warm and comfortable. She is only a maid, Bess, much too young to become cold clay."

Bracing himself for an ordeal, anticipation of which had already dotted his forehead with beads of sweat, he returned to the cave, carrying with him a saddle-bag from which he took out a towel and a thick mantle. Then, handicapped by uncontrollable tremors in hands and arms, he undressed her.

For a fleeting moment, before reverently swathing her in the garment, he gazed at her, looking at the soft curves of her body, the swelling of her breasts, the long strands of hair.

" She is so beautiful," he told himself, choked with emotion. " In all I have seen when abroad of the great masters' sculptures and paintings, never have I seen anything remotely of such perfection. O God, how divinely have you wrought in this maiden, and I thank you for this glimpse of the miracles you can perform, however forbidden it may be for me to do so."

Abruptly he turned away and, outside again, struggled upward in the darkness until he reached the highway, along which, one way and then the other, he stumbled for some distance, perceiving nothing and hearing nothing save the howl of the wind and the tumbling of water everywhere. It was only what was to be expected, in a wild and lonely countryside, and although somewhere there would be the cottages of wood-cutters and shepherds he had no idea where they might lie.

When once more down by the river, he entered the cave and, treading cautiously, approached the fire. As he knelt on the stony floor to look more closely at the maid her eyes opened. Mouth suddenly dry, momentarily speechless, Ughtred stared at her; and, wonderingly, she looked at him, apparently fearlessly.

" You are . . . you are safe now, lady," he faltered.

Her glance remained on him. " I fell from the cart . . . I remember that . . . and I remember the dreadful water . . . but nothing after that."

" Your forehead is bruised, lady," he said. " I think you must have struck your head on a rock."

" You saved me? "

" It was through God that the river widened here, and I could walk out to you, lady."

She started up. " My lady! " she said imperatively. " And dear Sister Katherine . . . and silly-willy Puchin? "

42

" Puchin! "

" Sister Katherine's monkey," she explained. " What has happened to them? Where are they? "

Ughtred shook his head. " I don't know, lady."

Tired by this effort the nun again laid her head on the pillow of bracken Ughtred had contrived. On re-opening her eyes, now wet with tears, her glance rested incuriously on the cloth of the Cistercian mantle in which she was wrapped; but then, chancing to notice more familiar clothing outspread to dry on a branch set up as a rail, realisation dawned, and her hand moved. Immediately she became aware of her nakedness underneath, rich colour invaded her cheeks, a flooding of blood which, before the sequent ebb left her deathly pale, crept from slender throat to hair-line on her forehead. Drawing on her courage, she turned to Ughtred.

" Sir Monk . . . for that is what I now recognise you to be," she whispered. " When you brought me in here . . . wet and my senses lost . . . you . . . you . . ."

Ughtred of Monkseaton bowed his head. " Yes, lady," he said simply.

For another long spell there was silence until, freshly-covered with rosy confusion, she forced herself to look at him again.

" I owe you much, Sir Monk . . . for everything," she said softly. " And with all my heart I thank you."

Ughtred mumbled, " You were frozen and half-drowned, lady. And I felt that unless your . . . unless you were warm . . ."

Not knowing what else to say, and wishing to save her modesty as much as possible, he went outdoors again. On returning, after allowing an appreciable delay, he brought with him crusty bread and a flask of wine. She ate a little and drank a little, and told him that already she was much better.

The fire was burning well, large enough to add thick logs which, when once ablaze, would keep the cave warm for some hours.

" After a good sleep, lady, perhaps you will feel yourself again," he said, making sure the fire was safe. " God willing."

" Where are you going? " she asked.

" To water and fodder my mare, lady. She will become very impatient if I neglect her any longer."

" Will you be long, Sir Monk? "

" It may take me a little time," Ughtred said, awkwardly. " But have no anxiety, lady. When I am cosseting Bess I shall not be far away, and no one shall harm you."

She smiled at him. " I have no fear that I would ever call to you in vain, Sir Monk. When I close my eyes to sleep I shall do so in content."

For long after that the sweetness of her voice lingered in his ears. It was still with him when, close to the mare, he settled on a narrow ledge to pass the long hours before first light brought an end to the night of storm. Some time later, just after deciding how imperative it was for the nun's good name to get her away before the woodmen arrived to start their day's labours, he became aware that the flickering light at the entrance to the cave was obscured. Slipping past Bess, he hurried towards the rough, projecting roof, beneath which he found her, hugging to herself a mantle which flowed copiously round her feet.

" Lady," he said worriedly, " I had hoped you were fast asleep before now."

" I might have been if you had come back," she said. " But you didn't, and I began to wonder why, and as I wondered I grew more wideawake."

This was the moment, Ughtred thought, when wordly advice was essential. Carefully picking his words, he explained how impossible it was for them to spend the night hours together. Even in a layman and a maid it would be wrong, and it would be far more wrong, a betrayal of everything each devoutly accepted, in a monk and a veiled nun.

" Then it is wrong of you to look on my face," the nun of Watton retorted haughtily. " And it was still more sinful of you to disrobe me. Tell me, what would your Saint Bernard have thought of that? "

" In . . . in the circumstances," Ughtred stuttered, " I think he might have understood."

" The circumstances are still the same," she said, her tone distant. " Moreover, Sir Monk, if your Saint Bernard is as wise as he is reputed by the doctors, he would agree with me that it is folly for you to remain in the pouring rain. Did he urge those who followed him to seek illness deliberately? "

44

" Perhaps not, lady," Ughtred of Monkseaton said uneasily.
" But he taught that Death is only a loving companion at our elbow
throughout life, and that we should never be alarmed by its near
presence."

She did not argue further but, her lips curved sweetly, held out
her hand.

" Come, Sir Monk," she said. " Between now and daybreak is
merely the briefest interval against what remains of our lives, and
soon after the day breaks we shall both be on the way to the cloisters
in which we are to spend the rest of our span. It would, in the
months and years ahead, be a comfort to me to remember that I
had a thought in these few hours for your well-being."

" I am not unused to cold and hardship, lady," Ughtred said
gently. " I shan't harm out here."

Her eyes became more luminous. " Please, Sir Monk," she
begged. " I could not rest if you didn't."

Protesting no more, Ughtred allowed himself to be led inside,
where he replenished the fire and, at her command, arranged a seat
of bracken for himself. For the next few minutes each of them, it
seemed, was either lost in a reverie to do with the golden flames,
or much too tongue-tied for speech.

" Sir Monk," the nun said eventually, "wil you tell me who
you are? "

Ughtred cleared his throat. " I am Ughtred of Monkseaton,"
he said huskily. " A monk of eight years profession, of the Abbey
of the Holy Virgin at Rievaulx in Ryedale, and of age twenty-four."

" And I am the nun Lazelle, of the Double Order of Saint Gilbert at Sempringham, of the Priory of Watton, in the wapentake
of Harthill towards the river Hull, of years eighteen."

" Lazelle! " Ughtred murmured. " *Lazelle!* It is a name I have
never heard before . . . a name which slips sweetly off the lips, lady."

" I don't know who gave it to me," the nun Lazelle said wistfully. " It could have been the choice of one of my parents, but as
I have never known who they were I have never been able to ask."

Ughtred saw her distress when, less nervous about looking into
her lovely eyes, he turned to her.

" These things happen when men are often in strife and plagues
every few generations sweep the land," he said consolingly. " A

child is orphaned, and frequently there is nobody to care for it."

The young nun nodded. " It may be so . . . Brother Ughtred. All I have been told is that I was handed into the charge of the nuns when only a babe, and ever since I have lived in one nunnery after another. And I also know that the Sheriff of Lincoln pays the priory threepence a day for my keep, and a mark annually for a robe."

" Then of certainty you must spring from a noble family, lady," Ughtred said.

She smiled faintly. " I have no family, Brother Ughtred, except the religious at Watton. But no more of me—tell me how it was you became a monk."

The picture of an everyday scene in the hall of his family's manor house flashed into Ughtred's mind, and his mouth curved with humour at many recollections—his smallest brothers and sisters romping noisily with the dogs; the wailings or the chuckles of delight of his nephews and nieces, the babies of his older brothers; the laughter of his mother, and unwed sisters, and sisters by mar-riage; the buzz of preparation for sporting forays; the glee and the excitement, the toastings and boastings about martial deeds to come, when blown horses raced in and exhausted riders gave news that raiders from the North were in the offing.

He told the nun Lazelle something of this. " It was a happy and boisterous family life. But I had only one idea—to paint." He shook his head wryly. " I couldn't when there, and I hungered for somewhere where I might have more seclusion."

" So that explains how you became a monk," she said. " It was just a yearning for the stillness and silence of the cloister."

" Not entirely, Sister Lazelle," Ughtred said gravely after a short space for reflection. " In itself I think I was attracted to the life of the religious. But," he smiled, " I have always been the odd one out, preferring to watch a sunset to breaking in a yearling . . . or *anything*," he ended almost inaudibly.

The young nun had been intently watching the play of expres-sion on his face.

" You are very happy now that you can paint? " she said.

He frowned slightly, the firelight causing two creases on his brow to appear deeper than they really were as he talked to her about

Citeaux and elsewhere, and of the many masterpieces he had seen, and of how he had soaked in the effect of the more intense light of a southern climate.

" All the way home I have been thinking of the works I would try to do," he went on haltingly. " And praying that to the glory of God and of Rievaulx I might reach a little towards the wondrous paintings which have enraptured me. That has never been out of my mind, and I have been longing to reach home to begin the attempt. Yes . . . yes, I have been happy enough."

" But you are not as happy as you were, Brother Ughtred," Lazelle said gently.

He found it hard to furnish a rational explanation for the feeling of disquietude he could not shake off, but, in fits and starts, he succeeded in conveying to her how much he had been shaken by the remarks of a Franciscan friar recently met, remarks which had in truth sprung from the outpourings of a down-at-heels street preacher.

" In my travels," he continued slowly, " I have seen incomparable riches and treasures in a few places, and poverty beyond description in many more places. It was this preaching Lollard's opinion that Holy Church and the great abbeys might well use their wealth, even to the extent of impoverishing themselves, to improve the lot of a multitude who from day to day do not know from whence their next pittance of food will come."

" Even I have seen something of that," Lazelle said sadly. " Poor souls in rags, carrying babes they are too enfeebled to suckle, pleading pitifully at the almonry for an extra pittance to take away to feed other children."

" I have seen mankind reduced to more horrible straits than that," Ughtred said, shivering with distaste. " Starving and ill husks who, stomachs void, claw for the dole and cram the food into their mouths with the ravenousness of wild beasts."

Lazelle closed her eyes. " It is so very dreadful, Brother Ughtred."

Ughtred sighed. " I don't know what the answer is, my sister," he said. " It is all very well for the Lollard to urge the religious to surrender their revenues, but even so I am quite certain that this grievous state soon would be with us again, and then who would

47

there be to succour the needy and distressed? For it is in human nature for some to be weak and slothful, and weakness and sloth lead to abject poverty and a lack of pride which makes easy the acceptance of charity."

" But it would be a step, wouldn't it, Brother Ughtred?" Lazelle said. " Did not Christ teach us to share with others even to the last crust? "

" Yes," Ughtred of Monkseaton murmured. " Yes, He did, lady."

Another squall howled past the entrance to the cave. When the sound died away the nun Lazelle spoke very quietly.

" I think the preaching of the Lollard affected you very power-fully, Brother Ughtred. Or else you—who willingly gave yourself to a life of seclusion and contemplation—would not fret yourself about the outer world's things."

Ughtred shook his head. " It was much more the Franciscan," he said. " He was sarcastic at my expense, I know, but although I could not comprehend his barbed shots some glimmering is now entering my mind. Vaguely, perhaps, but it is there."

Disturbed by the worry and uncertainty in his expression, Lazelle put her hand on his arm.

" What can you do? " she said. " You, who are not of the world? Besides, you owe a duty to yourself, a duty to what God has entrusted to you—your power to paint."

The lines on Ughtred's face softened. " Would that I were as gifted as you imagine me to be," he said. " So I must tell you, Sister Lazelle, that never yet have I painted a holy picture which satisfied me when done. I was always disappointed."

" That merely proves what I say," the young nun replied with some energy. " It is the indifferent craftsman who is smugly pleased with his workmanship."

It was a long time since Ughtred of Monkseaton had laughed aloud. He did now, more heartily than he had done since leaving his home more than nine years before.

" Your support, Sister Lazelle," he said, still smiling broadly, " would be more convincing if you had seen a single fresco of mine."

" I don't even need to see," the nun Lazelle said obstinately. " Somehow I *know* you have great skill."

Ughtred's smile faded. "Would that I had," he said longingly. "Would that I could grind and blend my colour to the shades I conceive in my head, would that the strokes of my brush could lay down the glories I picture in my mind's eye."

With a steadily growing intimacy, they continued quietly to talk in the firelight; for so long beyond Compline and into the Great Silence that, when Ughtred of Monkseaton rose regretfully, it could not have been more than a few minutes short of midnight, when the monks of Rievaulx would be rising from their beds, for Matins and Lauds.

"Sister Lazelle," he said as he fed the fire, "you have undergone a very trying experience and now I think you should rest. Will you try to sleep?"

Her eyes were bright. "I will try, Brother Ughtred. But if I don't succeed it is only because . . . because I am excited about this night, and so happy, too."

Ughtred's voice was shaky. "I am also happy, Sister Lazelle. It has been wondrous to unburden myself freely, without watching over my shoulder for a guardian of the cloister in his soft-soled boots; wondrous to talk without fear of a scourging in the chapter house the next morning."

The nun Lazelle's lips were quivering. "Brother Ughtred," she began tremulously, "might we say together the last prayer of Compline, as each of us would before going to bed in our convents?"

"It . . . it would be a fitting conclusion, my sister," Ughtred murmured.

She rose from the bracken and, hands in the attitude of prayer, they knelt side by side, close together.

"O Lord God," said Ughtred.

"O Lord God," Lazelle whispered.

They continued in unison, the sweet voice and the deep voice:

"O Lord God, save us waking, guard us sleeping, that awake we may watch with Christ, and asleep we may rest in peace—grant us a quiet night and a perfect end."

No other word was spoken. In this fashion a monk of Rievaulx and a nun of Watton, in a small cave above a fast-flowing stream, while the wind howled and the trees dripped, entered into a Great Silence of their own.

*     *     *     *

To the man with the cross-bow the end of the stalk had been an unnerving experience and, still down on one knee, he stared in horror at the couple now disappearing into the distance—at the nun riding on the mare and the monk who was walking alongside. To have a nobly-antlered hart pause, look round and feed within range, and then to have the quarry frightened away well before the shot could be loosed off, was infuriating enough; but to be gently told that this was no morning to slay one of God's most beauteous creatures . . .

"She was a virgin wife, to that I will swear," the bow-man muttered, knuckling his eyes, "but if she was, what was she doing abroad? And why was there a grinning monkish fellow with her? If . . . if either of them was there," he groaned aloud. There would be no more sport for him this day. Visions were grim portents and he must seek solace without delay, even if it meant the burning of many candles.

Scared and unsteady, with a distant shrine in the forefront of his bemused mind, one containing a fingernail of Saint Pancras, the foiled marksman rose to his feet.

Meantime the mare Bess was plodding on patiently, her ears pricking occasionally as if she were listening to the conversation taking place in her vicinity.

"Oh, I'm so glad he got away, Brother Ughtred," Lazelle said. "I couldn't bear to think of a creature so lovely being killed on this morning."

The sun was shining and she had opened her hood again. Still smiling, Ughtred of Monkseaton glanced at lace-like threads of water, the aftermath of storm, which were running down the hills, before looking up at her.

"He was a very shaken man, I fear," he said. "I doubt if he will miss Sunday Mass for many weeks to come."

Lazelle smiled. "His mouth opened, and I swear he gaped at us as if we were spectres from some unhallowed region."

Ughtred laughed, and nodded. "Sister Lazelle, there's one

matter, a very different one, you must satisfy my curiosity about. Why was your lady in these forlorn parts, particularly at this late season? "

Momentarily, wondering about her companions' fate, Lazelle's expression clouded.

" We were returning from the wilds of Richmondshire, where My Lady had been staying with her friend, the prioress of Marryck," she told him. " But for the mishap we should have laid with the nuns of Keldholm for the night, going on to the abbey of Rosedale the next day, where My Lady has another friend."

" One of the convents Cistercian and two Benedictine," Ughtred commented. " Your lady does not confine herself to your own Order of Gilbertines."

Lazelle laughed. " My Lady, for herself, does as she wishes, though she can be less lenient with others. If it pleases her to net badgers in the night she ventures out, and if it amuses her to shock the good ladies of Holderness with a daring head-dress she does— they often are invited to the priory for great festival days."

" I should have thought that a lady of decidedly sporting inclinations would not have spared a thought to matters of dress," Ughtred said, amazed.

" Oh, she does," Lazelle said, very seriously. " My Lady is a most fashionable lady."

Their route took them up hill and down dale, in and out of the forest, over narrow, high-arched, pack-horse bridges below which streams foamed, and past cascades leaping down stony terraces. It was a joyous journey, abruptly ended at the top of a brow beyond which the bents and heather of a moor showed. A rider was approaching them from below, attired in a manner Ughtred was now able to recognise.

" Sister Lazelle," he said, " I fear we shall soon meet one of your canons regular."

Lazelle's brightness faded. " So it is over, Brother Ughtred," she said, beginning to busy herself with her hands. " Now I must be veiled, and my hood must be so nearly closed that——"

" Not yet," Ughtred said imperatively. " Let me look at you."

Many seconds later she whispered: " Why do you stare at me so hard, Brother Ughtred? Oh why, Brother Ughtred? "

"Because I want to remember everything—the colour of your eyes, the long lashes fringing them, the curve of your lips," Ughtred said. "Everything, Sister Lazelle, because——" At that moment he had the inspiration. "Because, Sister Lazelle, when I am home again, My Lord willing, I shall paint a picture of your face, a picture that shall be, God giving me a power I have never had before, the greatest work I have ever done."

Fumbling through haste, she had eventually undone a thin chain round her neck, from which hung a tiny box containing a holy relic.

"Take this, Brother Ughtred," she said quickly. "Within it is a small piece of manna from Heaven which was fed to the Israelites."

"I have one also," Ughtred said, as quickly. "It is a fragment of stone on which the Baptist John once sat."

They had exchanged their treasures, and she was circumspect to all outward appearances when the canon of Watton reached them, a middle-aged man with shadows under his eyes and a bitter, discontented mouth. Over a black habit he was wearing a white cloak, furred at the neck, lined with lambskin.

"How is it with My Lady and Sister Katherine?" Lazelle asked.

"They are safe," said the canon regular.

"And Puchin?"

The canon frowned. "Making as big a nuisance of himself as ever," he said sourly. "But what of you, my sister? Where have you been? How have you spent the night?"

"She spent the night in as much comfort as may be expected when a gale blows over a wilderness, Sir Canon," Ughtred said sharply.

"I am not addressing myself to you," the canon regular retorted.

"I passed the night unharmed, and in perfect safety," Lazelle said haughtily. "Sir Monk watched over me most carefully, and God could not have given me a more proper guardian."

"You will be more respectful, Sister, or you may repent your naughty tongue," the canon snapped.

"I will be respectful to My Lady, and will gladly answer her questions," Lazelle said icily. "But no more of yours."

The canon regular's cheeks flamed with anger, but he contained himself. " Very well, Sister," he said thinly.

There was another clash after Lazelle had dismounted from Bess and Ughtred had seated her on the other horse. She firmly declined to permit the canon to ride with her.

" I cannot walk back all that way," the canon spluttered. " It is miles to where the Dame Philippa lodges."

Lazelle expressed regret, but reminded him that if he enforced his will one of the strictest Rules of their Order would be broken; faithful adherence to these, she added, had always kept the two communities of Watton free from shame.

" What My Lady would say I don't know, Brother Canon," she wound up. " But I fear the canon superior would issue instructions for a flogging the like of which your chapter house has never wit-nessed before."

Had the circumstances been different, Ughtred would have been amused by the departure of the pair, the enraged canon at the pre-scribed distance to the front, his charge riding behind him. But, after bowing as Lazelle passed by, he was in too melancholy a state to do other than throw himself on to the grass, where he looked for a long time at the relic he had been given before fastening the slim chain round his neck.

It was the same when, at long last, he resumed the journey. Lost in his thoughts, he saw little of the countryside about him and, when close to home, almost failed to recognise a small market town and the once proud castle overshadowing it. A few miles farther, well beyond a tall stone cross on a green-turfed lane, he began to try to pull himself together, and stopped where a gap in the forest permitted a view of Rievaulx and its surroundings which, however much it might have repelled the Sieur Newburgh of long ago, made a most verdant sight now.

" Home again," he muttered, staring at familiar things.

The abbey, surrounded by a watchtower-studded, battlemented wall, outside which was a small cluster of the dwellings of the land-servants, lay in a lovely, wood-encompassed valley, along which stretched well-kept meadows and pastures. Owing to the restricted nature of the site, the line of the grey church ran appreciably at variance from the accepted east and west, though this departure had not been allowed to affect the names of the walks of the cloister. From this point after the final, circling approach, there was a fine view of the severe, west front of the stone-slated nave, but the low bell-tower hid to some extent the more ornate and later-erected quire, with its steeply-pitched roof and fancy pinnacles.

" Yes, home again," Ughtred repeated, clicking his tongue.

Scenting home also, the mare moved with alacrity, soon reaching another tall cross, of wood, which indicated the way to abbey-bound travellers. From there she quickly came to the first gate and the outer court beyond, across which she headed unerringly towards the gate-house in the main wall. Breaking into a canter, she passed various buildings: the wax-house used by itinerant candle-makers annually, the store where lambskins, catskins and cloth were kept, and the workshops of cobblers and tailors. To her extreme left were the piggeries and cart sheds, and, nearer, a huge, newly-constructed barn with a porch enriched with carvings of saints.

The porter, with several assistants, was already waiting to receive Ughtred at the gate-house. All smilingly bowed, but there was a touch of inquiry in the porter's tone when he spoke. The testy auditor, Roger, had passed in unquestioned on arrival, but from the younger newcomer information might be obtained.

" *Deo gratias*, Brother Ughtred," he said. " It is good to see you home again. But . . . er . . . what of My Lord? "

" We bring news of him," Ughtred said after dismounting. " He will be with us in a few days."

" Praise be," the porter murmured as he beckoned to an under-porter and nodded at the saddle-bags. " Take them to Brother Ughtred's cell in the dormitory and remain with them until one of the honoured obedientiaries arrives."

When Ughtred had finished fondling Bess, and a groom had led her past the kennels and hawk-mews in the direction of the hay-house and the stables, he walked across the paved inner court towards the arcaded porch at the west end of the church. On his way he went by the granary and the massive guest house, and, on the other hand, the pudding house, the shambles, and the stock-fish place.

After entering the porch, where he had to skirt a blue marble coffin lid projecting a few inches above the floor, Ughtred went inside.

For a few moments he stood just within the doors, looking down the immense length of the church towards the tall and slender windows at the east end which silhouetted a magnificent silver crucifix, rising loftily above a beautiful screen behind the High Altar, and a large figure of Our Lord, surmounting the rood screen.

Advancing slowly, he passed the massive Norman pillars of the nave. The light was not good, although the interior, save for thin red lines representing the courses and divisions of masonry, was wholly coloured in white; the windows, both in the barrel-vaulted aisles and the clerestory, were small, the bubble glass in them of a greenish hue.

When a few paces short of the nave altar and the superb, wrought-iron screen beyond it, Ughtred halted to stare at a fresco in the south aisle, of *The Descent of the Holy Ghost on the Day of Pentecost*. Sadly he shook his head—now, after his travels, he was even more dissatisfied than he had been two years before, when this task was completed.

. " I am ashamed," he muttered. " Much too crude and garish."

Beyond the ironwork screen, lovely little chapels filled the aisles; each beautifully-fashioned altar was raised, holy relics were built into the walls, and the basins, for washing the holy vessels, were exquisite.

Ughtred entered St. Paul's, always his favourite. From it he could perceive the soaring arches of the crossing which, rising to dimly-seen heights, supported the tower. Kneeling, he prayed.

" Jesus Christ, our Saviour, take this thing from me, give me the calmness I yearn for. O Redeemer, cause me to forget her, to think of her no more . . . no more, no more."

After a time, spent with emotion, he rose and, closing the open-carved door of the chapel, went forward to the crossing. As he looked about him, into the transepts and up the quire, he murmured to himself.

" For a church with its arms, O Jesus, is the shape of the cross on which you so cruelly died, to save others. Of them I am one, and never has my need been so great. Please, O Jesus, help me never to think of her again."

From there he wandered to the end of the north transept, where he eyed a picture on boards, in oils, from his brush. It was *Our Lord's Pity*, showing the dead Christ on his Holy Mother's knee.

Hearing footsteps ringing on the tessellated pavement, Ughtred turned and saw a monk of somewhat less advancement than himself who, plainly, had been in trouble for speaking when it was not permitted. His cheeks bulged, forced out by a stone which, both as reminder and for punishment, he would have to keep in his mouth for a week or a fortnight, save when eating, sleeping, or during the Offices.

" So you're home again," Brother Giles said indistinctly. " It was only by chance I came hither, in the hope that in an out-of-way corner I might assuage the pain in——"

Ughtred shook his head slightly but emphatically before bowing as two of the abbey's most important officials, the sacrist and the cantor, came from the quire, through the doorway in the massive pulpitum. Simultaneously Brother Giles took his cue, conducting a conversation by signs, which was permissible. He pointed upwards to *Our Lord's Pity*, rubbed his hands, and clapped Ughtred's back as if in congratulation.

Ughtred waited until the two seniors had passed through the south doorway into the cloister.

" I'd take greater care, Brother Giles," he said. " You know what it means when you're caught out—double of what anybody else gets."

Brother Giles's pleasant face darkened. " You're out of date, my friend—though we're not allowed to have friends who might distract us from absolute devotion to the Rule, are we?—yes, you're out of date." He touched his mouth. " Two days more—in my fourth week."

" Sssssh," Ughtred hissed.

A number of monks had entered from the cloister, and for a few moments, during which Brother Giles slipped away, he was kept bowing. Meantime an odd remark made by the Franciscan friar came into Ughtred's head, possibly because he was back in familiar surroundings, and now away from a world in which only the minority were clad as his own Order. Yes, the grey habits of the

Cistercians were cumbersome—the sleeves, in fact, fell to below the knees, and were a yard or even more wide.

After this not very rewarding thought he passed through the pulpitum, from which the Epistles and Gospels were read. Beyond, he looked into the quire, with its double-banked stalls at each side, where he had sat for so many hours in these past nine years, night and day; and at the presbytery, with three steps leading to the magnificently-appointed High Altar.

After a while, Ughtred returned to the crossing, from which he glanced towards the south transept, with its three great windows through whose small, delicately-leaded panes a rich ruby light filtered. The clock-house was below the centre window, and he at once went out to the cloister on noticing that the period devoted daily to work and recreation had been longer in course than he had supposed.

The abbot's seat near the church door was unoccupied, and so he had to await the prior's arrival. From that point he could see the full length of two of the cloister walks. Along the north walk to his right, sheltered by a lean-to roof extending from the church, the scribes, copiers, rubricators and illuminators were busy in their carrels, small compartments separated from one another by wooden partitions. Each carrel had a window which looked on to the grassy, rectangular cloister garth, where a grave was dug in the middle, a permanent reminder of the mortality of man.

In front of him was the east walk, at the far end of which the novices, entirely clothed in white, had been reciting the *De Profundis* under the supervision of the novice-master, another senior official. The proceedings were momentarily suspended—the novice-master, so Ughtred gathered, had taken exception to a pupil's pronunciation of the Latin. The culprit, grabbed by the hair, was being shaken, and it appeared as if tufts might shortly be pulled out, so much was his tutor's vigour.

" So you have returned, my son," the prior said, sitting down.

Ughtred hastily bowed. " Yes, Most Revered Father," he said.

The prior had thin lips, and was the most feared disciplinarian in the convent. It was believed he was not in accord with the abbot in many matters, but there was no proof of this.

" Why did you not come back with Brother Roger? " he asked, promptly putting another question after Ughtred had briefly explained. " How did you safeguard this nun you speak of? "

" I passed her to the care of one of the canons regular of Watton, Most Revered Father," Ughtred said.

Nodding, the prior dismissed both that matter and the monk. " You know what you have to do now? " he said.

" Yes, I go to my cell in the dormitory and wait there. And then I go into retreat for three days."

The prior waved him away, and Ughtred, after bowing, crossed the east walk, passing the library, chapter house, parlour, and treasury. When near to the novice-master he stopped to bow, and bowed again after the obedientiary, rising from a carved wood chair, had inclined to him. Then he went up the day-stairs to the dormitory, an immensely far-extending apartment divided by wainscot at each side into a long range of cells. Half-way along the mat-covered passage was a cross, where trivial violators of ordained silence did penance for a few hours at a time.

The under-porter was in Ughtred's cell, and both stayed there until the sub-prior arrived about twenty minutes later.

The sub-prior responded to Ughtred's bow, but spoke to the under-porter first.

" The bags have not been touched? " he said.

" No, Revered Father," the under-porter said.

" You are aware that a monk can have nothing he can call his own? " the sub-prior said sternly to Ughtred. " You are to be naked in imitation of Christ, and in obedience to the precepts of our Gospels."

Ughtred bowed. " Yes, Revered Father."

" Very well," the sub-prior said.

The bags were opened. Additional clothing, loaned for the journey to Cîteaux, was put to one side, to be taken by the under-porter to the chamberlain's department. The remainder was checked against the official maximum: three shirts, and three pairs each of drawers and stockings; two habits, one scapular, and two hoods; one pair each of leather boots, clogs, sandals, and night boots, the latter warm in wear and felt-soled for silence. The smaller items consisted of an extra girdle, a pouch with handkerchief, tablet and style for writing, breviary, comb, knife, needle, bodkin and hank of thread.

A number of sketches, done in France, were impounded.

" My Lord knows of them, Revered Father," Ughtred said, when sternly asked for an explanation. " They are intended as a basis for pictures for me to do now I am home."

The sub-prior did not relent. " I shall speak to My Lord on his return," he said, signing for the under-porter to leave. " If he confirms what you have told me you shall have them back, my son."

Ughtred bowed, and bowed again as the senior left.

Before making an essential call, he looked about the cell. Nothing had changed. All was the same: the oaken bed and head-perch, tester, sheepskin coverlet; the bench at the foot of the bed, and the round mat.

" But nothing is the same," he told himself desperately as he went into the passageway. " O God, grant me the calmness of spirit I had."

The necessary, off from the dormitory, was a long and very narrow compartment divided on the right into small, open-fronted cubby-holes. The drain, through which a strong stream of water ceaselessly flowed, was against the wall, and over the channel wood seats were fixed. It was spotlessly clean, and each recess was pro-vided with a supply of clean, soft hay in a box.

After leaving the necessary, Ughtred went down to the cloister again, and in the south walk, at one of the lavatories flanking the handsome doorway of the refectory, washed his hands. As he was drying he heard, muted, noises coming from behind the warming house, and so he went through the song school to the novices' court. They had been excused from lessons and, with a few very junior monks of scant advancement, were playing foot-ball. It was a very rough game, an opportunity for young men, who for so many hours in the twenty-four were at prayer or under instruction, to release pent-up energy.

An idea about a much more thrilling way to spend his time struck Ughtred and, steps eager, he hastened to the north walk where, hiding impatience, he waited at the entrance to Brother Robert's carrel. When noticed, he mimed his requirements.

The old chronicler understood him, and pointed with a large knife used for trimming sheets of vellum.

" I've been saving my off-cuts for you, my son," he said. " Under *De Proprietatibus Rerum*—very interesting, that. Pay you to read."

Ughtred bowed his thanks.

The chronicler grunted. " I shall be wanting a talk as soon as you are permitted to speak," he said. " So think up anything unusual you may have seen or heard. All grist to my mill."

Ughtred again bowed and then leisurely, to disarm suspicion, went up to the dormitory where, when certain no one was either going to or returning from the necessary, he darted into his cell. After taking off his constrictive habit, which left him arm-free in a sleeveless, tunic-like scapular, he pulled from under the bed a wooden box containing drawing and painting materials. Time passed swiftly then and, lost in what he was doing, the bell was ringing for Vespers before he could believe it. But he had achieved what he had set out to do—a woman's face stared at him from the oblong of vellum, Lazelle's.

" I have not done ill," he said thickly.

Absorbed, he again examined the likeness before hiding it in the bottom of the paint chest. Then, first glancing furtively into the passageway, he returned to the cloister where his fellows were assembling in line before walking in procession to their stalls in the quire as soon as the great bell tolled.

After Vespers, immediately the supper bell rang, the community filed from the church in pairs, washed their hands at the lavatories, and then went into the refectory, a most handsome chamber.

With the exception of the abbot's table, which stood on a dais at the remote end, the tables were close to the side walls, high officials, monks and novices sitting with their backs to fine wainscoting which extended upwards as far as the sills of tall, lancet windows.

At the table opposite Ughtred's there was a vacant place, with a small wooden cross where a plate should have been. Someone had died, and for thirty days after his death his food was reserved, and the almoner would give it to any needy passer-by. Shading his eyes against the nearby candle to look across, Ughtred at once knew that Brother John of Yarm had joined his Maker.

The big dishes had been placed at the head of each table, for passing along; and the reader, who had climbed a spiral staircase in the wall to reach the pulpit, had begun, at a signal from the prior, to read from the pious legends collected by the Dominican, Jacobus de Voragine.

For a traveller who had eaten nothing that day except a small piece of bread and a mouthful of wine, the meal was not extravagant, an apple alone following the main course, an egg dish overflowing with a thick sauce flavoured with cumin. But before the fruit was handed on one of the servers, Brother Hubert, a young man with a strained expression, appeared before Ughtred with a platter of baked herrings. Conversation was never allowed in the refectory, and he indicated by signs that the fish came from the prior's table. A certain well-defined routine followed: Ughtred offered the dish to his neighbours on each side before helping himself, and all three before eating bowed to the prior. The extra was very welcome to them—the next day was one of abstention, which meant that sixteen hours would elapse before there was even a pittance of food again.

In due course, when the prior gave another signal, the reader marked his place and the community walked in procession to the church. After grace had been said a move was made to the lavatories, where washing again took place, in order of seniority. This done, the brotherhood ascended the day-stairs to the dormitory, where day habits were changed for older ones and soft-soled night boots put on before a return was made to the cloister, speech in a low tone being permitted until the bell rang. The whole company then went into the chapter house, occupying the finely-carved stalls at each side, the abbot's tall-backed chair, crucifix rising from the top, being at the innermost, rounded end. The reader was already standing at the stone lectern near the door and, when the prior had seated himself, began to read from the Book of Exodus.

The real severity of winter had not begun, but the chapter house struck chill, as did all the domestic apartments, refectory, dormitory and cloister. But not until All Saints' Day came in November would a fire be lighted, in a chamber adjoining the refectory, so that the members of the Order could warm themselves occasionally.

After the reading, the brethren went out to the cloister where, some shivering, they waited until the bell summoned them to church for Compline.

When that Office ended the brothers left their stalls, filed through the pulpitum doorway and turned towards the south transept, where the clock showed it was still short of half-past seven. The prior had taken up position at the foot of the night-stairs, and as each of his sons passed he sprinkled him with holy water. The Great Silence had started, and in silence the monks of Rievaulx mounted to the corridor above, along which, passing a sinister prison cell, they walked to the dormitory.

Some few minutes later the third prior made his routine round, glancing into every cell to assure himself that each occupant was abed, and that faces were covered by hoods.

Ughtred of Monkseaton could not sleep that night, and not very much more than four hours later, when the door of his cell was violently struck with a wooden mallet, he was only dozing uneasily.

" *Benedicamus Domino*," the sub-sacrist called sharply.

" *Deo gratias*," Ughtred said wearily.

He got out of bed and put on his night boots. And, as Christ was born at midnight, he stood and said the *Ave Maria*. Sitting on the bed he waited until the bell began to toll, when novices, each with a candle, lighted the brethren in parties of a dozen to the church.

The bell ceased when the prior was in his stall, and Matins began. The Office lasted almost an hour, when there was a brief interlude, during which the younger brothers warmed themselves by rapidly walking round and round the four walks of the cloister, and many of their elders got themselves to the necessary as quickly as possible. Lauds followed Matins, the Nocturns ending about two o'clock in the morning, when the community, candles bobbing in the darkness along its strewn-out length, ascended the night-stairs and wound in procession back to the dormitory.

For Ughtred of Monkseaton the only life he had known since attaining manhood was now resumed.

# 2

It was shortly before seven o'clock on the first morning after the conclusion of Ughtred's period of retreat, and the bell for Prime was ringing. As the tolling would be for the span of a *miserere* psalm only, the brethren on rising from their beds had to hasten. Slipping off night habits and tunics they snatched black scapulars and day cowls, murmuring a short prayer when donning each garment— gratitude because the former represented armour against the Devil, and thanks because the latter signified the all-encompassing protection of God.

After Prime the community left the quire to wash, meantime a bell began to send out a deep, reverberating summons. This was for the Early Mass for indoor and outdoor servants, who would crowd into the nave of the church before starting their diverse duties.

For the religious there was now an interval for reading or reflection, and the cantor, after ceremoniously opening the door of an aumbry recessed in the wall of the east walk, began to distribute books on loan. Now and then he glanced at a monk who seemed to be standing about irresolutely.

It was Ughtred, who was gazing across the cloister garth towards the west range. Through the windows at the far side he could see a bevy of white-clad novices, some of whom were practising walking with becoming decorum; others, under their master's tutelage, were attempting the deepest bow of all, the profound, the art of which was to bring crossed arms down to touch the knees without loss of balance.

Thinking unhappily about an immensely dull encyclopædia he had mistakenly chosen some months before, Ughtred turned to the book cupboard.

He bowed, a profound one. " Reverend Father," he said apologetically, " if it pleases you I would prefer to re-borrow."

The cantor, a plump individual, made several pungent comments, but was nevertheless lenient enough to lead the way into the library, opening an iron gate in the inner wall of the walk and the stout wood door beyond it.

"Well now, what shall be entered in the ' Out ' book this time which perhaps may satisfy you? " he asked caustically. "Look round, my son."

Books and manuscripts filled the shelves, some newly-bound and others scuffed with the usage of over a couple of hundred years. There were the works of the Jewish historians, geographies, copies of the Vulgate, the Greek and Latin Fathers, and many others. Bindings were generally in calf or sheepskin, many of which were stamped with the arms of the abbey, and the majority of the great volumes had locks on them.

"I was wondering, Reverend Father," Ughtred said, "if there was anything from the pen of the learned writer, Wycliffe."

"Wycliffe!" the cantor said sharply. "John Wycliffe? "

"Yes, Reverend Father. The . . . the doctor of divinity."

The cellarer, coming in briskly with sleeves flapping, caused a diversion. When buying provisions at Malton, he told his fellow obedientiary, the erudite Lord of the Manor of Hinderskelf had inquired if he might borrow the *Analytics of Aristotle*.

"Not without his bond in advance," the cantor said promptly.

The cellarer nodded. "I understand the difficulty, Reverend Father. He is absent-minded, it is true, but I would remind you of what you know better than I—he has bequested his library to us."

It was a dilemma and the cantor considered it, tongue thrusting out his cheek. The merest suspicion of a tight smile appeared on his face when he found a solution.

"I will send him a letter by post-messenger," he murmured. "I shall . . . er . . . advise him that the work is in the hands of Brother Ambrose, our book-binder, but will be despatched to him immediately when available. I shall also ask him to entrust to the messenger his set of the Venerable Bede's *Ecclesiastical History of the Nation of the Angles*, to which we have urgent need to refer."

"Excellent, excellent," the cellarer remarked appreciatively. "Naturally you would know these volumes and be aware of their value."

Completely poker-faced again, the cantor nodded. " I venture to assert we should be well on the right side if anything untoward happened. Gems! Amongst the earliest copies of King Alfred's translation."

This little problem neatly settled, the cellarer hastened off to his duties and the cantor turned to Ughtred.

" What do you know of the scoundrel, Wycliffe, my son? " he demanded.

" Very little, Reverend Father," Ughtred replied. " I am aware, of course, that he translated the New Testament into the common tongue so that those ignorant of the Latin might read it."

Brow beetled, the cantor looked at him searchingly. " And that, my son, is enough for you to know about a rogue who tried to destroy the very foundations of our society," he snapped. " Understand? "

" Yes, Reverend Father," Ughtred murmured.

The eventual outcome was that, when in the cloister again, Ughtred turned the pages of an ancient geography, *De Mensura Orbis*, until the bell rang for the Lady Mass. The assembly point for this, the *statio*, was at the nave end of the west walk, which increased the distance of the processional walk to three of the four sides of the quadrangle.

After Lady Mass, for so long as the great bell tolled for the Daily Chapter, the community stayed in the quire stalls " thinking, " as was laid down by the Rule. Then, juniors in the van, a move was made to the chapter house, where the brethren took their seats.

After the reading, the prior made the familiar announcement: " Let us now speak about the affairs of our house." This was also a signal for the novices, who had been standing in the aisles, to leave.

The cantor rose, to face the figure of authority in the high-backed chair at the apse end.

" Most Revered Father," he said, " this day the great bell should be rung."

" In whose memory, my son? "

" That of the noble Wulfstan of Kirkdale, who endowed our beloved foundation with seventeen hereditaments and three benefices."

" So be it," said the prior. " May his soul, and the souls of all the faithful, by the mercy of God, rest in peace."

On this, the sub-sacrist made a note on his tablet about ringing the bell, and the cantor instructed an assistant to enter the details on the *tabula*, so that anyone not present would know the reason for the ringing.

Next, the auditor Roger complained about the quality of the ale, and was handsomely supported. In reply, the cellarer did his best with a bad case, as also the kitchener when yesterday's over-baking of the bread was severely commented upon by a succession of angry speakers.

While this wrangling continued Ughtred was staring across the chapter house, at scenes from the Apocalypse painted above the round arches of the lower range of windows more than a century and a half before. He envied the dead artist's purple and, as often before, regretted that the archives failed to give the slightest hint about the composition of that amazing colour.

Nearby, Brother Hubert had risen. He was trembling.

" Yes, my son? " the prior said.

" Most Revered Father, we are instructed that all inward thoughts must be admitted publicly," Brother Hubert opened shakily. " I have to confess to a misdemeanour."

The prior pointed to the offenders' trunk, a wood platform in the middle. Close to it a beautifully-carved Greek cross rose from the floor : manacles were attached to the extremities of the horizontal arms, and on the upright were two sets of chains.

The monk Hubert had taken his place as directed. " I have had evil thoughts again, Most Revered Father," he faltered. " Last night."

" What were they? " the prior asked sternly.

" I . . . I thought overmuch of Saint Mary Magdalene and of Mary of Egypt," Hubert whispered, hanging his head. " They had no other cover to their bodies save their long hair."

The sub-cantor had already checked the records and, at the prior's nod, disclosed to a gathering now decidedly more alert that the offender had received twenty-five stripes as recently as Michael-mas. His self-confessed error then had been of dreaming about putting his hand into a maid's bosom.

"Forty stripes," said the prior.

This heralded a burst of activity. The *flagellum*, a handle to which leather thongs were attached, was taken from its place on the wall; and Brother Hubert, stripped to the waist, was secured to the cross.

When the sentence had been completed, the monks entrusted with carrying it out—Eustace, a constant weeper and groaner about his own faults, and Aubrey, who was inclined to writing poetry—helped the moaning victim into his clothes and half-carried him back to his place.

The incident did not end at this. Brother Godwin, the barber and weather-man, charged Brother Aubrey with not laying on hard enough, and as a consequence Brother Aubrey received fifteen stripes.

It was a day for talking and it began when the prior, entering the cloister a little later, picked up the *tabula sonatila* and shook it. The musical tinkle had barely died when Ughtred's arm was firmly grasped by the chronicler, who drew him to his carrel in the north walk.

"Well now, my son, what have you to tell me about your journey to France?" he inquired. "What interesting events did you witness? Has your path crossed that of great personages? Any strange rumours you may have heard?"

While toying with a piece of pumice used for rubbing parchment, Ughtred did his best to satisfy. But it was not very long before the chronicler was blowing his full cheeks in and out, as he always did when disgruntled, until an explanation occurred to him.

"My son," he said, "you must understand this is a matter of official business, in so much as it is my duty to write up everything appertaining to this holy house, and to those who are dwellers in it. I am *not* asking you to gossip, from which I know you are debarred as well as you know it yourself—or should do. Now come, my son, have no hesitation."

Ughtred shook his head. "Apart from the wonders of travel I don't know that I have seen or heard of anything outstanding, Brother Robert. Though . . . though . . ."

"Yes, yes?" said the chronicler eagerly.

Dubiously, decided already that his tit-bit of news lacked the exciting quality Brother Robert plainly sought, Ughtred mentioned a hasty detour round a small town in France where a case of feverish pestilence had been reported.

"A case of pestilence, of paltry feverish pestilence," the chronicler said scornfully. With a finger horned with years of writing, he pointed towards the library. " If I took you in there, my son, I could show you what my predecessor fifty years ago wrote of a far more terrible visitation—' The Death ' as we here in England knew it in those dread days when whole townships were abandoned and crosses were laid on the highway to keep people away. He died of it himself, as his successor relates, but before rising to Heaven he described in telling phrases how this land was decimated; when cattle trod down the crops in the fields, because there was nobody to chase them away, and the dead lay unburied because hardly a grave-digger survived. We knew it at close quarters, too—half our lay-brothers—we had almost five hundred, then—half of our lay-brothers perished, I say, and a goodly proportion of the religious of this community. Only a little farther away the lord abbot of Jervaulx succumbed horribly, and such inroads were made into the number of parish priests that for years afterwards Sunday Mass was not said in many hundreds of villages."

" I have read that the country stank of putrification, Brother Robert," Ughtred said gravely. " It must have been a cruel ordeal."

The chronicler crossed himself. " Never to be forgotten, my son. Let us trust that God in his goodness and mercy may for ever prevent any repetition."

" Please God," Ughtred said devoutly.

Present requirements paramount, Brother Robert inserted a couple of fingers under his hood and scratched his tonsured head.

" Brother Roger had nothing titillating to report, and now you," he grumbled. " Surely, even if you didn't see it for yourself, you must have picked up tales of knights in tourney array, and of duels and the like. That's the kind of material I seek."

" I fear not, Brother Robert," Ughtred said regretfully.

He was impatiently dismissed. " I'll approach My Lord's chaplain and secretary on their return," the chronicler snapped. " And if I can't get anything suitable out of them I shall not scruple to try to dig something out of the servants. Good gracious, the world outside can't be as deadly dull as all that."

Belatedly, Ughtred had remembered this might be turning-out day in the dormitory, but on reaching there no one was about. Closing the cell door, he opened his paint chest and took out the sketch of the nun of Watton he had made.

" If it were only in colour instead of ink," he murmured after gazing for some minutes. " If I could only reproduce the glints in her hair, the wonder of her eyes, and the tone of . . ."

He was still puzzling about this on returning to the cloister, where a heated argument was in progress. The noise was at striking odds with the sign Saint Bernard was making in a fine portrait, by a long-dead Italian painter, which hung on the church wall in the north walk—the saint's finger was on his lips, reminder of the silence rule.

Those involved, members of the Parliament which, after the Daily Chapter, assembled to transact common business, were sitting on the stone benches close to the *statio*.

An aged, lantern-jawed monk was ending a tirade denouncing a laxity whereby younger brethren were allowed a day out to act as beaters when My Lord arranged a sporting expedition. He also relieved himself of several withering comments upon the lord abbot's new pastoral staff.

" Instead of everlastingly preparing for the hereafter, are we here for sport and foolish pomp? " he demanded, pointing across the garth. " No, my brothers, not if we are to believe the Blessed Saint Bernard, who said: ' The Holy Fathers, our ancestors, sought for damp and narrow valleys in order that the monks be often ill, and having death frequently before their eyes might not feel themselves to be in possession of any certain lease of life.' That was the way of it, with him."

" Would it assist," the sub-prior snapped back at him, " if we returned to the early days of Cluny, when the lessons of the Night Office were so lengthy that the Book of Genesis was read through in a week? "

Brother Luke scoffed. " Why bring in another Order, in which we have no part. All the return I desire is that we should once more conform to the simple, fervent faith of our saintly founder."

The sub-prior clapped his hands together. " If you were not as old as you are . . ." he bawled, before trying to control his temper. " But that will do, my son," he went on. " There is a vast difference in station between us, and I will not tolerate insolent behaviour."

Although agog, Ughtred had noticed the fourth prior, one of the cloister's guardians, edging past the carrels, and he decided it would be asking for trouble to remain where he was. Those with business with the Parliament might properly be there, but the idly curious received short shrift if caught.

The treasurer was standing in the east walk when Ughtred reached that side, and a beckoning finger summoned him into the treasury. This was a narrow, barrel-vaulted strong room in which the monastery's chief valuables were kept: gold and silver plate, censers, spoons, priceless relics, muniments and deeds, including documents deposited by noble families for safe keeping. The entrance door, of solid iron, had a peep-hole through which, at night, the light always burning within could be seen from the walk. For further security the treasurer and another brother slept there.

Despite this weighty responsibility, the treasurer attended to many small matters, amongst these the brethren's pocket money.

" Your last quarter's became due to you during your absence, my son," he said. " It shall be disbursed to you shortly."

Ughtred bowed. " Thank you, Reverend Father."

After speaking briefly to an assistant, the treasurer led the way to the western range, a two-storied building where lay-brothers of past years had had their refectory and dormitory. Since then the long apartment on the ground floor had been sub-divided for office pur-poses, one of which was used by the auditor Roger, amongst whose duties was that of scrutinising the expenses of each of the convent's main departments. There was also a legal branch, where monks versed in the law made leases, mortgages, assignments and convey-ances, and which for its size burnt more candles than any other place in the establishment.

The treasurer entered the chequer through a small room in which a bespectacled monk was totting up rent receipts by moving counters on a board marked off in coloured squares. He did not even glance up.

As his senior opened an iron-banded cash-box and dumped a

fistful of coins on a table covered with green baize, Ughtred glanced at the books on a shelf. These, apart from those kept there for professional reasons, included a complete set of Euclid, translated from the Arabic into Latin by a monk of Bath, Athelard. The treasurer's hobby was mathematics and as the flimsiest excuse only would cause him to burst into spate about its mysteries Ughtred was prudent enough to be looking elsewhere when the obedientiary addressed him.

"There you are, my son," the treasurer said, indicating a few silver pennies. "So now, when the itinerant traders next lay out their goods in the parlour, you can purchase a little gift to send to one of those many nephews and nieces of yours."

Ughtred smiled. "This time it is the turn of the wife of a brother, Reverend Father. From indirect inquiries, through a sister as yet unwed, I have learnt that she would esteem a small leather case with needles, and hanks of embroidery thread."

The treasurer wagged a finger. "Seek the cellarer's advice before you buy, my son. Through visiting every fair for sixty or seventy miles around he knows every merchant and peddler, and can tell you from whom you will obtain the fairest value."

Ughtred bowed. "That I will do. Thank you, Reverend Father."

Returning to the other side by the north walk, he paused at the copyist's carrel, to watch him at work. Brother Anthony nodded quickly but not unpleasantly, and did not break off—in forty years he had already copied seven hundred and thirty-five volumes, and it was his ambition to surpass the famed Maurus Lapi, who in just under the half century had copied a thousand books.

Marvelling at Brother Anthony's script, every stroke of which was perfection despite the challenge before him, Ughtred continued to the east walk where, stepping into a bay where clothing and underlinen requiring repair were left for the chamberlain's staff to collect, he opened the handkerchief pouch on his girdle and dropped the money into it.

This done he crossed the paved promenade, now being heavily strewn with straw for winter warmth, to inspect the cloister *tabula*, which was fastened to the inner wall between the library and the chapter house. Running a finger down the waxed surface, he found that from the following Sunday he was listed to serve for a week in the refectory.

Ughtred was thinking that, if My Lord had not arrived home by then, to decide what paintings he might do, this duty would hardly affect him at all, when a stiff forefinger was jabbed painfully into his ribs.

" I have it now, my son," Brother Robert remarked ironically, waving a small piece of vellum under Ughtred's nose. " Listen to this, my blind and deaf son. Are you all attention? "

Recovered from surprise, Ughtred bowed. " All attention," he said gravely. " All attention, Brother Robert."

After clearing his throat, the chronicler began to read. " In the fourth year of the reign of Our Sovereign Lord and King, Henry IV, a party from Rievaulx under the Lord Hugh, twenty-third abbot, again journeyed to the abbey of Cîteaux for the Annual Chapter of our Order."

" How does it sound, my son and brother? " Brother Robert demanded.

" Of great dignity," Ughtred said.

The chronicler was not appeased. " Listen now," he snorted. " Er . . . amongst this party was the auditor, Roger, and the monk, Ughtred of Monkseaton, both of whom went and came back without having heard or seen anything. This unique distinction, their incapacity to notice what was before their eyes, their crass inability——"

A small bell rang and conversation ceased everywhere. In the silence, the priest of the week and other sacred ministers walked to the lavatories, to wash their hands before making their way to the sacristy, where they would robe themselves for High Mass.

When the Jesus bell in the tower tolled, the community proceeded with heads bowed and arms folded to their stalls in the quire, where juniors appointed by the cantor opened a press and distributed graduals and psalters.

Standing at the raised stone lectern, the cantor found his note and led the singing. For once, Ughtred did not give himself as utterly as he might have done to one of the most solemn Hours in the seven. His glance wandered, from stone-ribbed vaulting to magnificent candelabra hanging by immensely long chains; from the tomb of Sir John de Roos, who died on a pilgrimage to Jerusalem, and of the Lady Mary his wife, to the doorway of the sacristry, where the ' eternal ' lamp, used to carry a light elsewhere, burned day and night, year in and out.

Dinner followed High Mass, the brotherhood remaining seated in their stalls until a bell in the tower-chamber rang. In the refectory the tables were laid with white cloths and mats, and the servers, wearing freshly-laundered over-sleeves, waited near a screen concealing the kitchen hatch. Loaves, crisp from the oven, were at each place, covered by a napkin; the reader was in the wall pulpit, and below him the sub-cellarer, carrying an immense jug of ale, had just reached the top of a newel-staircase from a storeroom in the basement below.

The chanting of grace after the meal signified the beginning of a period, of almost five hours, for work, outdoor exercises, and a short interval for recreation.

On leaving the church Ughtred noticed Brother Luke, who in two years, on attaining fifty years of advancement, would become a wiseman with comfortable quarters in the infirmary, where he would be subject to far less severe discipline. The sight of the old monk, who did not seem at all subdued by his difference with the sub-prior, reminded him of another even more aged monk, Godfrey, who had moved to the infirmary half a dozen years before. He decided to pay a visit to the old fellow.

At the end of the east walk, between the novice-master's chair and the song school, Ughtred turned into the Passage, but had not gone more than a few yards before hearing bestial cries coming from a gloomy recess. In the semi-darkness he went forward to a square stone with iron rings in it, the entrance to an underground vault in which, very occasionally, the worst of recalcitrant brothers was fettered. The abbey's ordinary prison cells were not pleasant, but the thought of ever being confined in either this dank chamber or in No Ease, another fearsome place near the top of the night-stairs, sent a shiver of terror through every religious in Rievaulx.

Unaware that anyone was absent from the regular life of the convent, Ughtred stooped. His footsteps must have been heard for, from below, a continuous stream of profanity reached him. Deeply shocked, he recoiled and quickly sought a more wholesome neighbourhood.

Crossing himself twice, and puzzling about the prisoner's identity, Ughtred continued along the Passage to the infirmary cloister, where he stood to one side and bowed until the infirmarian had gone by.

Entering the main doorway of the infirmary, he went along the hall as far as a fine brass crucifix let into the floor, and then turned into an aisle, flanked by beds, towards the parlour. This was a snug chamber, warmed more than adequately by a fire which, though big, was being replenished by a fuel carrier.

Old Brother Godfrey, whom Ughtred always thought had the face of a saint, was delighted to see him but, despite his gossip-inclined fellow wisemen's expostulations, immediately suggested a stroll. As he remarked smilingly a little later to Ughtred, whose arm he held, he had a thousand questions himself about the great journey to and from Citeaux.

" A wonderful adventure, my son," he remarked at the conclusion of the account. " Envy is forbidden to us, but I am sure our dear Saviour will forgive me for my backsliding."

This was near one of the fish-stews. The pond was alive, a condition which, amazing to laymen for generations, was essential to a community eating so much fish. But Rievaulx had certain monks who were as expert in pisciculture as those of any other monastery, and all of them zealously guarded their secrets of rearing from the outside world.

Brother Godfrey looked closely at his companion. " My son," he said affectionately, " you seem faraway."

" I am sorry, Reverend Father," Ughtred said apologetically. " I was thinking of how Saint Benedict, almost nine hundred years ago, changed so many things."

" It is indeed so, my son," the wiseman said. " From his foundation at Monte Cassino hundreds of Benedictine monasteries sprang, and we have many noble convents of that Order not too remote from here, tributes every one to pioneer exertions: Saint Cuthbert's at Durham, Saint Hilda's at Whitby, the renowned house at Selby, and Saint Mary's in York. A fine tally forsooth."

" Our Cistercian Fathers also toiled hard," Ughtred said.

The aged monk pointed. " There was a time, my son, when the river over there passed close to our home, but thrice, each time shifting its course farther away by the sweat of their brows, our honoured forebears removed it to where it is now. And those pastures and meadows, once foul and marshy, were drained after immense effort so that those early monks, singing Alleluia as their calloused hands steered their oxen, could plough the rough land and make it fertile."

" The Benedictines no longer labour," Ughtred murmured unhappily. " That being so have they declined from their true glory? "

Brother Godfrey, a considerable student, sighed. " Monastic systems throughout history have had their phases of decline—often irredeemable, I fear."

" Is that why," Ughtred asked, " our own beloved Order came into being much later, perhaps only three hundred years ago? "

" It was a breakaway by Benedictines, who yearned for the old austerities," the old man said, nodding. " The truth was that gaudy processions on feast days, fanciful altar cloths, gorgeous vestments, copes, albs and so on, were repugnant to them. So, calling themselves Cistercians, they set out their ideals in a new *Consuetudines*, rigorously observed them."

Ughtred's thoughts went back to the Franciscan friar. " But nowadays we no longer do, do we, Reverend Father? " he said.

Brother Godfrey paused to stare at him. " I agree, my son, that here the quire of the religious is not actively engaged in the fields, and that our Saint Bernard would have spoken sternly about our living on monies derived from revenues."

" Then we must have declined also, Reverend Father," Ughtred said huskily.

The wiseman looked at him again, searchingly. " My son," he said gently, shaking his head, " you are encroaching on dangerous ground. You must not."

Ughtred bowed, and nothing more was said on the matter.

As Brother Godfrey expressed a desire to visit the cemetery, which was a regular gathering place for many after dinner, they sauntered that way.

A score or more of bareheaded monks were praying over the

graves, which were marked simply by wooden crosses with initials carved on them. It was Brother Godfrey's whim, however, to descend to the crypt of the charnel house, where there was a collection of bones which came from burial places disturbed when making new graves.

" I always think those bits and pieces from the remains of many monks deserve special attention, my son," the old wiseman said with a smile when they emerged into full daylight again. " And now," he spoke with authority, " you must be away to your own affairs." He smiled again. " Small doses of an aged old fellow may cause you to wish to see him soon again, and that is how I like it, my son."

" Not until I have taken you back to the parlour," Ughtred said as he replaced his hood. " Indeed, I think you have done too much as it is. A chill can have serious consequences."

" Even so, what does it matter, my son?" Brother Godfrey said consolingly. " I have had a long and goodly life and I have the temerity to hope that my place is reserved for me in Heaven. A monk, my son, should not be frightened of death."

" Still . . ." Ughtred persisted.

The old man was adamant. He pointed out firmly that Brother Basil, with whom he had an appointment to play chess after his walk, was not more than a few paces away, and that the pair of them, each supporting the other, would manage splendidly.

Ughtred bowed both old men away and then, feeling sad about the inroads of age—and depressed about statements confirming certain of the Franciscan friar's views—set off in the direction of the conduit tower, from which water, channelled down from springs in the hillside, was piped to various parts of the monastery.

To be all-prepared for Abbot Hugh's return, Ughtred entered the church by the galilee and the west door, and walked slowly through nave, crossing and quire to the five exquisite chapels which filled the full width of the east end. Searching for available wall space suitable for embellishment, he also critically eyed banners, pictures and texts some of which might be removed to provide room for something better, halting every now and then to make a note on his tablet for My Lord's consideration.

The north transept, which from the view of perspective was very important, worried him most; it faced the community descending by the night-stairs, and was seen immediately on passing The Holy Three by those entering the church from the cloister.

" The picture there is not rich enough," he muttered. " Perceived in that position, where it catches the eye, it should be a jewel of outstanding distinction."

It was all very well talking, he told himself as he approached *Our Lord's Pity*, which he had begun with such enthusiasm. For some moments he gazed at his work, until, backing away, he started to reflect about the many painted Madonnas he had seen in his travels.

The conception struck him when, still retreating, his shoulder touched one of The Holy Three, sculptured figures, inlaid with precious metals and stones, standing on a marble base.

It was a conception so inspiring and yet so frightening that he seemed simultaneously to quiver with excitement and shiver with fear.

" A Madonna without the Babe," he whispered. " A Virgin for whom the Immaculate Conception still awaits. A maid whose face bespeaks innocence, a maid with purity shining in the limpid depths of her eyes. The face . . . the face of the nun Lazelle."

Senses swimming, he stumbled a few paces and, supporting himself with a hand on the smooth stone of a towering pier, lowered his head to dispel the dizziness. At his feet he saw one of the beautifully glazed yellow-and-green tiles which, the arms of Rievaulx and an inscription on them, had been laid at regular intervals in the floor of the crossing.

" *Benedicite Riavallis Domino*," he murmured. " And perhaps, in all humbleness, it might be the greatest mite my brushes could bestow on this, my home."

Exalted, he rose and stared at the north transept. His lips framed words, but no sound came.

" Please God, lend me the power I crave, so that I may create what I see when I close my eyes," he tried to say. " And, O Blessed Redeemer, if it so pleases you let My Lord be moved to give his gracious consent when I petition him about the Madonna painting I have thought of."

What impression he must have made on the prior, entering from the cloister with an apprehensive-looking party of monks trailing behind, is a matter of surmise. But there could have been no argument about the superior's manner.

"What are you mooning about here for, my son?" he asked sharply.

"Most Revered Father," Ughtred faltered. "I . . . I was thinking about a picture."

"You will attend me," the prior said sternly. "To toil with your soft hands, as our fathers toiled with their roughened hands, in the fashion insisted upon by our Blessed Saint Bernard."

The party left the church and was augmented whenever the prior perceived anyone whom he did not think suitably engaged. Outdoors, as they marched in file past the brew house, he started off his subdued followers into singing the Twelfth Psalm; and near a watch-tower, where the castellated defence wall reached the river, he peremptorily halted progress to castigate fiercely a white-faced young brother of just over two years advancement who, caught humming, plainly did not know every word perfectly by heart.

Tools were taken from the tool-house, and habits discarded, but before work began the prior, his bare-armed, scapular-clad flock standing before him in a crescent, led them into prayers, winding up himself with the versicle in Prime by which he implored the Lord's blessing on their manual labour. This, after all present had bowed to the prior and to each other, was the prelude to two back-aching jobs, with the superior as pacemaker: cleaning open drains and digging out rocks for an extension to the garden.

Afterwards, an exhausted company replaced their tools and hastened to the lavatories in the cloister, where readers had begun to replace borrowed volumes in the book aumbry.

While Ughtred scoured his hands with sand and rinsed them in the water flowing along a lead-lined trough, he had a quiet word with a neighbour in the next arcade, who was able to tell him that a monk of Jervaulx occupied the underground vault. It was a recognised system in the Order, where particularly stubborn culprits were concerned, to pass them to another house for correction. Done only as a last resort, it was an admission of failure on the part of the wrongdoer's convent.

The conversation was continued against the towel aumbry, a

78

large cupboard with a carved door cunningly slatted for ventilation.

" Only once been done by us since I came here," Brother Giles said as he dried his hands. " In my novitiate it was, before My Lord had been elected abbot, and I can recall one of the seniors and a junior being taken off under close escort to the abbey of Rufford— Rufford, mark you, not somewhere conveniently near. They never came back, either. To me it seemed a very mysterious affair, and I've never understood the why and wherefore of it."

Ughtred shook his head. " Nor did I, and I'd been accepted for quite a while then. Have you any idea what this fellow's done? "

Brother Giles tapped his forehead. " It isn't what he's done— it's what he is. *Non compos mentis,* my friend."

" He sounds it," Ughtred remarked. " Has he had the usual treatment? "

" Thirty at four consecutive chapters, and then a lay-off followed by sixty stripes, twice," Giles enumerated. " And I expect he'll be scourged again as soon as his back will stand it."

Ughtred spread his towel over a rail in the aumbry. " I don't suppose the prior is very pleased."

The bell began to ring for Vespers, but despite the sound and the stir of movement the monk Giles glanced about before cautiously replying.

" The most revered father isn't used to failures, Brother Ughtred, and I have no doubt he would prefer to have had the case successfully off his hands before My Lord returns. When will that be, by the way? I would have thought he would have been here before now."

" So would I," Ughtred agreed. " My impression was that he would lie with our brothers of Byland for the one night only."

The next day he and the remainder of the community learned that it would still be two or three days before the abbot Hugh reached home, and that when he came it would only be an hour or so in advance of the lord abbots of Byland and Newminster, who would be his guests for four or five days. Reading between the lines, it seemed that the three abbots had been having excellent sport in the forests and on the moors around the abbey of Byland, and now proposed further recreation with Rievaulx as their headquarters.

Immediately on hearing this news Ughtred obtained permission to have an easel set up in the west walk, whose windows facing the cloister garth enjoyed a north light.

For the next few days he worked diligently on the panel, though its theme did not appeal to him. Nevertheless when abroad My Lord had taken a great fancy to a picture he had seen in the refectory of the Cluniac priory of St. Martin-des-Champs, and so Ughtred strove his utmost to make the most of the main elements he had sketched from that picture: a cardinal, a child, and a moon.

If My Lord was gratified with the result of what he was doing, Ughtred thought as he plied his brush of mixed colours—meantime the brethren kept peeping over his shoulder—My Lord might be kindly when listening to a humble suggestion for a unique and glorious Madonna, God willing, to replace *Our Lord's Pity* in the north transept.

\* \* \* \*

It would have been difficult for the lord abbot of Rievaulx to have found fault with the reception he received from the community. From the west door of the church a single line of the brethren, clothed in albs in honour of the occasion, stretched across the inner court almost to the central arch of the gate-house, and clustered to either side, in an attitude of obeisance, were the paid servants, indoor and outdoor.

When My Lord descended from his horse the religious, snowy-white vestments flowing to their feet, began to move slowly forward, each in turn on reaching him sinking to their knees to kiss his hand. A procession was then formed for the walk into the church, where the holy water was given to him, and he, now in his turn taking the aspersorium, sprinkled each of his sons. Then the obedientiaries, the prior at their head, formed about My Lord and, chanting a *Te Deum* of thanksgiving for his safe return, conducted him to the High Altar, from which he blessed those present.

The ceremonial would have been more prolonged but for the impending arrival of the abbots of Byland and Newminster. They, too, were greeted by the whole community, but this was outside the gate-house, and the procedure was different. The newcomers, before slowly marching into church for prayers, were conducted to the almonry, where their host, attended by high officials carrying towels or bearing silver ewers filled with warm scented water, washed their feet.

For several days after that, for those concerned, the hours of daylight were devoted to sport. Hawks on wrists, the abbots rode out to fly their pets at pheasants, moor-fowl and herons; and, with a sea of hounds around them, set off in pursuit of nimble and suspicious deer.

On the fourth day snow fell, and My Lords rested.

None of this made any difference to Ughtred. As a server, much of his time was spent either in the kitchen or the refectory, and his name had not been included amongst those of the younger brethren who would beat for the lord abbots in their hunting pleasures.

That morning, with both dinners over, the main and secondary, the kitchen was a turmoil of orderly activity. Servers collected plates and dishes from the hatch into the refectory, carrying them to the big sink in the adjoining chamber to the west, where aproned servers were washing-up and placing the pieces on a lengthy draining rack alongside. Others, two pairs of deerskin-gloved hands required, lifted a cauldron of boiling water off the kitchen fireplace and bore it to the sink. In the kitchen proper, a room stone-vaulted in two spans, a monkly cook, peering into one side of a deep double oven, endeavoured to move fig tarts from the top shelf to the bottom, with a scoop on a handle twice a man's height.

It was a cheerful gathering, and hymns and psalms were sung all the time. That was extremely unfortunate for the baker, when the prior walked in by the door from the south walk. Just then, kneading a doughy confection in a deep dish, his voice was raised as lustily as the rest. It should not have been—for the sake of cleanliness, and the kitchen department had that aspect of cleanliness which is next to godliness, a baker was never permitted to sing at his work, lest saliva should ever drop from his mouth.

The prior had looked thunderous ever since the arrival of the distinguished visitors, who in one way or another disturbed the smooth routine of the establishment. For that reason, perhaps, the unlucky baker for the week, Brother Pagan de Bolebec, was left in no doubt as to what he would suffer.

It is almost certain that the prior's mood was worsened as he left the kitchen. At the doorway he nearly collided with a gardener bringing in dried herbs, and a step beyond that he did collide with the third larderer who, heading briskly for the buttery, was carrying a large basket of fish covered with damp reeds.

Three or four minutes passed after that before anyone attempted to sing, and their voices died quickly enough when footsteps were again heard in the cloister, which on that side was not covered with straw. A sigh of relief went up when the abbot's secretary came in to tell Ughtred, who was alternating between sharpening knives and hanging up big cooking spoons, that My Lord wished to speak to him.

" In the lodgings, Brother Ughtred," he added.

The chief larderer, who was sprinkling saffron on an eel bake-meat he had prepared for the fish-cook, pointed to the outer room.

" Wash in there, Ughtred, my son," he said. " The less time lost the better—as it is we're all in trouble here, judged by the fashion the most revered father looked at each of us before departing."

Room for Ughtred was made at the corner of the long sink, and a clean towel was found for him. He was helped into his cowl, his hood was squared off, and they would have girdled him had not his own fingers been quicker.

When near to the novices, who were in their usual place in the east walk, an idea occurred to Ughtred which shattered him by its daring. But after a moment of rational thought he sedately mounted the day stairs, until out of sight of the novice-master, when he scurried along to his cell in the dormitory and took out two small pictures of the nun Lazelle.

" I . . . I shall have to do it sooner or later," he told himself nervously, replacing the one drawn first. " So why not now? "

He retraced his steps, downstairs, bowing to the novice-master again before turning up the Passage, where his pace increased on hearing an eerie scream from the underground vault, his stride continuing lengthy until he had passed the prior's chamber, which looked on to the infirmary garth. Then, after walking under a pentise built out from the wall, he came to the main doorway of the abbot's lodging.

The secretary told him to wait in the ante-room, from which

he had a good view of one end of the spacious dining-hall, a fine apartment with a magnificent ceiling of oak and Spanish mahogany. It was very obvious that a banquet of some grandeur had been in progress. The main table and the side tables were still loaded with dishes tempting enough to make his mouth water: a side of ox, various game, the remains of turbot, sucking pig, goose, pigeon, brawn in a roll, several kinds of choice bread, ewe cheese from Jervaulx, fancy pastries of many kinds, dates and almonds. But what did make his mouth water was a block of butter, with the abbey's arms moulded on it—butter, allowed only in the abbot's lodging, the guest house, and the infirmary occasionally, was a delicacy he had not eaten for nine years.

The secretary came out of the abbot's parlour, to tell him he might now enter.

With the Lord Hugh were the abbots of Byland and Newminster, all sitting at their ease in front of a tiled fireplace. Goblets of wine were close to them on a table, near a large silver ornament, in the form of a lion's head, which reflected the flames of a coal fire.

Ughtred sank to his knees and bowed his head.

" Ah, my son," the abbot said genially. " I take it, my son, that you know that vanity and pride are besetting sins."

" Unques—— without question," the abbot of Byland remarked.

" Yes, My Lords," Ughtred said.

Abbot Hugh held up one of Ughtred's sketches. " Then I may tell you, my son, that my lords here have been most complimentary about your draughtsmanship."

" They are too gracious, My Lord," Ughtred murmured.

The abbot of Newminster rose, assisting himself out of his chair by the arms. His cheeks were flushed and he wobbled slightly when bowing to his host.

" My Lord Abbot," he pronounced solemnly, " the culinary achievements of your menials have been of such excellence, and your wines so superb, that I am in danger of disgracing myself by nodding off. Therefore, if it would please your lordship, I would propose that we take this walk round your noble convent that you have in mind for us."

Abbot Hugh chuckled. " So be it, My Lord Abbot, so be it," he said, furiously ringing a small silver-gilt bell. " And you, my son," he glanced at the kneeling figure, " you will accompany us. It is in my thoughts to select a number of places where we may further beautify our house."

The abbot of Byland belched. " To the glory of God, My Lord Abbot," he muttered.

Chaplains and secretaries soon appeared, and valets brought mitres and pastoral staffs. That was the beginning of a tour during which everyone in the path of the party, which was headed by the three dignitaries, each with his left hand high on the crook of his staff and right signing solemn acknowledgment or blessing, prostrated themselves until it passed.

The refectory was visited first, and there the three lords unanimously were of the opinion that a representation of *The Good Shepherd* could fittingly be shown on the wall above the linen and plate press; but in the vestibule of the chapter house there was controversy about the placings of *Herod's Birthday Feast* and *Christ and the Apostles*, which of them should be on the better favoured south wall. Abbot Hugh eventually decided to defer a decision.

The fine shrine of Saint William, the first abbot, and once secretary to Saint Bernard, was in the vestibule. The relics were preserved in a beautiful container resting on a massive stone slab; above the slab was a vaulted and gabled stone canopy, and below it a gap through which the more pious could squeeze, instead of entering the chapter house by the magnificent doorway.

The abbot of Newminster, who had been scrutinising the colour scheme of the panelled roof, gilt crosses upon a soft mosaic, looked for the second time at a figure beneath the slab, but made no comment. Brother Eustace, stretched face downwards, was groaning miserably as he bewailed his many faults.

A number of decisions were fairly promptly taken in the church. Thanks to the grandeur of the stonework in the quire, with its many smoothly-masoned ribs, embellishment might have spelled ruin, and the small touches of red on the carved capitals was entirely sufficient. The aisles, however, did lend themselves more advantageously, and Ughtred was able to note My Lord's choice for two wall paintings: one of *The Wise Men coming from the East*, the other *The Descent of the Dove*. For spaces in the aisles of the nave the lord abbot selected *An Angel laying hold of the dragon, Satan,* and *The Cauldron of Hell.*

The services for the convent's servants were held in the nave, and when the party, returning, had reached the stretch between the wrought-iron screen, where the tessellated pavement had tiles here and there marked with small circles to help lay-brothers of other days to find their positions when the Office was one of elaborate ritual, the abbot had an afterthought about the frescoes in that part of the building.

"Your work must be bolder than when you are similarly engaged in the quire, my son," he told Ughtred. "The servants are ignorant and for anything regularly within their view it is essential that you be more than ordinarily arresting, conveying as much terror as may be possible."

Ughtred bowed. "Yes, My Lord."

By the time the abbot had reached the crossing under the tower he had issued further instructions to his secretary, who was to seek the Custodian of the Fabric and arrange for the masons to strip off old plaster where necessary, in preparation for re-plastering.

"My Lord," Ughtred said, the palms of his hands damp with sweat, "perhaps it might be best, please My Lord, to wait until the winter is over. Should frost come before the plaster dried out properly, a subsequent thaw would rend the surface with many cracks."

"Yes, there is that, my son," the abbot said. "Though the full rigours of snow-time are not on us yet."

"And may the Almighty keep them away," the abbot of Newminster murmured. "I still have many hard miles before me."

After his superiors had jested about this, Ughtred nerved himself anew. He had drawn another little picture of Lazelle, thinking that the original would appear to My Lord far more as that of a maid than of the Madonna. The face was the same, but he had tilted her head and now she was looking with yearning at a cloud within which two angels were gliding downwards. They held a scroll between them, and on the scroll was a new-born babe.

"My Lord," he said, his heart thumping, "any changes in temperature would not harm if my pigments were mixed with oil and my brush were laying the paints on canvas or wood panels.

And, if I may be so bold as to speak on it to My Lord, I have the thought of a great picture and where it might rest to the most advantage. It . . . it is this, My Lord . . . and the place, My Lord, is where *Our Lord's Pity* now is."

"Remove *Our Lord's Pity* from there?" Abbot Hugh said. "My son, I have always believed that in that you added handsomely to the glories of our house."

"I tried, My Lord," Ughtred said simply. "But if My Lord would have the *Pity* in his lodging, as was My Lord's intention once, I think I might surpass it. I . . . I feel it so, My Lord. Perhaps My Lord would be gracious enough to inspect this."

The abbot examined the little sketch, and was joined by his guests.

"It is a very fine conception, my son," he said, musing. "In colour it might be magnificent. And certainly, my son, it is of an originality which does you credit. What do you think, My Lord?"

The abbot of Byland smiled. "If you can spare him to me, My Lord, this would be the first work he did for me."

Turning to Ughtred, the abbot of Newminster slowly shook his head. "God forbid that you should ever slip into grievous fault, for which your lord cannot cure you, but if it happens, and if your lord sends you to me for correction, I will tell you your fate, now." His voice momentarily became grim, before he chuckled. "You would be immediately chained, my son—to a brush."

"My Lord is very good," Ughtred said.

"H'mmm," the abbot of Rievaulx murmured, again eyeing the sketch. "Yes, I like this, my son, and perhaps later . . . but there is much elsewhere for you to do before this could be considered. And as for the difficulties about changes in the weather ruining your work . . ."

Beckoning, he instructed his secretary to bring the convent's barber to him. Brother Godwin, in addition to shaving the brethren and attending to their tonsures every three weeks, was the abbey's weather expert, keeping a daily diary.

Near the *statio* in the west walk he had various water creatures in large jars on a table in a bay, and over that, fastened on the twin shafts of the arcading so that they faced the grassy garth, were several devices relying on catgut, goat's whiskers, and seaweed. For additional assistance he studied the behaviour of hares, sheep and cows in calf.

Meantime the abbot of Newminster, drawn by the sound of weeping and muffled cries for heavenly help, wandered towards the clock house. His two colleagues followed him shortly.

" I have one of them, too," the abbot of Byland remarked as he looked beyond wooden tracery screening a small chapel in which, shoulders swaying in his agony, a monk was on his knees before the altar of Saint Blaise. " And that, my lords, is enough."

In the church of the abbey of Rievaulx there were in all sixteen private chapels, of which four were in the transepts, two at each side against the east walls. Brother Eustace, after crawling from beneath the shrine of Saint William, had chosen that nearest the door from the cloister. It was on the main traffic route.

" I *had* one," the abbot of Newminster said ambiguously.

About then his host's secretary arrived, bringing with him Brother Godfrey who, when asked, declared with the air of infallibility of all weather forecasters that mild days, without a semblance of frost at night, could be expected until at least St. Martin's Day.

" Beyond that, My Lord," he continued, still kneeling, "my prognosis is less certain."

" Thank you, my son," the abbot said, signing to him to rise and leave. " Let us hope you are correct in your assumption."

As if in complete agreement with the latter, both the other abbots nodded. An Ecclesiastical Council was to sit in York the following month, at which all the leading church dignitaries and abbots of the north would be present, and fair weather made travelling so much more easy.

Again Abbot Hugh looked at the drawing of the nun Lazelle, and then, eyes slightly narrowed, stared towards *Our Lord's Pity* in the north transept.

" I will give this my consideration, my son," he said a moment later. " Meanwhile you will proceed with the work on boards I have approved, without delay. From Sunday, after your week's duties as a server are completed, you will be excused all observance between the end of the Daily Chapter and Vespers, so that your tasks may be forwarded with all speed."

" Yes, My Lord," Ughtred murmured.

" That is all, my son," the abbot said.

" My Lord," Ughtred sank to his knees, " I ask and beseech God's mercy and yours. If it would please My Lord I crave that you will permit me to use as before the workshop near the gold-smith's where I store my materials, so that I may have space to mix and grind my colours."

" You always have that permission when works of appreciable size have to be done," Abbot Hugh said, waving him away. " But," he wound up benignly, " I commend you for asking, my son. It is always inadvisable to take anything for granted."

For the remainder of the day Ughtred's heart was singing, for if My Lord had not consented to the painting of the Madonna there had been no outright refusal, and indeed grounds for hope were by no means lacking.

His happiness had not diminished one jot later in the afternoon when he was assisting the refectorian, by taking spoons from the cupboard and placing them conveniently for the reverend father, who would distribute them when the brethren were seated. It was a day on which, as a treat, the community were to enjoy small loaves hot from the oven, and when the baker announced there would be a slight delay he did not fret or worry as did some of his fellow servers—they were anxious to have the meal over, too appre-hensive in advance about an error in the refectory: spilling the bean soup when carrying a large dish, leaving a thumb mark on a plate, any mistake of that kind—for which they would have to do penance in the middle of the floor.

And when, in his cell after Compline, before hanging day habit and scapular on the perch at the head of the bed, he stood in his undershirt praying, the prayer was of gratitude.

" Thank you, O my Redeemer," he said, with ardour but inaudibly, " for what you have done. And if in your wisdom, O God, you should so move My Lord in the future that he grants my desire to paint the nun Lazelle as a Madonna far out of the reach of earthly man, then give this poor limner the power to rise to heights he has never before attained. For this once, Almighty God. . . . Just this once, my dear Lord above who is so much mightier than My Lord here below, exalted though he be."

This inward glow was with him the next day, warming him

through all the Offices, from the cold, dark hour of Matins to the Daily Chapter so much later. For once, after leaving the dormitory passage to walk with eleven of his brethren to the top of the night stairs, lighted by a novice, he did not notice the low, barred front of No Ease, a prison so placed that an occupant could hear the services in the church—if, confined in quarters so small that it was impossible fully to stretch a limb, beneath a roof too low to allow him to stand, the unfortunate creature was in any condition to hear at all.

That inward glow was tinged with a morsel of impatience as Ughtred entered the chapter house the next morning, the impatience of one who, so near to his goal, is not immediately able to give himself to work he loves. To his relief, however, the presence of the abbots of Byland and Newminster, in chairs placed to either hand of My Lord's, did not unduly prolong the proceedings.

When the reader closed the Book on the lectern near the door, which was when the novices and any strangers invited to be present left the chapter house, My Lord's guests remained seated by my Lord's dispensation.

In the event, nothing of a private nature was bruited. Brother Stephen, an engrosser, asserted not too coherently that a mistake had been made in the singing of the canticle of the *Benedictus* at Lauds, but his argument was elegantly demolished by the cantor; the baker for the week, following upon an accusation by the prior—who seldom stood as mediator between father and son, as some considered to be a prior's function—was whipped for misdemeanour in the kitchen, and three more monks also, all senior to him, for permitting it; and Brother Aubrey was given permission for a slim volume of his poems to be bound in calf and placed permanently in the library.

Brother Henry, to whom life in a monastery had meant escape from the perplexities of a large estate, covetous neighbours, and endless law suits, requested permission for an extra bleeding. He was refused.

" No, my son," the abbot said sternly, " what you are seeking is a pleasant three days' holiday in the infirmary, not to lessen the strains and stresses brought upon a sinful man by overrich blood."

Notwithstanding the rebuff he had witnessed, Brother Eustace rose to beg that he might be allowed to wear, next to his skin, the coarsest hair-cloth shirt the chamberlain could provide. At this, it may have been of some significance that the guest abbots glanced at their host.

" Why, my son?" the Abbot Hugh said with apparent mildness. " What is your reason? "

To Brother Eustace, the invitation to unburden himself was meat and drink, and he promptly embarked upon what soon proved to be a catalogue of his failings, which were without exception of a very petty nature: in the refectory he had cracked nuts with his teeth or cleaned his knife on the cloth instead of using a piece of bread; when he had drunk he had occasionally forgotten to grasp the cup with both hands, and twice in one week he had been greedy enough to cover what was left of his loaf with his napkin, instead of leaving it bare so that the servers would collect it in the basket, to be given by the almoner to any who might be in need. And in church . . .

" I think that is enough, my son," the abbot said sorrowfully.

" I have fallen far, My Lord," Brother Eustace said miserably.

" So far, my beloved son, that the itching of a hairshirt is much too feeble a reminder," the abbot remarked gravely.

" What then, My Lord? " Brother Eustace mourned.

" Forty stripes," Abbot Hugh said crisply. " That should be a far more effective reminder."

Brother Eustace's dropped jaw, and his screeches long before the first blow from the whistling thongs fell upon his bare back, was evidence that he was of a similar opinion. Watched with grim satisfaction by a gathering long wearied by his pretensions, Brother Martin and the registrar, to the tune of twenty strokes each, did their full duty with the scourge.

Both the visiting abbots were leaving within the hour, after a special service in the church, and it was undoubtedly tactless of the auditor to bring up one particular matter, arising from a series of transactions between Rievaulx and the abbey of Newminster. Brother Roger asserted pugnaciously, oblivious to the Lord Hugh's scowl, that the accounts had been out of balance since the beginning of the year and it was full time a line was drawn.

Furiously, My Lord silenced him.

The cantor then read a mortuary roll received by messenger from the abbey of Meaux in Holderness, announcing the death of Simon of Hedon, an aged monk of the house; and the Daily Chapter was concluded with the *De Profundis* and a prayer for the souls of former brethren and benefactors of their own house.

Ughtred felt that My Lord's instruction released him from any obligation to attend the service of farewell and Godspeed for the departing abbots; when the community filed into the cloister he slipped out by the kitchen porter's door.

Rejoicing in a freedom seldom experienced, he walked across the inner court to the workshops reserved for the religious, which were beyond the granary. There were plenty of things for him to see: Coverham and Jervaulx-bred horses being exercised; the larderer and two assistants returning from the fish-ponds, dragnets filled; three of the abbey's carriers just returned from a fair, the wagons packed high and their armed guards relieved to have completed the journey without incident; My Lord's long chariot, freshly-washed, standing gleaming outside the carriage house; and a blacksmith at the forge shaping a red-hot iron-bar on an anvil.

Of great interest were these various sights to Ughtred of Monkseaton, as they would have been to any of the brethren, but he did not hang about watching them.

Filled with a resolve amply to satisfy My Lord, he entered his workshop and began to take stock of his pigments, colours and wash-powders.

" Yes," he told himself exultantly, " if I can but please My Lord now . . ."

Ughtred was breaking up a rocky substance obtained from Byland, an iron-powder from which hitherto he had made a very satisfactory red, when the movement of his hand ceased and he started to murmur.

" This," he looked into the mortar, " would serve me well for what I have to do now. But for what I think and dream of . . . I must have perfection in everything I use, and for one thing I must look to the west."

The monks of Furness made the finest red in England. Filled with determination, he resolved to beg My Lord to include in the post-messenger's bag a request to the lord abbot of Furness to send a supply of the quality needed.

" God grant that if it comes," he told himself wistfully, " I may be able to employ it for the real purpose I have in mind."

Not many seconds after that, optimism engulfed him and, joyously, he began to sing a song of praise.

# 3

In another three days it would be the great festival of All Saints', and there was intense activity throughout the abbey; even the prison cells at the extreme north end of what formerly had been the lay-brothers' range, though wholly unoccupied since the previous evening—when Brother Ambrose, the book-binder, a mild man generally, had been released after a fortnight on bread-and-water for twice swearing at the tanner about the poor quality of calf-leather supplied—were being swept so that fresh rushes could be strewn on clean floors.

Elsewhere, hundreds of cleaned-out sconces were being fitted with new candles; the sacred vessels were being washed, candlesticks polished, and copes and other vestments examined for tears or darns that had become unsightly. And, as All Saints' so often heralded cold weather, rushes were being scattered in the dormitory passage, thicker mats were being laid under the quire stalls, and the servers of the week were spreading straw under the refectory tables to a depth sufficient to warm feet a little.

When the sweepers bustled into the nave with their long brooms, Ughtred swiftly sheeted the painting on which he had been working and, collecting pots and brushes, left the church by the west door.

From the open arcade of the galilee he noticed a few slightly out-of-the-ordinary stirrings: smoke poured from the chimney of one of the buildings in the inner court, where the pudding wives were using the ovens; three farm carts piled with further supplies of hay, straw and rushes creaked across the paving; and from the shambles men were walking in pairs, carrying between them wickerwork hampers loaded with blood-red joints of meat and offals.

Ughtred then went to the workshops, where he cleaned and put away his brushes. In the next small compartment another of the brethren, a smile of pure joy on his lean face, was gazing at a mechanical contrivance, a mass of intermeshing wheels. Peeping in, Ughtred nodded towards a beautifully-fashioned dial and hour hand.

" Who seeks your services this time, Brother Martin? " he inquired.

Brother Martin did his utmost to look modest. " The Most Revered the Archipresbyter of Canterbury," he said.

This somewhat surprised Ughtred, though he was aware of the other's wide reputation as a clock repairer.

" I know a clock once came to you as far as from My Lord Superior of the White canons of Welbeck," he said. " But *Canterbury*, from the cathedral of Saint Augustine, Brother Martin! It is indeed a tribute to you."

Brother Martin blushed. " As to that . . . but it has been to London twice, and still is erratic, so I must strive to my best." His expression changed, becoming disparaging as he stabbed a finger at a cog wheel. " How even the worst of bodgers could allow that to remain is quite beyond me, and I shall cut a new one for a start."

" Is there anything you might need from the city? " Ughtred asked.

For a moment Brother Martin eyed him blankly. " Oh! of course, you ride in My Lord's train after the Blessed Feast," he then said, glancing at a small stock of brass sheets and metals neatly laid out on a shelf. " No, Brother Ughtred, thank you. It is most kind of you to make the suggestion."

" Well, if you think afresh you must let me know, and we will petition My Lord," Ughtred said.

He liked Brother Martin, and as a result of joking about each other's all-absorbing interests a smile was still lingering on his lips as he entered the cloister by the kitchen porter's doorway. Beyond, in the least used west walk, a very junior monk, Lionel, was limping along painfully, but when another of the brethren of the same year, Peter, tried to lend him an arm he petulantly threw him off.

Ughtred did not pause to make an inquiry. One of the chamberlain's assistants, passing by with a pile of towels, was a reminder to him that the hour for feet-washing was not far away, and so he hastened to the nearer lavatory, to scour colour off his hands.

The next morning, shortly after the daily reading in the chapter house, Brother Lionel accused Brother Peter of deliberately kicking him at foot-ball the previous afternoon. The abbot heard him out and then turned to the accused, who bowed his head.

" You have my permission to defend yourself, if defence you have, my son," My Lord told him.

Brother Peter, an open-faced young fellow, blurted out: " I kicked him, My Lord, but it was an accident."

" It was done with malice, My Lord," Brother Lionel said nastily. " How else could he have kicked me in the behind and the ball not near? "

" I slipped on the wet grass, My Lord," Brother Peter said stoutly. " But I expressed regret to my brother afterwards, and he would have none of it."

" Because he roared with laughter, My Lord," Brother Lionel said shrilly. " Until his eyes streamed."

The abbot glanced sternly at the novice-master who, a very tall and spare figure, rose flurriedly to speak: " I was not present, My Lord, or I would have dealt immediately with an offence that did not need proving—this unseemly laughter."

" Why were you absent from your duty? " the abbot demanded.

" I have a disorder, My Lord," the novice-master said wretchedly. " It causes me to visit the necessary in great haste."

" Into whose hands did you entrust your charges? "

" Into the hands of no one, My Lord," the novice-master replied. " I realise I was in error, My Lord, but the call was acutely pressing and the game appeared to be proceeding without any undue vigour."

The Lord Hugh pronounced judgment. The monk Peter received twenty stripes on the spot, and this was not the end of his punishment. Both he and his accuser would not be allowed any recreation until after St. Stephen's Day, almost two months away; and during recreation periods until then, be it rain or shine, gale or snow, they were to stand facing each other across the open grave in the middle of the cloister garth, where both were to recite the Office of the Dead without ceasing.

The abbot signed the culprits to leave the chapter house. " And should it ever be seen by the guardians, or other of the brethren, that your lips are not constantly moving," he concluded, "you are to be brought before me again."

Dejectedly, heads turning as they passed, the two young men walked down the chapter house, between the stalls of the community. As soon as the vestibule door closed behind them, the lord abbot addressed the novice-master.

"As for you, my son," he said coldly, "your feet shall be bare until the day preceding the Nativity, your pate shall be uncovered, and whenever you walk your attitude shall be of that extreme humility as is prescribed the most absolute under our Rule."

Mouth quivering, face flushed dully, the novice-master bowed.

More general business followed. The terms of a deed were read out, whereby the Abbot of Rievaulx and his Chapter, in consideration of value received, engaged themselves to remit eight hundred marks to Annotus Puisaquille of Genoa on the first day of September of the following year, payment to be made at the New Temple in London.

Apart from one dissentient, Brother Luke, the community approved of this, and the treasurer and the sacrist, each with an assistant, left for the treasury and sacristy respectively, returning in due course with the abbey's seal and the eternal lamp. A taper was then lighted, wax melted, the cantor sealing the document with the arms and legend of Rievaulx.

Brother Luke also played a lone hand in the next matter, a proposal that the east windows of the church should be modernised by the introduction of pictures in stained glass. This became an argument between two people. The prior, expression dour, notably took no part in the controversy, and the lord abbot towards the conclusion only.

"How much more," Brother Luke demanded, "must we seek to emulate Fountains, whose abbot is now reported to desire a lofty, ornate tower instead of a low bell-chamber which is the limit our venerable statutes permit?"

"This has nothing to do with the abbey of Fountains," the subprior snapped. "And could we employ our monies more profitably than in glorifying God's house, howsoever the means of it?"

The old monk's lined face was scornful. "Monies we should not have—from lands we should not own, from tithes we should not be enjoying, from fat benefices we should not possess."

" Without money this abbey and most others would never have been erected as we know them," the sub-prior said furiously. " Or do you contend our fathers acted unwisely? "

" The money was Aaron of Lincoln's, a usurer, but despite that our forefathers were wise to borrow," Brother Luke retorted. " Nevertheless the Jew Aaron was quickly repaid—through frugality, by the diligence of our monkish shepherds, by the sweat and toil of monkish farmers labouring in our fields."

" We are discussing the east windows, not loans," the sub-prior shouted.

His old eyes hard, Brother Luke stared at him. " But before that, only a few moments ago, we were talking about a loan, Reverend Father. For myself, on that, I would be glad to be told precisely what that money was required for—if not for fatuous embellishment."

There were imminent signs of a most improper uproar, with nearly a score of obedientiaries and others jumping to their feet to declaim passionately. But the abbot, from his crucifix-surmounted, high-backed chair, quelled them with a raised hand and, silenced immediately, brethren on both sides bowed submissively to him.

" Less of this unseemly behaviour," he said sternly before singling out the old monk Luke. " As for you, my son, you will either hold your tongue or you will be disciplined for your mischief as a novice would be. Nor shall your years excuse you. You understand? "

Brother Luke bowed.

The lord abbot rapped his staff on the floor. " Let us now think, my sons, of the great day soon to be upon us, when we honour all saints, whether known or unknown."

Towards celebrating that day, the next was also one of preparation, of fasting, and vigil; by evening nothing remained to be done, save by the sacrist and his assistants, when after Compline the community filed in the Great Silence to their sleeping cells.

So that the brethren might carefully dress themselves in the appropriate garments, distributed by the chamberlain's department earlier, the sub-sacrist called them sooner than usual that night. It was still a quarter of an hour from midnight when he drew his arm back to hammer on the first door with his mallet.

When robed the brotherhood sat on their beds, waiting. For this once, candle-bearing novices would not be in attendance, and as the great bell began to toll each went into the dormitory passage which, like the stone-flagged corridor beyond, was brilliantly illuminated with torches. Moving off, night shoes making no more than shuffling sounds, the monks of Rievaulx, in snow-white albs and winter-wear fur caps, walked towards the night stairs, so passing No Ease, now starkly revealed as a barred prison cell of proportions more fitted for confining a hound than a human being.

From end to end the church blazed with light; the altars of the nave chapels shone behind the delicate tracery of wooden screens, and smoky, yellow flames leapt up from the standards to give another kind of beauty to colourful wall paintings, rich tapestries, and texts scrolled in gold. And in the transepts the glow, though failing to rise to the mighty height of the crossing, softly shaded the corbelling of piers, the tooth moulding round the triforium windows, and the quatrefoils between the spandrels of the arches; it caressed the sculptured forms of The Holy Three, and added wonder to figures of saints and martyrs carved on the rood screen.

On passing through the doorway of the pulpitum the slowly-advancing file of monks saw double lines of waving light on each side, a silver candlestick marking every stall; and between these, bringing out the brassy gleam of gravestone crosses sunk in the floor, cressets flared in the draught. Hanging from the stone-vaulted roof, magnificent candelabra glittered; and a silver lantern, suspended from a ceiling-rose too high to be discerned, shone on the parchment pages of a chained Antiphony opened on the stone lectern, vividly lighting up square notes and large letters.

Beyond, enclosed by its decorative screen, was the presbytery, brightest part of all from an array of many-branched candlesticks, lamps, candelabra, cressets, and a profusion of large candles on the High Altar. As the chapels at the extreme end had deliberately been left in darkness, this concentration of light invested the crucifix, rising high against the barely seen east windows, with a new magic, and gave an eerie quality to various effigies farther westward in the aisles.

Last of all to come to the quire was Abbot Hugh, who was received by the brethren on bended knees. Be-ringed hand on staff, vestments gleaming with jewels, mitre reflecting a hundred pin-points of light, he walked majestically to his stall. He raised his arm, the bell ceased to toll, and Matins began.

The short interval between the conclusion of this Office and the beginning of the next Hour was passed most pleasantly by the community, in novel comfort. From All Saints' a fire was kept burning in a common-room adjoining the refectory, and when Matins ended the brothers, chilled to the bone after being in church, headed as one man to this warming house, where a log fire crackled and sparked in an immense double hearth.

Throughout All Saints' Day bells pealed joyously, and forever there were processions: in church, round the cloister, through the domestic portions; and several outdoors, one of them alongside the castellated wall, which took in the cemetery, where a brief Office in honour of the departed was sung. These processions differed in rank, but most were of grandeur, with brethren bearing the Cross and the Taper, carrying banners and holding aloft the abbey's holy relics, all present chanting both then and during the final solemn walk from the west door of the church to the presbytery, where ceremonial positions were taken facing the High Altar with its superb reredos as background to priceless images and reliquaries.

Dinner was correspondingly impressive, and in the refectory faces were beaming and mouths already watering when the lord abbot, the kitchener at his elbow, inspected dishes on a table near the hatch to decide whether or not they were of a quality suitable enough for that day of festival: vast platters with legs of mutton, sirloin, geese, swan, plover, pike, salted salmon, venison pasties, and lobsters succulently garnished.

Supper also was of noble proportions and even the ascetics did full justice to it, knowing that from that evening until Advent, with the exception of St. Martin's Day, it would be a repast in memory alone. The refectory was brighter, too. From All Saints', until the winter was over, a candle was shared between three brothers, instead of one to a table.

The meal ended, grace said and hands washed, Ughtred and the other brethren who were riding with My Lord to the city left in a body for the wardrobe chamber, where the chamberlain provided each of them with a pair of superior drawers, two pairs of white cloth hose, somewhat better cowls and scapulars than normally worn, and a mantle.

Under the leadership of Brother Stephen, the engrosser, the party picked up these various articles of clothing and, walking behind one another, went to the dormitory, where each made a few modest preparations for his journey on the morrow.

\* \* \* \*

Brother Godwin's weather forecast had been accurate, and the abbot's party was making excellent progress. Many miles of bleak moorlands and dense woodlands were behind, and several fords and at least three high-arched bridges whose condition was better than anticipated. Nothing much had been encountered since leaving Rievaulx: once a group of pilgrims bound for the tomb of St. Cuthbert at Durham; and a considerable number of cattle and sheep, on their slow way to the city market, was overtaken. However, drovers and dogs acted sensibly—the herd and the flock were driven amongst the oaks and sycamores flanking the narrow track, and the riders' progress was not unduly delayed.

Ughtred was very happy, but with that happiness a sense of guilt was occasionally coupled. Was it wrong, he asked himself now and then, to have this feeling of release? Should he be so amused by rabbits scuttering across the rough road? Was it his business to speculate about the lives of riding foresters and bow-bearers, guardians of the King's game preserves, who halted respectfully to receive My Lord's blessing? How had it come about that at a village, while the church bells rang out in lively greeting, he had wondered what it must be like to dwell in such a community? Was he falling into the sin of envy when a ploughman and his goadsman, zestfully competing in singing the Canticles of David, thought nothing of leaving their oxen on sighting My Lord's little cavalcade?

" Is it because I lack freedom—the freedom to paint what I will? " he asked himself. " What do I care for copying the works of other men? Nothing! Nothing at all."

It was on this vexing issue that the lord abbot Hugh sent for him a little later, when the party again moved off after brief devotions for a canonical Hour. At the time the scholarly Edgar of Heslington was pointing out to Ughtred, with most unscholarly excitement, the city he had just glimpsed. It lay far ahead, in the midst of a far-extending plain, and its salient features were difficult to perceive at all clearly, but with the emotion of one sixteen years absent from a place well known in happy boyhood he persisted.

"Away to the left is the castle, Brother Ughtred," he said, his eyes welling. "There is the keep—it stands on a mound, but you can't see that. And over to the right is the holy pile so famed in our land that I need not even name it to you, while just so little again to the right, close to the Minster, naming it now, Brother Ughtred, is the Benedictine house of St. Mary's, where we are to lodge."

"With the tower capped by a spire?" Ughtred inquired.

Brother Edgar nodded. "It is a great convent, as could be expected in this northern capital of ours, a convent which for generations the sovereign lords our kings have visited when affairs of immense moment brought them to these parts, which was often. York is a city of outstanding consequence, Brother Ughtred, barely secondary to London, if secondary at all."

The great Forest of Galtres was thinning out, and here and there were glades through which grey baronial castles, cultivated monastic lands, and small estates with manor houses at their middle, could be seen. But as Brother Edgar was still expounding with a most unbecoming pride the view was cut off by a long extending stand of beech and elm; in any event Ughtred was attracted to the abbot's secretary, who had reined in his mount and waited until he had drawn alongside.

"Brother Ughtred," said the secretary, "My Lord desires to speak with you."

Through the kindly offices of the groom-in-charge Ughtred had been given Bess again, and the old understanding between man and mare had not been lost. Neatly, without barging against those in front, she took him to the abbot Hugh.

"Ah, my son," My Lord said. "You have brought your drawing materials?"

As the result of long journeyings Ughtred had mastered the art of bowing with reasonable skill when riding.

"Yes, *Domine*," he said. "As My Lord's reverend chaplain instructed me."

The abbot nodded. "You will be in my company in the morning, when with His Grace the Archbishop and others of the Council we raise our voices in praise to Him above, my son, but after that I have other intentions for you."

Ughtred guessed what was coming. "Yes, My Lord," he said, suppressing a sigh.

"You will then spend all the time that is feasible, my son, in making drawings of whatsoever you consider will add further glory to our house of Rievaulx," the abbot continued. "In these you will include statuary and other objects of art, not merely confining yourself to holy pictures—we have, as you know, my son, brothers in our convent who can turn their hands to fashioning in clay or chiselling in marble, and others who know the secrets of enamelling and those of the goldsmith's and silversmith's trade."

Ughtred bowed. "Yes, My Lord."

The track turned sharply, revealing York much more clearly. Now, in addition to the three most prominent features pointed out by Brother Edgar, the keep of the castle, the bulky Minster, and St. Mary's steeple, it was easy to discern, squeezed amongst a huddle of dwellings and larger public buildings, the towers and spires of two score or more churches. With the exception of the Benedictine abbey, all was contained within a massive, fortified wall, which was given a more striking impression of impregnability by being raised on a line of earthwork at whose foot, continuing throughout with it, water gleamed in a broad moat.

"After leaving the Minster you will not again be required to attend me," the abbot resumed after he had taken in the scene. "You will then lend yourself as I have directed, and to avoid interruption you are to be excused bodily presence at all the Holy Offices between the conclusion of Prime and supper, though you will not omit a *Gloria* at each Hour wherever you may be."

"No, My Lord," Ughtred murmured.

"In the main you will obtain the most noble rewards in the Minster, my son," the abbot went on. "But you must neither be contemptuous of the churches or indifferent to chapels and chantries, however trivial. 'Seek and ye shall find,' my son—perhaps a unique little carving here, possibly the garnishing of an otherwise humble shrine there. And always remember to what your labours are leading, as I have already said—to the further glorification of our home, so that by God's will we shall make its fame, power and authority ever extend."

Dismissed, Ughtred encouraged Bess to the side, waiting until Brother Edgar drew level, when he allowed the mare her head.

For a student who before leaving had talked of little else save the books he hoped to see and handle at St. Mary's and in the Minster library, Brother Edgar behaved strangely. Taking immense pleasure in acting as a guide, he pointed out the gateways to the city, each a fortress in itself, with barbican, portcullis and gate.

" We don't enter by Goodramgate Bar because that would take us into the city, Brother Ughtred," he continued. " You see, St. Mary's—oh, and over there——"

Arm outstretched and ranging, he indicated the four liberties of the city, each with a prison, court and gallows. He mentioned other things of interest, some of which certainly were not visible from there—the royal mint at the castle, the gaol and place of execution for offenders against the forest laws of Galtres, and the little plot of Jewbury, where Hebrews were interred.

"Not that Jews have been interred there for a long time, Brother Ughtred," he said informatively. " Not since Our Sovereign Lord, Edward the First, wise ruler and brave warrior, expelled them for coin-clipping and extortionate usury, and that is more than a hundred years ago. That is why, when borrowing has to be done, we nowadays always approach the Italian merchant-bankers."

The party was now riding close to the massive walls of the city and Ughtred's attention was more concerned with slits towards the summit from which an archer, sheltered himself, could aim and shoot at attackers. As he nodded to his neighbour he was thinking that the slender apertures, beautifully made in the form of a cross, were related only to sudden death, and had no connection with the holy appearance they presented.

Those unfamiliar with the district drew their hoods closer. Bootham Bar was near, but there, instead of turning towards the archway, the monks of Rievaulx and their abbot skirted the castellated defence wall of St. Mary's, which joined the city's wall, until the gate-house of the monastery was reached.

It did not require an acute observer to become aware that the Benedictine convent was very accustomed to receiving visitors, and that the gate porter could assess at a glance the precise quality of the reception to be accorded to those who sought hospitality. This was natural. His lord abbot was fully mitred, with a place amongst the Lords Spiritual in Parliament, and had control both of a private mint for coining and a prison whose cells he had the power to use for purposes beyond the domestic; and the abbey, in the second city of the land, was on an important thoroughfare which constantly saw the comings and goings of those of the highest degree.

Everything went with the smoothness of long practice—the feet of the travellers were washed by those of equal standing, and in the same manner they were escorted to the chapel for prayers. And after an appetising repast a number of the Black brothers, apparently without an order being given, offered to show the newcomers, excepting those on Abbot Hugh's personal staff, the treasures of their house. In this wise the eyes of the monks of Rievaulx came to open wider at the spectacle of much that was of an extravagance they had never perceived before: chalices adorned with rubies and emeralds, clasps of gold for copes, chasuble brooches gleaming with sapphires, and the manuscript of a Gospel with a picture on the cover of the Crucifixion, solidly created in glittering diamonds. And, though the reason came out as the result of inquiry and was not told for the sake of bragging, a heap of silver spheres which were in everyday use for warming hands when the Offices were likely to be lengthy and the weather at all chilly—a comfort indeed.

Later, before darkness fell, while Brother Edgar remained behind, engrossed in the vast library, two brothers of St. Mary's took Ughtred of Monkseaton and a companion monk, Ailfy, to the top of the tower. From there, looking out between pinnacles and with the spire rising behind them, there was a magnificent view: of the archbishop's noble chapel, the canons' walled close, and the minster of St. Peter, where clusters of tradesmen were at work— some on the roof of the newly-enlarged quire and others close to the crossing, over which there were indications that a great central tower was to be raised.

From another side the city unfolded before them, divided into two walled parts by the broad river which flowed past the well-tended grounds of St. Mary's. The strangers stared at Ouse Bridge, which connected the two sides, and at the chapels, wooden houses and workshops which were erected on it; farther down, the river was joined by a smaller stream which bellied out into an expanse of many acres of water before narrowing again to enter the main flow.

"The King's Pool," one of their escorts explained as he smiled. "Excellent for fishing for bream, but actually designed to maintain the castle and city ditches at a correct defensive level."

Various other things of interest were pointed out, but to Ughtred, who was entranced by the play of light on roofs of tile, stone and thatch, it was no more than a catalogue until shortly after the Benedictine nunnery of St. Clement's was spoken about. This was across the city, outside the walls, on the far side of the Ouse opposite to the point at which the Foss joined it.

"The sole nunnery of import in the city," he vaguely heard one of the Benedictines say. "A small establishment, rather too small for the crush there at this moment, but it can rejoice in that it possesses a relic of immense renown—a few drops of the milk of the Blessed Virgin."

Brother Ailfy glanced at Ughtred, once again hoping he would soon take more part in the talk; and again also, thinking with regret of the family life at Rievaulx. He wished he were back home, preferably in his workshop, shaping a handle for the silver pot he had been making. His upbringing, however, had been good, and so, despite shyness and a feeling of awe about the Black monks, who seemed so fluent and wordly, he strove to his utmost not to allow the conversation, on his part, to languish entirely.

"Why is there a crush?" he asked.

"My Ladies the prioresses who are attending the Council are lodged there," he was told.

To Ailfy's relief, Ughtred began to take his share. "Ladies attend the council?" he asked, surprised.

"Most surely, Brother Ughtred. As representatives of their illustrious houses."

" They will all be of your own great Order of Benedictines, I imagine," said Ughtred.

" By no means, Brother Ughtred. As I remarked a few moments ago, though possibly you missed hearing me, St. Clement's is the only nunnery of any consequence here, and the lady superiors of all the Orders stay there—and, of course, our Benedictine and your Cistercian prioresses."

" Absorbed by the view, I have been somewhat inattentive," Ughtred explained apologetically. " But I have a notion you mentioned a Gilbertine house, and I am rather puzzled."

The Black monk who had been doing the speaking smiled. " I did, my brother of Rievaulx—it is St. Andrew's, across the river from St. Clement's in point of fact. But, unlike Sempringham and Watton, it is not a double house and canons alone reside there."

" So My Lady the prioress of Watton will be lodging at St. Clement's? " Ughtred said, adding hastily: " And the lady prioress of Sempringham, of course."

The younger Benedictine monk put on a grave expression. " I don't know, my brother, but if it is of interest to you I think inquiries might be made."

Ughtred flushed. " Of interest to me, Sir Monk? "

The other chuckled. " That was unpardonable, my friend—to tease an honoured guest. But we Benedictines hold that a little humour adds salt to life." He coughed. " Er . . . it is not always the same in other bodies of the religious."

Ughtred laughed so heartily that the monk Ailfy, who in every aspect adhered conscientiously to his Order's Rule, began to squirm with embarrassment.

" Think no more of it," Ughtred said, largely. " My observations were so ill-framed that I deserved all I got, and more."

The Benedictine bowed. " I am indebted to you for your kindness, Brother Ughtred," he said.

Ughtred bowed in response. " Far from it, my friend. But if debts are to be spoken of, then place me further in your debt by continuing to describe this city you know so well."

" It will be a pleasure," the Benedictine said warmly.

From that elevated vantage point much could be seen. The tide was on the flood and water was slowing rising to cover the broad, shelving banks of the river. Small, single-masted vessels, high at stem and stern, were coming into the city, sails filled with the breeze, their destination the quays near Ouse Bridge, where discharge of cargoes would be made into the warehouses thereabouts. Where the ships came from the narrators obviously could not say, but some would undoubtedly be inward-bound from the ports of the Continent, the Baltic, and the Low Countries.

"Berwick, London, King's Lynn, our merchants do much business with them," one of the Benedictines murmured. "As for farther afield, they have, I believe, a most profitable trading with such places as Dantzic, Veere, Calais, Dordrecht and so forth."

Even to the monk Ailfy, to whom the outside world had always seemed to be a chill and unsympathetic place, these and other matters made absorbing listening, and the bells in every quarter of the city were ringing for Vespers before it was decided to return below—the tellers of the tales, for all their sophistication, delighted at their success at entertaining these pleasant but simple fellows from the country.

Before Ughtred left the stone-flagged platform he paused to stare towards the castle keep and a faint cluster of lights in a building lower and beyond: the Benedictine nunnery of St. Clement's.

The younger brother of St. Mary's mistook the direction of his interest.

"The Franciscan Friary in Castlegate, Brother Ughtred," he said, his lip curling. "The abode—when they are not indulging in the coarsest sins elsewhere—of the most impudent beggars in the land."

"I believe," Ughtred said tentatively, "that there was a time when St. Francis's followers unswervingly adhered to the highest ideals."

"If that be so they have long fallen from them, as have all the other Orders of mendicant friars," the other remarked tartly. "But of one thing I am quite assured—in far-off days they strove through their sermons and preachings about the countryside to do as much damage to Holy Church as they could."

The slightly more senior Benedictine joined in crisply. "It is true. That is why, if I could find a word in support of the miscreant

John Wycliffe, it would be to admit that at least he hurled his most vicious barbs at the friars."

" Nevertheless, may he still be choking for breath in Hell. We have to thank him for the intolerable presence of these Lollard vipers, who seek to destroy us just as the Dominicans and the Franciscans did."

" And with more prospect of success, slight although I concede that is," the older monk growled. " But it is not hard to obtain converts when the bait is quick money at the expense of others."

The exchanges continued, for a little longer, and in that short time, listening enthralled, Ughtred learned much that he had never known before, on questions which had perplexed and worried him ever since he had ridden into Ripon. Simultaneously he drew a comparison between his own Order of Saint Bernard and that of Saint Benedict, marvelling that their guides could speak so freely on subjects forbidden in his own home.

When the discussion was petering out, he endeavoured to prolong it.

" I know very little about this John Wycliffe," he said. " Save that he was a doctor of divinity."

The Benedictines assured him there was little else to know, but one of them suggested very solemnly that if he was still curious it might be wiser not to try to satisfy that curiosity if he met any of the canons or priests of St. Peter's.

" Why not? " Ughtred inquired.

It was another Benedictine joke, and both smiled broadly. " Because, Ughtred, my brother," it was explained to him, " because it is only fifty years or so since the caitiff was ordained in the Minster, and it is still a *very* sore point with them."

" I see," Ughtred said.

Alarmed, Brother Ailfy turned hurriedly to say he believed a city church was on fire. When he pointed towards a tower in which a flickering light steadily increased in brightness, the two Benedictines were again heartily amused.

" No, that is an experimental beacon at All Saints', Pavement, and if found to be useful to distant wayfarers a stone lantern will be built on the tower in course of time, Brother Ailfy," the younger man said. " As you see, they have lighted the lamps, but if you would care to wait a minute longer you will hear another means of guidance to serve those who might go astray."

It was slightly more than that before the monks of Rievaulx heard a bell with a majestic depth of tone. The single stroke was repeated at regular intervals.

" The bell of St. Michael's in Spurriergate, my friends," the other Benedictine monk told their abbey's guests. " And on many occasions it—and the beacon already—has guided travellers lost in the forest to one of the Bars, where at least they might remain in safety until the gates of the city were opened the next morning."

Brother Ailfy shook his head. " Many are the perils of journeying," he said lugubriously.

One of the Benedictines affected to shiver. " I propose we descend, my friends," he said. " The night airs off the river are becoming a shade insistent, and I think we all would savour a goblet of mulled wine. What say you, Brother Ughtred? "

Ughtred pulled himself together. " I can promise that I for one would relish it. Yes, truly."

As bewildered as ever before, he went down to enjoy the lavish hospitality of the princely monastery of St. Mary's, where the worship of God was not regarded in quite the same manner as in many other convents he had known.

\*     \*     \*     \*

On the following morning the lord abbots paraded solemnly and, by way of Bootham Bar, walked to St. Peter's, where the lord bishops of the Northern Province awaited them in the Minster close. The city's constables and the sheriff's men were out in full strength, using their staffs as rails to keep a large crowd at a respectful distance. From the nunnery of St. Clement's the prioresses had already arrived, but as was more seemly had gone without pause into the cathedral church.

A combined procession, monastic and ecclesiastic, then proceeded with pomp and dignity into the Minster, received at the west door by the dean and canons, resplendent in robes of many hues: red, blue, white, green, black and purple. With them was the archbishop, a figure of breathtaking magnificence from head to foot—an enormous ruby on one of his rings caught the light, his superb pastoral staff caught the eye, his beautifully embroidered robe was enough to make onlookers marvel, and although his mitre must have been made of fabric the material was virtually obscured by a wealth of diamonds, sapphires and pearls.

Ughtred's first impression on entering the nave was of the profusion of shields on the walls, but after that, with almost every step towards loftily-canopied stalls and the amazingly rich frontal of the High Altar, he had much more to gasp about: jewelled crosses, silver and gold arks, a figure of St. George on a silver horse, a life-size silver lamb, gold censers, and delicately-chased silver basins obscurely placed to allow room for the many basins beaten out from gold.

At the end of the service another procession formed, for the short walk to the archbishop's town residence, where the first meeting of the Council was to take place in the great hall. Later, all the dignitaries were to ride out for a banquet at the archiepiscopal manor at Bishopthorpe.

His duties finished, Ughtred returned to the Minster, to pick up a portfolio left there earlier. Drawn by the gathering of notabilities, there were still too many people about for him to look round with the idea of doing any work; but for a short while he did linger: watching an artist craftsman putting in glass, wood carvers happy to have resumed their life's tasks, and in listening to a clerkly teacher who, pointing towards a window, was tutoring a number of small boys and girls by means of a biblical story told in stained glass.

There was also plenty of activity outdoors, much of it far noisier and more strenuously purposeful in every way. The corner made by the nave and north transept was being used as a builder's yard, and chips of stone were flying as masons in tunics, aprons and gloves hammered at their chisels. Bustling about in clogs, their foreman was eloquently indicating to the driver of a four-horse sledge, just arrived with sparks flying from the runners, precisely where a load of fresh-cut stone should be placed, beneath a hook suspended from a jib dizzily-high up in the building. These proceedings were being watched with interest by a throng of townspeople and—all granted leave of temporary absence from St. Leonard's Hospital, which as Ughtred now knew was just over the city wall from St. Mary's—orphans, pensioners of the King, and scholars from the grammar school.

Knowing little more of York than he had gleaned from St. Mary's steeple tower, Ughtred wandered down an ill-paved street from which now and then there was a glimpse of the river. Used to cleanliness and the decency of sanitary arrangements at home, he was soon picking his way fastidiously, trying to avoid the worst of the filth in the gutters: excrement, stinking remnants of food, and ghastly-looking offal at which legions of crows, each fearless of him, were picking.

As My Lord Hugh had told him, he quickly discovered that religious institutions abounded, and he was able to glance round four churches in fairly quick succession, without finding anything suitable. But a few yards beyond a trio of shops, a fishmonger's, spicer's, and hosier's, all with shutters down and goods displayed on them, he came across another church, and went inside.

"Yes," he muttered. "That's the kind of . . . of *thing* likely to appeal to My Lord. It should not take long, either."

He placed a bag of food, which the Benedictine brothers had so kindly insisted he must have with him, in a musty recess near a simple little shrine. Opening his portfolio, he took out ink-horn, quills, pen and small knife for scraping. After arranging these conveniently and clipping a piece of parchment on a board, he sat on a bench and scrutinised the tympanum carefully before making the first stroke. It was horrific—of a company of ape-like devils brutally bearing away the soul of a terrified and dying man.

Ughtred was a swift worker. "Mmmm," he mumbled when finished. "I think I have largely captured the ferocity. "Yes . . . yes, I think so."

As soon as the ink dried he stowed the drawing away and went out again. Ambling through the winding streets, he came across more churches, houses of religious instruction and hospitality, craving permission to enter where it was necessary. In this manner he added several other drawings.

Gradually he reached a busier quarter, along the backs of houses and merchants' warehouses which at the other side abutted on to the river quays. People hereabouts were better and more colourfully dressed, and the sombre clothes of the religious stood out more markedly. Cloaks were more dashing, doublets had fuller sleeves, and the pointed shoes of the real dandies were so long as to require slender, silver support-chains between toe-caps and knees.

At St. Michael's, on the end of Ouse Bridge, Ughtred was able to make a sketch of *The Coronation of the Virgin*, thanks to the helpfulness of the chantry chaplain, who would have remained with him far longer than it took him to make it.

The Ouse, though salt water influenced it, was not the sea, but Ughtred, apart from the fabulous journey to Citeaux, had neither seen ships nor sea since leaving home, so it was perhaps not surprising that when in the middle of the bridge he idled, delighted by such small sights as the current below rippling against the stout stem of a craft, even persuading himself that the old smell of tar was in his nostrils.

His interest was noticed by a tradesman, and before another five minutes had elapsed Ughtred was much better informed about the nature of the main sea-borne foreign traffic carried on from there: wines from France, glass and fine stuffs from Italy, and furs and timber from the Baltic ports; outward—wool, leather, and the red cloth for which the weavers of the city had far-flung renown. It is an astonishing phenomenon how all cobblers can maintain a flow of conversation while waxing a length of thread with one end in the mouth.

"Red cloth, good shoemaker," Ughtred said, checking the spate. "Do you know whence they obtain their dyes?"

"Their dye," the tradesman rumbled. "That I do not, though I suspect it may be a craft secret. That makes good sense, doesn't it, Sir Monk? If clothworkers everywhere were privy to these private matters it would be a secret no longer. And if it were a secret no longer . . ."

Before Ughtred managed to escape from this pleasant but decidedly garrulous person, which was not until a barge laden with new-cut stone had at long last been manœuvred into position against a low-lying wharf, he had decided to have a word with the cellarer about this dye as soon as he was home.

At the other side of the water he looked into a bridge chapel of some quality, but found nothing inside nearly so striking as two widely-differing head-coverings he sighted on coming out, one of them the tallest and broadest as could be conceived, the other merely a jewelled net fitting tightly as a skullcap, the incongruity being that the two gentlemen were together.

Ughtred's attention was next taken by another kind of skull, a human skull speared on a stake. As he averted his head hurriedly he was extremely startled at feeling someone endeavouring to take his arm.

" These sleeves, Sir Monk," that someone said disparagingly. " Unless my memory is faulty I am certain that once I told you they were a yard wide and dangled to your knees."

Mouth opening, Ughtred gaped at the Franciscan he had seen at Ripon and, as before, the fellow succeeded in throwing him off his balance.

" Did we exchange names? " the friar inquired gravely. " If so, I fear I cannot recollect what yours is."

" Ughtred of Monkseaton," Ughtred said, and could have kicked himself.

The Franciscan bowed. " Friar Jerome, at your service. Now if you wish to do me a favour," he wagged a finger solemnly, " you must on no account tell me why you are here. Allow me to guess, Brother Ughtred . . ." His eyebrows went up. " Of the famed abbey of Fountains, is it? "

" Of the abbey of Rievaulx," Ughtred replied stiffly. " Equally famous."

" Ah," said the friar, " and your presence here is connected with an event which is throwing all our socially-ambitious city fathers into a dither—the Ecclesiastical Council of the North. Am I right, eh? "

" Perfectly," Ughtred said coldly.

The Franciscan's worn face shone with gratification. " How splendid it is to put the shaft into the middle of the target. However, we are warned against the iniquity of conceit, aren't we, Brother Ughtred, so with your permission I will betake myself elsewhere on errands that will speedily dispel my complacency."

" Is that so? " Ughtred said.

" You appear to doubt me," Friar Jerome said. " That being so, suppose you accompany me? "

" I have other affairs," Ughtred told him.

The friar mused. " When a man in all essence calls another man a liar . . . still, you are quite safe, Brother Ughtred. We are both men of God and I am debarred from smashing the back of my hand against your mouth. Nevertheless, in fairness, I would have thought that a disciple of the honest and ever-truthful Saint Bernard——"

" I will go with you," Ughtred interposed angrily.

That was the last time, for nearly two hours, that either of them spoke to the other. During that period, his feelings ever becoming more agonised, Ughtred followed the gaunt figure of the Franciscan from one wretched habitation to another. He passed through alleys so noisome he could hardly breathe, and entered chambers into which light barely entered. In dingy courts he went into tumbledown, one-storied dwellings, and when the friar sank to pray by the side of the ill, the fearsomely diseased, or the dying, he sank to filthy floors to pray also; and again and again marvelled at the love and compassion in the Franciscan's voice, whether he was coaxing a sickly child to swallow a pill, or tenderly supporting a stricken man or woman while administering a dose of medicine from one of the phials he carried.

As ordeals do, the ordeal ended, and eventually Ughtred found himself standing with the friar in a street which two hours earlier he would have thought disgusting, now never noticing its abominable condition.

" Well, Brother Ughtred," the Franciscan said a little wearily. " I trust you will now believe I am cleansed of all conceit."

" I also," said Ughtred. He swallowed. " I am sorry, please accept that I am excessively sorry."

Friar Jerome smiled. " Say no more, my brother," he said.

In truth Ughtred was so emotionally drained he had nothing to say, but found speech on remembering the bag pressed on him earlier at St. Mary's.

" Friar Jerome, it is surely dinner time now, and I have an abundance of food with me," he said eagerly. " I . . . I don't feel very much like eating, but even if I did there is plenty to spare. Won't you share it with me? "

The Franciscan poked a finger into the bag. He found a loaf, a flask of wine, raisin pasties and several rounds of beef. The loaf was cut into two halves, each half being partially scooped out; butter was stuffed into the holes that had been made.

"I knew our chance encounter this morning was auspicious," he said. "The kindliness of your greeting, the—let us away to the churchyard of All Saints' in North Street, where we can enjoy our repast in comfortable circumstances. Ah, yes, indeed it was well met this morning. Your expression was so indicative of ... genuine pleasure, shall we say?"

For the first time in their acquaintance Ughtred did not fall into a trap, and with something of satisfaction he told himself he was beginning to understand this queer fellow much better.

It was starting to rain, but as they went through streets so narrow that the progressively more overhanging stories of tall dwellings on each side hardly left much more than a slit of sky visible, they did not get at all wet.

At All Saints' the Franciscan led the way through the graveyard to a well-sheltered spot, where they began to eat.

After some time, as he handed the flask to the friar, Ughtred began to try to clear the confusion in his mind.

"Brother Jerome," he said haltingly, "do you believe with the Lollards that if Holy Church and the monastic Orders surrendered their wealth much of the miseries I have just seen would be no more?" He sighed. "I realise now, as never before, what an immense income the Church must have, to possess the treasures she has and for her dignitaries to live as they do, and I know for myself that the monasteries own properties as far-extending as any baron's in the land. Would a sharing out, bringing greater equality, make all that difference?"

The friar shook his head. "Not as you state it, Brother Ughtred," he said slowly. "But Mother Church, if she only would, could use a substantial part of her vast revenues to alleviate the distressed instead of wasting so much money on costly fripperies and pomp."

"And the monasteries, Brother Jerome?" Ughtred asked. "If they were no more how would travellers fare, to whom hospitality is given freely and generously? And who else is there to give alms to the poor who pause at their gates?"

When he spoke, the Franciscan went off on a very different

track. Quietly, he made the point that the highest culture in England was reposed in the monasteries; that the cloisters were packed with scholars the most learned there were; that here and there amongst the monkish community dwelled the most skilful engineers and scientists of all, as had been so for centuries.

"Otherwise your well-conceived foundations would neither have come into existence nor have been maintained," he continued. "In this great city the privies are evil, the breeders of fever and worse, while in your abbeys the rere-dorters have running water, and the nauseous matter is carried swiftly away. Here, as you may have noticed, the crows are never molested, because they are the sole scavengers we have, whereas your Cistercian forefathers dealt with the problem in a more sanitary way. You wash the dirt off your hands in a lavatory with a tidy stream, but within a stone's throw of where we are even the well-to-do have less hygienic methods."

Ughtred shivered. "It may be so, Brother Jerome," he muttered. "But . . . but, even if monasticism bereft itself, how would these matters you refer to be advanced?"

Momentarily the friar's mouth tightened. "If your abbots could be less extravagant in their mode of living the surplus saved might be employed to greater advantage. And if, abandoning the seclusion of the cloister, the most suited amongst your brethren, those of scientific and mechanical bent, went out into the world—to attend to the correct disposal of that surplus—then humanity would be benefited to an unbelievable extent."

"Yes," Ughtred said thoughtfully.

Then, eyes widening with astonishment, he stared more searchingly at a square tomb. Part of the slab of stone at the side had broken away, and in the aperture, turned to them, was a face. It was pallid, grimy, and a tangle of hair fell over it—and it was an aged woman's face. Shaking with horror, he drew his companion's attention.

To his surprise the Franciscan merely smiled. "She is an anchoress, Brother Ughtred, with a reputation for saintliness, and is often consulted—the fee is a morsel of food. We have also a hermit in one of the chapel garths, but he is often abroad on good works."

Ughtred shivered. "What a gruesome existence, in the confines of a tomb. And you say, Brother Jerome, that persons consult her?"

The friar nodded. "As you could yourself, if you have troubles."

Aghast, Ughtred eyed him. "I . . ."

"You have many perplexities I think, my brother," the Franciscan said gently.

The old woman's face had vanished before Ughtred replied. "Yes, I have many perplexities," he admitted soberly. "So many that my brain is in a whirl. And what you have recently spoken about has not lessened my confusion."

"Perhaps it may reduce that if I put my ideas more simply," Friar Jerome said. "Setting aside all questions to do with the worship of God, and reducing the matter to the earthy—I contend that if the standards of monastic life could be spread more widely infinite good would result."

"We are bespoken to a life of meditation," Ughtred protested.

"So it would seem," the Franciscan said dryly. "But I can tell you that others are beginning to see the light, beginning to perceive that education must not remain the sole prerogative of a limited society. Until recently nobles and wealthy merchants have sought to save their souls by enormous bequests to Holy Church and the monasteries, but now they are much more inclined to found schools where grammar and the humanities are taught, and to endow the colleges of Oxford and Cambridge."

A strange thought occurred to Ughtred. "Brother Jerome," he said, "do you agree with the tenets of the doctor of divinity, John Wycliffe, and of his followers, the Lollards?"

"In part but not the whole, my brother," the friar said, his face clouding. "It still disturbs me greatly that I conjecture whether the bread I receive at the holy table can truly have been translated by mortal man into the Body of Our Lord Christ, which is what I was taught to believe."

Ughtred was more shocked than ever in his life. "But it is sacrilege even to question it," he gasped. "You can have no doubt."

"I wish it were so," the Franciscan said regretfully. "But, on that, I am as muddled as you tell me you are in other ways. As for the remainder . . . well, my brother, I think there is much in favour of the Lollardist beliefs."

Ughtred, though still reeling about a sinful and monstrous

assertion, noticed the Franciscan's face was taut and his hand tightly clenched.

"Is anything wrong, Brother Jerome?" he asked.

"Yes," the friar said, his expression ineffably sad, " to-morrow I shall be at the stake, standing at the side of a Lollard when the flames begin to sear his flesh, and I am frightened. Frightened, my brother, lest in my anguish I may fail to afford him the comfort he will so sorely need."

Cold sweat covered Ughtred's brow as in his mind's eye he saw the intelligent, tired face of a man in a tattered university gown, for it could be no other.

"The Lollard at Ripon," he said unevenly. "He is to be burnt?"

The friar sighed heavily. "He has been burnt already, and I was with him. No, this is another, Brother Ughtred—burnings, my brother, are becoming more frequent as the weeks pass."

Feeling dizzy, Ughtred heard snatches only of what the Franciscan next said, but he grasped that an act had been passed, *De Heretico Comburendo*, whereby heretics lawfully could be burnt alive. It was to the king's eternal shame, he picked up also, that in return for support which had brought him to the throne he acquiesced in the destruction of men for their religious beliefs.

"I ... I know little of these matters, but ... but surely the king alone does not bear the responsibility," he stammered. "The commons of our land must be in agreement or it would not be so."

The friar turned to him. "In the land you speak of there are three Estates, and one of them is that of Holy Church," he said, his voice angered. "It is by the authority of ecclesiastical courts, them only, that these men die horribly ... ecclesiastical courts in which the judges are those to whom I—and you, Brother Ughtred—owe allegiance, duty, and homage."

"Why do they do these things?" Ughtred said strickenly.

"Out of fright, my brother. Fright that if the Lollards grow in power and stature they will despoil the churches and monasteries of their treasures."

Several minutes passed. Both were lost in thought, thoughts which though they differed were as painful.

"Friar Jerome," Ughtred said at length, embarrassed by what

he was about to say, "please understand that I speak with no dis-
respect towards you personally, but in the twice we have met it is
nevertheless true that you have insinuated ideas into my head that
could, if I were weak enough, undermine my faith in my Order and
my faith in Holy Church. And this, from you, who . . . who . . ."

"Go on, my brother," the friar said.

Ughtred nerved himself. "It has for long been instilled into me
that the mendicant friars are no longer what they were, that they
are rascals and cheats and drunkards. I don't think myself you are
that, but I am baffled why, with the views you have, you are still
a Franciscan."

"H'mmm," the friar murmured, unperturbed. "So that's it,
eh? Well, I realise now I must talk to you a little longer, and I will
begin by telling you that my faith is as strong as ever. I have not
departed from the ideals of my Order—it is others, those leaders
who for decades steadily abandoned the reasons for which Saint
Francis of Assisi brought us into being. And my contention is that
Holy Church and the monastic bodies, beginning long before us,
have followed the same downward path. Did you ever, my brother,
discover how your Cistercians came to be? If I remember rightly
I suggested to you at Ripon that such an inquiry might furnish
you with a profitable line of thought."

Ughtred nodded slowly. "Yes . . . yes, I made some inquiry,
Brother Jerome," he said reluctantly.

"Let us leave it at that, my friend," the friar said.

Companionably, he started to talk about himself; about his
life in England and abroad, and, smiling occasionally, he spoke of
his studies at the University of Ravenna, where he had obtained a
doctorate in physic and surgery. Gradually he came nearer the
present, how he had tried—and it had been hard—to look objectively at the scene about him, revealing also those deeper matters
which had caused him so much agonising appraisal. From that
he described how a handful of the younger men of his Order had
gradually drawn together, Franciscans of a kind unlike those so
universally denounced.

"New Franciscans perhaps, though our aim is to live our lives
as the earliest Franciscan friars lived theirs, in poverty, chastity,
and obedience." He smiled faintly. "But we think it will be wise,

having regard to the unsavoury reputation Franciscans now have, if we give ourselves a new name, and that of Believers or Observants has been mentioned so far."

Ughtred's head was aching, and wearily he put his hand on his forehead. "You are a good and honest man, Brother Jerome, of that I am certain," he said, adding pitifully: "But I am so confused that I do not know where I am."

The friar rested his hand on Ughtred's shoulder. "It has been much easier for me, my brother, for I have been out in the world, whereas you have for long dwelled in the peace and seclusion of the cloister, where every thought is channelled and rigidly directed, until little will is left at all. But be not afraid—let your conscience be your guide, and perhaps one blessed day you may know the sublime truth. If that happens the light will shine on you suddenly, and it will be a bright light, for it will be God's light."

Ughtred sighed. "I think now that I wish I had never travelled with My Lord. It has brought so many unbearable complexities into my life."

"They will be resolved, my brother," Brother Jerome said tenderly. "Have faith that they will be resolved, as surely as day follows night."

Ughtred stirred. "No—No!" he said with sharp intensity. "I am glad of my journeying, because it has brought to me something I shall always cherish, forbidden though it be."

Curiously the friar looked at him, but did not seek an explanation. He was inquisitive, however, about the reference to travelling, and before they parted Ughtred gave him an account of the visit to Burgundy. "I would that we could talk again, Brother Jerome, often," Ughtred ended wistfully. "But that will never be."

"You will be in my prayers from this day, my brother, as I hope I shall be in yours," the friar said gently. "Friends may be apart, but separation does not mean they cannot commune."

The despair in Ughtred's eyes lessened. "If . . . if I am in omeone's thoughts . . . and she is constantly in mine . . ."

"She!" the friar said sharply.

Ughtred looked at him unflinchingly. "She is a maid I met by chance when returning from Citeaux. Nay, she is more . . ." His voice fell. "She is one who is espoused to the Lord Christ."

Never before had he seen the friar look either astonished or disconcerted. But that was Brother Jerome's expression both then and throughout the tale which followed.

" I have never heard anything like it," the Franciscan exclaimed.

" It is the most wonderful thing that has ever happened to me," Ughtred said. " But I suffer grievously because I have never unburdened myself to my confessor, as I should."

" What are your thoughts about this holy nun? " the friar asked, looking at him searchingly. " Are they evil thoughts, lustful thoughts? "

Ughtred half rose. " No, they are not," he said. " She is pure and lovely and as innocent as the Babe, and I could not think sinfully of her. I . . . I just remember her, remember her very often, too often. That is why I have decided that when I am at home again I shall do as I should have done long ago, unburden myself to my confessor."

" You must not," Brother Jerome said urgently.

" Why not? " said Ughtred. " I have deliberately broken the Rule and I should be punished."

" What good would that do? They would whip and whip you, perversely striving to break your spirit. And to what end? Afterwards you would still be thinking of her, wouldn't you, my brother?"

" Perversely! " Ughtred said coldly. " In my Order, Brother Jerome, scourges are administered in the hope of restoring the wayward to the path from which they have deviated."

The friar eyed him oddly. " Perhaps so, perhaps not, but we will not argue that, my friend. Let us examine the whole circumstances from another aspect. Has it not occurred to you that the incident with the nun Lazelle passed off very smoothly?"

" It is true there were few inquiries," Ughtred admitted.

" It could be different if you carry out your intention. The suspicion might arise that if you think of her so much it is because forbidden things took place."

Aghast, Ughtred stared. " That we sinned? As a man and a maid not joined in holy matrimony may sin? "

Brother Jerome nodded several times, with immense solemnity.

"There is a distinct possibility. That is why I, more wordly-wise than you, if you will forgive me, urge you not to confess."

"I should be continuing to break a Rule to which I am dedicated," Ughtred said.

"Would you do so if you knew it would save her from harm?"

For a while Ughtred stared round the graveyard. "A thousand fold," he said eventually. "God forgive me."

The friar leaned towards him. "Then break it, my brother, break it for her sake. After all, it is only trivial at the worst."

It seemed as if Ughtred miraculously had lost all doubts and misgivings. "I shall," he said resolutely.

Satisfied, Brother Jerome rose, saying he must be about his business.

"Good-bye, my friend," he said. "May the Almighty be with you now and for always."

"And with you, good friar," Ughtred said huskily. "To-night I shall thank Our Lord and Redeemer for bringing us together. Never before, even in my youth, have I known anyone to whom I found it so easy to speak freely, and my gratitude is unbounded."

Brother Jerome took one of Ughtred's hands between his own. "Good-bye, my friend, good-bye."

He smiled as he left, and Ughtred watched the gaunt and barefooted figure until it passed from sight. Even then he stayed on the stone bench, motionless, until a thought struck him and he opened the bag of food. He had not eaten well, and most of a half-loaf, an untouched slice of beef, and a whole pasty still remained. Impulsively he crossed the rough grass to the anchoress's habitation.

"Lady Hermit," he called out nervously, "I have a pittance of food if it would please you to accept it."

Talon-like hands first appeared, to snatch away his offering. Next, he saw her face again, hair falling over it. With the side of her head almost resting on the ground, her ear touching the coffin slab below her, she looked up at him with a pair of eyes which were astonishingly virile.

"Be of good heart, my son," she croaked.

"Be of good heart!" Ughtred gaped.

"Many grave trials await you," she muttered. "But you must be of good heart, my son." And with that, leaving him gazing down in stupefaction, she disappeared within the lichen-encrusted tomb.

Bewildered and scared, contrasting a life of orderly routine with a world of horrors and surprises, Ughtred left the graveyard. While the light lasted, working feverishly, he completed another five small sketches before starting towards St. Mary's, through streets swarming with people clad in so many, to him, bewilderingly different colours of clothing: shades of red, green and brown predominated, with many in white and few in black apart from the religious who, in small numbers, were everywhere. By cloth and cut it was possible, for those versed, to distinguish the attorney from the leech, and the nobleman from the merchant prince. Cheerfulness, strange also, was in the air; quite half the men and youths were whistling, and hucksters bellowing their wares were being subjected to badinage by passers-by. It was all such a contrast to Rievaulx.

The city's constables were taking up their positions, lamplighters, after lighting wicks, were hoisting lamps to the top of tall hold-posts, by ropes; housewives, from upper windows and doors, were adding slops and refuse to garbage already in the street; and nearer St. Mary's the ward's watchmen, using barbs on long poles, were pulling burning thatch from the roof of a house.

Ughtred was not in the mood to linger. Past monks had instilled into succeeding generations the belief that the inhabitants of York were vulgar churls, addicted to quarrelling and given to fighting on the least provocation.

\*　　　\*　　　\*　　　\*

There was very little whistling that day in the streets of the city, and not a smile was to be seen on the faces of the hundreds who, passing out by Micklegate Bar, trudged towards Tyburn Gallows and the Knavesmire.

Earlier that morning Ughtred had begun his round at the opposite side of the city from St. Mary's Abbey, beginning with the Templars' Chapel at the castle. From there, while working back towards Ouse Bridge, he loitered twice, once to stare longingly at the barbican and drawbridge over the castle moat, beyond which men-at-arms and armourers were winching a massively-timbered portcullis up and down repeatedly, as if the mechanism were at fault.

He itched to set the scene on parchment, but it was a project My Lord would certainly have frowned upon, and so, shaking his head, he resumed his way.

Apart from sitting in a church porch for a snack provided by the hospitable Benedictines, his next halt for self-enjoyment was in an alley not far from Ouse Bridge where, granted permission by the various owners, he watched tradesmen intently engraving gold and silver chalices, and others shaping holy images in wood, stone and wax. It was a district catering for ecclesiastical needs and elsewhere effigies were being made, and sepulchral brasses cast.

Wandering again, Ughtred soon found another church, which was always easy. At the extreme side of the graveyard he saw an enormously high wooden erection on wheels, divided into three spaces. He walked over to it and was standing, puzzled as to what it could be, when a woman, who had been drawing water from a well, spoke to him. She was slatternly, not ill-looking, and possessed a pair of eyes of a boldness most alarming to him. Nevertheless, quite civilly, she explained that the contraption was stored there until needed for a pageant, and that the middle compartment was the stage. *Noah and the Flood* was the last play to be performed on its boards.

" You're a Cistercian, aren't you, Sir Monk? " she said. " We're used to friars, Dominicans, Carmelites and the rest, and Benedictine monks are around in droves, but we don't often see a White monk."

" Our houses are remote from the city, and we seldom come, good housewife."

She laughed. " Yes, I'm wed, Sir Monk, but my good man went early to the forest, if you know what I mean."

" No . . . yes," Ughtred muttered.

" No, you don't," she said, winking as she sidled nearer to look more closely at him. " He's after a bit of something tender for the pot that his lordship the king will never miss."

Ughtred flurriedly began to close his hood. " Oh! " he said, his heart beating.

She giggled. " Why stop me seeing you properly, Sir Monk. I was thinking that you were a real pretty fellow—and if you weren't so nervous . . ."

Gathering up the voluminous skirt of his habit, Ughtred fled, pursued by a raucous scream of laughter.

Composure gone, he reached the sign of the Bull in Coney Street before realising he was covering old ground. Turning, he hastened to Ouse Bridge, his aim to get to the other side of the river as quickly as possible.

This encounter had its effect. In Micklegate, as he now knew the narrow thoroughfare to be, he did not immediately connect the stream of people passing along it with the reason which since rising had filled him with desolation. But when, in still another church-yard, he saw a man sitting in the stocks quite unmolested, with not a single mischievous, offal-throwing apprentice in the vicinity, he knew the throng's destination.

" O Jesus," he groaned, raising the crucifix on his girdle to kiss it, " help him if it has to be, let his pain be small and his end quick."

Trembling, he entered the church but, finding little of value in it, soon left. Shortly after that he did come across a carved motif in the timberwork of a wood-and-plaster faced mansion, which well merited recording, but his hands were so shaky he had to desist.

Stragglers only were in Micklegate now, all of them either running and walking alternately, or taking long raking strides. As he watched their progress a most daring thought entered his head.

" Should I go to see for myself? " he muttered. " I know so little of what happens, and maybe my imagination has built a fiendish horror that is not so. Mankind cannot be so callous, and perhaps, after all, these unfortunates are plied so much with strong liquor or potions beforehand that . . ."

He was irresolute for a few seconds, and then, filled with purpose, he started towards Micklegate Bar, his footsteps soon ringing out in the tunnel-like, vaulted spaces of the massive entry point as he stepped out towards the highway beyond, which Brother Edgar had told him was the main road to the south.

The country was green and peaceful immediately outside the city walls, pasture and common land on which horses and cattle were grazing. Habitations were few and mean, and the sole building of any consequence was a wayside chapel, which he reached after walking for some time. Shortly after that he sighted a vast crowd, in a field off the road.

As he drew closer he saw the stake, and could faintly hear the voice of a man addressing a very silent throng. Near him were sheriff's officers, a clerk in holy orders, and the lean, brown-clad figure of Friar Jerome.

The highway was becoming blocked, and it seemed that traffic in both directions had been halted. Scores of horses, riding-horses and pack-horses, were tethered to anything that might serve, whether the side-stakes of four-horsed wagons piled with victuals and merchandise, the hand-grips of long carriages, or the sockets of banner standards on two-wheeled carts trundled laboriously from town to town by mixed companies of jugglers and strolling players.

As he joined the fringe of the assembly Ughtred was startled by a mass outcry so menacing that the closely-knit body of sheriff's men ringing the stake, not looking very happy themselves, grasped their weapons more tightly as if aware that an attempt at rescue might not be far off.

" Let him finish, let him finish," was the angered roar.

The crowd was composed of all qualities: beggars, minstrels with their cases, merchants, journeymen, retainers with the badges of their lords embroidered on jerkins, tradesmen, labourers, foresters, nobles, chapmen, tumblers, and city fathers.

A sheriff's officer signed imperatively to the men who were holding the venerable Lollard and he was allowed to step forward again.

" As I have already tried to tell you, my friends, the Reformation has already started," he said in a thin but steady voice, " and nothing the clerics may say will stay its progress. So let me again remind you of the imperishable words of the blessed John Wycliffe, the bright shining star of that Reformation. He it was who taught that the Pope's claim to be God's vice-regent on earth was no more than a blasphemous usurpation. And why, *why*, dear friends and brothers, did this learned divine, sometime Master of Balliol College—why did this deeply-studied man assert that? I will tell you, my brothers —because he devoutly believed that all of us, and each one of us alone, is responsible to Heaven for his own acts and thoughts. We do not require intermediaries here below, whether they be father confessors, absolute lord abbots, proud prelates, or parish priests.

"I will not detain you much longer from your affairs, my friends, but this I must say before I submit myself to what awaits me. . . .

"I die, I hope, not without semblance of dignity, but should I cringe, and howsoever my poor spirit may fail me, I die with the knowledge that I have done my poor utmost to convey a message to you and others that will bear repeating. It is this, my dear friends and brothers, that each one of us—*alone* and with the aid of none— is responsible to Heaven for his own acts and thoughts.

"May God bless you all."

He turned and walked firmly to the stake, to which he was quickly bound. The end was not yet, however, for the clerk-in-holy-orders still had a duty to perform.

"In this last moment, foul traducer and liar, betrayer of Holy Church, you have the opportunity of saving your knavish life," he shouted. "Will you, before these good people—will you withdraw, will you confess that all you have said is untruth?"

"No, Sir Clerk, I will not."

The parson's tone became shrill. "For the last time, pest and evil defamer, by-blow and spawn of Hell," he shrieked as, face transfused with rage, he shook his fist at the still figure on the stake, "will you recant? For the last time, vile heretic and sinful liver, will you abjure?"

"Never, my friend," the Lollard said. "Life is still sweet to me, but never would I pay that iniquitous price to save it."

"Then die," the cleric screamed. "And may the torture you suffer now be merely a foretaste of what awaits you in the inferno below."

The rising growl of the crowd died into an uncanny silence as a wisp of smoke spiralled upwards. Then, very clearly, the crackling of the thinner kindling could be heard. Flames, small at first, began to rise, and Brother Jerome, who was as near to the condemned man as was possible, started to pray.

"Into thy merciful hands, O Lord," the Lollard cried out steadfastly, "I entrust myself, sure——" A fierce red tongue, leaping up from the fire, seared his cheek. He faltered, a small anguished sound escaped from him, and his head briefly lolled. As the blaze increased he made a desperate effort to resume, but in vain.

A howl of fury went up from the gathering, which seemed to sway forward as though it meant to perform the one act of mercy that was left. A thunderous demand resounded:

" Give it the green . . . give it the green . . . pile it on, you inhuman varlets."

The sheriff's officer barked at several of his men, and they, driven to urgency far more by the clamour than by the command, grabbed armfuls of damp straw and vegetation and threw it on the fire. Suffocation was quicker and more kindly, and as smoke rose thickly the tumult died.

The last words of the Lollard, now unseen, came faintly from within the ascending column.

" Into Thy merciful hands, O Lord, I gladly entrust myself . . . in the certain knowledge . . . ." He choked, and fought for breath. " . . . in the certain knowledge that . . ." After this no more was heard.

Ughtred of Monkseaton turned, his hands over his face, and staggered back to the highway. Legs jelly-like, he returned to Micklegate Bar, but afterwards remembered nothing either of the walk or how he had come to be where he was, when he found himself praying at a chapel altar in a city church.

Utterly spent, he rose and walked slowly to the doorway, now seeing, as he had not seen before, a coffin on a bier, and the waving lights closely encompassing it. Six paid mourners in black knelt round the coffin, three psalm-singing clerks and three widows who alternately offered up pleas for the soul of a testator sufficient well-to-do to will that eight torches, each of ten pounds weight, should burn by his mortal remains.

Ughtred paused to pay respect to the dead, and then, chilled by inactivity and strain, went to his chamber at the abbey of St. Mary's.

A knock on the door aroused him more than two hours later, long after the bell of St. Michael's in Spurriergate first started to send out its homing message to travellers who might have difficulties in mist creeping insinuously from river to plain. Miserable and wan, he responded to the summons, to be told by one of the guest master's corps of assistants that his lord abbot required him at once.

Ughtred quickly dashed water over his face at the guests' lavatory, before hurrying outdoors to fumble his way across to the fine lodging of the abbot of St. Mary's, visibility blanketed by coldly-penetrating vapours rising from the river at the foot of the lawns.

Abbot Hugh, in the cosy parlour of one of the suites St. Mary's had of necessity for its many distinguished guests, was benign enough not to refer to what might have appeared to be dilatoriness.

" Ah, my son," he said, " you have been busy carrying out my instructions? "

" Yes, My Lord," Ughtred said.

Relaxed by a sufficiency of good red Gascony wine in his belly, My Lord chuckled.

" I will examine the sketches on our return to our beloved home, my son. Meantime, to-morrow, I have another mission for you. After dinner you will go to the nunnery of St. Clement's and present yourself to my cousin, the Dame Philippa, who is staying there." The abbot chuckled again.

While not losing too much dignity the Lord Abbot of Rievaulx was quite amusing about women in general and the Lady Philippa in particular. It seemed that the prioress of Watton had taken an inordinate fancy to his new pastoral staff, and was avid to have one comparable. My Lord, very indulgently, had promised a number of designs for her to choose from, to be sent her by the monastery's post-messenger when ready.

" That is the sum of it, my son," he concluded. " But she desires to see you, I suspect, merely to insist upon a few details of scant relevance." He laughed loudly while ringing a small silver bell. " These ladies and their foibles, my son."

His chaplain and secretary hastily entered, and the latter, in response to a peremptory signal, filled a goblet with wine. Both left almost at once, dismissed with a wildly fluttering hand. My Lord then drank deeply, smacked his lips noisily and, leaning forward, tapped the side of his nostril.

" My son," he resumed gravely, now raising his first finger to waggle it vehemently, " I have also a commission of the utmost importance for you in the morning, and the nature of that commission you will keep locked within your bosom."

"Yes, My Lord."

The abbot wagged his finger again. "My son, you are serving me in my desire to further beautify our abbey, so that the name of Rievaulx may have far carrying renown. Is it not so?"

"Yes, My Lord."

The deep voice became deeper. "I regret to have to tell you, my son, that I have latterly discovered it is essential in one important aspect that amends must be made, lest what we are doing in our convent may be largely lost by how we appear abroad. You understand, my son?"

There was only one reply to be made. "Yes, My Lord."

Abbot Hugh picked up the goblet, drained it, peered inside, replaced it on the table, glanced at the bell, thoughtfully picked his nose, and issued his instructions. On the morrow, at the Minster, Ughtred was to make drawings of all the mitres bequeathed by former archbishops at their deaths.

"This will tell you what to avoid, my son," he went on warningly, "for by avoidance, by not copying what has gone before, and by remembrance of what His Grace the present Archbishop of the Northern Province now wears, you will create something very different. You understand, my son?"

Ughtred swallowed. "My Lord, I ask and beseech God's mercy and yours," he said. "I don't, My Lord."

By now My Lord was becoming a trifle goggle-eyed. "You don't, my son?" he exclaimed.

"No, My Lord," Ughtred said.

Frowningly, the lord abbot thought that out; but his brow smoothed when, reflecting aloud, he came to the conclusion that it is not in the nature of artists to be clear-sighted about mundane matters.

"The fault was mine, my son," he said magnanimously, beating the breast of a robe embroidered throughout with figures of the saints. "I should have been more plain at the outset. I shall be now, so listen carefully, my son."

"Yes, My Lord."

"To the greater glory of our dear abbey of Saint Mary the

Virgin at Rievaulx," Abbot Hugh pronounced with immense solemnity, "and for the sake of those abbots who will succeed me, my son, I propose to have a new mitre."

" Yes, My Lord."

The abbot wagged his finger again. " You will strive with all your might to furnish me with a pattern from which our goldsmith and jeweller brethren can work, that when the mitre is completed it shall be of such awesome dignity and magnificence as shall instantly attract the eyes of all beholders."

" I will do my utmost, My Lord."

" I am assured of it, my son," the abbot said, signing him to rise, " for I am aware that all your thoughts are given to God and to making His convent at Ricvaulx more glorious. You now may go, my son."

Ughtred had nearly reached the door when the lord abbot, ceasing to ring the bell furiously, called to him.

" My son," he said, " I need not remind you that as between the brethren of our blessed Order of Saint Bernard, there can be no singling out for favouritism. But it is permitted that I tell you I am pleased with you."

Ughtred bowed. " Thank you, My Lord."

The abbot smiled. " Very pleased, my son," he said.

Bowing again, Ughtred left the parlour as the bell started to ring again, though chaplain and secretary, each looking apprehensive, had already scurried in.

Food was not in Ughtred's mind, but as he had had nothing at all since mid-morning he obtained a sweetened drink before retiring to his chamber, which was not at all difficult in a house with the facilities and attitude of St. Mary's.

When in bed he tossed for hours, unable to forget the Lollard's hideous passing. Occasionally he wondered about My Lord's latest project, but more often he thought about the prioress of Watton, and one of her nuns, Lazelle.

*       *       *       *

The scene in the Minster was the usual weekday morning one: priests saying the Mass at candle-lit altars, pilgrims clustered reverently at the tomb of Saint William, canons clattering about in cold-defying clogs, and ordinary visitors moving from one holy shrine to the next, humbly prostrating before various relics of renown—the finger of Saint Dionysius, the bones of Lazarus and his sister Martha, and the sandal of Saint Peter.

A dreary task finished, Ughtred slipped into his portfolio the last of the drawings of archiepiscopal mitres, stepping aside to allow a party of palmers to pass, each with a scallop shell in his wide brimmed hat to show that the Holy Land had been included in an itinerary of far-distant travels. Then he went outdoors.

With a little time to spare before returning to St. Mary's for dinner, Ughtred made a circuit of the great cathedral, often pausing to stare in admiration at its beauty of conception. This round took him past the archbishop's prison in the Minster, and included liberty, a halt in a position well back, from which he was able to see pigmy figures at work on the tower. Later, as he walked towards Bootham Bar, he was hoping that if opportunity allowed and he were spared long enough he might still see the fully completed edifice.

Outside the gateway's barbican, guards were assembling. Their duty, in severe winter, was to ensure a safe passage for travellers crossing the forest when it had been reported that starving wolves were haunting the highway; on this occasion, he gathered, two men had been killed by a gang of armed robbers, and precautions were now in force for that.

As a religious, Ughtred could eat in the monastery's refectory if he so desired; pressed urgently, by one of the Benedictine brothers who had taken him up the tower for a view of the city, he acquiesced, but was soon thinking that an excuse would have been better. As at home, talking was not permitted during the meal, and the reader could always be distinctly heard; but signs, as at home also, were allowed. To each side of him, down the line of crisp, white tablecloths, his hosts were silently clapping hands at each other, or patting one another's shoulder, the expressions on their faces implicit of satisfaction that still another heretical dog had been put to the flames.

Now much more familiar with the city, Ughtred had no difficulty, when grace had been said in the abbey church, in finding his way through the tortuous streets to Ouse Bridge, which he had to cross to reach the nunnery of St. Clement's. At the other side of the river, where many alleys and courts lay just off the narrow main thoroughfare, he kept a sharp eye open for Brother Jerome, but saw nothing of him. But he did see a Franciscan, and what he saw made him realise that there was sound reason for the mendicant Order's bad name—the fellow, a scurvy specimen indeed, was demanding money from a gentleman whose arm he was vigorously tugging and whom he seemed disinclined to release.

At the road which went out to Bishopthorpe and the archiepiscopal palace Ughtred's progress was stayed by a train of wagons bringing in peat-turves. The country was opening out, and not far ahead of him was the convent of St. Clement's.

At the lodge of the nunnery it soon became obvious that male callers, even those garbed in the habit of a monk, were thoroughly scrutinised and checked before being allowed to proceed farther. But in due course the senior porter escorted Ughtred across a courtyard, and then handed him over to an even more suspicious-eyed lay-sister of advanced years, who conducted him to a small room in which there were three doors, four chairs, and nothing else. On leaving him, she made it sternly clear that he must remain seated until Dame Philippa came, however long that might be.

It was not an encouraging prelude to a meeting which Ughtred was viewing with some nervousness. The prioress of Watton ranked equally with My Lord Abbot, and personages of their power and position were always to be feared. Moreover there were facets to the Dame Philippa, gleaned both from Brother Roger and the nun Lazelle, which were both strange and disquieting. She was a lady who enjoyed sporting activities; she was a most fashionable lady; and she was a lady who could be sweet with those who pleased her and as suddenly cruel to those who thwarted or disobeyed her.

Ughtred was thinking that Sister Lazelle had perhaps not used the word "cruel" when a slight sound, of a door opening, broke his reverie. He jumped up and, eyes popping, watched a woman in a white cap and black flowing habit entering the chamber. Her back was to him, and everything, including soundlessly closing the door, proclaimed secretiveness. When she turned his senses rocked.

"Sister Lazelle!" he gasped.

"Ssshhhh," she hushed him, touching her lips.

Terrified for her if she were caught with him, and unveiled at that, Ughtred pointed to the door.

" You must leave me, Sister Lazelle," he said, trying to keep his voice low while being insistent. " If you were found here with me . . . I don't know what trouble you would be in."

She shook her head. " I shan't be, Brother Ughtred. My Lady is surrounded by bolts of silk from Italy brought to her by a merchant and she will be ages in making her choices."

The controversy did not end until Lazelle slightly opened another door, through which the Dame Philippa would come. Beyond the gap Ughtred could see a lengthy, stone-flagged corridor, and he placed himself in a position to watch.

" No one would believe you could ever have the courage to jump into a swollen river," the nun Lazelle commented. " But I so wanted to thank you properly for saving my life, and I'd made my mind up that if the least chance offered I would come to you."

" I didn't jump into the river, Sister Lazelle," Ughtred said. " I only walked in."

" My Lady is perfectly sure you saved my life," Lazelle said firmly. " So am I."

He was looking at her; at her eyes and the long eyelashes fringing them, seeing again the sweet shape of her mouth and the pleasingness of her nose. She was as lovely as ever, more lovely in reality than he had dreamed. But, under his gaze, a flush was investing her cheeks, displacing a pallor as frightening as the one she had when he saw her unconscious in the light of a fire.

" Are you ill, Sister Lazelle? " he asked.

She tried to smile. " I slept fitfully, Brother Ughtred, and I can't forget something dreadful. It . . . it haunts me." Her lips quivered. " Brother Ughtred, I . . . yesterday I saw a man being burned to death."

Stupefied, Ughtred stared at her. It seemed impossible that a Gilbertine nun could have been in the crowd. The explanation he was given, however, was simple enough. During an interval at one of the meetings of the Ecclesiastical Council, of which she was becoming heartily weary, Dame Philippa had heard that the Prince Bishop of Durham proposed riding a few miles south of the city to inspect, later in the week, two greyhounds about whom he had a glowing report. Stealing a march on him, she had driven off the previous day and bought the two dogs. On the way back her cart had been held up by the gathering at the stake.

The nun Lazelle shivered. " I peeped through a chink in the screen once only, Brother Ughtred," she said miserably. " But I think from now on I will never cease to have nightmares."

" Try not to think about it, Sister Lazelle," Ughtred said. " He is at peace now."

" I . . . I marvel that anyone can be strong enough to endure such agonies for his convictions," she whispered. " And I would," she fired a little, " that his judges could suffer a slight taste of the same medicine."

" Sister Lazelle," Ughtred said hollowly, " his judges were prelates of Holy Church, and no other."

He felt she looked as much shocked as he must have done himself when told the same thing.

" Prelates of Holy Church? " she repeated.

Ughtred nodded. " A Franciscan friar informed me they were, and at St. Mary's, where there is freer speech than I am accustomed to in my cloister, the monks also told me that it is so—appearing to think nothing of it."

She gasped. " But . . . but to condemn anyone, even a malefactor, to hideous death is against our Saviour's teaching. And their lords the bishops, and abbots and prioresses and other superiors, stand for Him on earth. When they speak to us it is the voice of Our Lord Jesus Christ who speaks."

" Not according to these Lollards, who preach the words written by a dead cleric known as John Wycliffe." Ughtred sighed. " He affirmed that no one can be an intermediary between ourselves and God, and that no one here can direct us as if he were God."

Lazelle's eyes widened. " That our prioresses and abbots are not transmitting to us the desires and commands of God? And cannot? "

Ughtred nodded. " That is what the Lollards assert."

Wonderingly she looked at him. " And they are willing to die for that belief? "

" I know of it twice," Ughtred said sombrely.

Slowly the nun Lazelle shook her head. " I . . . I am ignorant of these grave things," she said. " But I am sure there must be evil in those who sentence these poor creatures to such an inhuman end."

" Sister Lazelle! " Ughtred said imperatively. " You must not say that."

" Why should I not? " she asked.

" Because lately I have learned something of the harshness there is at this time in these matters," Ughtred went on passionately. " You could suffer intolerably."

Her chin was raised proudly. " If I accepted anything heart and soul, Brother Ughtred, I would not shrink if I had to pay the price."

" Sister Lazelle, please," Ughtred begged. " In these affairs you must never be heard either to criticise or question."

She smiled at him. " I think we are making a great bother about nothing, Brother Ughtred," she said, " I have no knowledge of the Lollards and their doctrine—and all I say is that there is wickedness in those who send them to a fearsome death."

" Oh, Sister Lazelle," Ughtred said despairingly.

Lazelle laughed at his rueful expression, but clapped her hand over her mouth as he signalled frantically. It turned out that his action was not due to the Dame Philippa's approach but out of fear that she might be heard.

" I am very ignorant, too, but less ignorant than I was," Ughtred continued. " Or rather the little I have acquired perplexes and worries me immoderately, and I shall be glad to be home again to think things out peacefully."

" Yes," she said, understanding.

" Sister Lazelle, you remember I told you about a Franciscan friar I thought was a pert fellow, but who, despite his oddness, put some strange ideas into my head. He is the friar I have just mentioned."

" At Ripon it was," Lazelle said.

" Yes, but I have met him again, here in the city," said Ughtred. " He is still odd, but beneath his oddness there is gentleness and humility and the true godliness."

He had told her a great deal about Friar Jerome, and something of what had been said by the only two Lollards he had ever encountered, when the latch of the door along the corridor clicked. He stepped quickly to one side, at the same time pointing to the corner from which Lazelle had entered. She slipped away, but in the doorway turned.

" God be with you, Brother Ughtred," she whispered, and was gone.

Ughtred, heart still thumping, fell to his knees when the prioress of Watton came into the chamber majestically, her clothes rustling and the odour of a musky perfume accompanying her.

" You are the monk of Rievaulx, Ughtred of Monkseaton," she said, " Sent to me by the Lord Abbot Hugh? "

" Yes, My Lady."

Dame Philippa seated herself and, holding her staff erect, grasped in the middle, stared at the prostrate figure.

" Lift your head, my son," she said sharply. " I find a face more interesting than the top of a hood."

" Yes, My Lady," Ughtred muttered.

The prioress surveyed him much longer than he cared for. " H'mmm," she said. " And it was you who rescued one of my daughters, eh? "

" I was able to aid her, My Lady," Ughtred said. " It was no great thing."

" Nonsense," the Lady Philippa scoffed. " I know what those swift mountain rivers can be even where it is shallow and when it is only the beginning of the spate. I don't spend all my leisure hours sitting at a spinning wheel or a tapestry frame."

" No, My Lady," Ughtred mumbled.

" My daughter tells me that you were gentle and considerate, and for that I have a small gift for you."

" It is not necessary, My Lady," Ughtred said, more firmly.

The prioress's tone was autocratic. " I am the best judge of that, my son. I am also aware that your Rule does not permit you to own anything, and so I have arranged with your Lord that you hold the present in trust for your convent."

" You are very kind, My Lady."

In more youthful days Ughtred had encountered one or two ladies of high birth and frightening presence, but never before had he seen one remotely comparing to the Lady Philippa, and she a holy prioress. Her habit was of velvet, not cloth, and its shade the blue of a cold northern sky. And her veil was so much a web of gossamer that it was possible distinctly to perceive the whiteness of powder on her cheeks, the shading of paint near her eyes, and the hard dominance of expression in greenish eyes.

He was bewildered when she laughed musically and unexpectedly. " My Lord," she said, straightening her face, " has informed you what I desire you to do? "

" Yes, My Lady."

" You will create and paint a number of designs so that I may select the one which pleases me best."

" Yes, My Lady."

She drummed her fingers on the carved arm of the chair. " H'mmm," she murmured thoughtfully.

It soon became evident that the pastoral staff was to depart from My Lord's in two features. It was to be so provided that a veil-banner could be attached, which presented no difficulty, and the curve of the crook was to be reversed, which did present a problem.

" My Lady . . ." Ughtred said hesitantly.

Sharply instructed to say what he had to say, he respectfully told her that only bishops' crooks were turned outwards, signifying authority over their wide-ranging flocks, as opposed to the inwardly-bending crooks of the abbots of monastic Orders, which meant an authority limited to the convent.

" Thank you, my son," the Dame Philippa remarked tartly. " But what I desire is that it shall curve outwards. Do you comprehend? "

Ughtred bowed. " Yes, My Lady," he said.

" How long will it be before your Lord's messenger will bring the pictures to me? "

" It will depend, My Lady. I would not care to part with anything which either was not satisfying to me or which I thought would not please you."

She shrugged. " It is of no moment, my son. The creation of an object of unique beauty is not to be hurried, and that is what I require."

" I shall do my best, My Lady."

The prioress of Watton was in the midst of graciously assuring him that she was amply sure he would, when she vented a thought which wholly contradicted a previous assertion.

"About a month, perhaps?" she said.

"I don't know, My Lady," Ughtred said. "My Lord has much for me to do when we return home."

"It is to be expected, from what the Lord Hugh confided to me," she said, a slight edge in her voice. "As I have told you, my son, it is of small moment."

She rose and, repenting of the flash of ill-humour, extended a white, heavily perfumed hand for him to kiss. Then, ordering him to remain where he was, she left.

The same vinegary lay-sister came shortly afterwards, but took him out by a different route, as far as a small yard enclosed by a very high wall. There, while watching Ughtred as though convinced that every boy-child grew to be a lecher, even a dedicated monk, she rang a large hand-bell vehemently, continuing without a pause until the porter appeared. Within a minute of that Ughtred was outside the closely-guarded precincts of St. Clement's; an iron-banded, arch-shaped door slammed behind him, followed by the sound of bolts being rammed home.

Filled with joyousness about a meeting more blessed than any other could have been, Ughtred remained motionless for some little time, recapturing that meeting as he stared at Gilbertine canons walking in the confines of St. Andrew's across the water, and while looking up-river on the far side where, with no place shoreward for building, extensions to merchants' premises jutted out into the Ouse to varying extents.

"Please God," he murmured, clasping his hands in supplication as a frightening thought entered his head, "never allow her to be open-mouthed as she was with me. Guard her, O Lord, from dangers she cannot understand. O Saviour, grant this to me, Thy humble and devoted servant."

Ughtred had got as far as the Bishopthorpe road before he remembered that, squeezed under his arm, was a package wrapped in soft, purple-dyed hide. It contained a metal box of Florentine craftsmanship; inside were requisites for 'painting in little,' including a range of pens, brushes with tiny heads, vials of pigments, and a hand-glass for magnifying.

This handsome present would certainly have caused any illuminator of manuscripts to glow with pleasure, and an explanation did not strike him until he began to reflect about the donor. The prioress of Watton was a lady, he decided, who would not pay much attention to others, and might not properly have grasped the nature of the work he did.

" Still, it is over-generous of her," he mused, his lips curving into a smile. " And of a surety Sister Lazelle, apart from speaking of me far too fulsomely, must have related to her something of the love I have for what I do."

This notion kept him busy until another occurred to him, a most thrilling one. " It shall be," he told himself. " I will experiment, I will try to master the difficulties—I will try to paint pictures in miniature, of holy events in the Book and of scenes at home. I . . . I might even strive to paint Sister Lazelle, though never could I do her justice . . . *never*."

After replacing in its velvet-lined cavity the last of the vials he had lifted out, Ughtred rose from the tree-stump and resumed his way. In the city it was Thursday Market but, excitedly preoccupied by a prospect which might fill in any little extra leisure with delight, he neither saw the crush beyond the toll-booth or heard the cries of poultry dealers, cheesers, and medicine men.

When Bootham Bar was behind him, and as he walked outside the defence wall of St. Mary's towards the gate-house, Ughtred thought of the breviary on his girdle. Much had happened during his stay with the Black monks, none of which he would forget while breath was in him, whether the horror or the wonder.

By God's goodness he was now more nearly at peace. He started to read.

# 4

Between arriving home and the eve of St. Martin's Day, on the sound principle that it is less irksome to break the back of disagreeable jobs first, Ughtred made four sketches of a pastoral staff for the prioress of Watton.

Within the same period, working also in the seclusion of the bell-chamber, he completed a miniature painting of Lazelle, based to some extent on the first drawing he had done of her. The latter, having served its purpose, he now tore into pieces for subsequent safe disposal, probably by burning on the warming house fire when no one was looking.

The new picture, of head and shoulders only, was startlingly different from the pen-and-ink drawing the lord abbot had seen—without hint of halo, cloud, or angels bearing the Holy Child. Simply, it was the face of a very lovely maid in a pretty, white cap, the same cap Ughtred had seen at St. Clement's Benedictine nunnery.

The last tiny stroke done, Ughtred slowly put down his brush and stared at his work. After a while, sighing with relief, he decided that the pigments and emulsions entrusted to him by the Lady Philippa had served him well, and that within reason he had successfully portrayed the soft bloom on Sister Lazelle's cheeks, the redness of her sweet lips, and the almost indefinable colour of her beautiful eyes.

" It could have been worse," he told himself. " But . . . but with such skill as I have I . . . I think it is the best I could ever do."

To his annoyance his eyes began to tingle. Impatient with himself, he rose from the bench on which the bellringers sat to eat their pittances, and walked to a window on the west side of the tower. Vision misty, he looked over the roof of the nave towards the inner court, where sheep and beasts were being penned near the shambles in anticipation of St. Martin's Day, a day of slaughtering and salting for the winter, when black puddings and other delicacies were made, and the tit-bits of the offals pickled in brine.

Returning, Ughtred gazed again at the likeness, and then, carefully picking up the picture between outstretched thumb and finger, placed the oblong of stiff vellum in a thin box he had made, so that the surface of the portrait could not be rubbed while still wet.

Shortly afterwards, the treasure stowed inside his habit, he descended a corkscrew staircase squeezed within the massive stonework rising from the transept, treading as quietly as possible. At the bottom he glanced out cautiously, coughed gently, and stepped forward only when the sole person in sight turned to nod to him. This was Theobald of Guisborough, a middle-aged monk whose mild appearance did not suggest he was likely to play the part of accomplice in anything unlawful.

" Thank you, Brother Theobald," Ughtred said gratefully.

Brother Theobald smiled. " Only too glad to help, Brother Ughtred. I am an artist of sorts myself, and I know full well there are times when intruders are a nuisance, however kindly their interest."

Feeling himself a cheat, Ughtred muttered vaguely in response. It was one thing to be supposed to need a little privacy to do a few special designs, as Brother Theobald supposed, but quite another to use the major part of that privacy to paint a picture of a maid.

" Well . . . well, let me see how you have got on in my absence, Brother Theobald," he continued, kneeling on the shining pavement for a closer view of the tracery of a door into one of the chapels. " Oh! you're beyond the stem by now. Another cluster of leaves? "

" Yes, Brother Ughtred. I shall now repeat the last but one."

Theobald of Guisborough, from boyhood, had always wanted to serve the Almighty, but was happiest of all when paying tribute with his hands. His skill at woodcarving was such that it was freely acknowledged he was not a whit inferior to the best craftsmen either of Durham or York, which was renown indeed. He had been responsible for the exquisite carving on the bosses of My Lord's new staff, and at the present was adorning the openwork screens of the transept chapels with a thin band of naturalistic foliage. Each leaf curved as in life, and not a vein or serration was missed.

" Wonderful, Brother Theobald," Ughtred murmured, his sincerity unmistakable. " Superb! It really is."

Brother Theobald's face glowed. " You think so, Brother Ughtred? " he said. " You think that, you who has travelled so far? "

" And never seen work to improve on it," Ughtred said, fingering a tiny wooden flower. " No, not in one of the great cathedrals and monasteries I have been privileged to enter."

" You fill my heart with joy, Brother Ughtred," Brother Theobald said, very nearly overcome.

Conversation was always easy between them and, while Brother Theobald continued to whittle, they talked low-voiced but animatedly. For their respective reasons both were deeply content.

At the second rising, after Lauds, shortly before seven o'clock the next morning, Ughtred's mood was no less happy as he signed his forehead with the cross, and said the *Credo* of the Prime of the Little Office of Our Lady; and silently, beneath his breath, he hummed a favourite hymn when turning his bed and on going down to the cloister to wash and comb his hair.

St. Martin's Day, in its earlier part, passed smoothly. After Prime there was a perambulation. Beginning by climbing the night-stairs, the community walked in single file as far as the cresset standard in the dormitory, where the leader turned and marched slowly back to the day-stairs. Rounds of similar pattern were made of the chapter house and refectory, these proceedings reaching their conclusion after a complete circuit of the cloister when, between the book aumbry and Saint Bernard's portrait, the prior halted and faced the windows looking on to the garth.

This was the cue for a white-clad novice much farther down the ranks to step forward to call out the name of the day, the month and the year. Imagining himself the focus of all attention the youth carried out this duty, but his voice quavered, a misdemeanour which did not escape his master's notice.

A short breather followed before Lady Mass. In this interval a know-all brother, Edmund, started an argument on the philosophy of Philo of Alexandria; Brother Martin, the wizard with clocks, who had belatedly come across Friar Bacon's writings, buttonholed Ughtred to tell him excitedly about an engine which could be used for sailing and flying; Brother Giles, in a moment of aberration, rested himself on the abbot's seat near the church door, but shot up again when a pair of gimlet-like eyes, the third prior's, were fixed on him; and in the song school the offending novice, tied to a stone pillar, was thrashed with a rod taken from the wall.

Throughout this the bell had been ringing. When it ceased the brethren assembled at the *statio*, and from there walked round to the church; on entering each kissed the crucifix, took holy water, and bowed to The Holy Three.

After the Lady Mass the community moved off in pairs to the chapter house, with one exception all using the fine doorway. The exception was Brother Eustace who, resuming his old moaning and weeping, had crawled under the slab upon which, beneath its gabled canopy, the receptacle containing the relics of Saint William stood.

From the prior's attitude it was at once realised that the lord abbot was to be present, and two lines were formed. The Lord Hugh arrived a few minutes later wearing an all-white furred robe, which indicated he would be presiding over the Parliament afterwards. As he advanced his sons sank to their knees to kiss his hand.

When the daily reading ended My Lord announced that it was now the time for them to speak about the affairs of their house, an intimation for the novices to leave the aisles behind the stalls, where they had been standing; and, on that morning, a signal for the novice-master to bring in two postulants who for three days had been living in the guest house.

The applicants, throughout those three days, had been under a far more severe scrutiny than they would have guessed, and several of the obedientiaries were able to furnish My Lord with a report. Designedly, the novice-master was called on last of all. Barefooted and bareheaded, flushed with the ignominy of his punishment, he humbly expressed an opinion.

None of this was very interesting, and Ughtred's attention wandered. Unfortunately, when lowering his head after marvelling at the ability of the masons who had fashioned the ribs of the vaulted roof, he glimpsed the expression on Brother Giles's usually pleasant face—that young man was eyeing the would-be novices as though utterly convinced they were crazy.

Hastily Ughtred gave his attention to an inscription cut in the mottled-grey marble of a coffin-lid in front of him. It read:

*Hic requiescit Dominus Ailred Abbas de Riavallis*
*qui obiit vii Die Decembris MCLXVI*

Abbot Ailred, recognised by Rome as a saint, had been the third and most famous of the convent's abbots, and so it was very proper for a junior monk to pay close attention to where he rested. Ughtred, frightened of laughing if he glanced at Brother Giles again, steadfastly continued to look at the hallowed place until the postulants, accepted on trial for twelve months, had been ushered out by the novice-master.

" And now the next item, my sons," the abbot said.

This proved to be a controversial issue to one member of the community. At first the discussion was concerned with the main points: whether a proposed new crucifix for the misericord in the infirmary was to be of gold or silver, and should a design be invited from goldsmiths and silversmiths in the city.

" Personally I have scant doubt," the abbot remarked, " that within our own religious we have, thanks to the Almighty, an artist fully capable of doing all that is required." He bowed graciously towards Ughtred.

" Thank you, *Domine*," Ughtred muttered, reddening with confusion as he prostrated himself. " My Lord is much too generous."

The tight-mouthed sub-prior also agreed. " It is indeed so, My Lord."

" I heartily concur, My Lord," the guest master grunted. " But first impressions count most, and were Brother Ughtred to confine his attentions for the time being to embellishing the lodgings to which I have the honour to lead so many distinguished personages——"

The abbot waved for silence. " The quarters over which you preside are not forgotten, my son," he said smoothly. " In due course our son and brother, Ughtred, will serve you as you so ardently desire."

"The church should have the first consideration," the sacrist said indignantly. "Our most solemn prayers ascend from it and every inch should be resplendent."

The refectorian irascibly slapped the book table before him. "In all the abbeys I have seen or read of, My Lord," he snorted, "it is the aim to make the refectory the most handsome chamber."

A monk mid-way down the chapter house, portly despite the many fastings granted to him, sarcastically observed that a refectory was best judged by two things, one of which was the drink.

The cellarer shot up. "What is your complaint now?" he demanded. "In what manner does the liquor fail to suit you?"

Ralph of Scarborough, an expert in polishing precious stones, stood his ground.

"The wine latterly," he retorted. "So sour that when it is gulped down I notice a score of mouths twisted horridly."

The kitchener joined in. "For one who frequently petitions to be excused at board you talk too much," he said sharply. "Why prate so often?"

Pendulous jowl wobbling, Brother Ralph admitted that in his search for purification he did abstain greatly from food. But this, he added, was all the more reason that the trifle he had should be of the best.

"Yesterday's broth," he ended succinctly. "No substance to it. Dishwater! Dirty dishwater at that. There was a hair in it, too."

All the essentials for a ding-dong row were present, but the lord abbot, who had been listening with a suspicion of amusement in his dark eyes, imposed silence with an admonitory hand. He then reminded his hearers that they had been debating about a crucifix for the misericord; and what it should be made of came first, he wound up.

"Wood," said old Brother Luke.

"*Wood*, in the infirmary," the infirmarian said furiously. "My Lord," he appealed, "with all respect it must be either of gold or silver or I shall be shamed to eternity."

"Silver or gold, for the decoration of an apartment that is a disgrace to those who conceived it," Brother Luke said passionately.

To the ill-concealed impatience of many, he embarked on an

account of early days when, by the wisdom of the architect of their Order, meat was denied forever to those of his followers who were able-bodied and well. Four generations afterwards, he reminded them, the sly found a means of evasion—a second dining-hall was built elsewhere, and named misericord, where red-flesh could be eaten on three days in the week.

" By that scurvy trick," Brother Luke thundered on, " the statute about the refectory allegedly was not broken. Now, however, in our hypocrisy and brashness, we go further, not even troubling to walk to the misericord for our sirloin and lamb."

Viciously the sub-prior turned on him. " The issue has nothing to do with what we consume. It concerns whether, in our homage of God, a sacred object shall be of silver or gold."

Stepping forward, Brother Luke almost spat out his words. " Have you lost all recall, Reverend Father, of the Blessed Saint Bernard's bitterness about the Cluniacs? ' Tell me,' he said to them, ' tell me, O ye professors of piety, what does gold do in a holy place? What has all that to do with monks, with professors of poverty, with spiritual lives? ' "

" My Lord," the infirmarian cried, " let us hear no more from him."

Doggedly Brother Luke went on : " The holy Saint Bernard decreed that candlesticks should always be of iron, and crosses of wood. He did not say that the crosses might not be lovingly carved or that——"

Abbot Hugh, spots of colour on his cheekbones, held up his hand. " That is quite enough, my son," he snapped. " You will remember I have warned you before. Is that so? "

Brother Luke bowed.

" Continue for your own sake to remember, my son," the abbot said. " I promise you I shall not be as lenient on another occasion."

There was no further argument about the crucifix for the misericord. It was to be of gold, and Ughtred was to create the design.

The next matter discussed was that of the recalcitrant monk in the underground vault off the Passage, about whom the Abbot of Jervaulx had been inquiring. It was a bitter pill for the prior to have to admit that he had failed completely with the fellow, who had been thrashed until in no condition to be thrashed any more.

" I see no alternative other than returning him to Jervaulx, My Lord," he said, white with chagrin.

Abbot Hugh toyed with him. " So you confess to failure, my son? " he said silkily.

" I can do no more with him, My Lord," the prior muttered.

" Thereby publicly admitting that we have failed, my son." The lord abbot shook his head regretfully. " I had not thought to hear such words from you, my son."

" I have done, to the limit, all that may be done short of taking his life, My Lord," the prior said, his cheek-bones prominent. " The reverend father our infirmarian will support me in that, I am certain."

The abbot glanced at the infirmarian. " Well, my son? " he inquired.

" It is so, My Lord," the obedientiary replied. " Without exception the learned doctors prescribe the same treatment for lunacy, and the most revered father, after consulting me, has carried it out faithfully, as I have witnessed for myself."

" What is the essential feature of this treatment, my son? "

" The shock of many scourgings, My Lord," the infirmarian said with an air. " In lunacy evil vapours collect round the brain, and the sole means of elimination is to force them out by acute pain."

The lord abbot stroked his chin. " This would be the first time this house has been disgraced since Our Lord God and the brethren in Chapter elected me to my august office," he mused, a faint smile beginning to appear on his lips. " But perhaps, Our Father above willing, we may avert this even in these last hours."

More ordinary matters were discussed later, when Parliament assembled in the cloister. Elsewhere in the walks activities usual to all breaks between the Offices were continued: some of the brethren read, and others quietly chatted about obscure points encountered in devotional volumes; the novices, very much subdued by the hiding received by one of them, listened attentively while Brother Stephen, an engrosser, explained the meaning of a passage in Scripture, and, as always, the ever-watchful guardians moved silently about.

For his part, Ughtred, cornered by Brother Robert, was compelled to sit on a stone bench at the north end of the west walk, close to where the Parliament had gathered.

"I had no idea, Brother Ughtred," Brother Robert remarked reprovingly, " no idea at all, my son, that when in the city you attended upon the Dame Philippa, prioress of Watton."

"No," said Ughtred. "Yes, I mean, Brother Robert."

The chronicler lifted his tablet from his girdle and examined the point of a style. " Not until Brother Ailfy chanced to mention it to me, quite by accident."

"It was of no importance, Brother Robert," Ughtred muttered. " Nothing worth informing you about."

To be honest, he had one ear cocked towards the Parliament, who were discussing a letter in which the abbot of Newminster requested that the auditor, Brother Roger, should visit him for a stay of some length. This was for a far more important purpose than merely to clear up a muddle between the two convents—it was My Lord of Newminster's intention to have a completely new system of book-keeping started, and he wrote to the effect that, from what he had seen of him, Brother Roger was just the man to carry this out effectively.

Brother Roger was pointing out that if the affairs of Newminster were in the mess he suspected he might be absent throughout the winter, perhaps until the Spring. He sounded gruff, perhaps too gruff, and Ughtred wondered if he were secretly pleased about what, after all, was a considerable compliment.

"Yes, yes," Brother Robert said testily. " Brother Ailfy told me you were to design a pastoral staff for the Lady Philippa, but that is only the small centrepiece around which I hope to build an entertaining story. Begin from where you reached the nunnery, my son. Did the porter remark upon the fame of our house? "

" The porter made very few remarks, Brother Robert," Ughtred said. " In fact, his manner towards me was one of grave suspicion."

The chronicler sat up. " In what wise? " he asked eagerly.

" He was careful about my credentials before admitting me," Ughtred explained.

" Ah," said Brother Robert.

" There was nothing out of the ordinary about it," Ughtred said hurriedly. " In his position he has to be cautious . . . there are holy nuns there, whom he must safeguard in every way."

The chronicler, style cutting into the wax, had already started to make a note which proved to be far more voluminous than these brief remarks would seem to have merited. But he broke off momentarily to deliver a pregnant observation.

" Brother Ughtred," he said, " his inquiries had nothing to do with you personally. It is once again an example of the mistrust and jealousy of the Benedictines for our Order. They seek to conceal it, but it is always there."

" He was only doing his duty," Ughtred protested.

" Then why did he not admit you without so much senseless parleying? " Brother Robert demanded. " Why should you, a monk of Rievaulx in attendance upon My Lord, be kept standing in the filthy road while he pestered you with a string of foolish questions? How else can such a grievous slight upon our house . . . but cease interrupting me, my son. I have many notes to make."

Inwardly sighing, Ughtred gave up, occupying himself surreptitiously with the business of the Parliament, where it had been decided that a message should be sent informing the lord abbot of Newminster that the auditor would leave Ryedale during the second week in Advent. Everyone seemed pleased about this, and Ughtred gleaned that the whole affair was regarded as distinctly a feather in Rievaulx's cap. The whole point was that Newminster, although a daughter house of Fountains, had preferred to apply for assistance elsewhere. It was, as the third prior commented not without pleasure, just another illustration of the fact that in many quarters the community of Fountains were being increasingly considered as too big for their boots.

" Flocks of sheep in their tens of thousands," Brother Roger grunted. " Yes, that's precisely what they tried to rub into me when I was there, and if I hadn't been of a courteous disposition . . ."

" In what other gross manner were you insulted? " The chronicler jabbed his elbow into Ughtred's ribs.

Ughtred had to suffer the older monk's probings and even more wild distortions for another ten minutes, during which the lord abbot, who had withdrawn from the Parliament, went round the cloister to his seat by the church door, where, his expression grim, he talked to the sub-prior for some time, apparently giving instructions.

When a small bell was rung for High Mass and silence, Ughtred thankfully excused himself to the chronicler—a bow sufficed—and, leaving while the chance availed, went round the cloister to the east walk, where books were being put away in the aumbry, under the eye of the sub-cantor.

The brethren then went into church, the senior members taking their places nearest to the altar. When the tower bell ceased to ring the lord abbot entered, to take the stall closest to the presbytery steps, opposite to the prior. From that position he signed to the cantor, already standing at the lectern, to lead the singing.

When this most solemn of Offices was concluded Abbot Hugh left, first of all, for the cloister, where he shook a small bell to summon the community to dinner. This bell-ringing, taken over by the sub-sacrist, continued until the moment arrived for procession into the refectory, where each fresh arrival bowed to the crucifix above the picture behind the dais.

In the refectory the procedure was as always when the lord abbot dined. The prior and the third prior assisted him to wash his hands in a marble basin on the wall, and the fourth prior and the almoner, each holding a spotless towel, waited his pleasure. When seated My Lord rang a silver-gilt hand-bell, and the reader in the wall pulpit at once read the first sentence, always selected for shortness.

My Lord then rang the bell again, and the meal began. Servers appeared from behind the screen effacing the kitchen hatch, and a junior monk cut My Lord's loaf in two while another filled his goblet with wine.

For the servers, with the lord present, it was an ordeal, and one, Brother Aymer, a rubricator, was so nervous that he spilled from a dish he was carrying. The refectorian glared at him, but the abbot punished him on the spot—after banging on his table with the haft of his knife, My Lord pointed with the business end to a place on the floor, close to the table at which the novices and their master sat. There, kneeling, the culprit did penance for the remainder of the meal.

Abbot Hugh was to use the haft of his knife thrice more, at the conclusion of the meagre repast: to summon two juniors, with their baskets, to collect leftovers and any bread not covered by a napkin, during which Brother Eustace made sure that everyone was aware he was handing in an untouched loaf; as a signal to the servers to collect the spoons; and as an instruction for the reader to sing the words of praise which marked the finish of all public readings. After that, grace in church stood alone between worship and the hours of work and recreation.

Afterwards, in the cloister, the prior invited Brother Luke to his room for a glass of wine; Brothers Peter and Lionel went into the cloister garth where, in pouring rain, they faced each other over the open grave; and Ughtred decided to pay a visit to the infirmary, thus killing two birds with the same stone.

Near the Passage end of the east walk a few novices, tongues out in their concentration, were laboriously writing in their copy books; while in the song school the sub-cantor was teaching choral parts of the service to another white-clad group, who were making sufficient noise to drown any sound which might have come from the underground vault not far away.

However, Ughtred heard nothing from the monk of Jervaulx, and anyhow was soon too far away, hastening to escape a wetting as quickly as his flowing habit permitted.

At the infirmary, instead of continuing towards the hall and parlour, he turned into the misericord. It was a fine apartment, ludicrously too large for the trifling number of the community who used it for dining: ordinary patients, monks who had been bled, and wisemen as yet not bedfast. Its size bore out old Brother Luke's contention.

" H'mmin," he murmured, staring at the present crucifix, of silver with a brass inlay. " It could do to be taller in a room of this height, and more slender would be an advantage."

Thinking it out, he wandered about the room, pausing once to examine a portrait of Sir Walter l'Espec, in Cistercian garb, a distinguished knight who had lived the last two years of his life as a most ordinary monk of Rievaulx; and again to look at a fine reading desk, which had been immensely improved by Brother Theobald's carving.

" Yes, much more delicate," he told himself, glancing towards the crucifix. " That is much too squat to have any real presence."

His mind made up on this, he returned to the hall, and from there, passing through the long dormitory, entered the parlour, where Brother Godfrey and two fellow wisemen, glad to see a fresh face, greeted him warmly. The four of them then settled down to a pleasant chat. Ughtred was able to furnish a few snippets of gossip, and they, with many a chuckle, told him of incidents which had amused them in their junior days.

Later, with a duplicity calling for a visit either to a confessor or St. Paul's chapel, Ughtred led the conversation first to the Franciscans and then to the Lollards.

" I heard in the city that there is a new Order of mendicant friars," he remarked. " A group of Franciscans who have split off from the main branch."

" I have been told of them also," one of the old men said dourly. " Observants they name themselves, and I believe they are pledged to a return to primitive obedience." He shook his head. " But they spring from rotten stock, and I would doubt the outcome."

" Nevertheless, in their youth the Franciscans, who at their beginnings termed themselves Minorites in their desire to be considered the most humble of the Orders, worked zealously for the Lord," the other old man murmured. " In their preachings they carried the word of God to the loneliest hamlets, and in the towns spent themselves in the service of the poor."

" I suppose, Revered Father, that it is the responsibility of each of us to decide, according to his faith and conscience, how best we may serve the Almighty," Ughtred said. " We believe we can come closer to Him by meditation and prayer, while the early Franciscans cherished the opinion that the Divine Will could be forwarded to the greatest advantage by active work in the haunts of men."

Brother Godfrey spoke with such vehemence that his elder companions shifted themselves to stare at him with palpable surprise.

" My son," he said severely, " I find these speculations both unprofitable and tedious. Let us have no more of them."

Ughtred bowed. " As you will, Revered Father," he said.

This rebuke had a dampening effect generally, and for some minutes the exchanges were most desultory. Conversation became more lively, however, when Ughtred mentioned that a Lollard had been burnt while he was in the city.

"As he should have been," one of the wisemen snapped.

"Miscreants every one of them," the other declared heatedly. "Liars and perverts who would undermine the foundations of Christianity. Let them to the stake, I say, every man-jack one of them—let them feel the excruciating agonies of the flames for their iniquitous conduct."

"That was the hope of the Benedictine brothers of St. Mary's Abbey, who were decidedly more free in discussion than I am accustomed to," Ughtred said gravely. "It was from them, Revered Fathers, that I learnt that the Lollard preachers were sent to their doom by ecclesiastical courts, and none other."

Brother Godfrey again astounded his more elderly companions. Trembling, he rose and fanned his face with his hand.

"My son," he said apologetically, "if you would lend me your arm to the main doorway, facing the garth, I would be most grateful."

Ughtred sprang up. "Certainly, Revered Father. But it is raining hard and it would not be wise for you to venture out."

The old wiseman shook his head. "No, no, my son, all I propose is to draw a few breaths of fresh air at the door. I . . . I find the heat and the fug in here a trifle stifling."

"Aren't you feeling well, Revered Father?" one of the other wisemen asked.

"Too hot and close in here? " the third elder said with surprise. "Why, Revered Father, it is always you who has asserted that old bones need to be on top of the fire."

Brother Godfrey smiled wanly. "It is nothing, my dear friends, and as soon as I have cleared my lungs I shall be my former self. Come, my son Ughtred, your arm if you will."

Ughtred assisted him to the hall, past the doorway of the misericord at one side, and those leading to the chapel and *flebotomaria*, where blood-letting was carried out, four times in the year for everyone, at the other.

At the outer doorway, the expression in his faded eyes tragic, Brother Godfrey stared at two sculptured figures in the infirmary garth, one representing The Fall and the other the Annunciation.

Rain dripped from them as it dripped everywhere, a dreary sound.

"My son," the wiseman said brokenly, "until now, for the length of a long lifetime, I have been as truthful to my God as I have been with my fellow men. And now I have lied."

"Revered Father," Ughtred said anxiously, "I don't know what you mean, but——"

Feebly shaking his head, the aged man silenced him. "I have lied, my son, out of fear for you, fear of what in your imprudence you might say. Fear which arose out of my love for you ... for you, my son Ughtred, whom in my thoughts I have always regarded, ever since the first months of your novitiate, as if you were a blood son of mine. That is why I lied just now, so that I might at once speak to you alone, so that when speaking I might once again warn you."

"Warn me?" said Ughtred, deeply concerned for the old man. "Oh, Revered Father, you must not worry about me."

Even a small crisis plays havoc with a very aged man, who for a long lifetime has lived in seclusion, remote from the stresses of the outside world.

"I have worried about you ever since we talked on the day we went to visit our dead brethren in the cemetery, my son," Brother Godfrey said, his lips quivering. "And now I am worrying far more because I discern in you something I fear may be . . . may be critical both of our Order and of Holy Church."

"I . . . I cannot help my thoughts, Revered Father," Ughtred said miserably. "I wish I could, for they plague me intolerably."

"You should have no thoughts save those of implicit obedience," the wiseman said with a pathetic attempt at severity. "To that you have been trained, and woe betide you if you are ever found to falter. What do you think our most revered father the prior would do to you if he suspected you of waywardness?"

"His discipline would be hard, Revered Father," Ughtred admitted.

"But as nothing to what——"

The old monk broke off on hearing the sound of footsteps at the dormitory end of the long hall, to which his aged companions had walked to inquire how he was faring. He did not resume until it seemed certain they were out of earshot.

"Evasions, trickeries . . . with old friends," Brother Godfrey murmured. "To that I have committed myself, my son, and it hurts me acutely. Nevertheless, my son, having sinned so far I will sin a little more. What was I saying, my son?"

"You were speaking of how the most revered prior would punish me," Ughtred said.

"Oh yes," the wiseman murmured. "And, my son, it would be of the utmost sternness, although it would be just according to the tenets of our early Cistercian father. But that sternness would be as nothing compared to what you would endure at the hands of the lord abbot."

"My Lord!" Ughtred exclaimed.

Solemnly Brother Godfrey nodded. "Yes, my son, even if he holds you in great esteem for your merits as an artist, as he does. But that . . ." he looked over his shoulder before continuing, "but that would not prevent him from bringing you close to crucifixion if he deemed it necessary for the good name of our house."

Nonplussed, Ughtred stared. "My Lord!" he repeated.

Brother Godfrey, looking frightened, nodded again. "Sheltered as I have been my judgments of men cannot be too sound, but there have been occasions, very few in all, when I have sensed in him a quality of . . . a quality of . . ." He leaned to whisper in Ughtred's ear, "a quality of barbaric savagery . . . and God forgive me for uttering such sentiments about him."

Conscious that the old fellow must not be distressed any more, Ughtred asked if he would answer two questions, promising never again to broach any of these matters which confused his mind.

"Very well, my son," Brother Godfrey agreed, brightening perceptibly. "What are they?"

"If you were in your youth again, Revered Father, desirous to serve God as you must have been, and knowing as you now know what your life here would be," Ughtred said earnestly, "would you still come to Rievaulx or would you take your religion into the world?"

For more than a minute Brother Godfrey stared across the infirmary garth, at the high line of the many evenly-spaced windows in the monks' dormitory.

"I don't know, my son," he said eventually, sighing deeply.

" For nearly fifty-seven years I have lived here faithful to the Rule and I cannot conceive anything different."

" I can understand that, Revered Father," Ughtred said gently.

" And what is it next, my son? " the old man asked.

" Oh! never mind, Revered Father," Ughtred said.

Brother Godfrey smiled. " Now come, my son," he said encouragingly. " A bargain is a bargain and I must keep mine if you are to keep yours."

Ughtred tried to pass it off. " I think I have talked overmuch already, Revered Father. Instead, let us forget——"

" Your other question, my son," the wiseman interposed, shivering slightly as he pulled his hood closer. " No more excuses, my son."

Ughtred drew a deep breath. " Revered Father," he said abruptly, " is it according to the Lord Christ's teaching that prelates of Holy Church send their fellow men to a hideous death at the stake? "

Mouth tremulous and his expression betokening the direst pain, the old man looked at Ughtred.

" No, my son, it isn't," he said unsteadily. " And . . . and I don't know how . . . how great ecclesiastics can lend themselves to these cruel ends."

Nothing more was said between them. Ughtred assisted his aged friend back to the parlour, and then, thinking with relief that for months he had much to do, returned to the cloister. Even the exasperations of satisfying My Lord about a design for a mitre would be better than brooding about issues which appalled him.

At the corners of the walks the cressets had been lighted, and those of the brethren who wished to read had crowded nearer to them. There was the hum of low-voiced conversation; near the entrance to the Passage the novices, now at liberty, were playing a game of Knockings In and Out; farther along the walk the treasurer, illustrating on his tablet, was endeavouring to explain conic sections to Brothers Aubrey and Henry, without any success; and nearer the church door a group were arguing the merits of the famous controversy between Saint Bernard and Peter the Venerable.

Ughtred paused to glance at the *tabula*, which was fortunate, as he had forgotten he was due for a shave and tonsure before Vespers. As he turned towards the church to find what time he had in hand Brother Anthony bumped into him—the cold weather was anathema to the copyist who, with a record to beat, required supple hands. In consequence, as the temperature fell, Brother Anthony was constantly seen racing between the warming house and his carrel.

Before Brother Godwin required his attendance in the cloister, Ughtred did several things, amongst them a visit to his workshop, to check his stock of paints. In the half-light, when hastening through the rain, he saw the sub-prior riding through the gate-house arch-way, and wondered where he could be going at that hour; at the workshop he had a few words with Brother Ailfy, who was pottering about with the small crucibles he used when engaged with precious metals; and when back in the convent he went up to his cell, where he removed from his neck the relic Lazelle had given him, hiding it away until shaving was over.

There was something of a commotion in the east walk when Ughtred went down: Brother Giles, at the prior's command, was being taken into the chapter house for a whipping. It seemed that, to save himself a journey to apply for a new candle, this always-in-trouble young monk had stuck a small piece of candle on the stub of another. There could hardly have been a more heinous offence in a place where dry straw, hay and rushes were strewn so prodigally on the floors everywhere for warmth—one mishap, and much of the monastery might have been gutted by fire.

The punishment was not immediate, and Ughtred had risen from the chair under the cresset when it began. Shaving was a semi-religious ceremony and it was fortunate that—while Brother Godwin attended to the next monk's chin, stropped the razor afresh, spoke testily to an assistant who was holding a dish of hot water, and transformed the ragged circle on the top of his client's head into a well-defined and shining expanse—those remaining were singing *Verba mea* and other psalms, so that the gruesome sound made by flails whistling down to strike thin flesh was largely drowned.

Brother Giles's face was pallid and drawn when, in drawers only and bare to the waist, he staggered out of the chapter house.

Ughtred, who was waiting for him, helped him to the lavatory, where he gently washed his back.

" I think I'm going to be sick, Brother Ughtred," Brother Giles muttered. " And if I soil anything here . . ."

Ughtred picked up his fellow monk's scapular and cowl and, with the other arm, assisted him up the day-stairs to the dormitory floor. Neither attempted to acknowledge the cross in the middle of the passage, the turning point to reach the necessary where, Ughtred holding his brow, Brother Giles vomited freely.

After a closer inspection of the weals and broken places on his companion's back, Ughtred decided that a soothing application was essential. And so, after easing Brother Giles on to the wooden seat in a narrow stall, he returned to the cloister.

In the warming house the sub-cantor was drying at the fire a piece of parchment on which he had been writing; the sub-cellarer, working on the bench table, supplies of galls, gum and copperas around him, was making ink for the sacrist; and Brother Henry was waterproofing a pair of sandals with a compound of pig's fat supplied by the chamberlain. This was the same grease that Ughtred was searching for, but he found an untouched jar in a cupboard.

On his return to the necessary he spread the grease on Brother Giles's back as tenderly as he could. Later, he put the scapular over the enfeebled man's head, and helped him into his habit. About then, the bell began to sound for Vespers.

" Bells, bells, bells," groaned Brother Giles. " Rules, rules, rules, we live by nothing else."

Brother Aubrey had been for some time in the necessary, and his head was in sight above the side screens.

" Quieten down," Ughtred hissed.

His jaw stubborn, Brother Giles painfully walked down the alleyway as far as the occupied stall.

" Would you tell on me, Brother Aubrey? " he asked.

The poet shook his head. " No, Brother Giles, I should not, though in that I know I am in error."

" Then I'll tell you something," Brother Giles resumed doggedly. " What we're living isn't life, it's death without end. So if you want to land me in more trouble," he carefully resumed his way, " you can slip up the Passage as far as the lodging of our most revered father, the prior, and pass on to him a tit-bit he won't be slow to act on."

"Brother Aubrey isn't that sort," Ughtred said stoutly.

"I shan't say a word," Brother Aubrey said, looking a trifle worried. "Brother Giles has suffered sufficiently as it is."

"And another thing," Brother Giles growled before moving off. "If the prior was half a man he'd support Brother Luke's cries for a return to the simplicity of other days. The revered father is just as much in favour of the old austerities as Brother Luke is, as you can see by his face when the subject crops up, but he keeps quiet for fear of running counter to My Lord."

Ughtred screened his mouth with his hand. "He's too much in pain to know what he is saying, Brother Aubrey," he whispered. "No one should take notice of the words of anyone in his dazed state."

This little suggestion had a most happy effect upon Brother Aubrey. "Of course not, Brother Ughtred," he said, as if he had seen an honest way out of a trying dilemma. "I knew it, Brother Ughtred."

In church not long afterwards, Ughtred found himself paying more attention to Brother Hubert than to the Suffrages of the Saints. It was not a day of festival, and the illumination was not good, such light as there was coming from the High Altar, the hanging lamp over the chained book on the lectern, and the array of candles along the stalls of the novices, who could not be expected to know their Offices completely off by heart, as did the brethren at the other stalls, which were in darkness at both sides.

But he could see that Brother Hubert looked ill, and he wondered if he were still dreaming about things that were forbidden. Still another misfit, he told himself, and sighed as he realised with what frequency he was having the most dangerous thoughts.

After Vespers, Ughtred noticed that the sub-prior had returned from whatever errand he had been on. Almost simultaneously he heard several brethren nearby talking about the monastery's third most important personage. Although far from interested, he gathered that one of the carriers, returning with a load of materials bought by the cellarer at East Witton fair, had seen the reverend father riding out of the Lord of Ryedale's grim castle a few miles away. Gossip was never countenanced, but as small talk to do with the convent was not prohibited Brother Stephen and a few others were enjoying themselves heartily in making guesses about the reason the sub-prior had been there.

There was no supper that evening, but in due course the bell rang for the Collation, which was served in the refectory. It consisted of a small piece of bread and a cupful of the liquid from a fish stew, with a herbal flavouring added, poor fuel which did little to assuage gnawing belly pains.

Then came the reading in the chapter house, presided over by the prior, and afterwards, in search of the only creature comfort left to them, a mass move by the community to the warming house.

The juniors, occupying stalls which were the most remote from the double fireplace, had hardly benefited from the flames leaping and curling from big logs when a scream was heard, so sustained and agonised that momentarily the hearers were petrified. Change followed swiftly: the most senior obedientiaries jumped from their stalls, and the novices, precedences forgotten, darted towards the door, but recoiled when, seen outlined by the fiery cresset near the entrance to the Passage, they perceived the tall figure of the lord abbot.

Again, and still once more, that ear-piercing scream arose, and then silence; a strange silence broken, two or three minutes afterwards, by the tread of feet as the sub-prior, followed by two brothers on the infirmarian's staff, came out of the Passage. Led by My Lord, the quartette began to cross the east walk, and it was only when they were beyond the parlour and the treasury that the youthful witnesses in the forefront of the crowd jammed in the doorway of the warming house felt it safe to breathe.

The tolling of the bell immediately began to summon the community to Compline.

Probably never in the long history of the abbey of Rievaulx had her sons ever given less of themselves to a holy Office; even Brother Theobald, who had grasped that something horrible had taken place in the underground vault, was wondering instead of spending himself in prayer right through to the end, when the *Pater, Ave,* and *Credo* was said.

There would be no further chance for discovery that day. The Great Silence began when the lord abbot made a sign; then a long column started to move, from the quire to the pulpitum doorway, across the south transept towards the clock house and the night-stairs.

The progress of this lengthy line, with candle bearers at every sixth, was starkly arrested when its leading member had left the stone-flagged corridor to enter the dormitory passage-way, and the tail-ender was placing his right foot on the third step of the night-stairs.

Shocked by the sound of bawling and cries of blasphemy, the long line halted. None dare speak, but many expressed their consternation and dismay in the only manner left to them. The cantor clasped his brow, the antiphoner of the week stuffed his fingers in his ears, Brother Ranulf reeled, and Brother Bernard put his palms together in supplication. But Brother Giles, for all his aches and pains, grinned slightly, and Brother Robert, the chronicler, eagerly snatched tablet and style.

An order, spoken by each in turn, was passed along. My Lord had absolved his sons from silence, and all were to return to the crossing.

In the church, lighted only by shafts of moonlight, two candles on the High Altar, and those held by novices, the lord abbot gravely told the community that the monk of Jervaulx had freed himself by drawing on maniacal strength to overpower two of the infirmarian's assistants who had gone to try to restore him to consciousness. He must be recaptured so that their house might not be disgraced.

Dispositions were swiftly made. Parties were told off to search the domestic buildings and those of the inner court, a precise hunting ground being allotted to each. The big bell was also to be tolled, to arouse and warn servants living in the cottages outside the wall; the sacrist's department was to light every lamp and candle throughout.

The operation was called off shortly before nine o'clock, when it was reported that the monk of Jervaulx had been seen on the top of the castellated wall, from which he had jumped outward when a hue-and-cry was raised. That ended matters, to the regret of a few youthful spirits, and within ten minutes, when the abbey of Rievaulx would soon be in darkness again, the community was marching to rest, the majority relieved that My Lord had decreed there should be no midnight rising for Matins and Lauds.

Shortly after that, as was customary, the third prior entered the dormitory on his nightly, but belated, round, to make sure the brethren were abed, their faces hooded. Hearing him, Ughtred, who had been trying to look at the painting of Lazelle in the moonlight, quickly replaced this precious possession in his paint chest, and tumbled into bed.

Disturbed, and ever wondering what those fearsome screams from the underground vault had meant, Ughtred could not sleep. When tossing and turning, time passes deceptively slowly, and he had just come to the conclusion that soon he would be aroused by the mallet for Prime when he thought he heard a cough and a shuffling sound. Raising himself on his elbow, and opening his hood wider, he turned and saw the door of the cell close.

Heart thumping, he swung his legs out of bed, bent to put on his night boots, and tip-toed to the door. Looking into the passage-way, he saw a figure beyond, stooping as if feeling the bars of No Ease. Taking advantage of the shadows and avoiding when possible parts bathed in moonlight, Ughtred edged along in pursuit.

If it were the monk of Jervaulx, he vanished after that, and Ughtred, with the solid walls of the corridor to each side, was able to proceed rapidly. But care was needed on reaching the top of the night-stairs, which he descended slowly, his glance switching from one side to another as he did his utmost to probe the darker patches. He was nearing the bottom of the stairs when the thought struck him—a most inconsequential thought in the circumstances—that the church, illuminated by bright shafts of moonlight piercing the windows at one side and silvery stretches alternating with degrees of gloom elsewhere, would make a wondrous picture. Afterwards, as the gap between the pulpitum and the corner of the south wall of the quire began to open out, that conviction became more profound when, pausing to marvel, he looked at the east windows, soft grey jewel-pieces bordered in sapphire blue and ruby red, and sprinkled with colourful medallions, the shimmering silver cross rising above the sanctuary screen outlined against them.

Ughtred was brought abruptly to the present when the flame of one of the huge High Altar candles, always kept burning, was fleetingly obscured. On tip-toes, he crossed to the south aisle, stealing along it as far as the break between the screen behind the nearer stalls and the screen of the presbytery. From that position, concealed by the tomb of Sir John de Roos and his Lady, he watched intently, his range of vision extending forward to the first marble shafting beyond the socket for the reading desk.

Several minutes had passed, so many that Ughtred was thinking he must seek elsewhere, when he heard footsteps in the quire. A few seconds later the monk of Jervaulx came into view, a man whose emaciated face had elements both of youth and extreme age. Extraordinarily, he was not skulking, but walked as if with a supreme purpose to the steps of the presbytery where, facing the Holy of Holies, he knelt as if he were about to pray.

He did not pray, however, but began to shoot out his tongue at the High Altar—in and out, in and out, a terrible grimace on his face.

Sick with horror, Ughtred crept away, hurrying only on reaching the crossing. From there, still trying not to make a noise, he went past The Holy Three, opened the door into the cloister, and ran along the east walk to the treasury. It was lighted, as always, and Ughtred, as he hammered on the iron door, saw through the peephole that the treasurer and his assistant were asleep.

Admission was not immediately granted, and when Ughtred was at last allowed in, he noticed that the guardians were still gripping most unpleasant-looking knives. Theirs was an immense responsibility, it must be said, and a startling summons in the dark hours might well be more due to a raiding party from the Border than to a call from a peaceful member of their Order.

Both accompanied Ughtred back to the church, where it was at once seen that the monk of Jervaulx had disappeared. When a quick search of the church brought no result, the treasurer went into the sacristy to shout for the sacrist, who slept high above the charge after which he was named. Alarmed in his turn, and perhaps sleepy-headed, the sacrist looked down to the church, from a quatrefoil opening in his chamber; Ughtred and the treasurer's assistant saw his face, a small white blob high in the gloom.

It was while waiting for their superiors that the treasurer's assistant, Brother Left-handed Thomas, discovered that a small, narrow door was slightly ajar. This was the opening which gave access to a tightly-winding staircase, and through it the bell tower and the leads could be reached.

" I'll go up," Ughtred said.

Brother Left-handed Thomas looked dubious. " I think, Brother Ughtred, it might be advisable to wait for the others. He is possessed with ten devils."

" It may save time, Brother Left-handed Thomas," Ughtred said. " If he is on the roof I shall see him at once in this brilliant light, and if he is not, for there is no place where he could hide, I shall come down."

It seemed reasonable for the treasurer's assistant to remain to tell the others where Ughtred had gone, and that is what he did.

When Ughtred reached the roof of the nave he drew a blank, but saw his quarry when only a few paces along the catwalk running at the side of the tower. The monk of Jervaulx was astride the ridge of the quire, about two-thirds of the way towards the east end of the church. He was moving in fits and starts, shuffling along. Ughtred, sweating on noticing the steep pitch of the stone slates to each side, began to follow in the same fashion.

Fortunately there was a breeze in his face, and slight sounds would not travel forward.

He was discovered when about a dozen yards away. The monk of Jervaulx turned his head, glared, and released a stream of profanity.

Desperately trying not to show how shocked he was, Ughtred attempted to start a conversation.

" I am Ughtred of Monkseaton," he said. " A monk of this foundation."

In the light of events, this was not the most happy of introductions and he was rewarded with another torrent, this time obscene.

" A Cistercian like yourself," Ughtred persisted. " Of the junior rank and so of no great consequence."

He shifted a trifle farther forward, but the movement caused much larger repercussions. With a screech of alarm the monk of Jervaulx jumped to his feet and, balanced precariously on the ridge, took two or three paces backwards. Then, his expression more animal than human, he looked down the tiles, as if considering leaping to the lead gutters below.

Perspiration trickling on his brow, Ughtred knuckled moisture from his eyes.

" I am not here to harm you, monk of Jervaulx," he said gently. " I shall do you no hurt."

The crazed fellow threw his head back to laugh, though the sound was nearer to a howl. But there was surprising sanity in his eyes when, mutely, he held his hands out, as if for inspection. As hands they were virtually unrecognisable, swollen to three times normal, and the thumbs, despite a covering of newly-dried blood, could be seen to be lacerated deeply.

Sickly realisation dawning, Ughtred shuddered. " Where did that happen to you, monk of Jervaulx? " he asked unsteadily.

He was not to have a reply or semblance of one. The monk was looking beyond Ughtred who, turning, saw that reinforcements had indeed arrived, their leaders on each side of the roof, almost level with him; those behind them, within touching distance of each other, followed along the gutter. From the tower the sub-prior began to issue instructions—they were simple enough, no closing in until the gable end was reached.

Meantime the monk of Jervaulx retreated as far as he could retreat, still on the roof peak.

" Reverend Father," Ughtred called, funnelling his hands " he is as nervous as a rabbit in a snare. If you would but allow me to try to coax him awhile——"

" There will be no coaxing," the sub-prior said sternly. " Let me hear no more of such womanish talk from you, my son."

Impotent, sensing with absolute certainty the outcome, Ughtred could only wait. And, as he had imagined, so it happened. As soon as the brethren, many of them terrified as much by what they were doing as by the fear of what their punishment would be if they failed to obey, left the comparative security of the wide guttering to claw their way up the tiles, the monk of Jervaulx rose. Swaying, he remained until the nearest pursuer was nearly within arm's length, and then, with a shrill and desolate cry, cast himself into space.

That was the end, in all ways. At a sharp command those on the roof slid down to the lead gutter in their various fashions, some with a head for heights, boldly, and others, troubled by vertigo, fearfully. Then, on both sides, they began to move along the edges towards a manhole near the tower, bald pates prominently showing in the moonlight.

But Ughtred, lost in anguished thought, remained on the ridge above, and was still there when the last prayer for continuing safety died away.

" I know nothing of these cruel implements, and it is wicked to condemn without proof," he told himself strickenly. " But I believe the Reverend Father, the sub-prior, at My Lord's order, rode to the castle for a fell purpose, and I think the monk of Jervaulx was tortured hideously in the vault."

At length, tired and shivery, he descended to the church, where he went to the little chapel of St. Paul, to pray for the soul of the dead monk.

Then, indifferent to the stares of brothers who had returned from carrying a broken body to an outhouse from which the burial would take place in unconsecrated ground, he crossed the east walk of the cloister and wearily climbed the day-stairs.

*     *     *     *

Although the last month of the year was not many days ahead, the weather still continued to be surprisingly mild, so handsomely upholding Brother Godwin's weekly pronouncements. None of this went to the monkish meteorologist-cum-barber's head, but on the day after the beginning of Advent—during which fasting would be as rigorous as Lent—he plunged to the extent of predicting, with a few ambiguities, that conditions would remain unseasonable for some time to come.

Two nights after this forecast it froze sharply, and the sub-cellarer sweated throughout the cold, dark hours. The next day, finding that no damage had been done in the undercroft beneath the refectory, he fervently chanted a song of thanksgiving while winding broad, thick bands of straw round the beer vats; the same afternoon, the lord abbot sent for Ughtred, to whom he conceded with some reluctance the inadvisability of attempting further wall paintings until spring.

That night it snowed, but the white world of the following

morning was speedily changed when the wind veered to the south-west shortly after dinner, and by the next morning the outlook was restored to what it had been.

Just over a week after Brother Godwin had had this most embarrassing forty-eight hours, following the day on which the community had given themselves to processions in honour of the Martyr Daria, Ughtred was working on a high stage in the nave of the church, putting the finishing touches to a painting on wood. The representation was of St. Christopher, picked out with enthusiasm by My Lord from the sketches done in York.

" I care not for the subject, and I dislike the gaudiness of the colours My Lord insisted upon," Ughtred muttered to himself. " The shoulders are the width of an infant's and the head the size of a monster's."

Disgustedly he descended to the floor where, standing back, he looked up, eyeing with distaste the saint, the orb on which the saint's hand rested, and the gnome-like angel perched on the saint's narrow shoulder.

" Primitive," he thought, ill-temperedly. " Would that I had no connection with such a caricature."

Climbing up again, he did a little more, but soon decided that additional treatment was futile. The picture was horrid, and nothing could be done to make it less offensive.

About then he heard voices at the remote end of the quire, and the sharp click of a latch as the aisle-door leading to the abbot's lodging closed. He glanced that way, but saw two persons only, the same persons he might have seen at any time within the past hour: Brother Theobald carving the screen of a transept chapel, and Brother Martin still at the top of a ladder leaned against the clock house where, hood thrown back, he was fiddling with the hand of the clock.

Ughtred was wiping off his brushes when he heard a sound he had never heard in the church east of the crossing, a woman speaking. Immeasurably startled, he twisted round and saw, emerging from the south aisle, the lord abbot and the prioress of Watton. My Lord had his pastoral staff, but the Lady Philippa, who lacked hers, was holding her cousin's arm at the other side. They were chatting gaily, but paused occasionally to examine pictures, sculptures and other treasures added during Lord Hugh's abbacy. Their stroll, over a tiled pavement in Moorish pattern laid by a long dead soldier-turned-monk who had been on a Crusade, took them as far as *le standard* near the west end, where they turned back.

As a few moments before, Ughtred braced himself to bow low when the notabilities passed, which was quite a feat of balancing on a narrow plank twenty feet above the ground.

This time My Lord stopped and, with a hint of laughter in his tone, asked whether the designs for the Lady Philippa were ready for her.

" Of course, my son," he went on, now very gravely, " we shall have to consider about sending them to My Lady's convent at Watton before long. No doubt, as with any artist, my son, you will wish to complete them to your full satisfaction before parting with them."

There was only one reply to that. " Yes, My Lord," Ughtred said.

Subsequently, in the crossing, there was a certain amount of byplay between the illustrious cousins, which Ughtred, from a commanding height allowing him to look over the rood screen, both saw and heard—My Lady stamping her foot and shaking My Lord's arm, and My Lord's: " Not surely now, my sweet coz? " Then Lady Philippa's cross: " You know perfectly well why I am here to-day, and I have known you far too long, my dear Lord Abbot Hugh, not to be aware how you enjoy being cat to a mouse."

The squabble had ended when My Lord, his features in their customary authoritative lines, instructed Ughtred to bring the drawings for My Lady's pastoral staff to his lodging.

" Yes, My Lord," Ughtred said, bowing from the swaying plank.

As Ughtred hastily packed his rags, vials and jars into a deep-sided wooden tray he heard further exchanges, of a nature that made his hands shake with apprehension. His attack of nervousness began when My Lady firmly expressed the opinion that the picture of *Our Lord's Pity* in the north transept was too small for the wall it was on. In reply to that My Lord explained he was contemplating replacing it by a large Madonna, unique in its conception.

The lord abbot did not have the afterthought Ughtred feared, and thanking the Almighty for this escape he left the church and went to the dormitory, where he tucked into his portfolio the designs needed. Before leaving the cell he looked at the coloured miniature of Lazelle, and at the drawing of her, with the angels and the Babe, the lord abbot had seen.

" If My Lord had asked me to bring it," he shivered, " and if the eyes of My Lady had fallen on it . . ."

Desperately hoping that nothing untowards might happen, he went down to the cloister where luckily, before it was too late, he noticed what he was still wearing. Hastening into the church, he pulled off a paint-streaked overshirt which protected his scapular and kept his arms warm, and slipped into his habit. Then he returned to the cloister and, portfolio under his arm, hurried to the abbot's lodging by way of the Passage and the Long Gallery.

The lord abbot's chaplain was crossing the reception apartment as he entered, and told him to await My Lord's pleasure in the ante-room.

" Yes, Reverend Father," Ughtred said.

Still jumpy, he wandered about the adjoining chamber, lingering once at a window to stare at the lofty east end of the abbey —until he remembered the fate of the monk of Jervaulx. Shuddering, he turned away and then gave cursory attention to a sixth-century topography of the world compiled by Cosmas Indicopleustes, an Egyptian monk. The next volume, *Treatieses Pertayninge to Hawkynge, Huntynge and Fysshynge* interested him a little more because it was by the Dame Juliana Berners, prioress of Sopwell, near St. Albans, and he was reflecting that the Dame Philippa was not the only great lady amongst the religious to have sporting instincts, when My Lord's secretary beckoned him into the parlour.

The lord abbot and the prioress were sitting in high-backed, beautifully carved chairs, drawn close to the herring-boned pattern tiled fireplace.

" No, my son," My Lord said, restraining Ughtred from the usual obeisance. " Set your drawings on the table so that My Lady of Watton may scrutinise them."

Lifting a silver lion's head to one side, Ughtred arranged the designs, but had hardly finished before Dame Philippa was at his side. She quickly expressed herself as delighted with what had been done, but was a long time in narrowing her selections down to a final choice, and to that she asked for a trivial amendment; My Lord, after commenting upon the arrangement for a veil banner and the outward turn of the crook, was less forthcoming, but became jovial enough later under his cousin's jesting.

"Could you show me what it would look like, my son, with the alteration I have proposed?" Dame Philippa asked Ughtred.

"With but little effort, My Lady," Ughtred said. "If My Lord would permit me to seat myself at the table it would be a matter of a few minutes only."

The lord abbot nodded. "Proceed, my son."

Ughtred rummaged in his portfolio and soon was scraping and re-smoothing portions of the parchment. Meantime, My Lady excitedly recapitulated the steps she would take about the staff. She named various Italian and Dutch merchants, resident in England, whom she would summon to Watton with their collections, and emphasised the celerity with which the jewels, when picked, would be despatched to Rievaulx. The question of who would supply the necessary gold and silver was also discussed, and arranged, thanks to My Lord's kindly interest.

"It is most loving of you to have this made for me here, my dear cousin," the Lady Philippa said softly. "Alas, my canons have few skills."

The lord abbot smiled. "Save in exercising their tongues, eh?" he said.

Dame Philippa's tone changed astonishingly. "Oh, they still whine and complain whenever an opportunity affords," she said harshly. "But Saint Gilbert in his wisdom ruled that the female chapters of his double foundations should control the purse-strings, and so long as I am prioress I shall retain the whiphand."

"I don't know that I would take kindly to the arrangement if I were in their shoes," Abbot Hugh soliloquised. "It must be galling to have to seek permission to buy or to sell, and to have to render account for each and every transaction. No, I don't think I would care about being in your prior's shoes, even though I might be the nominal head of the convent. A strange arrangement, my dear coz."

"I am in my own shoes, and that suits me very well," the

prioress said, her voice brittle. " Nor will I ever allow even a thin shaving of my power to be whittled away."

A few moments after that Ughtred rose, to turn and bow and respectfully say that the changes required had been completed. Despite what he had gleaned about My Lady's nature it none the less surprised him that she, after what had just gone, was smiling sweetly at My Lord. There was no doubt about it, either, for she was not wearing a veil, and he could see the curve of her reddened lips and the moist expression in her pigment shadowed eyes.

The Dame Philippa was enraptured with the modifications to the pastoral staff and crook, complimenting Ughtred on the skill with which he had interpreted her wishes; and, remaining with him at the table, her heady perfume reaching his nostrils, she was gracious enough to inquire how the work on the staff would be carried out and who would be concerned in it.

Behind them, the lord abbot had rung a hand-bell, and when his secretary arrived gave him instructions to ensure that the canons regular escorting My Lady were given any refreshments they desired.

The secretary bowed. " Yes, My Lord," he said.

" The Lady Philippa will be riding away to Keldholm within the hour, but before then, my son, we have affairs of great moment to deliberate," Abbot Hugh went on gravely. " I shall therefore require you to remain in the reception chamber until I ring for you, and while there it will be your duty to make sure we are not disturbed."

" Yes, My Lord."

" For any cause whatever," the lord abbot wound up sternly. " Time is limited, and I have much ground to cover with the Lady Philippa."

Dismissed, the secretary prostrated himself until his folded arms touched his knees and the peak of his cowl almost scraped the floor. Sent out also, Ughtred hastily replaced in the portfolio the drawing materials he had been using, bowed both to Dame Philippa and the lord abbot, but was recalled before reaching the door.

" The drawing you showed me for the Madonna, my son," My Lord said. " You still have it? "

Ughtred's heart sank, but not for fear of grievous trouble for himself. Since overhearing what the Lady Philippa had said to My Lord under the crossing he knew why she was there that day; and as she had never previously visited Rievaulx in all the years since his own acceptance into the community he thought it extremely unlikely she would do so again. But if Sister Lazelle's superior saw the drawing of his Madonna he knew how infinitesimal the prospects would be of the picture of his dreams ever appearing on the north wall of the transept.

"Yes, My Lord," Ughtred said.

"You must do another, but painted in the colours you would employ, so that I can judge better whether a much larger one would advantageously replace *Our Lord's Pity*, my son," the abbot said, holding his hands apart both horizontally and vertically. "About that size."

"Yes, My Lord," Ughtred murmured, hiding his joy.

"You will begin to work on it at once," Abbot Hugh continued, "putting aside all else."

The prioress of Watton intervened. "You forget my staff, My Lord Abbot of Rievaulx," she said, pursing her lips in what Ughtred thought to be a strange and affected manner. "Your son Ughtred is responsible for the design and I shall hold you responsible for the speedy outcome, dear cousin."

My Lord laughed. "Have no fear, My Lady Prioress of Watton," he said. "We shall honour our obligations, and without delay."

"The picture will not take me long, My Lady," Ughtred said.

She favoured him with a brilliant smile. "I think I can trust you, my son," she said.

Waved to the door, Ughtred bowed again, twice, and then left the parlour, crossed the ante-room, and entered the reception chamber, where My Lord's secretary was sitting. Although a most businesslike individual, the secretary was a very pleasant fellow who enjoyed a chat, but on this occasion had nothing whatsoever to say. His manner was so odd that Ughtred glanced back at him when closing the door—the secretary was staring fixedly towards the ante-room door while gnawing with what seemed senseless savagery at a knuckle, which made his behaviour all the more inexplicable.

But Ughtred was too happy to dwell long on anything except

the picture he would soon be working on, and so, rejoicing, he returned to the church to collect his painting-tray, carrying this outdoors to the block reserved for those of the religious who had proved themselves gifted in the use of their hands.

Adjoining the brew house, the workshops even in severe wintry conditions were never nearly so perishingly cold as the church and the brethren's domestic quarters, with the exception of the warming house; consequently materials could safely be stored in them, and enthusiasts used them all the year round.

When Ughtred went inside he noticed two brothers who would be concerned in making Dame Philippa's staff, but before going into their cubicles for a word with them he checked his own stocks, the greater of two projects always in mind. Estimating weights in his hand, he lifted dryers and other materials from the shelf: *viridus*, *ochre*, *argentum* and *oleum*: scratched his cheek about *plumbum album et rubeum*, and frowned at *aurum*: and, taking out tablet and style, made notes on *azure*, *vernix*, *collis*, *synople* and *vermilio*. That was all he could do for the present.

In the next cubby-hole but one, the monk Ralph of Scarborough, ruddy-complexioned and pot-bellied, was grinding a lens for a pair of spectacles for Brother Stephen, the engrosser, not handling a precious stone as he would have preferred. He was delighted to hear the news about the pastoral staff for the prioress.

" But you won't be involved just yet, though I shall have a talk with Brother Theobald, who might well make a start with the staff as soon as he likes," Ughtred continued. " Your part will begin when the post-messenger brings the jewels from Dame Philippa."

Brother Ralph popped another raisin into his mouth. He saved them whenever they were on the table for dinner, to stave off the pangs of hunger at other times. As only the flimsiest of excuses was needed for him to draw others into an inquiry as to why he, who ate so little, should run so much to fat, Ughtred was at pains not to comment about the sheep-like motion of his heavy jaws.

It also happened that another monk, who would also be similarly concerned, was tidying up his cubicle at the extreme end of the building. Brother Ranulf, notwithstanding his Norman blood, was a gentle creature who had no desire to spend his days in the saddle either fighting, in feats of knightly arms, or at the chase. He was an exceedingly fine craftsman in enamels, and continually experimented in his art.

" If you have the design might I look at it, Brother Ughtred? " he asked eagerly.

Ughtred stayed with him until the bell rang for Vespers, and then they returned to the cloisters by way of the back of the guest house and the kitchen porter's entrance.

Earlier, when at the abbot's lodging, Ughtred had perceived that My Lord initially was far from pleased that Lady Philippa's crook was to be out-turning, and until the tolling for Compline he half expected to be sent for.

By a strange coincidence, however, the issue of the humiliating difference between the crooks of bishops and those of the majority of abbots was ventilated, or should have been ventilated, at the Daily Chapter the following morning, as a result of a letter received from the lord abbot of Byland.

Before this, at the Lady Mass, there had been a most pleasant little ceremony, the opening by Abbot Hugh of the hood of a novice who, three days before, at the end of his novitiate of twelve months, had been voted as acceptable for full membership of the brotherhood of Cistercians. Now, after a retreat equal to the time Our Lord lay in a tomb, he had entered the world again. He received the kiss of peace from all.

If the community had gained young Brother Richard, its number was not augmented. In the chapter house later, the sub-sacrist had sensational news. During the night, sometime between the second retirement after Lauds and the signal to rise for Prime, Brother Giles had run away. He had left his tablet on his bed, with a message scratched on it. The tenor of this note caused a gasp of horror to spring up when it was read out.

" He has broken his sacred vow, so let the impudent rascal's name be struck from the roll of the brethren of our house," My Lord thundered. " Forthwith he is dismissed from the Order, and I charge you never again to permit his name to sully your lips."

Abbot Hugh's overbrimming anger might have been responsible for the harshness that ensued shortly after he had acquainted his sons with the views of the lord abbot of Byland, who had written asking for support for a petition he intended forwarding to Rome.

My Lord of Byland was fiercely convinced that the insignia of all abbots, whether applying to staffs, pastoral rings, or mitres, should be of the same pontifical grandeur as permitted to their Lords Spiritual of Holy Church. He also intimated that he would press this matter at the next meeting of the Council at Pisa.

"My sons," said the lord abbot, "before I express my views I should be glad to hear yours."

"I am entirely in agreement with My Lord of Byland," said the refectorian. "It would wipe out a slur which has borne down far too long on monasticism."

The sacrist rose. "I would not dissent in the slightest, My Lord, with the words of wisdom we have just heard from the reverend father," he said energetically. "It would be to the greater glory of this our house of Rievaulx, towards which we are always striving."

Brother Luke, struggling to his feet, waved his right hand above his head.

"How much farther must we go in our folly?" he asked passionately. "What do these fatuous baubles mean to men of God?"

"Enough," the cantor shouted.

The guest master growled. "He does nothing but stir up strife."

"Are we to copy the Grandmontines?" Brother Luke demanded. "As they saw their superior, are we soon to see our own lord abbot painting his cheeks?"

"We have heard too much from him already," the almoner said angrily.

"Let us with lighted candles strike him with anathema," the kitchener bawled.

"Towards what greater fatuousness do you all propose to reach?" Brother Luke cried. "What has foppishness for My Lord to do with our adoration of Our Saviour and Lord? Would it advance the——"

The sub-prior appealed to Abbot Hugh. "My Lord, deal with him. With respect, My Lord, we cannot forever allow the voice of a crack-pate old man to interfere with the rightful advance of our beloved house and Order."

"Destroy the false gods," Brother Luke persisted. "Destroy

those we sinfully have, and do not add to them, I beg of you, my dear brothers."

Expression forbidding, cheeks dully red, the lord abbot pointed to the wooden trunk. Promptly Brother Luke was hustled to the place for offenders, and there, watched by all, a solitary figure, he stood facing My Lord, waiting on his pleasure.

" My son," the lord abbot began grimly, his dark eyes narrowed, " have I warned you before to guard your tongue? "

Brother Luke bowed.

A few moments later, My Lord again pointed, to the wonderfully carved Greek cross with its manacles and chains; and a gasp went up, for Brother Luke, for all his faults, was aged and soon to become a wiseman living out the remainder of his days in the comfort of the infirmary.

" Secure him," the lord abbot said.

In a silence all the more telling after the hubbub preceding it, the old man was stripped to the waist and fastened to the cross. Meantime, obeying My Lord's finger, the new brother Richard fetched the *flagellum* from its place on the wall, and Brothers Bernard and Eustace slipped out of their habits to ensure their arms a greater freedom when in scapulars only.

Brother Bernard knelt to receive instructions, speaking when My Lord nodded permission.

" How many stripes, My Lord? " he asked.

" Until there is a copious effluence of blood," the lord abbot said coldly.

The punishment began. At its conclusion Brother Luke, head on his breast and arms hanging limply, was dressed and assisted to his seat, where he collapsed and fell in a faint. He was then, at My Lord's order, carried from the chapter house by four of the brethren. A fifth, an obedientiary, was delayed while instructions were given to him.

" You will treat him with all tenderness," the lord abbot said to the infirmarian. " And to the utmost of your skill."

" Yes, My Lord," the infirmarian said.

My Lord shook his head sadly. " He has been grievously naughty, and what he has received is for his own sake, my son," he said, sighing profoundly. " But use all your skill to restore him to

177

health, my son, so that sufficient are left of his declining years for him to make adequate amends for his many mistakes."

The incident adversely affected a few, and certainly Ughtred, who for once had little heart in painting, was relieved when told he would be outdoors the greater part of the next day, as a beater at a hunt My Lord had arranged at short notice. This happened after None, which had not been recited in quire before dinner, the omission being repaired following ablutions at the lavatory when the meal was over.

As the community came out of church, with a welcome change before them of a few hours for work and a little recreation, the abbot's secretary sought out fifteen junior monks, though not the most junior. Last of all to be marked off the tally, Ughtred was not unearthed until the secretary went out to the workshops.

" My Lord sporting with the Lady Philippa to-morrow! " Ughtred exclaimed. " So early? "

The secretary glanced sharply at him. " Why do you speak so strangely about My Lord and the Lady Philippa? " he asked.

" Strangely! " Ughtred echoed, surprised. " That was not my intention, my brother, but I own to being puzzled. My Lady is not lodging here to-night as far as I know, nor would it be proper, but how else can she ride out with My Lord so soon after the light?"

The confusion was straightened out when the secretary explained that My Lord's blood cousin would not be seen at the abbey. Insistent upon trying out the quality of the game on Rievaulx's preserves, Dame Philippa was leaving her bedchamber at Keldholm before darkness ended, and would be meeting My Lord some miles away on the moors.

Ughtred had been in the grip of depression ever since the scene in the chapter house, and it did not lessen with the secretary's departure, when he started to think about that and many other matters which troubled him so sorely. But imperceptibly his mood changed as soon as he started to make preparations for the sample picture My Lord required of the Madonna; and shortly, his mind entirely concentrated on an undertaking in which the nun Lazelle figured so prominently, he was at peace, lost in what he was doing.

*     *     *     *

By special dispensation, the monks whose driving would provide the lord abbot and his guest with satisfactory sport, it was hoped, broke their fast after Prime. It was still dark and candles were needed in the refectory, where the atmosphere was startlingly different from the normal. For one thing there was no reader in the wall pulpit, and for the other: well, it was a fairly youthful company and guarded but cheerful conversation was the rule rather than the exception whenever the sub-refectorian and the under-kitchener were absent.

On leaving the refectory each was given a bag of food for elevenses, and then, keeping in a body, visits were paid to the necessary first and the wardrobe chamber second, where one of the chamberlain's assistants handed out thick mantles.

Although the sky to the east had only just begun to break, there was a great deal of activity in the inner court: at the stables, the kennels, and the hawk mews, all lighted up. The abbot's fine hunting horses were being walked; the slip-gear of falcons and kestrels was being checked; and vain attempts were being made to silence hounds, harriers and mastiffs who, scenting what was in store, kept up a continuous baying and barking.

That was not all—making the pressure on this department all the more acute, it was also the morning on which Brother Roger, the auditor, was leaving with three companions for the abbey of Newminster, and horses had to be readied and in trim for them. In addition, for some unfathomable reason, there was a baggage mule with a fine chair hanging on each flank.

Day was fast getting the upper hand of night when the monkish beaters, who were to separate later into three parties, rode through the middle archway of the gatehouse, across the outer court, and up to the Rievaulx cross, where the woods came down. From there their route followed the rough road which eventually, much farther than they would go, joined the easterly highway, if highway it could be termed, leading to Stockton, the castle of the Bishop of Durham, and the kingdom's most northerly outpost, powerfully fortified Newcastle on the River Tyne.

In these lonely regions where forest alternated with ling, bracken and heathery crags, where there was no one to see excepting animals and birds, hoods were thrown back. The sun was rising, the day promised to be fine, and hearts were gay. With no body of authority near to frown, jokes were passed when fording streams, and always there was constant talk—in the circumstances, as was natural, mainly about Brother Luke's punishment and Brother Giles's wicked foray into the world, about which there was much speculation.

But in due course, when two contingents had left the road, it soon became the duty of Ughtred to take up station, and Brother Henry—who knew about these matters and was familiar with the terrain—began to watch keenly for a sheep-trod along which he would lead the others, to form an extended line up-wind from the hunters.

About then the road curved sharply, to run for a short distance at the edge of a rocky escarpment before bending away. In the little valley below, gained by a high-arched bridge over a river, was a small settlement completely surrounded either by a broad ditch or a lofty wall with a few breaches in it.

" Our long abandoned grange of Riggs, Brother Ughtred," said Brother Henry when he noticed Ughtred's interest. " Have you not seen it before? "

" No, never," Ughtred said.

" Everything's there—church, chapter house, refectory, everything we have at home but on a small scale," Brother Pagan de Bolebec chipped in. " Though why so much for a place used only to allow sickly members of the community a change of air, or to confine others, is beyond my understanding."

Brother Aubrey affected to shiver. " A dismal place . . . weeds, dilapidation. I did start a poem about it once, but it would have read more like a dirge and so I abandoned it."

" As our forefathers abandoned Riggs even when it must have been much less gloomy," Brother Left-handed Thomas remarked. " I applaud their judgment. It was obviously an impossible proposition."

" I would have thought no more so than when much earlier our pioneer fathers first set eyes on Ryedale," Ughtred murmured. " Or those who created Byland, and Jervaulx, and Fountains, all out of a wilderness."

Brother Left-handed Thomas nodded towards the grange. " What was the advantage in struggling on with it? " he asked.

" Our honoured predecessors already had a magnificent home, so why exert themselves unduly in the back of beyond?"

" Our Cistercian founders had a belief that once the furrow is begun it should be added to until the whole field is finished," Ughtred said levelly.

Pagan de Bolebec chuckled. " Perhaps the generations of monks succeeding them became somewhat softer."

" Perhaps so," Ughtred said. " And perhaps attitudes have changed."

Brother Hubert sighed. " I find nothing soft in our life," he said. " My belly is flat with fasting and that is why I am glad to be here to-day."

Head back, Left-handed Thomas watched a game bird which had risen with a harsh cry from a low copse and raced past with a whirr of wings.

" It might be better for you, Brother Hubert, if you fasted even more," he murmured.

" Why so? " Brother Hubert snapped.

With wide-eyed innocence Brother Left-handed Thomas looked at him. " My brother," he said, " surely you know from your reading that the greater the denial the more is sinful man imbued with His holy spirit. Grossness vanishes, and true purity takes its place."

By then, Brother Henry had spotted the winding track. " This way," he cried. " Follow me, my brothers, and when I raise my hand drop back in turn, until we cover almost half a mile of ground."

Most disappointingly, Ughtred and his companions saw little of the sport. In the early stages the prioress of Watton, hawk on her wrist, and the lord abbot were quite near, their scarlet saddlecloths standing out strikingly against the greens and browns of the moor. But My Lord, who was wearing the clothing of a country gentleman, soon turned away from the cascading stream towards which it was Brother Henry's duty to guide his extended team of riders at the opposite side, and the hunt, with its bow carriers, falconers and sea of hounds, quickly vanished from view, lost in a fold of the ground. It was seen once again only, a mere collection of dots several miles distant.

It was a strange experience for Ughtred and his fellows to have nothing to do and, as strange, they occupied themselves as they pleased, gathering together in full three times only: to say a *Gloria* for the Hour of High Mass, to water and fodder the beasts, and to sit down for a dinner of bread, ale, and a couple of grilled, red herrings, cold. That made messy eating and when grace had been said they washed themselves in the stream before sitting again.

Lost in contemplation of the landscape, staring at the ranging forest and at hills large and small, Brother Left-handed Thomas began to murmur in wonder about a God so omnipotent that He had created the earth, with an Eden in which he put the man into whom He had breathed life.

" And then," Left-handed Thomas continued piously, " made He a woman, and brought her to the man, and they were both naked and were not ashamed. But later the Almighty, in his wisdom, caused that man to know the woman . . . and she conceived. Yes, my brothers, they came together, that man and woman, so that . . ."

Brother Henry, who was interested in geology, excused himself, anxious to examine rock strata farther up the stream; Ughtred did likewise, because of curiosity about the grange called Riggs, which he was convinced from its lay-out was originally intended as a monastery, though small, in its own right.

Thanks to a kindly understanding, Ughtred had been given Bess for the day, which he hoped was as much pleasure to her as it was to him. He rode to the highway, and then along as far as a cross marking the side track to the grange. For a short distance this took him across a peat swamp and, as the land fell, a spur of the forest. When the little monastery came into sight he frowned, trying to remember what he had been told about the place.

" Yes, the soil is supposed to be poor, and the climate hard . . . but the same could have been said against our own Rievaulx or Byland," he told himself. " And crops often failed and cattle often died . . . but so did ours in the early years, and yet our pioneer fore-fathers refused to be discouraged." He sighed. " I think that Friar Jerome was right in what he thought but barely vouchsafed—the generations that followed lacked the early fathers' spirit and resolu-tion, until . . . until our purpose is to study and meditate, but never *do*."

By then the downhill path had brought him nearer to a grange which was regarded, as he now recalled, as being so remote that even the royal tax collectors had never visited there to ascertain whether there was value to assess.

On rounding a mixed stand of birch, pine and ash he came to the river; its bed, a natural pavement composed of immense blocks, would have interested Brother Henry, but Ughtred, a seasoned traveller, was more concerned with the condition of the bridge. Much of the parapet had gone, but the arch seemed reasonably sound at the moment, though there were signs that a few periods of alternate frost and thaw might make it much less so.

The gatehouse was ahead, the double doors open, and after riding through Ughtred found himself in a weed-overgrown court-yard. Determined upon a complete circuit of the premises before exploring on foot, he urged Bess to the left, leaving on the other hand a building which had been clumsily opened out to full width at one end to allow for the entry of carts. Cistercian abbeys were always in the same pattern, and he was quite sure the building had once been used as the chapter house; and that, when he turned Bess down the other side, the two-storied building on his right would be the former refectory and dormitory, with the kitchen adjacent and the cloister garth behind.

These speculations ended at the corner. Dumbfounded, Ughtred stared at a hooded cart, with four horses tethered to the wall near it.

" It is similar to those the Lady Philippa uses," he gasped.

The shock of surprise over, Ughtred leapt off Bess, secured her near the other animals, and then approached the cart, clearing his throat loudly when a few paces away. As there was no response he advanced a few short steps, stopping to cough violently. Ultimately he went forward and pushed the screen a little to one side with a shaky finger. No one was within the bulkily upholstered interior.

" I cannot understand it," he muttered. " I have seen nobody, but there must be a servant or more here."

Noticing a narrow doorway, he went through and found himself in a chamber with a sink and the remains of racks for draining plates. It *was* the kitchen, and sure now of his orientation he crossed the long neglected cobble-stones of the western walk and entered the church. It, too, was in a sorry state, but the altar at the east end was intact; the five brass crosses in the marble top were green, but it had a superb frontal and required only water and elbow grease to be made resplendent.

This thought passed through Ughtred's mind in a flash, forgotten when, through a window, he saw that a stone bench in a small apartment off the east walk was covered with a cloth embroidered in gold. On the cloth was a silver basin, a silver jug, eight or nine small ornamental phials and as many tiny, lidded coffers made from silver, glass, and green, blue and white jade.

" What does this mean?" Ughtred muttered. " Why . . ."

He faintly heard his name, heard it again more strongly, heard the sweet voice that sometimes interfered with his duty to God, as the lovely face of its owner frequently interfered. With an incoherent cry he raced out of the church.

They met in the middle of the untidy cloister garth, Ughtred and the nun Lazelle.

" Sister Lazelle," Ughtred exclaimed.

Her eyes were shining. " I was in the church and I saw you riding across," she said breathlessly. " I chased you, but you were always round the next bend."

" Oh, Sister Lazelle, it is good to see you again," Ughtred said. " I . . . I never dreamed I would."

" Nor I, Brother Ughtred. It is almost too wonderful to be true."

" Yes," Ughtred said huskily.

" Yes," said Sister Lazelle, nearly inaudibly.

Ughtred sternly admonished himself. If he were not careful, he would be acting towards her as he believed men act towards a maid. Moreover, his presence could involve her in desperate trouble.

" What are you doing here? " he asked. " If you are by yourself, and I now think that is so, why has your lady left you unattended? True, few will ever come this way, but there is always the exception."

Lazelle smiled at his vehemence. " I was not left by myself, Brother Ughtred," she said. " Sister Maud and Old John were to remain here, but they fidgeted so much that I assured them Jesus would protect me, and so they took two of the horses and rode off."

Until Ughtred had learned about Old John, who drove the cart, and of Sister Maud, he looked bewildered. Both were devotees of the chase, so much so that they were prepared to risk the Dame Philippa's wrath, though when watching the sport they did not intend to approach close enough for accurate identification; each, Ughtred was told also, was by way of being a favourite of the prioress.

"They just want to spy from a distance, and Old John is very crafty, so I don't think they will be caught, Brother Ughtred," Lazelle ended. "And My Lady is aware they love hunting as much as she does, so even if they are caught I don't think it will mean more than a furious scolding."

Anxiously Ughtred glanced at the track leading to Riggs, from that switching to the clear-cut line of a rocky scaur, on the top of which the highway ran for a little way. If he were seen anywhere between the grange and the cross it would be known where he had been.

"Sister Lazelle, for both our sakes I must be away with all speed," he said. "Days are short and if your Lady is to return here before driving to the abbey it cannot be long before she is in sight . . . and from what you tell me of them your Old John and Sister Maud will take pains to be present to receive her."

Lazelle shook her head. "None of them will be here for a long time yet, Brother Ughtred," she said. "My Lady will wish to do all the hunting possible, and then she and your lord are to dine."

"Dine!" Ughtred said.

It soon became apparent that Lazelle knew far more of the arrangements for the day than he did, even those stemming from his own convent. It seemed that My Lord's servants, his cook and valet with them, were to set up a tent in which the lord abbot and his cousin would sit down to their repast. After that, if time allowed, there would be more hunting, until My Lord escorted the Lady Philippa back to the grange, where she would remove the blemishes caused by hearty exercise and offer him a goblet of wine before leave-taking.

"My Lord is coming here," said Ughtred, a trifle dazed by the programme he had heard. "Bringing your lady?"

"The Lord Hugh always guards her most tenderly," Lazelle said. "Even though My Lady is one who knows her own mind, she frequently says she would be lost if she had not your Lord to lean on.

That is why he visits us at Watton several times in the year. To offer his advice, I suppose, on matters we hear briefly about at the Daily Chapter or in Parliament—loans from the Italians and so forth."

Ughtred could only marvel, until he reflected how little he and all the brethren knew of the affairs of My Lord, who lived a life so much apart from them.

"Brother Ughtred, there are two things I should like to do with you," Lazelle said gaily. "That is, if you will cease to fret about me and the whipping I may have if you don't flee."

Ughtred smiled at her. "What are they, Sister Lazelle?"

Her desires were very simple: to look round the quaint little monastery, and to speak again to Bess, who had carried her so gently on a ride she would never forget.

Ughtred laughed. "If I tell her that she will hold herself even more proudly," he said. "So surely she must be first."

They crossed the garth, and passed through the kitchen.

"Bess," Lazelle cried, running ahead.

All unconscious that behind him, silhouetted on the skyline, a horseman had halted to stare, Ughtred watched the nun Lazelle as she fondled and talked softly to his mare. In the solitude of Riggs, Lazelle had discarded her veil before he came, and he could see the lovely lines of her face, the beauty of her eyes, and the sweetness of her lips. A lump came into his throat.

Lazelle nuzzled Bess again before turning away. "There, Brother Ughtred, she tells me—what is the matter, Brother Ughtred? Why . . . why are there tears in your eyes?"

"I am mourning my inadequacy, Sister Lazelle," Ughtred said huskily and, without realising to what he might be exposing himself, told her about the Madonna painting for My Lord, and his hopes that the lord abbot might in due course be so moved as to allow him to do a larger picture for the glorification of the north transept. "If I feel sad, Sister Lazelle," he ended, "it is because I know I shall fall far short of my ideal."

Her expression changed gradually. "You must not think of using my face, Brother Ughtred," she said, impulsively clutching his arm in both hands, "because if you do the day may come when you are condemned for it, and would suffer hideously. It is not

186

enough to tell me that My Lady has only been once to your convent, because she was impatient about the designs, and that she has never been before and won't ever again. She might, Brother Ughtred, and if she did you would be undone."

"I would have sound excuse for my misdoing, if it is misdoing to strive with all my power to pay homage to the Holy Mother," Ughtred said gently. "Surely it would not be so serious, Sister Lazelle."

"Brother Ughtred," Lazelle said desperately, "would your Lord take it lightly if he discovered later that the face of the Madonna he esteemed was the face of a nun of Watton?"

"I don't know, I don't know," Ughtred said passionately. "But I do know that a vision rarely comes to an artist, but if it does he must try to pin it down with his brushes or else it is better for him to rot. I have a vision, Sister Lazelle, and though I cannot hope to attain the glory I picture in my mind, yet I must try should the Almighty decide I am to have the chance."

Her mouth quivered and she did not speak for a while. "I . . . I think I understand, Brother Ughtred, so I will say no more," she said at last.

She was very quiet when they looked round the kitchen, and remained so as they walked the length of the refectory. In the cloister garth, however, hiding her fears, she seemed much more her own self as she pointed to an outdoor staircase which led to the chamber above the refectory. In its day the ascent had been roofed and covered in with wood, but now all that had vanished.

"Let us climb up there next, Brother Ughtred," she said.

"It will be to the dormitory, Sister Lazelle," Ughtred said hesitantly.

She laughed. "Brother Ughtred, since being a tiny babe I have lived in nunneries, and so have never had an opportunity of looking into a monkish bedchamber. It is full time I repaired the gap in my education, and that is what I intend to do."

Ughtred bowed. "Very good, my impetuous lady," he said, throwing his arm towards the steps.

If Lazelle was filled with anxiety about Ughtred's intention to portray her as a Madonna, the situation was reversed within the next few minutes, during which she nearly scared him out of his life. It all began so simply, when they talked about Ughtred's design for the prioress's staff, the details of which My Lady, as well as she was able, had confided to both Sister Maud and herself, though not to the two canons regular who were at the hunt.

"It will be very costly, Brother Ughtred, won't it?" she commented. "Oh, I am certain it will . . . just as I am certain there was too much senseless extravagance when the Lord Bishop and his mighty retinue came a-visiting to Watton a few days before we sent up our prayers for Andrew the Apostle, who was crucified for his beliefs. Never could there have been a banquet of more splendour than My Lady gave, and all the time I thought endlessly how much more Christian it would have been if the money had been devoted to the poor."

"Sister Lazelle!" Ughtred said uneasily, "you revealed none of these thoughts to anyone?"

Her lips curled. "No, Brother Ughtred, but I would have had I not lacked courage. And I would also have declared boldly that the hands of our lords spiritual are stained with blood when they send men to the stake."

"Sister Lazelle!" Ughtred tried to check her.

It was in vain. "I have thought constantly of your Franciscan friar, and of the soul-searching he has caused you," she continued almost without pause. "And I have thought of much you did not tell me, Brother Ughtred. I have thought of the learned doctor of divinity, John Wycliffe, whom so many of our Holy Church would be glad to drag out of his grave in order that they might wreak vengeance on his remains—I have thought he did well to translate the New Testament into English so that those who are without the Latin, but can read, may be able to absorb the holy words, and I do not believe that the noble doctor did ill, as our chaplain and the canons regular fiercely assert; for I do not think, as they do, that those holy words will be misunderstood by those they term as ignorant, and used contrary to the interests of Holy Church." She had spent herself, and, the strength gone from her voice, ended very quietly and sadly: "Perhaps I am wrong in that, Brother Ughtred, for no one imbued with the Scriptures could do other than speak censoriously about the simony, corruption and evil-living at the Holy Father's court."

Aghast, speechless for the moment, Ughtred stared at her. "How . . . how did you learn of these things, some of which are unknown to me, Sister Lazelle? "

Tired now, she told him about two ladies who now lived in her convent: Dame Eleanor, whose husband and two sons had been slain by the Scottish rebels, and Dame Jean de Warke, the widow of a rebel gentleman from the Border who had been killed on a foray.

"They were on opposite sides, and sometimes I think they hate each other," Lazelle said sorrowfully. "But they have been out in the world, and are at one in condemning the merciless persecution of the Lollards. Sometimes they talk quietly on these matters, and I listen if I can."

Ughtred was so disturbed that he stretched out and, holding her by the shoulders, drew her nearer.

"Sister Lazelle," he said urgently, "you must swear to me you will *never* express your doubts to anyone as you have done to me just now. I beg of you, Sister Lazelle."

She smiled faintly at him. "I don't think I ever shall, Brother Ughtred."

"That is not enough, Sister Lazelle," Ughtred said firmly. "There is much cruelty about us, perhaps even in our own Orders, and you would suffer the venom of your superiors if ever you were found out. They would not spare you—because all prelates and dignitaries are of the same mind about stamping out what they consider are evils."

Their faces were very close as she looked into his eyes. "Brother Ughtred, would you promise me to forget the vision of your Madonna if I pleaded with you? "

"That is very different," Ughtred insisted. "There is no comparison."

She shook her head as she placed her hand on her breast. "No, Brother Ughtred, not so very different," she said. "Because I have something here, too, and it would be as difficult for me to dismiss it as it would be for you."

"Oh, Sister Lazelle," Ughtred groaned.

"Don't worry, Brother Ughtred," Lazelle said softly. "All will be well. . . ." Her eyes began to shine. "I know it, Brother

Ughtred, because my trust is in Him and He will not fail me."

" Yes, but . . ." Ughtred muttered.

She laughed, accused him of lacking faith, and told him, as she had told him before, that the happening he feared would never arise because she would never have the courage to speak her mind. Then, smiling, she reminded him that he would not be with her much longer, but that while he was it would be more pleasant if they ceased wrangling.

" Besides, I haven't seen everything yet," she said. " Come, Brother Ughtred, let us go down to the garth again."

The prison quarters were hardly the most enlivening choice, but the buildings of the western range were nearest and so they went inside. There were several single cells and one double one, and while they looked at the cloister from the barred windows Ughtred explained their purpose in former days.

" They would have much more to see than we have in our cells," Sister Lazelle remarked. " Ours have a very dreary out-look."

" Nuns are confined in cells? " Ughtred exclaimed.

Lazelle laughed. " Before we left My Lady confined Sister Isabella to one for three months, and denied her communion for the same period."

Surprised, Ughtred stared at her. " You take it very lightly, Sister Lazelle. She had done something deserving of that? "

" Not really," Lazelle told him, apparently still amused. " But Sister Isabella is always asking in chapter if she may mortify herself, and My Lady got tired of it. But I am quite sure Sister Isabella will be released when we reach home again."

" I suppose your Sister Isabella is a favourite of your Lady's, as you must be when she brings you abroad so frequently? "

Lazelle sighed a little. " I suppose I am, Brother Ughtred, but I have seen many in My Lady's favour out again as quickly as they had become favoured. It can be likened to certain of the players My Lady sometimes has in for our entertainment—they walk on stretched ropes."

" You must take all care, Sister Lazelle," Ughtred said, fright-ened again.

" Oh, Brother Ughtred," Lazelle said in mock dismay.

Time was passing all too swiftly, as Ughtred saw from the position of the low-down winter sun.

" I must leave you now, Sister Lazelle," he said. " And when I go you should remain within the small chamber where a cloth and basin are arranged for your Lady, until you are certain I am beyond the highway, when no one would connect me with you."

" What if you were seen half-way and someone asked whether you had spoken to me? " Lazelle said.

" I would lie, Sister Lazelle," Ughtred replied briefly.

For a few seconds, Lazelle looked at him. " I ... I think you are changing, Brother Ughtred," she said.

Ughtred nodded, a trifle grimly. " Occasionally I wonder about that myself, Sister Lazelle."

" Perhaps we may still meet again," Lazelle said wistfully. " But if we never do, Brother Ughtred, I have my thoughts and a chip from the stone the Blessed John the Baptist once sat on."

" As I have your holy relic, Sister Lazelle," Ughtred said. " A piece of manna received by the Israelites from Heaven hangs always round my neck save when it is shaving and other days."

" As with me, Brother Ughtred. Except when it is bath night."

Ughtred found himself flushing, too. " I must say farewell, Sister Lazelle," he said hurriedly. " God be with you, always."

Lazelle rested her hand on his arm. " Brother Ughtred, it is still far from the end of the day ... but if we could go into the little church and together say the last prayer of Compline ... as we did in the cave above the river ... it would make me very happy."

" As it would me," Ughtred said huskily. " Yes, it is well thought, Sister Lazelle."

In the church, using the skirt of his mantle, he wiped the dust and dirt from the floor before they knelt in front of the altar. Then, in their differing voices, the one so sweet, they began:

" O Lord God, save us waking, guard us sleeping, that awake we may watch with Christ, and asleep we may rest in peace—grant us a quiet night and a perfect end."

Before rising, Ughtred looked at her, and as he looked at her the sinful and yet wondrous thought occurred to him that they were as a man and a maid being joined in the bonds of holy matrimony. Whether her thoughts were the same he could not know, but her lips parted and she stared at him with an expression he had never seen before. Somehow, simultaneously, their hands met and clasped and tightened.

" Oh, Brother Ughtred," Lazelle whispered

" Sister Lazelle," Ughtred said strickenly.

Limbs as water, he left her there. Stumbling across the cloister and out by the kitchen entrance, he mounted Bess and sped her over the weedy courtyard to the gatehouse. Without once glancing back he took the bridge, never noticing that from that side it seemed more rickety than from the other, and from there raced almost as far as the cross at the wayside, where the land began to rise steeply. So far he had met nothing, and his good fortune continued to the second cross near the highway, from which, his heart still throbbing, he headed towards the slight hollow in the moor where he had left his companions.

At first, he saw Left-handed Thomas only, laid out snoring, but then Brother Pagan de Bolebec, who had been sitting with his back against an outcrop of rock, came to him.

" Where is everybody, my brother? " Ughtred asked.

Pagan de Bolebec, who seemed to have something on his mind, pointed first to Brother Henry, who, making his way down the stream, was carrying in a handkerchief pieces of spar and stone to add to his collection, and then to Brother Aubrey, who was writing a heroic ballad in a dell.

" Where is Brother Hubert? " Ughtred asked.

Brother Pagan passed his tongue over his lips and, without replying, drew Ughtred to a small rise from which there was a view of a place where the foaming beck leapt over a shelf to make a waterfall ten or so feet in height. Nearby, naked, was Brother Hubert. As they watched he stepped under the chilling downpour.

Ughtred crossed himself. " He will catch his death. Why is he doing it? "

" To purify himself," Pagan de Bolebec said heavily. " It is because of his sinful dreams, but . . . but . . ."

" But what? " Ughtred pressed.

Persistence succeeded, and once Brother de Bolebec started he was not sparing.

" It is all because of Brother Left-handed Thomas," he said.

" Whenever he is with Brother Hubert it is always the same, because he knows so surely the effect of tales of whoremongers and fallen women upon him. It is evil of me to say it, but there are times in the cloister when I believe Brother Left-handed Thomas studies the Book for no other purpose."

Ughtred nodded. " Go down to Brother Hubert, Brother Pagan. Do your utmost to dry him, and slap and rub him to get him warmer. Then help him to dress, for he will be numb, and then bring him up here."

When Brother Pagan had left on this mission, Ughtred, filled with cold, purposeful rage, went back to where Brother Left-handed Thomas was sleeping. He roused him roughly, telling him to get to his feet.

" What is the matter with you, Brother Ughtred? " Brother Left-handed Thomas cried angrily. " You are behaving as if soon the Devil will have you as he had the monk of Jervaulx."

Ughtred grabbed him by the mantle and shook him as a terrier shakes a rat.

" Remember this, Brother Left-handed Thomas with a pervert mind," he said. " Never again disturb Brother Hubert with your tales of harlots, or it will be the worse for you."

" For a Cistercian brother to lay hands on another is an offence earning the most severe penalty, Brother Ughtred," Left-handed Thomas said shrilly.

When releasing him, Ughtred thrust him away, and then advanced on him, his manner so menacing that the other retreated.

" Unless the Lord strikes me down beforehand I am more than inclined to lay my hand on you less lightly than I have already," Ughtred said. " It would be a pleasure, too, Brother Left-handed Thomas, even though an unchristian one. Nothing would gratify me more than to pound your smug, self-righteous face."

" I shall accuse you in chapter for this in the morning," Brother Left-handed Thomas bleated.

" Do so," Ughtred snorted. " Then I shall petition My Lord to speak and I shall tell him why I have acted as I have. I might be scourged, I know, but, as certainly as the Almighty is looking down on us now, I am certain you would be punished, perhaps more severely."

Brother Left-handed Thomas sneered. " As a favourite of My Lord's you think you would escape lightly. But, my brother, favourites are sometimes kicked out of their seats."

Ughtred clenched his hand, and Left-handed Thomas, seeing the tight fist, backed away.

" That is what I think, too," Ughtred said. " It . . . it may surprise you, Brother Left-handed Thomas, but that dire thought will constantly be in my mind from this day."

" It happens," Brother Left-handed said. " But even if you are favoured now, My Lord would not overlook your violence against me."

" What happens to my hide is immaterial, so long as yours is whipped into a pulp," Ughtred remarked grimly.

Unhappily Left-handed Thomas digested that. " I see no advantage in both of us being thrashed, Brother Ughtred. I had, of course, no notion that my references to Holy Writ had the effect you claim on Brother Hubert, but if it will pacify you I will promise not to mention these matters to him again."

" Take out your crucifix," Ughtred snapped. " And when you have, swear on it to stand fast to what you have just said."

Brother Left-handed Thomas fumbled beneath his mantle, and in due course meekly did as he had been bade.

Ughtred nodded. " You will do well to keep to your oath, Brother Left-handed Thomas," he said. " For if you ever falter and I hear you, I will smash my hand against your slack mouth, be it in the cloister or elsewhere, as the Lord Jesus is my Saviour."

Plainly scared, Brother Left-handed Thomas had not a whisper of defiance left, and was not long in edging off.

Away in the distance, along a track across the moor which curved constantly and often dipped from sight, the lord abbot Hugh and his cousin the Dame Philippa led a small cavalcade towards the abandoned little monastery of Riggs.

Ughtred of Monkseaton clapped his hands briskly, and at the signal his companions started towards him from their various places, Brother Aubrey alone having to be rooted out. Then they rode together to Rievaulx, reaching home as sleds arrived with the hunters' substantial bag of the day: pheasant, moor-fowl, woodcock, hares and rabbits. There were also two fine does, which it was known were to be salted and sent to Watton.

At the stables Ughtred said good-bye to Bess, thanked the groom-in-charge for allowing her to him, and then, his mind filled with precious thoughts, walked across the inner court towards the guest house and the kitchen porter's entrance.

Two novices, one with a taper and the other carrying the eternal lamp, were lighting up the cressets in the cloister as Ughtred began to wash himself in the shadowed interior of one of the arcaded lavatories in the east walk. Shortly the Jesus bell would begin to ring for Vespers.

# 5

One of the most important days in the calendar of the abbey of Rievaulx was the anniversary of Ailred, the third abbot, an event always celebrated with pomp and pageantry. The present year was no exception and, as on a dozen or more festival days annually, the church's prevalent smell of mustiness was masked by an overpowering odour of incense.

It was usual, before the Collation, for the lord abbot to sit in the parlour awaiting those of the brethren who might have requests to make, and on the next evening Ughtred petitioned My Lord to be allowed to show him the sample picture for the Madonna, now completed. Permission was granted, and on the day following, soon after grace had been said for a sparse dinner, Ughtred made his way in a howling wind to the abbot's lodging.

My Lord was so pleased with the specimen picture that he took immediate steps to ensure there should be no delay in starting on a larger Madonna, and his chaplain and secretary were despatched to summon various high officials and senior servants.

As the most severe part of winter lay just ahead, the knottiest point to decide was where the work should be done. My Lord was insistent that the painting should not be seen by the community until placed in position, and that ruled out the warming house; and although there were spare rooms in the lord abbot's lodging, where a fire could be lighted, none of these had large windows with a northern aspect.

Ultimately the *custos fabricae* had a brain wave; in consequence, the head carpenter, whose responsibility was now to provide seasoned panels for Ughtred, was sent to bring the kitchen porter who, in addition to guarding the entrance to the cloister, had charge of the *locutorium*, a large chamber adjoining his lobby where the brethren could talk to visiting relatives and friends. The significant factor was that the kitchen fireplace, with a hearth large enough to hold three huge cauldrons, for boiling beans, vegetables and heating water, and two spits sufficient for the biggest joints, was at the other side of one of the walls of the *locutorium*.

On arrival, the porter confirmed that the temperature in the *locutorium* was always reasonable, even when it was icy outdoors. Before being dismissed he was instructed on two counts: never to give the key of the *locutorium* to anyone except Brother Ughtred until the order was cancelled; and to make certain personally that the chief fuel carrier, who tended to be forgetful, always replenished the kitchen fire handsomely every night. Two novices were also to heap-up the fire later, between Matins and Lauds, so that the flow of heat through the thick wall never faltered.

When all the arrangements had been completed those concerned with them bowed to My Lord before leaving, including the sacrist who was to see that the *locutorium* was scrubbed out and thoroughly cleansed, and the *revestiarius*, whose duty would be to furnish a hanging ample enough to protect the painting from dust.

Ughtred was detained a little longer, sufficiently for My Lord to inform him that, while engaged on his great task, he would receive a special dish for breakfast, over and above the slender fare usually provided, four ounces of bread and a third of a pint of wine. As even then it would not be full light he would join his brothers at the Lady Mass, but at the conclusion of the Office would not be required to remain in his stall " thinking " until the bell tolled for the Daily Chapter.

" After that, my son," the lord abbot continued, " you will be excused all set devotions until the sinking sun stays your hand."

" Yes, My Lord," Ughtred murmured.

Within a minute or so he was hastening excitedly towards the infirmary, to tell Brother Godfrey the wonderful news.

He began work on the Madonna on the first day of the Ember Season and, self-critical though he was, grudgingly conceded by the fifth afternoon, when a hailstorm darkened the sky, that his progress could have been worse.

Ughtred had changed into his habit, and was locking up the *locutorium* when his shoulder was tentatively tapped. Brother

Richard, the convent's most junior monk, had just arrived in the lobby, and had either not been sufficiently tutored by the novice-master in the nice grading of bows or was determined to be on the safe side. There was, of course, a considerable gulf between the advancement of himself and Ughtred, but he bent unnecessarily low, his folded arms quite definitely touching his knees, and that was the ultimate.

"The reverend father, the treasurer, tenders his compliments to you, Brother Ughtred," he said, on straightening. "When it is agreeable, he would take it kindly if you would present yourself to him."

This hardly sounded like the treasurer, Ughtred thought, but concluded that Brother Richard was adding a few flowery touches of his own.

"It is agreeable immediately, Brother Richard," he said.

"The reverend father, the treasurer, would not wish to disturb you when engaged on a work to My Lord's desire," the young man told Ughtred earnestly. "A work of splendour to the glory of the Lord, to the glory of His Son Jesus, to the glory of the Blessed Virgin Mary."

"We must wait upon that, Brother Richard," Ughtred suggested as they entered the cloister. "It is wisdom never to count the chickens until they are hatched."

"And to the glory of this noble house, to the glory—Yes, of course, Brother Ughtred," Brother Richard said belatedly.

Ughtred decided it would be easier if he shifted the youngster off his lofty plane, but the effort proved futile. The only difference was that Brother Richard expressed noble and holy sentiments on another subject, the sad accident sustained by Brother Roger when a few miles short of his destination in Northumberland. The auditor had been thrown from his horse and, unconscious throughout, had been carried on a litter to the abbey of Newminster. It was believed his skull was fractured.

"There was a fresh report of him by messenger this morning, Brother Ughtred," Brother Richard said. "Thanks to the Lord God, who in His infinite and all-embracing mercy has so ordained it, the reverend father is showing signs, faint as yet albeit, that his senselessness may be passing."

"That is very good news, Brother Richard," said Ughtred.

Brother Richard shook his head. "He is still gravely ill, and paralysed, Brother Ughtred, and we must spend ourselves in praying to the Almighty for his recovery. If our pleas to the Lord of Lord, King of Kings, Ruler over All, are strong enough, surely we may save our beloved brother—if that is His will."

They had come to the iron door in the east walk. "We must hope so, Brother Richard," Ughtred said when preparing to turn in. "And not so low, my brother."

Brother Richard, who had deeply prostrated himself, rose more rapidly than his training should have taught him to do.

"Not so low, Brother Ughtred?" he said.

Ughtred smiled. "Neither for me nor for many others amongst the brethren," he said. "Excellent for My Lord and the most revered father the prior, but after them I'd taper off."

Brother Richard became nearer the boy he almost was. "I am overdoing it, Brother Richard?" he said, crestfallen.

"Overdoing it," Ughtred confirmed. "So let us try together, my brother. Your back to be less than horizontal, mine somewhat higher."

Solemnly each bowed to the other, neither knowing that the fourth prior, who missed nothing, was quietly advancing up the north walk.

"Most fitting, my brother," Ughtred commented. "You put in neither too much nor too little."

The young monk bowed again. "Thank you *very* much, Brother Ughtred," he said gratefully.

Ughtred was also commended by the fourth prior. "I applaud you, my son," he said warmly. "It should not be that the higher officers alone teach the willing but as yet not wholly instructed."

Again Ughtred went down, in a response that would have pleased My Lord himself. "You are too generous, Reverend Father," he said.

"Far from it, my son," the fourth prior said cordially, bowing in acknowledgment. "Not at all, my son Ughtred."

Reflecting that the favour of the lord abbot circled wide, Ughtred went about his business.

On entering the treasury, his glance was drawn at once to a

spread of precious stones—rubies, emeralds, and diamonds—laid out on a piece of dark blue stuff, and he quickly learnt that a receipt for these had been given to the prioress of Watton's post-messenger shortly after Parliament had dispersed. Moreover, the treasurer had instructions to transmit from My Lord, who despite the weather had ridden off to spend the night with the lord abbot of Byland. Work was to begin at once on the Lady Philippa's staff, and those concerned were to be informed.

"Yes, Reverend Father," said Ughtred. "Brother Theobald has already started on his part, and the others are only too eager about theirs."

Used to valuables of immense worth, the treasurer casually rolled up the piece of blue stuff, with its contents, and dropped it in an iron-bound coffer.

"You will know, my son," he said, "that My Lord has authorised a fire for the workshop block?"

"Yes, Reverend Father," Ughtred said.

"Very well, my son," the treasurer said. "Arrange a gathering of those involved, and let the work proceed."

Ughtred bowed and left the treasury. As he paused outside, looking round, he saw that Brother Aymer was at work in his carrel in the north walk, and so he went round to him. The rubricator, in the middle of writing the heading of a chapter in red, was blowing into his cupped hands.

Brother Aymer, a most dexterous engraver also, was delighted about the task awaiting him and gladly promised to be present at a meeting proposed by Ughtred for the following afternoon.

Ughtred next went outdoors to the workshop, where he found Brother Theobald fitting together the three sections of the staff, each the length of rather more than twice a man's handspan. As yet the work was in the rough, and next would come the refinements: making sure that, howsoever quickly the staff was put together at the end of a journey the joinings would not show, and the carving of the rings and boss, with provision for the insertion of small gems.

Brother Theobald, when told of what was intended, also looked forward to a round table conference with colleagues with whom he would share the responsibility of creating an object of great beauty to the glory of the prioress of Watton and her convent. This arranged, Ughtred chatted a little longer while luxuriating in front of the fire, and then went into the stinging hail, where he fell in with the larderer who, keys swinging from girdle, was returning from inspecting the hay house.

Those present at next day's meeting were Brother Ailfy, for the silver and goldsmith's part, and Brother Ranulf, enameller; Ughtred himself, of course, and Brothers Theobald and Aymer. Brother Ralph, skilled with precious stones, completed the roll, and it was he who remarked, when either Brother Ranulf's or Brother Ailfy's stomach rumbled—there was a slight argument on this—that My Lord would have given them an invaluable tool if, in addition to the workshop fire, he had ordained that each of them should be strengthened by a more privileged diet.

It was a bitterly cold day and when the party met in the east walk their first undertaking was to pile more straw on the long, stone bench near the bay in which clothes to be repaired were left for the chamberlain's assistants to collect. The severity of the conditions, however, was forgotten as soon as Ughtred's design started to pass from hand to hand. The whole conception was examined from tip of the crook to ferrule, and as heads came closer together differences of opinion about procedure were ventilated, some so heated that if there had not been a great deal of traffic one of the guardians would certainly have sternly intervened. But brethren elsewhere, particularly those engaged in sedentary work either in the carrels or the chambers of the chequer, were constantly seeking the necessary or a short spell near a fire, and their movements in and out of the warming place, and up and down the day-stairs to the dormitory, set up a counter noise.

Craftsmen are tetchy individuals, and as soon as Ughtred was sure his design was fully understood, he excused himself.

When glancing into the cloister garth, where Brothers Peter and Lionel, faces blue with chill, were standing at opposite sides of the open grave, as they had been doing for so many afternoons, Ughtred noticed Brother Godwin scrutinising his meteorological indicators near the *statio* in the west walk. He walked round to inquire about weather prospects, passing through the north walk, where Brother Robert, the chronicler, holding a pricker in a stiff and calloused hand, was making dots for lines across a sheet of parchment; and Brother Stephen, another stalwart, was busy in the next carrel with the third volume of a bible he was engrossing. Both were wearing warm headgear and fur-lined amices and, bundled up, looked enormous.

Brother Godwin had no reservations about next day's weather.

" Colder still, with snow the day after, Brother Ughtred," he said. " In fact, Brother Ughtred, I am staking my reputation that we are due for heavy falls until at least the Vigil of Christmas Eve, whatever George of Pontefract may assert to the contrary."

Ughtred knew of the rivalry between Brother Godwin and the monk of Kirkstall. Their forecasts were taken regularly by post-messengers round the northern abbeys, priories and nunneries.

" What does he say, Brother Godwin?" he asked.

With four major victories in a row, Brother Godwin was inclined to forget a disastrous reverse at the hands of the monk George two years before, when he had scoffed at the latter's warning, posted out as early as the Feast of the Nativity of Our Lady, to the effect that shepherds should take great care of their ewes with the approach of the next lambing season, then many months ahead.

" Green days of festival," Brother Godwin said scornfully. " George of Pontefract has never bottomed the learned Alhazen on twilight or the renowned Vitellio on the rainbow, and the crudeness of his devices, Brother Ughtred, would have raised eyebrows when Julius Agricola governed this land."

Ughtred nodded towards the two young monks in the garth. " If you are correct, Brother Godwin, the worst of their travails is still before them."

" I refuse to go beyond the Vigil, Brother Ughtred," Brother Godwin said, wagging a finger. " But by then, mark you, it will be up to their middles. A green festival season, forsooth! "

This conversation did not make a strong impression on Ughtred, but he did recall it on the afternoon of the Vigil of Christmas Eve when, owing to the lengthy devotions awaiting the community, he finished earlier than usual in the *locutorium*. Before sheeting up the picture of the Madonna he took a stool to the opposite wall and, standing on it to obtain a more level perspective, stared hard at the painted face of the nun Lazelle. Nothing else mattered, whether the angels or the Babe—all must be subordinate, and nothing allowed to detract from it.

" I . . . I believe it is coming," he muttered. " Perhaps . . . perhaps with your divine help, O my Maker, I may be permitted to draw near to the vision I have."

Partially thrilled with this hope, partially fearful that in the later stage his performance might fail, Ughtred locked up the *locutorium*, left the key with the porter, and went into the inner court by the lobby door. It was a very white world outside; a broad carpet of snow bulged over gutters high and low, branches were weighed down and the paths cut between the various outhouses were trenches more than four feet deep. In the all-pervading lightness the sole contrasts were provided by the trunks of trees and the dark line of the river. It was still snowing.

In the workshop the Lady Philippa's staff was slowly but surely advancing towards its destined form. Brother Theobald was meticulously cutting out a lozenge-shaped recess into which a stone, at present being trimmed and polished by Brother Ralph, would fit; Brother Aymer, singing a Psalm of David, was pouring hot wax on to a sheet of silver; and Brother Ailfy was intensely preoccupied with the snake-like curves of the crook.

As to Brother Ranulf—he was heaping coals on a fire, already large, whose heat permeated every one of the little cubicles off the wide passage-way running along one side.

As usual, Ughtred was invited to see how each was getting on. He finished up with Brother Ranulf, who desired his opinion on a number of crosses and medallions. They were made of gold, with claw edges as a precautionary measure to hold the enamel for all time once it had been fused on the surface of the metal contained by them.

" You have done well, done superbly, Brother Ranulf," Ughtred assured him. " And I will confess that as I drew the designs I wondered whether what I was asking would be impossible to execute."

Brother Ranulf's beam of pure delight vanished as he started to enumerate the many problems still facing him.

" I pray God that I may not shame myself before you and my brothers, Brother Ughtred," he ended hollowly.

If Ughtred had let the least hint slip that this might be the case—

which never entered his head—Brother Ranulf would have flown into a mighty tantrum, not become more dejected. It was the same with the others; each would mourn his own incapacity, but woe betide anyone who might challenge his artistry and ability.

" And how fares it with the painting we know so little about, Brother Ughtred? " Brother Theobald inquired.

" I am trying hard, Brother Theobald," Ughtred said. " Sometimes my heart leaps with joy because I think I am succeeding, and sometimes an icy band of despair constricts me."

Five heads were nodded solemnly. " It is the same for all creative beings, Brother Ughtred," said Brother Aymer, speaking for all. " And it is well that it is so. Were we clottish, pursuing the even tenor of our ways, none of us would ever have had the small triumphs the Saviour has decreed we should have."

" Words of great wisdom, Brother Aymer," Brother Ailfy murmured.

It was warm and pleasant there, the blanketing snow transforming the workshop into a place apart, a haven in which the happiness of a small group need not be restrained as they laboured at tasks they loved. So Ughtred lingered until, thinking of his own undertaking, he decided that another glance at the miniature of Lazelle might not be unprofitable at this crucial stage.

He rose, bowed all round, received a bow from each in turn, and then left for the cloister. It was when he was under cover again, brushing snow off his habit at the junction of the west and south walks, that Brother Godwin's prediction was recalled to mind by the sight of two snowmen in the centre of the garth, seen only from their waists upwards. Both Brother Lionel and Brother Peter might or might not have been reciting the Office of the Dead, but their lips were certainly moving, Peter's the more rapidly as, his pleasant face decidedly contorted, he glared at his companion in distress.

Feeling amused, Ughtred turned towards the day-stairs, but took care that his face was expressionless when pausing to prostrate himself as the third prior stealthily advanced to cast a searching glance at the delinquents.

In the dormitory, Ughtred lifted the miniature portrait from its hiding place, but could not gaze at it for as long as he would have wished. This was a very special evening for the community, all of whom, before Vespers started, had to collect snowy-white albs from the wardrobe. There was also an extra shaving and tonsure, a painful experience when skins were goose-flesh with the cold.

Severe cold was to be the lot of the community for many hours. The Office for the Vigil of Christmas Eve was lengthy, and, although the church was brilliantly lighted from end to end, the cressets, the standards, hanging lamps and candles gave off such little heat comparatively that the breath of the brethren was always visible. When the Midnight Mass ended, the bells in the tower pealed joyously as the half-frozen religious made their way to the warming house, where it had been the chamberlain's duty to ensure a large fire and plenty of hot water for washing.

Christmas Day was a day of immense rejoicing, of endless bell ringing, of procession after procession, both indoors and out in the snow, led by bearers of the holy water and the cross, with others supporting magnificently-shrined relics; and novices carrying candles, and the lord abbot, in colourful pontificals, at the tail-end of a double line of cope-clad brethren; a day of the most solemn participation in the Lord's Supper, a day on which the blessing of the salt and the subsequent addition of a pinch to each salt-cellar in the refectory and kitchen was carried out by the sacrist with much more than the usual ceremony.

It was a day also on which those tenants who could reach the abbey were royally entertained in the large hall of the guest house, providing each brought a quantity of firewood estimated as being sufficient to cook his meal—an ancient statute not insisted upon, though a token stick had to be offered.

Christmas Day was also the day when bellies shrunken by the fast of Advent could have an abundance, to the subsequent discomfort of many of their owners; a day when those weary of herbs and pulse, of dishes of salted and dried fish, whose taste could never be disguised by mustard sauces in various guises, were able when filing decorously into the refectory to feast their eyes on the service tables outside the screen of the kitchen hatch. There were vast platters with sides of fresh ox, and legs of home-grown mutton; roast geese and swan, and decorated bakemeats of ling and plaice from the ice-house and not too long out of the sea; and to fill up any odd corners: blancmange, pastries, cakes, fig tarts, cheese, dates and almonds.

Drink was not forgotten—two choices of wine, French and from the Vale of Gloucester, a potent home-brew of ale, and buttermilk if desired.

As always at dinner, the reader of the week was in the wall pulpit and silence had to be strictly observed, but this did not prevent the brethren from communicating with one another—by toastings with upraised goblets, stomach rubbing, the smacking of lips, and even acting repletion by leaning back against the wainscot as though collapsed, with eyes closed.

Afterwards Ughtred went over to the infirmary to pay seasonal greetings to Brother Godfrey. The old man received these with distinct reserve and appeared more inclined to harangue about the painting, charging him with thinking too much about it, to the exclusion of his duty to God. It was not the first time recently that Ughtred had discovered a certain waywardness in the wiseman, and as he returned to the cloister he puzzled about the change in his old friend. Sometimes, it seemed, Brother Godfrey was feeling his way towards subjects he had forbidden Ughtred to discuss, but no sooner was a trifling advancement made on these paths than he withdrew like a scalded cat.

In the east walk Ughtred paused to glance at the *tabula* on the wall, discovering from it an item of information he would have known already had he not been otherwise engaged during the Daily Chapter on the morning of the Vigil. He found that those at his table in the refectory were due to be bled two days after Holy Innocents', an operation to which all the brethren gladly submitted themselves four times in the year. It meant three full days of holidaying while convalescing in the infirmary; three days of absence from the regular daily and nightly grind of devotions, with food unstinted and no bar to conversation so long as it was not sarcastic or likely to cause quarrels.

Ughtred was far from pleased. " For the best part of four days I shan't be able to touch a brush . . . unless I can persuade the reverend father, the infirmarian, that painting is a gentle exercise which will not bring me out in a sweat."

This feeling of annoyance had its repercussions. He began to think about Brother Godfrey's accusation, and the more he thought about it the more he realised that the painting was standing between himself and the Lord. On rising the next morning he had decided to submit himself to the Sacrament of Penance.

After Prime, a confessor was always available in the chapter house for the next hour, and Ughtred went there after leaving the church.

Brother Bernard, a senior monk and priest with a reputation for salutary sentences, was sitting in a front stall near the lord abbot's chair. Sighting him, Ughtred almost had second thoughts, the more so as Brother Bernard was sipping hot water, presumably affected as many others by over-rich food on digestive systems unused to it. But it was too late then, and so, committed, Ughtred bowed before kneeling between the trunk and the gravestones of William Punchard, 6th lord abbot, and Peter, the 20th.

" Yes, my son? " Brother Bernard asked.

It was a simple enough tale, told by a man who, following Friar Jerome's advice, had locked the nun Lazelle in a separate compartment of his mind, to which no one should have entry.

" In all your waking hours you dwell on nothing save the painting of the Madonna, my son? "

" Yes, Father."

" You are painting this picture at My Lord's desire, my son, so that if it should please Our Heavenly Father to guide your hand and eye, you will be adding to the glories of our convent. Is that not so, my son? "

" Yes, Father," Ughtred murmured.

Brother Bernard winced before proceeding. " Then I do not hold you guilty of erring unduly, my son," he said. " Is it not said that the house which is divided shall fall, and He, who has given you the rare gift you have, knows that part of that gift is a single-minded purposefulness towards the ends you seek? He will not condemn you, my son, nor shall I."

Ughtred must have looked surprised, for Brother Bernard went on: " Our Order of the Blessed Saint Bernard is strict, my son, but its compassion and understanding is second to none, so great that if a former Brother—with whom I have often seen you in conversation but must not name—were to return with humility, he would be received, after severe punishment naturally, into the brotherhood again, and for twice more after that if he faltered further."

" Yes, Father," Ughtred said.

Brother Bernard's hand flew to his chest. Between groans, he lowered the water in the beaker. His tone was less considerate when he spoke next.

" But at least you have said a *Gloria* at each canonical Hour, my son? " he snapped.

Ughtred bowed his head. " Not always, Father."

" Then He above," Brother Bernard said forcefully, " would expect me to punish you, my son. And so it shall be."

Probably a mighty belch, followed by a series of much smaller belches between sips of water, saved Ughtred from anything condign.

" My son," said Brother Bernard, sounding more human, " for the next two days you will be denied the Collation."

" Yes, Father," said Ughtred.

Brother Bernard had never been seen to smile, but the harsh lines on his face smoothed a little.

" I trust, my son," he said, " that the punishment, slight though it is, will be more trying for you than it would be for me. Now go, but remember in future that when you are painting a few moments for devotion will not fatally impair your work. So remember, my son, a prayer to the Almighty at each holy Hour."

" Yes, Father," Ughtred said respectfully.

Feeling much lighter hearted, he went to the workshops, where he suffered a leg-pulling, his cheerfulness being attributed to entering the infirmary shortly, where he would be free to laze. He enjoyed the badinage, but got his own back when, as opposed to relaxing in the infirmary, he compelled each of the brothers to admit to a preference to working on the Lady Philippa's staff.

Officially, blood-letting was deemed to release evil spirits and tone up the stomach. More practically, in the founder's view, it was devised to cool blood too hot as a result of a farinaceous diet, thereby subjugating bestial passions of the flesh.

No solemnity was discernible on the faces of Ughtred's table companions on the day and at the hour appointed, when he had splashed through the mud of the thaw to join them at the infirmary, in the *flebotomaria*, where a bright fire burned. Brother Eustace was neither weeping nor groaning; Brother Stephen, the engrosser,

looked as if already he was savouring plenty of gossip, and Brother
Edgar, who had brought books with him, as if happily anticipating
a long, undisturbed read. Brother Anthony, the copyist, carrying
manuscripts, quills, iron style, ink and leaden parchment-weight,
appeared as if he hoped to complete his 737th volume before
returning to the ordinary life of the community; and Brother
Edmund, always a show-off, was expatiating on *Disputatio Judae;
cum Christiano*, an account by an abbot of Westminster of a discussion
which converted Jews within the hour.

Even Brother Edmund's spate died when Brother Edgar
announced that he could faintly hear music in the chapel adjoining.

" It is a harp," Brother Anthony said.

As could be expected of him, Brother Stephen slipped into the
hall. On returning, he reported that Brother Luke, upon whom
melancholia was known to be descending, had been carried to the
chapel. A novice, with a trick in these things, was playing to
cheer him up.

A tear slid down Brother Eustace's cheek. " Our dear brother
has been bedfast ever since he was whipped," he said miserably.
" Perhaps he is close to the blessed gateway, whereas I, a sinner
who——"

A man suspected of enjoying belabouring the backs of others is
not popular, and Brother Anthony checked him very sharply.

" You will cease your snivelling," he said, " and not resume it
while we are here."

A mild person always, Brother Edgar lent support. " This is a
welcome change, Brother Eustace, during which I can read almost
uninterruptedly, *if* I am at peace. I shall not be if you are wailing
interminably."

Brother Eustace appealed to the others. " My beloved brothers,
how can I smother within my breast the knowledge that I am guilty
of——"

The infirmarian and three assistants came in, and Brother Eustace successfully smothered any further observations. One painful
experience had taught him that the higher hierarchy was not sympathetic towards his revelations.

" My sons," said the infirmarian, " you will listen attentively."

A homily followed, known to all by heart, the infirmarian first satisfying himself that his patients had fortified themselves within the past hour, by taking a little bread and wine in the refectory. He then reminded them that, towards facilitating a swift return to vigour, they were not to bend unnecessarily; and if, instead of attending any of the Offices in the infirmary chapel, they went to church, they must leave before the others and not walk out in rank.

" Because," he explained, as if none had heard of it before, " if you are walking in rank there is risk that the wound might be knocked. Brother Eustace! Off with your habit and into the chair."

It was all rapidly done, with the efficiency of regular practice. A vein was opened in the arm, two measures of blood were drained into a vessel; a styptic was applied, and then the bandage.

By permission, Ughtred's cupping was done on his left arm. With the others, he was put to bed in the lengthy, dormitory chamber; a little later he was given a draught of salted water with dried sage and parsley in it and, much more palatable, a dish of soft-boiled eggs.

The next morning, wan but cheery, the patients were up and about.

During his stay in the infirmary, Ughtred had many conversations with old Brother Godfrey, and two remained in his mind. The first was at dinner in the misericord on the second day, when he and the wiseman shared a table—which was not difficult, as there were many spare tables in a chamber large enough to seat the whole community.

To Ughtred's astonishment, Brother Godfrey prefaced his remarks strangely. " I shall keep my voice low, my son," he said. " Because I am aware that what I shall be saying would be frowned on."

" Revered Father," said Ughtred, " do not speak on matters which I believe may pain you. For that reason I regret having ever allowed you a glimpse into a mind that is confused."

" Never mind about that, my son," Brother Godfrey said. " True, I am here to live my last days in peace and comfort, without a care, but thanks to the benevolence of Our Lord and Saviour I am not senile yet, and I have a conscience which tells me that I must gird myself to speak freely."

It sounded very formidable, but was much less so. Reduced to its essentials, Brother Godfrey confirmed that just as the Cistercians had come into being because the Benedictines had not retained their austere ideals, so had the Orders of the mendicant friars arisen because neither Benedictines *nor* Cistercians conceived it their affair to help suffering humanity, save that small portion presenting itself at the abbeys' almonries. To that extent he criticised his own Order.

Their conversation was resumed at supper, although Ughtred, from sitting down, had studiously avoided anything controversial.

" My son," Brother Godfrey said suddenly, as a servant re-filled his goblet with wine, " do you remember once asking what I might do were I youthful again, but had the advantage of then knowing what my years here have meant to me? "

Apprehensive that the old man would be overheard, Ughtred began to perspire; and in the parlour afterwards, where everyone was close together, he was even more uneasy. Fortunately, Brother Godfrey's friend, Brother Basil, saved the situation—refusing to accept " no " for an answer, he brought the chess board and a set of pieces beautifully carved from a walrus's tusk, and challengingly made the first move.

On the last day of convalescence Ughtred obtained permission to do a little painting. The " little " turned out to be the beginning of a burst of inspired work which kept him going until shortly after the Feast of the Epiphany when, realising all virtue had gone out of him for the present, he cleaned his brushes, sheeted the Madonna, locked the door of the *locutorium*, and, in a penetrating east wind, walked to the workshops, where his sudden arrival so startled Brother Ralph that not only were several pearls swept to the floor but he also choked—over a piece of almond lodged in his throat, as he explained when able to speak.

Brother Theobald, his contribution to the staff completed, was now carving the stalls in the warming house as conditions were too severe in the transept. But Brother Ranulf, who had been enamelling the top ring, and Brother Ailfy—leaving a piece of silver he had been beating out—came running from the two cubicles most remote from the door to ascertain what the commotion was about. They found Ughtred thumping Brother Ralph's back.

All insisted that Brother Ralph, under the impression that the newcomer was the kitchener, had swallowed a stolen pork chop, bone and all. It made a rib-tickling joke about a brother whose extra fastings never reduced his weight, and everyone roared with laughter, even the victim after an initial flare-up of hoarse-voiced indignation.

When the gathering calmed, the talk was about the staff and crook. General opinion was that it would be finished in a week's time.

In fact it was five days only. That morning, after grace, Ughtred had gone to the necessary and was sitting in a cubicle when Brother Ailfy came in for a quick call. All too casually, before leaving, he asked Ughtred to look into the workshop when he had a moment to spare; and if this were not enough to arouse Ughtred's curiosity a similar invitation from Brother Ranulf a couple of minutes later undoubtedly was. The enameller exuded mystery, which certainly was not his intention.

"H'mmm," Ughtred murmured as he went down to the cloister to wash. "I think Dame Philippa's staff is finished, and I think they are proud of what they have done. And if they are proud I am sure, knowing their skills, that they have wrought wonderfully."

Frightened of his hands chapping, which would affect his work, he dried them thoroughly before hanging the towel in the aumbry. Then he started off for the workshops.

The pastoral staff was magnificent and, though prepared to some extent, Ughtred's breath caught when Brother Aymer, not lacking the air of a showman, took it out of a cloth.

"My brothers!" Ughtred gasped.

Marvelling, he stared enraptured at what they had achieved— the serpent-like head of the crook, with a pair of glowing, red eyes and gleaming scales enamelled in shades of green and soft blues outlined with delicate threads of silver; the beauty of the engraving, and the perfection of countersunk, diminutive figures of saints made of gold; the exquisite carving on such wood as was visible, and the artistry of the bosses, scintillating with light.

Ughtred blinked. "My brothers," he said huskily, "the Lady Philippa is to come into a possession whose glory the like I have never before seen. Never, my brothers, can there have been a staff and crook so superb."

"Brother Theobald fretted about the carving, Brother Ughtred," Brother Ailfy said despondently. "As for myself, I am conscious that there are many defects in the details of the saints' faces."

"My hand slipped once or twice, Brother Ughtred," Brother Theobald said apologetically.

Brother Ranulf pointed. "My hand slipped more than once or twice, Brother Ughtred," he mourned. "See there how the enamel has crept."

"My acid crept, too, Brother Ughtred," Brother Aymer said dejectedly. "Notice how the vein in this leaf thickens the wrong way."

Impatiently Brother Ralph elbowed him away. "That is nothing, Brother Aymer. But inspect *this*, Brother Ughtred." His tone became tragic. "Look at it—where in cutting the diamond I chipped the underlie, so that it is as a pebble out of the river."

Reassuring those whose temperaments make them difficult to assure is exacting toil, but Ughtred soon had them grinning with delight. A businesslike conference was next held, at which it was decided that Brother Theobald, as the senior, should petition My Lord for permission to show him what they had done.

Swathed carefully, the staff was then taken by the whole company to the treasurer, for safe keeping. The obedientiary, however, refused to accept the package until he had seen what was inside.

"I must adopt the same custom as when a messenger from outside delivers a bag of silver angels or a valuable tome for the reverend father the cantor—or what purports to be a valuable tome," he explained gravely. "Or how would I stand, if it were not as described, when a claim was made later for its return? You appreciate my point, my sons?"

"Yes, Reverend Father," the murmur rose.

In this wise the treasurer satisfied his curiosity, and so further praise was heaped on the makers of the staff. Proud as peacocks, they went their various ways, to take up more mundane affairs.

For his part, Ughtred returned to the *locutorium* where, perhaps the aftermath of a triumph in which he had shared, he shook his head dispiritedly after staring at the Madonna.

"I think it may be that occasionally my brushwork tends to be too bold," he told himself. "Yes, that could be it."

His mood was entirely different the next afternoon, and when a decline in the light ended his work he was buoyant, confident the painting would be completed within a few days, and that he need not shrink from others viewing it. Indeed, he was trying to whistle, though softly, as he had heard men and boys in the city whistle, when there was a knock. After throwing down his painting-shirt and putting on his habit, he went round a tall screen, placed so that no one in the lobby could see inside. On unlocking the door he saw Brother Left-handed Thomas on the threshold.

"Stretch your neck too far and you will be defying My Lord's orders," Ughtred remarked conversationally.

Brother Left-handed had not relished his errand, and was anxious to escape immediately on discharging it. In truth, he was completely innocent of any attempt to pry, but Ughtred was now firmly of the conviction that he was a sly customer who should be kept on the jump.

"I had no such intention," Brother Left-handed Thomas said loudly, glancing over his shoulder to ascertain whether the kitchen porter was within hearing. "From what the reverend father the cantor wrote on the *tabula* I am aware of My Lord's strict command, which I would be the last in the convent to try to break, surreptitiously or otherwise."

"When the reading desk was being set up in the sanctuary last night I noticed you looking at Brother Hubert," Ughtred remarked as he went off to leave the key. This somewhat odd remark was completed when he rejoined the treasurer's assistant, who was gaping. "I thought at first you had an unholy glint in your eye, Brother Left-handed."

"It is . . . it is impossible for me not to glance at Brother Hubert now and then, for his stall is opposite mine," Left-handed Thomas spluttered. "And I had no unholy glint in my eyes anyhow."

Ughtred nodded. "Fortunately for both of us I came to the same conclusion, praise to the Lord," he said, endeavouring to thin his lips as the prior did on occasion. "Otherwise, unless the Lord Jesus had restrained me—which is doubtful, for He will be on my side—otherwise I would have darted from my seat, and hurled myself across the quire between the cresset and the grave of our esteemed benefactor Thomas de Roos—bless his memory, may he——"

" Why . . . why would you have done so? " Brother Left-handed stammered.

" To seize you by your miserable throat," said Ughtred. " Digging in my thumbs at both sides of your windpipe."

Brother Left-handed Thomas's pasty face seemed even more lardy. " Brother Ughtred," he said anxiously, " have I not sworn that never again will I utter a word that shall cause Brother Hubert unease? "

" You have, but nature will out," Ughtred said sadly, closing his eyes and holding his hands together for a short and audible prayer. " Please, God, I beg you to let me be there when Brother Left-handed Thomas back-slides. And if I be not there at the moment of his crime give speed to my legs so that I may throttle him with all despatch. Grant me this, Saviour."

Convinced his brother was insane on this particular issue, Left-handed fumbled in his pouch for a handkerchief. He was wiping his forehead when Ughtred asked him why he had come.

" The reverend father the treasurer desires you to attend him. With him are several brethren who have been joined in the enterprise you know of."

" They will be at the treasury, not the chequer? " Ughtred said.

" At the treasury," Left-handed Thomas replied.

Unhappily for him, as it chanced, Brother Hubert was busy in the nearer lavatory in the east walk when they reached the iron door of the treasury. He was sharpening his knife on a whetstone, a commonplace spectacle Ughtred chose to misinterpret.

" See how he thumbs the sharp point to test its merit," he remarked sepulchrally. " Do you think that when you caught his eye in quire he conceived you were pondering fresh torments for him? There is a limit to even a Christian's endurance."

Horrified, Brother Left-handed Thomas stared at him. "You... you mean, Brother Ughtred . . ."

" I have nothing to go on, nothing whatsoever," Ughtred murmured. " But it is squally outdoors, and stealthy footsteps would not be heard in the dark hours of the night . . . and but three cells separate you."

Brother Left-handed's teeth were chattering. " You suspect he would strike me down while I slept? Brother Ughtred, I beg you to speak to him, for he takes note of you. Assure him I have no intention of serving him ill, either now or ever. I swear it as I swore it before."

" Death, as we are taught, is not to be feared, my brother," Ughtred reminded him gently.

" But violent death is," Brother Left-handed said frantically.

Ughtred shook his head reproachfully. " You should always be prepared, my brother, however swift the end."

" There are always things left undone," Brother Left-handed Thomas urged. " Small sins undisclosed."

" It may be so with some," Ughtred said disparagingly. " Still . . ." he considered. " Very well, Brother Left-handed, before we ascend in the Great Silence I will converse with Brother Hubert. But now I must seek the reverend father."

All those concerned in the making of the staff were in the treasury. As custodian of the Lady Philippa's property while it was in the abbey the treasurer accompanied the party through the Long Gallery to the lord abbot's lodging, where the chaplain escorted them through the private suite, from reception room to ante-room and thence into the parlour. My Lord was in the bedchamber beyond, but was expected in a few moments. Meantime the staff was unwrapped and placed on the table.

Within five minutes, rarely could a company of craftsmen have been more delighted. Abbot Hugh was unstinting in his praise, and even when he mentioned the out-turn of the crook there was more amusement than rancour in his tone.

" I fear the Lady Philippa has stolen a march on us, my sons," he remarked. " But before this year is out I fancy the slur on many of the monastic houses will have been removed, and to you, my sons, I shall entrust the designing and creation of insignia more appropriate to our convent's authority and power. As to the present, you may be sure that I shall instruct the chronicler Robert to record your deeds in the annals, and when I write the Lady Philippa, as I shall before a second dawn, each of you will be mentioned by name."

This was most gratifying, but My Lord assured a more public

recognition at supper in the refectory, when, unprecedented honour, he sent two dishes from his table on the dais to each of them, dishes doubtlessly arranged for in advance with the kitchener. And so the Brothers Theobald, Ailfy, Ranulf, Aymer, Ralph and Ughtred twice stood up, their fellows' eyes on them, to bow deeply to the lord abbot who, commanding figure outlined against a large picture of *The Last Judgment*, graciously responded in kind. There was also a general ovation, a hand-clapping in which the palms never met, for the treasurer, with permission, had placed the staff on show for all to behold.

Ughtred felt glad and yet intolerably sad, both then and when the community filed out. As he bowed to the aproned servers of the week and the regular officials of the kitchen, who were standing in a line near the screen of the hatch, he was far away, wondering if his Madonna would earn him as much as he had earned that evening.

" It will not be many days before I shall know," he told himself with a sigh. " But I am not seeking the congratulations of my fellows . . . all I seek is perfection."

The brothers with whom he had collaborated on the staff were gathering together, and more with them. In no mood for rejoicing, he turned towards the shadows in the north walk. After a while he entered the church by the seldom-used south-west doorway, and aided by no more than a faint glow from the candles on the distant High Altar, walked slowly up the dark nave to the little chapel of Saint Paul.

\*　　　\*　　　\*　　　\*

The painting of the Madonna was finished six days before Septuagesima, eleven minutes before the prior came to the door of the refectory to signal that the bell ringing for dinner should cease. For two of those minutes Ughtred stared at what he had done and then, lips quivering, covered the Babe and the angels and the face of Lazelle. For three or four minutes more he sat on the bench, shoulders bent and eyes closed. Next, rising wearily, he cleaned his board and brushes, before packing them and the paints and jars into his painting chest.

The thought of food impossible, he remained in the *locutorium* until the community came into the cloister after grace in church, and then, too indifferent to bother about breaking long established custom, went to the abbot's lodging, where he requested an outraged chaplain to inform My Lord that the Madonna had been completed. He was sent away sharply.

It was a dry day, and the novices had gone to their court to play ball when the lord abbot's secretary found Ughtred leaning against the canopied shrine of Saint William in the vestibule of the chapter house, apparently lost in thought while gazing at an inscription on the stonework above the inner door: *Nulla quae Deo pertinent nogotia a me puto aliena.*

" I have had a business searching for you, Brother Ughtred," the secretary said in a near-panic. " Thanks to God I have now succeeded."

Ughtred smiled faintly as he nodded towards the deeply-cut words. " All God's business is my business, too, Brother Secretary," he murmured.

The secretary shook his shoulder. " My Lord is coming to view the Madonna," he said imperatively. " He may reach the *locutorium* in advance of us if you do not collect your wits and hurry."

" My Lord is on his way? " Ughtred muttered. " My Lord is——"

He jumped up, the dazed expression in his eyes vanishing. Striding out in the van, the secretary trying to keep up, he reached the kitchen porter's quarters as the lord abbot, all prostrate as he passed, progressed from the east walk to the south.

That allowed sufficient time. When Abbot Hugh entered the *locutorium* with the chaplain the picture had been lowered from the trestles and was supported nearer the floor, more in line with a bench dragged hurriedly to the opposite wall.

Ughtred knelt. " My Lord, I ask and beseech God's mercy and yours," he said, his heart fluttering. " If it will now please My Lord I will uncover the Madonna."

" You may, my son," said the lord abbot.

Ears buzzing, arms trembling, Ughtred stood on a stool, stretched upwards, and the broad sheet fell, forming rough folds where it lay. Not for what seemed an age was a word spoken.

The silence was broken by My Lord. " She lives," he muttered.

"The Holy Virgin is alive . . . it is as if she were there." Turning to his chaplain, he added, his voice charged with awe: "What think you, my son? You have travelled widely through the cities of France and Italy—how does this compare with the masters you have seen?"

"My Lord," the chaplain said, deeply moved, "only recently I had reason to rebuke Brother Ughtred for seeking you at your lodging instead of petitioning you at the proper hour in the parlour, as is laid down. But now, My Lord, after seeing what I have seen— and in all humble obedience—I venture to say I would not upbraid him had he dared to approach you even more directly."

The lord abbot was still staring at the picture. "Such purity I have never known in a face before," he marvelled. "Ughtred, my son, you are surely blessed in that the Almighty has used you as his instrument on earth, a poor mortal whose God-given art, even if you never touched brush again, will by this single picture bring joy to our community and them who follow in our footsteps."

"Its beauty will become known far beyond our convent, My Lord," said the chaplain. "This is a gift to the world, a gift in which the world will rightly demand a share."

"Never have I seen such tranquillity in eyes, never a mouth which so bespoke compassion for all men," the abbot murmured. "She is the Holy Innocence as we might imagine her in our hearts, and to my son Ughtred's genius in transferring his vision we owe much, and still more to the Saviour who inspired him."

The secretary coughed. "I fear, My Lord," he said, "that regrettable though it be, this will give rise to jealousy in certain quarters. Neither the abbeys of Fountains nor Furness will take kindly to our possessing a picture which will surely bring many princes and nobles to feast their eyes on it. The city of York, which is the second capital of the land, may be somewhat remote from us, but as My Lord is aware there is a tendency to a patronage of arts outside the religious foundations, and a more widespread desire to be informed on it."

"I agree, my son, that there will be much jealousy," Abbot Hugh remarked cheerfully. "When our distinguished visitors see this superb picture raised on the wall of the north transept—it is far and away the most fitting place for it . . ."

Ughtred broke down. Again without permission, or thinking of it, he sank on the lord abbot's bench and, shoulders bowed and head in his hands, quietly wept. Almost simultaneously Abbot Hugh rose, but this was not because he was either offended or annoyed. Excitedly, dimly heard by Ughtred, he paced to and fro, detailing his plans. The picture should be provided with a sculptured portal laid in the wall, and must not be seen, except by those intimately concerned, until the unveiling, when invitations would be issued to highly-placed personages, many of them.

" A portal, My Lord? " Ughtred said, wiping his eyes.

" Either a recess or protruding, with stone border of effective design. As you will have little time before you leave here, my son, you will submit a pattern to me with the least delay."

" Before I leave, My Lord! " Ughtred exclaimed.

Abbot Hugh nodded. " You will now attend on me, and shortly I shall acquaint you with my desires," he said, continuing most kindly: " And soon also, my son, there will be wine for you, for I perceive you are in need of a restorative."

" It is the reaction of the artist of true talent, My Lord," the chaplain said. " He has just completed a great undertaking, and for a while will be no more than a husk."

Remaining respectfully to the rear, and wondering what was in store for him, Ughtred returned with the small party to the superior's lodging, where My Lord, after stalking through reception chamber and ante-room to the dining-hall, rang a hand-bell briskly. Both cook and barber answered the summons, and were instructed to place wine and two goblets on the parlour table. Chaplain and secretary were then dismissed.

For Ughtred it was a nerve-racking experience to be sitting at one side of a fireplace with the abbot at the other, though My Lord was genial enough as he spoke about a letter from the prioress of Watton.

" Another measure, my son? " he broke off to inquire hospitably.

" With respect, but no thank you, My Lord," Ughtred said.

" So, my son, as the Lady Philippa writes in such eager terms we must acquiesce to her wishes," My Lord resumed. " That is why you will start out for the priory of Watton on the day of the Conversion of Saint Paul, to convey the staff to her. With you, for security,

will be a small company of the brethren, amongst them your brother
Martin." This seemed to amuse him, the creases near his dark eyes
becoming more defined. "The Lady Philippa's clock is misbehav-
ing, and she is not well disposed to those who have failed to remedy
its errors. I trust your brother Martin may have better fortune."

"He is exceedingly adroit with mechanisms, My Lord."

The laughter creases deepened. "We must hope, my son, that
his skill does not desert him," said the lord abbot.

Ughtred was then told that his companions would remain at
Watton two nights only, unless snow-bound, sufficient to allow
Brother Martin a full day's finicking, but that he himself would be
staying in Harthill long enough to complete a number of pictures
for the embellishment of the convent. He was to take his painting
chest and materials enough for several large wall paintings.

"My Lord," Ughtred said anxiously, "it is as I explained to
My Lord, this is no season for working in wet plaster, and if that is
the Lady Philippa's intention for me —"

The lord abbot roared with laughter. "Don't pester me with
objections, my son," he said, "but save them for the Lady Philippa.
I daresay," he chuckled, "she will pay you satisfactory attention,
and accept your advice."

"Yes, *Domine*," Ughtred said, feeling dubious.

Abbot Hugh picked up the flagon. "Away to your affairs, my
son," he said, pouring. "There is the edging of the portal to be
limned for the masons before you depart, and it must be in keeping
with the beauty and purity of the Holy Virgin it is destined to
enclose."

"Yes, My Lord," Ughtred murmured.

My Lord took a long draught. "That is all, my son," he said
affably. "Submit the drawing to me when ready, without previous
petitioning, and as you have not much time in hand you will continue to be excused bodily presence from certain Offices as hitherto."

Ughtred rose and placed the silver goblet on the table. "Thank
you, My Lord," he said, before bowing himself out.

Stirred by what was before him, and heady with a wine of a
potency he had not experienced before, Ughtred returned to the
cloister. For seclusion, he went to the south walk, and tried to collect his thoughts.

" Soon I shall be dwelling under the same roof . . . no, that cannot be," he said to himself, trying to conceal excitement. " But wherever she is we shall both be in the same priory . . . and if God is good . . ."

The excitement gone, he shook his head soberly. Lazelle was a bride of Christ, and the Lord God, however understanding about other frailties, could not be expected to lend His help to furthering an illicit meeting.

After a while, he grew more optimistic. " It could happen, by chance," he muttered. " And if it should be that I do speak to her, I can tell her about the Madonna painting—how it pleased My Lord, and how it is to be placed in the north transept."

He shook his head again, much more decidedly. That would never do. Far from being delighted, Sister Lazelle would worry.

The words quietly escaped him. " She would be worrying for *me*," he said, his expression rapturous. " For me, Sister Lazelle would . . ."

The fourth prior was advancing slowly from the direction of the Passage. Idleness was a serious offence against the Rule—hastily Ughtred lifted his breviary and gave close attention to it, ostensibly.

His reverie, during which he continued to wax both hot and cold, did not last much longer, and shortly afterwards, towards the drawing My Lord required, he climbed the day-stairs to his cell. On returning with his portfolio he went round to the chronicler's carrel, where after very liberal coaxing he obtained a few sheets of parchment—Brother Robert was firmly convinced that with a little application anyone could be a competent news-gatherer, and turned a jaundiced eye on those who had failed him.

The *locutorium* was a refuge from all interruptions and, pleasantly warm, Ughtred began to sketch ideas for the bordering of the Madonna, which he peeped at before starting. His object throughout was simplicity; the painting must be clothed, but there must be nothing to draw attention from the centrepiece. In the end he decided it would be the most appropriate of all if the design were based on the architectural features of the transept: quatrefoils at the corners connected by tooth moulding adapted from the surrounds of the triforium windows.

" H'mmm," he murmured, eyeing the drawing when finished.

THE FACE OF A MADONNA

"I fear My Lord will not consider it sufficiently ornate, but if I ensure the reverend father the chaplain has a sight of it first . . . My Lord respects his opinions in these matters."

His mind was not wholly given over to the lord abbot's command, for in the midst of wondering how best to obtain in advance the support of an ally he was overwhelmed by a daring notion: that of presenting Sister Lazelle with some small token of his esteem.

"It is next to impossible that I shall speak to her again," he muttered. "But surely it is not beyond inventiveness that I can manage to pass to her whatever it is I may take."

It was not until he had been staring at the wall for some minutes, pondering about the nature of the gift, that it occurred to him that his own hands might create the most acceptable gift of all.

"A painting in little," he whispered. "As I painted a picture of her with the tiny brushes and the magnifying glass her Lady entrusted to me."

Impulsively rising, Ughtred wandered about, the scope of his ambitions steadily increasing. It should be more than a picture, this representation of the Lord Christ he had determined on.

"A locket, an open-faced oval locket with Our Saviour looking from it," he mused. "I know the structure of the relic box she wears, for it was mine, and it will be easy to devise a catch for her to join them herself, so that it will also rest on her bosom, hanging from the same chain."

Before the light failed he had made a drawing, preliminary to starting the next day. Happy about this, he tucked the other design, for My Lord, into the portfolio, where it would remain hidden until his work for Sister Lazelle was finished, so that no one would question why he locked himself into the *locutorium*.

It was bath day, an event once each quarter, and when Ughtred entered the cloister the community was assembling in the warming room. Inside, novices were lighting extra candles at the fire, and carrying them to the partitioned-off aisle behind the stalls at one side, along which were a dozen large tubs; servants were bringing cauldrons of hot water from the kitchen, the chamberlain's assistants bustled in with stacks of towels and fresh underlinen, and a carrier heaped more logs in the double fireplace. A few of the most important obedientiaries, the cantor, sacrist and third prior, had drawn

223

up a bench and were toasting their feet on the stone kerb, but the remainder of the brethren awaited their turns in the stalls at either side.

Then, and during bathing, and when drying himself as he stood on a thick layer of hay spread on the floor near the tubs, Ughtred thought of the locket. Before dressing, the picture was clearly in his mind—the Lord Jesus should be sitting beneath a canopy, in a robe of rich colour, an Italian scarlet he had revelled in ever since trying out the pigments in the Florentine box.

This picture, with a brilliant diaper as background, was completed on the third day. Next, fortunate to find an oblong piece of hardwood in the workshops, he shaped an oval; in the face of this he dug out another oval, undercutting the edges so that the parchment he had chosen would snap into it, though later he added a touch of glue for security. Then he smoothed the rim of the locket, before persuading a length of triple-twisted gold embroidery thread through a minute hole. The remainder was done in the *locutorium*, with gilt and a brush.

These nefarious activities made the remaining days before departure very busy ones. Thanks to the chaplain's respectful but firm interventions My Lord consented to accept the portal-design Ughtred showed him, but this was merely the prelude to long, drawn-out consultations with the *custos fabricae*, his senior assistant, and the master mason, during which a dummy of the Madonna painting, made to the measurements Ughtred specified, was placed in various positions on the north wall of the transept, with numerous standings-off from afar to view how it appeared.

Ughtred had other preoccupations, too, one that his paint chest had to be bulging with materials. Better quality habits and scapulars, a thick mantle and an additional pair of drawers, had also to be obtained from the wardrobe, and he went along for these with others who, in addition to two servants armed to the teeth, would bear the pastoral staff to the prioress of Watton. There was Brother Henry, late to become a monk, and countrywise, and Brother Aubrey, born in Holderness and guide along the route; Brother Martin, who was taking tools, and Brother Ranulf, chosen to represent the makers of the staff.

On the last afternoon before leaving, Ughtred set off to the infirmary to bid farewell to Brother Godfrey, but he had only just left the Passage behind when he pulled up, appalled by what he saw. Carrying a jar, the old wiseman was tottering across the remote side of the infirmary garth, towards a stick stuck in the ground. It was a punishment Ughtred knew, the watering of something which could never grow.

" Brother Ughtred! " a voice snapped.

It was the sub-infirmarian. " Yes," said Ughtred, too non-plussed and upset either to bow or respond correctly.

" The reverend father my superior wishes to speak to you, Brother Ughtred," the sub-infirmarian said sternly. " You will follow me."

Ughtred was escorted through the infirmary hall to the infirmarian's chamber, where he was left to cool his heels. Until footsteps sounded, he looked about cursorily: at mortars and measures on shelves, and strangely-shaped instruments for operations; at an open cupboard containing ginger, peony, cinnamon, and other comforting cordials; at books on leechcraft and the veterinary art; and at standard works on medicine, the most important of which was John of Mirfield's *Breviarium Bartholemei.*

The infirmarian closed the door. " You were intending visiting Brother Godfrey?" he said sharply.

" Yes, Reverend Father," Ughtred said.

" You are not to approach him again, my son, either now or on your return from Harthill. Repeat that."

Ughtred swallowed. " I am not to approach him again, either now or after my return from Harthill."

" What else? " the infirmarian thundered.

" Reverend Father," Ughtred said hastily. " I ask your pardon for the omission, Reverend Father."

" You are aware," the infirmarian said hectoringly, " that our Rule forbids friendships. Why is that so wisely ordained? "

" Lest our devotion to anyone on earth should be at the expense of the wholehearted devotion we must have for God, Reverend Father."

" But your visits to the wiseman, Godfrey," the obedientiary stormed, " are they not an act of friendship? "

A seed of rebellion began to germinate in Ughtred, and with it a perilous chain of thought: the abbot had crushingly dealt with the equally overbearing novice-master, and the infirmarian might well prefer to shun anything which could involve him in a matter vexing to My Lord.

"As is your duty, Reverend Father," Ughtred said, risking it, "you have pointed out my error, for which I suppose I must be punished, though I shall also punish myself."

The infirmarian stared. "How so?"

"I shall explain to My Lord why I am not fitted to rest at the priory of Watton," Ughtred said coolly. "He had plans for me, on behalf of his blood cousin, the Lady Philippa, during my sojourn there, and if I thwart him I suspect my back will bloodily reflect his annoyance. But I shall have deserved my pains—by visiting Brother Godfrey as I have, without invitation from him, I have condemned him to what I have just perceived he is undergoing."

The infirmarian's expression had strikingly changed. "No, no, my son, that has nothing to do with you," he said quickly. "In his dotage Brother Godfrey has acquired strange fancies, and when an aged man babbles foolishly he must pay in kind, by being compelled to do foolish things for a few weeks."

Regretfully Ughtred shook his head. "Excuse me as you will, Reverend Father, but it is plainly my fault that the revered father would still be despondently pouring water on a dead stick when I should have been endeavouring to paint to the desires of the Lady Philippa, and that is why I must sink before My Lord forthwith, however enraged he will be."

There was an edge in the infirmarian's voice. "My Lord must not be troubled with this trivial affair," he said.

Sadly Ughtred shook his head. "If I rode forth to-morrow, leaving Brother Godfrey suffering for what I believe is my responsibility, the melancholy possessing me would weigh on me throughout my days at Watton, and my painting would be a sorry thing. With respect, Reverend Father, I must petition My Lord."

Abruptly the infirmarian walked to the window, remaining for some time looking out. When he turned again to Ughtred the skin on his cheekbones had tightened and he had lost colour.

"Had you been less loquacious, my son," he said harshly, "you would have learnt by now that I have been considering ameliorating

Brother Godfrey's state. His disgracing is to end with the passing of this day."

"Reverend Father, I am overjoyed," Ughtred murmured.

"To be overjoyed for another is an indication of friendship," the obedientiary snapped.

"I fear you misunderstand me, Reverend Father," Ughtred said. "I am overjoyed because through your clemency I shall leave contentedly to-morrow, which I must be if I am to please the lady prioress of Watton and My Lord."

The infirmarian's eyes were pitilessly hard. "It is to be hoped you do, my son," he said with an effort. "Although in this life on earth we cannot always attain our expectations."

"That is so, Reverend Father," Ughtred agreed dutifully.

"You may go, my son," the infirmarian said tersely.

Ughtred bowed low. "Yes, Reverend Father," he said.

Consumed by anger, but trembling also, Ughtred walked along the hall. Nevertheless, on meeting the old wiseman, Basil, he was self-contained enough to tell him the good news about Brother Godfrey, repeating this on encountering the sub-infirmarian again. The latter made no comment, partly because Ughtred spoke so wordily about the infirmarian's humanity, and partly because he had been flabbergasted on seeing Ughtred pull up and toss away the stick in the garth.

The next morning, after Prime, special prayers were said for those leaving the abbey, and then the travellers went to the refectory, where they were served a hearty meal. Following that, all made a round during which various necessities for journeying were collected: to each a flask of wine and two loaves, a blanket and a candle. A move was then made to the stables in the inner court, where everything was in readiness, including the mare Bess which, favouritism prohibited elsewhere or not, had been allocated to Ughtred.

Left-handed Thomas, carrying a well-padded package wrapped in ox skin, came from the cloister with the treasurer who, addressing admonitions all round, handed the pastoral staff to Brother Ranulf. During this interlude Ughtred stared so fixedly at the treasurer's assistant that the latter, unnerved, sidled alongside to whisper.

"Do you seek to cast an evil spell over me?" he said. "If it is to do with Brother Hubert have I not sworn never to say anything that might cause him to dream sinfully? "

Ughtred bent to him. " It is as well, Brother Left-handed, because the Lord has promised to tell me in a vision if you slip."

Awed, Left-handed Thomas gaped at him. " The . . . the Lord has spoken to you, Brother Ughtred? " he stuttered.

Ughtred nodded. " In the little chapel of Saint Paul."

The exchanges were interrupted when Brother Robert, the chronicler, came puffing up, so out of breath that he could not speak until he had pushed seven or eight wax tablets into Brother Aubrey's saddle-bag.

" There, my brother," he wheezed. " On those I charge you to make a complete record of all that happens between now and your return home."

" Me! " Brother Aubrey said incredulously.

" There are those," said Brother Robert, glaring at Ughtred, " who are indifferent to the importance of the chronicle I assiduously keep. But you, my son," he went on, " are used to scribing your thoughts on wax, and I have every confidence about entrusting the pleasant task to you."

" Pleasant! " Brother Aubrey virtually closed his hood.

The poet spoke three times only during the first eight miles of the ride. " Me, to be regarded as a vulgar news-gatherer," he cried out when the hooves of the party's horses were ringing beneath the arch of the gatehouse. " Me—supposed to have an ear for tittle-tattle."

He was next heard when the company was passing the castle to which the sub-prior had raced on the afternoon the lord abbot decided to take stern steps about the recalcitrant monk of Jervaulx.

" Me," he stormed. " Me, who has a copy of my poems in the library, well bound by Brother Ambrose."

His next offended cry came near a cliff where falcons bred, when Brother Henry alighted to pick up a specimen of glittering rock.

" And yet Brother Robert compares me with a busy-body poking his nose in everywhere," he announced bitterly. " Me, who has had a ballad approved by monkish composers as far afield as Rufford and Sawley. O Lord God, grant me a semblance of justice."

His next words, some considerable distance farther on, were of an entirely different nature. This was in the forest beyond Hovingham, where eight or nine retainers of a lord were examining the carcass of a stag, recently killed. It was not the men's arrows which had struck a noble beast, however; wolves had pulled it down, and worried it to death.

"Antlered monarch of the . . ." Brother Aubrey murmured thoughtfully. " . . . monarch of the . . ."

Since leaving Rievaulx, Ughtred had not joined in the general conversation. Lost in gloomy introspection, he had reached the conclusion that he was fast becoming an arrant liar. It was all very well striving to protect Brother Hubert, but when that involved deceit it was a different affair. Even the Lord Almighty, with all His magnanimity, could not pardon such conduct.

This mood persisted until, the character of the country steadily changing, they came to Malton, where Brother Martin pointed out the convent of the Gilbertines. Turning, Ughtred saw a religious clad similarly to the canon regular he had met when with Sister Lazelle—in a white cloak, furred at the neck, over a black habit.

". . . of the heathered hill," said Brother Aubrey.

"What? " said Ughtred.

The poet waved a hand impatiently. "Don't interrupt me, Brother Ughtred. Can't you appreciate I am in the throes? "

With no one of authority present, the party had been making the bright, cold day into an enjoyable outing, but the light was fading and it was now necessary to press on across the Wolds if a farmhouse near Wharram-le-Street, which was under contract to provide hospitality for travelling monks, was to be reached before nightfall.

The last stage was not easy. Candles were too dear for common use, and the sole light in the windows of habitations was a flicker from a fire, which did not carry far. In the end the monks of Rievaulx stumbled upon their mid-way resting place when fear was rising that they might not find it.

\*       \*       \*       \*

Suddenly, on the second day out, the forest ended, and there was a village, with a cluster of houses, a communal field, a little stream, a few lean oxen, a scattering of poultry, and a church . . . a wooden church.

The small company from Ryedale, who had been expecting a church fairly recently built of stone, brought their beasts to a halt. Behind them the two servants were grinning broadly.

" So this is Bainton," Brother Henry remarked dryly.

Affecting terror, Brother Martin crossed himself. " There is only one explanation, my brothers," he said. " An emissary of the devil has been here before us, and by his accursed magic has transformed God's house into a construction of aged timber."

Heads turned towards Brother Aubrey, whose lips were moving. He was scowling occasionally, and once, his expression lightening, he snapped finger and thumb.

" Brother Aubrey," said Brother Ranulf, repeating himself deafeningly when completely ignored, " Brother Aubrey, there is grave talk that you are in league with Belial."

" And other Satanic denizens of the bottomless pit," Ughtred supplemented.

" Of a truth we are learning much about you, Brother Aubrey," Brother Martin said sadly. " To our dread and dismay."

There was no doubt that Brother Aubrey was now paying them full attention. " What have you learned? " he asked.

Ughtred recited impressively: " Antlered monarch of the heathered peak, proud-standing with the vale below, God's own no less than . . . than . . ."

Brother Ranulf chuckled. " Within the past hour he has shortened the choice. Now he is only undecided between ' sinful man ' and ' heaven's stars above,' though if it is supposed to be night I cannot comprehend——"

" I should not expect you to," the poet said hotly. " There is a *curiosa felicitas* in the realms of pure and noble invention which is far beyond your capacity to appreciate."

Scathingly he added several more remarks to this, but most of them were drowned by laughter. " Have you done? " he said haughtily, when able to be heard. " If so, I suggest that we proceed."

Brother Henry scratched his nose. " But whither, Brother Aubrey, whither? "

"A reasonable enough inquiry, Brother Henry," Ughtred approved.

"To the point," said Brother Martin.

"Succinct," said Brother Ranulf. "Brother Aubrey, with his capacity for appreciation, will soon grasp why we pause in some doubt. Say by Vespers."

If the game had not already been given away, it was then given away by the mirth of the servants, one of whom, in his exuberance, unsheathed his sword and, with a mighty swing, clove the skull of an imagined opponent. In consequence, surprised by the flash of the blade, and delighted to have an excuse, the horses indulged themselves in spirited frisking and snorting.

"I know not this place," Brother Aubrey admitted lamely when his mount's prancing was diminishing. "I fear, my brothers, that I am lost and I ask for your forgiveness."

Ughtred smiled. "Be off yonder and make inquiries, O reliable guide to Harthill and beyond," he said. "Then we may be disposed to mercy."

The mistake was not serious, and, following a bridle path, Bainton was soon reached. The tower of the priory of Watton was seen shortly after that, just as the riders were somewhat noisily jesting about Brother Martin's anxieties—the clock expert had confided in his companions his apprehensions about what the Lady Philippa might say if he were unable to coax her clock out of its ill-humour during the limited time he would be there.

"My brothers," Brother Henry said as the gatehouse drew nearer, "we must now ride with far more decorum."

"Assuredly," Brother Ranulf agreed, pulling his hood closer.

"It would be wrong to give our orderly house an undeserved reputation for levity," Brother Martin observed righteously.

"Without question, Brother Martin," the poet Aubrey said. "But it is not ill if we conceal within our breasts that we still have a great joy in store, the thought of our ride home together. All save Brother Ughtred, for whom I am sad."

"Yes, there is that," said Brother Henry, brightening. "For myself, I do not care for lying in a strange convent, and I shall count the hours until we begin our return journey."

"And if the Almighty is as merciful to us again in giving this

231

crisp weather," said Brother Ranulf, " we shall have two more days of leisurely bliss on the road."

Experiencing a rising thrill of excitement, Ughtred's glance roved over the strange priory. What struck him immediately was the striking difference between the two halves of a very extensive range of buildings facing on to a broad courtyard, each with an arched entrance at its extreme end; the part to the left had the usual complement of windows, whereas the walls adjoining were blank, without an opening pierced in them.

This peculiarity was noticed by the others, but having regard to the intervening distance it hardly seemed essential for Brother Ranulf to lower his voice to a whisper.

" Those will be the dwelling quarters of the spouses of the Lord Christ," he said. " In the absence of windows they cannot ever inadvertently show themselves to the eyes of man."

" It is a prudent precaution," said Brother Henry. " Many ungodly wayfarers will call for alms or hospitality, and it is as well to remove temptation from the sight of the lustful, whose eyes might otherwise stray towards that upon which they are forbidden to look."

Brother Martin, who fancied his voice, called for attention by loudly clearing his throat.

" Let us sing the psalm to the chief musician, Maschil, for the sons of Korah," he proposed. " The forty-second."

" It would be fitting for us to be heard as we arrive," Ranulf said.

Brother Henry nodded to Brother Martin, who promptly began: " As the hart panteth after the water brooks, so panteth my soul after thee, O God." Then the others joined in, the volume rapidly swelling: " My soul thirsteth for God, for the living God: when shall I come and appear before God? "

So, chanting away, the monks of Rievaulx came to the Gilbertine priory of Watton; and still chanting, Brother Aubrey stooped to hammer on a wooden doorway decorated with a lacework of iron. That chanting was continued when the porter, coming out to receive them, sank to his knees, remaining on them until the final verse had been magnificently rendered.

" Why are thou cast down, O my soul? " Brother Martin sang,

starting them off. " And why art thou disquieted within me? hope thou in God: for I shall yet praise him, *who is* the health of my countenance, and my God."

The porter bowed again. " *Benedicite*," he murmured.

With slight variations only, the reception of visitors was much the same at Watton as at Rievaulx. After the usual ceremonies in the almonry the saddle-bags were taken off the horses, who were later led by servants to the stables. The guest master then conducted the party to the chapel of the canons regular, where he sprinkled them with holy water and stayed with them for prayers.

Before starting out for the customary tour of the convent, the strangers looked round the chapel, a cheerless place whose most notable feature was an ante-chapel with a gallery. There was a modest amount of carving of the York school, outstandingly at the back of the stalls, and a passable sculpture of The Annunciation of the Virgin Mary.

Next, when in the cloister, the guests stopped at the north walk lavatory to remove travel stains. The basins were of marble, and fluted. Most attractive, they made a welcome talking point.

The refectory was not a handsome apartment, with hardly a wall decoration or picture. It was possible, however, to comment favourably on the pattern of a number of niches in the wall, each containing a novel feature hewn in the form of a bird. The most was made of these.

But the dormitory of the canons earned quite genuine approval. It was built over the warming place, and so heated to a limited extent.

" A great improvement on ours, Reverend Father," Brother Henry said emphatically.

" In our cells, Reverend Father, we have nothing to temper the chills of the night," said Brother Ranulf.

" Oh! that is not quite correct," Brother Martin said. " The novices do have a fire in the song school beneath us at snow-time."

" At the most, twice a week, Brother Martin," Ughtred said.

" And then it is never replenished within an hour of the bell ringing for Vespers," said Brother Aubrey.

" And if the novices are so comfortably accommodated."

Brother Ranulf remarked devastatingly, " why is it that we see them endeavouring to obtain a morsel of cheer at the back of our own warming place, farthest from the fire. By my faith, Brother Martin! "

Brother Henry snorted at the discomfited clock-mender before turning to their guide. " I must repeat, Reverend Father, that this fine dormitory of yours is an immense improvement on what we have."

The guest master was not deceived. " My own sleeping chamber is at the guest house, where I can ensure I am more pleasantly situated than the majority of obedientiaries and canons," he remarked, adding with distinct irony: " Nevertheless it surprises me to learn that here at Watton we have anything superior to what your great foundation can offer, at least on this side. Unhappily, after we have descended the night-stairs to the chapel again, our next stop will be at the chapter house, where I feel very safe in asserting that you will have nothing to enthuse about."

It was so, too. Fortunately the guest master was called into the east walk before the stage was reached when his charges felt themselves under the need to frame a suitably polite comment.

" Never," said Brother Ranulf after glancing at the door, " *never* have I known a convent in which poverty is cried out so much aloud. Have you, Brother Ughtred, who has travelled so widely? "

Ughtred shook his head. " It is so, Brother Ranulf."

" If you are to illuminate prettily as it should be, Brother Ughtred," Brother Aubrey remarked, " you will be here for years, not a few weeks."

" I doubt, unless Our Saviour is gentle to him, if we would ever see our beloved brother again," said Brother Henry, barely stifling a groan. " Moreover we still have to view the church the reverend canons share with the most blessed nuns, and I am fast running out of kindly platitudes."

" What perplexes me is how they can share a church, if they are forbidden to meet," Brother Ranulf muttered.

" I know nothing of their arrangements," Brother Henry said.

When the guest master returned it was with the news that the prioress desired them to attend on her. A second messenger would be sent when she was ready to receive them.

" In the meantime, my sons," he continued, " we will walk to the church, where I have intimated you will await the Lady Philippa's commands."

They left the cloister by an exit beyond the church door, a passage which, as soon as the prior's lodging had been left behind, became a pillared alley with a roof over. This parade, to the right of which was a bowls court and a cemetery, with the canons' garden on the left, kept in a straight line until it bent sharply at the east end of the church, where Brother Henry noticed that the stones of the fabric were of considerable interest, geologically speaking.

" Fossils! " he exclaimed, probing to the detriment of his finger nail. " Ammonites of the genus of cephalopods unless I am gravely at fault. Reverend Father, have you knowledge where these stones came from? Were they quarried not far from the sea? "

" I regret I cannot assist you, my son," said the guest master. " But it is possible you might obtain information from the archives in the library. Later, if you so desire, I will take you to the reverend father, the cantor, who I am sure will gladly help if he can."

Brother Henry bowed. " I would be most grateful, Reverend Father."

A larger vista opened out when round the corner of the building: a few upper windows of " the other side " of the Double Order of Saint Gilbert of Sempringham could be seen, but an extremely lofty wall, separating the two enclosures, cut off the prospect lower down.

" I suppose, Reverend Father," Brother Aubrey said, " that the gardens of the holy ladies will be over there? "

" That is so, my son. Latterly laid out in the form of the Garden of Gethsemane, or as near as lavish expenditure made it feasible."

" The gardens resemble Gethsemane? " the poet said, much intrigued. " What an enchanting conception, Reverend Father."

" Whether enchanting or otherwise it is a conceit of My Lady the prioress," the guest master remarked sourly. " And I regret to have to confide in you that the effort disorganised the routine of our out-door servants for two summers, to the considerable loss of the convent."

As a result of this ill-tempered disclosure there was a certain amount of eye-brow raising and trying to catch the eyes of companions as the monks of Rievaulx went into the church, but once inside everything else was forgotten in a common amazement. It was lengthy, but so restricted for width that there was only a single line of stalls at each side, so narrow its central gangway that the hems of flowing robes, such as albs for ceremonial occasions, must have brushed against the reading desks in front of each stall. In fact, it was a thin slice lengthwise of the whole building; the dividing wall, of well over a man's height, was carried to the flat roof by an open, stone arcade, and through the arches it was possible to see that the roof adjacent stretched farther than that above their heads.

" The nuns' church, my sons," the guest master said tartly, " is decidedly more commodious than this. It has also, which you cannot perceive, a separate High Altar of its own. "

" What is beyond the other side of the church, Reverend Father? " Brother Aubrey inquired.

" Apart from a private chapel, a precise facsimile of what we have to the east, my son," said the guest master. " Cloister with garth, chapter house, refectory, dormitory, kitchen and other domestic ranges."

The party had now reached the crossing, where there were two openings in the inner wall, one a massive wood door covered with a scroll pattern-work in iron, a mode of decoration the convent appeared to favour; the other opening was much smaller, filled with a turntable device none of them had come across before.

" The large doorway, my sons," the guest master explained, " is for use at funerals, and on days of feasts, when there are processions."

" On days of feasts, Reverend Father," Brother Aubrey asked, " do the canons regular mingle with the community at the other side? "

" The Lord God forbid," said the guest master, palpably aghast. " We are together, it is true, but there are the strictest safeguards against any manner of intercourse whatsoever."

Brother Martin, as always captivated by anything mechanical, was rotating the turntable. It fitted so snugly in its circular cavity that, as he remarked in all innocence after trying to peer at several places, it would be impossible to obtain the merest glimpse of anyone in the north portion of the church.

" That is why it is arranged thus," the guest master said cuttingly.

" What is it used for, Reverend Father? " Brother Aubrey asked.

The guest master was still staring austerely at Brother Martin. " It is where our sisters in the Lord take holy water and receive the *pax*. There they are communicated, too, the table serving for passing the sacred vessels."

Ughtred, who had gone as far forward as the steps to the presbytery, was thinking that the sacred vessels were not likely to be of prime quality if judged by the High Altar. He was becoming depressed; the only ornamentation of any consequence in the church were a few sculptures hewn out of large stones in the wall, amongst them an owl with a human face, and a fox racing off with a goose. To add a wall picture or two would merely emphasise, he decided, the dreariness of the whole.

Preoccupied, he did not hear Brother Henry until the latter had hissed thrice. Turning, Ughtred saw that his companions and the guest master were kneeling, and then he made haste. The prior of Watton, for it could be no other, was advancing up the aisle, habit flapping. His expression of discontentment and barely suppressed rage was that which seemed to characterise so many of the canons regular of the convent.

" My Lord," said the guest master, " these are the monks of Rievaulx, who have brought a new pastoral staff for My Lady."

" You have conveyed it hither safely, my sons? " the prior asked. " You had no misadventures on the journey? "

" None at all, My Lord," said Brother Henry.

Since leaving home, Brother Ranulf had refused to be parted from the precious package for even a second.

" I have it here, My Lord," he said. " Exactly as it was when we departed."

" No doubt I shall feast my eyes on it before very long," the prior remarked sarcastically. " Which of you is the monk Ughtred? "

Ughtred bowed. " I am, My Lord."

"You are here to embellish the convent to the Lady Philippa's wishes, my son," said the prior. "What think you of the task?"

"I shall do my utmost, My Lord," Ughtred said uncomfortably. The prior, laughing mirthlessly, threw up his arm. "Have no fear, my son," he said. "Your talents are not to be exercised at this side, where even a genius could make no impression . . . no, not if he had a score pairs of hands and as many lifetimes."

With that, he turned on his heel and swept away. No one spoke until he had left the church.

"Reverend Father," Brother Aubrey said with fetching courtesy. "If it would please you I would be overjoyed if you would satisfy my curiosity on certain matters."

"I will try, my son," the guest master said most amenably.

"One is this, Reverend Father," the poet said. "If I were wishing, as an example, to send a verse to the other side, how would I accomplish it? If I were carrying the parchment on which the verses were penned, by what path would I proceed?"

The guest master's expression had grown more forbidding, but he answered. If the processional door in the church were unlocked, he said, it was but a few steps to the nuns' cloister; if the door at the west end of the church chanced also not to be locked, the prioress's lodging could quickly be reached. And if it were merely the handing over of the parchment aforementioned, the speediest procedure would be to take it along the east adit as far as the turnover house, where the custodian would pass it through to the custodian on duty in the west adit.

"Reverend Father, what are these adits?" Brother Aubrey asked.

"By Saint Gilbert," the guest master growled. "Are you another?"

Startled, Brother Aubrey stepped back half a pace. "I don't comprehend, Reverend Father. I inquire about these strange adits, of which we have nothing of the name at home."

The guest master struggled to hold himself in, but failed. "Nor have you virginal maidens," he shouted. "But I warn you, my son, that I have smelled out your drift, and if it should be that you make any attempt to converse with them either in person or by a note, not even your lord abbot would be able to save you from our wrath . . . no, nor even the lady prioress, though I will allow that even she would never oppose the vengeance we should submit you to. We——"

"Reverend Father, you wholly misunderstand him," Ughtred broke in urgently. "To us, living our monkish lives, all this is novel and strange, and all my brother was doing was as he said—to satisfy his curiosity."

Terrified, ashen-cheeked, Brother Aubrey was trembling. "That is all it is, Reverend Father," he gasped. "I have neither the intention of intruding myself upon the Lord Christ's brides nor of writing about their beauty and charms as a knight engages a scrivener to write about his fair lady."

"What foul and decadent monster have we here in the guise of a saintly monk?" the guest master bellowed. "What talk is this of the beauty and charm of nuns? What——"

Ughtred intervened again: "With all respect, Reverend Father, he did not speak in that sense, and as the Lord is above us I declare to you that Brother Aubrey is no more than one who has an inquisitive mind."

The guest master ignored this. Savagely he pointed out that never had a breath of scandal hung over the convent, which spoke volumes for the careful watch that was always maintained.

"I tell you," he continued ferociously, "that if he attempts to penetrate the secrets of the veiled he will be seized before he has taken twelve strides in his design, and if he is so apprehended, monk of proud Rievaulx notwithstanding, he will suffer the torments of the damned, and none will dare interfere."

"Reverend Father," said Brother Henry, "we have lived for long with Brother Aubrey . . ."

"And we know him well," said Brother Ranulf.

"He is not of the base character you imply, Reverend Father," said Brother Martin.

"It is not even worth discussing, Reverend Father," Ughtred wound up, "but if it must be it would be as well if done temperately."

The guest master could not have looked more surprised if he had been struck. "You are rebuking *me*, Sir Monk?" he stormed. "You are charging me with being loud-mouthed? That is a gross insult and a lie to boot, and I shall at once lodge a complaint with My Lord the prior."

"And I shall accompany you on your mission, Reverend Father," Ughtred said grimly. "And when accompanying you I shall have no hesitation in restraining you if you attempt to wipe off the spittle which still dribbles from your chin."

Long-held breath, released by Brothers Martin and Ranulf, could be heard in the silence. But Brother Henry was of different metal.

"It is there, for everyone to behold," he grunted. "We would all accompany you, Brother Ughtred."

"There is another end to this, Brother Henry," Ughtred remarked easily. "Is this the rude fashion in which we, guests of the convent, should be treated by the guest master? Leastways, not how we were taught."

Brother Henry clicked his tongue. "A guest is to be honoured, Brother Ughtred, above all else."

"I think, Brother Henry, that if a personage even as exalted as our own most revered prior had so offended, My Lord would have had him on the cross for a whipping," Ughtred murmured.

Conflicting emotions had passed over the guest master's face, but he had not the appearance of one who would brave it out, and colour was receding from his cheeks faster than it came.

"Cistercians!" he whispered. "It has always been my opinion that it is a scurvy Order, and I tell you I am not without consolation in having my opinion confirmed."

Ughtred shook his head sadly. "The Loving Shepherd, who knows all our manifold weaknesses, is more kind to us, Reverend Father," he said. "But My Lord Hugh is a great and distinguished abbot of the Order, and I fear that the Lady Philippa, his blood cousin, will be less tolerant if we acquaint her with your views."

The guest master licked his lips. "I have fears also, my son," he said, with a travesty of a smile. "I fear that . . . that in my solicitude for our beloved virgin spouses I have become more heated than is proper."

"It is understandable, Reverend Father," Ughtred said. "You have, and all at this side, a most taxing and onerous responsibility."

"It bears heavily, very heavily, my son," said the guest master.

Differences had been patched up to this extent when footsteps were heard, those of a lay sister walking up the aisle. She came to inform the monks of Rievaulx that the prioress now expected them.

After bowing to the guest master, the five brethren followed her to the west end of the church, and through a dark passage. They emerged in an extensive, paved yard, with a solid, double-gate on the right and postern on the left, leading respectively to the outer court and the nuns' garden. The prioress's lodging, a fine building, was in the centre of the yard.

The interview with the Lady Philippa was short, but satisfactory enough for Brother Ranulf's face to be wreathed in smiles when they reached the church again, where he fumbled for his tablet and style to record her comments for the edification of his collaborators at home.

" Carving more exquisite than I have ever seen, and gold saints of incomparable delicacy . . . that's for Brothers Theobald and Ailfy," he was muttering when, glancing up, he saw Ughtred near. " Oh! to-morrow morning, Brother Ughtred, when you attend on the Lady Philippa after the Daily Chapter, will you have the kindness to thank her for her graciousness? She struck me all of a heap with the generosity of her praise. . . . I think she abashed me as well, Brother Ughtred. I have never heard of a lady religious like her, still less set eyes on one."

" It shall be done, Brother Ranulf," Ughtred promised.

Brother Henry, after a few words with the guest master, had gone off to find the cantor, and Brother Martin for his tools. And to Ughtred, reflecting, it seemed that at Watton they would be left very much to their own resources, which was extraordinarily different from the care and attention the Benedictine brothers of St. Mary's lavished on their guests.

With nothing better to do for the moment, he and Brother Aubrey started on a round of exploration, which ended in the refectory. While descending the steps to the north walk of the cloister both noticed a passage they had missed before, and as a canon was nearby the opportunity was taken to inquire where it went.

" It leads to the turnover house, and is called the east adit," he told them coldly before resuming his way. " There is nothing along there which will interest my brothers of Rievaulx."

Brother Aubrey shook his head. " Over haughty, aren't they, Brother Ughtred? " he said. " How does he know what will or will not interest us? Let us walk along and satisfy ourselves."

These were the hours for work and recreation, and there was a considerable gathering along two of the walks. The canons regular of Watton were reading or quietly talking, and the prior was sitting on his seat near the chapel door.

" By all means, Brother Aubrey," Ughtred said. " No prohibition is on us, so why not? "

The east adit was a lengthy corridor with a line of small windows too high to be looked out of, and to increase the light the rough stones of the walls were whitewashed. Mid-way between the two branches of the convent a doorless wall was built athwart the way; in the wall were two openings, one very small and the other containing a turntable similar to that the visitors had inspected in the church.

At the side of the adit, close to the barrier, was a stone bench, on which an elderly canon had been sitting, with his nose almost touching an illuminated copy of the Gospel of Saint Wilfred. Hearing footsteps, he turned, rose and peered at the oncoming couple.

" What is your business? " he demanded.

" We are monks of——" Ughtred began.

" God has not taken my sight from me and I can see who you are," the old man said irascibly. " I asked you your business."

Before Ughtred could deal courteously with this question, there was an interruption. A bell tinkled and, muttering with annoyance, the canon opened a shutter in the small opening, so disclosing a grille with tiny holes in it. An aged, feminine voice from beyond said: " Here you are, Father, and, praise the Lord, it is a very good brew this time, as I can vouch," and before the old fellow could get out another word after " Stay . . ." the shutter behind the grille clicked into position. Within a few seconds the turntable started slowly to rotate, and a brimming tankard came into view. A small incident, perhaps, but it transformed the recipient of the ale into a small boy caught in a misdemeanour.

Ughtred bowed. " Our regrets, good Father," he said. " With your permission we will now withdraw."

When a discreet distance on the way back, Brother Aubrey leaned nearer to Ughtred. " I have no malice in my heart, Brother Ughtred, but I am afraid I think there must be more kindliness at the other side than at this. What evil were we contemplating when we strolled along here, what harm would it have done had it been possible for us to glance at the adit leading to those described by Saint Paul in his writings as ' the virgins whom you shall call widows? ' "

Ughtred eyed him. " I am beginning to think the reverend father the guest master had grounds for wondering about your incessant questioning, Brother Aubrey. To me also you seem to thirst for knowledge of the Gilbertine nuns."

" I do," Brother Aubrey said promptly.

" How so? " said Ughtred.

" I am writing a poem, Brother Ughtred, and without bragging I believe it is destined to be an epic."

Ughtred smiled. " What of the other, the one that kept you in a trance for the greater part of our ride? Is that discarded? "

" For the nonce," said the poet. " At the present I am engaged in the preliminaries of a much nobler affair. Listen, Brother Ughtred."

" I am all attention," Ughtred said gravely.

Brother Aubrey began:

> " In yonder green oasis, sinful man,
> Virginal brides in an unseen Gethsemane,
> Barred from such as you, they be
> Who live as monks bespoke to God!
> Those holy maids, how sweet they are,
> How very sweet those holy maids."

" No more," Ughtred said sharply.

Four of the Watton brethren, arms clasped behind their backs, were approaching. Bows were exchanged as the parties met, when Ughtred noticed that none of the canons looked at him. Four pairs of eyes gazed piercingly at his fellow Cistercian, heads even turning as they passed by, perhaps to ram home more clearly an unspoken warning.

" They stared at me most oddly, Brother Ughtred," the poet said. " I did not care for it at all."

" You were declaiming mightly, on that which would rouse them," Ughtred said. " Moreover I think they followed us here because they had heard of your interest beforehand from the guest master."

" It is right that they should guard the widows of Christ zealously," said Brother Aubrey. " But I mean no harm."

Ughtred sighed. " Yes, they guard them with zeal," he murmured.

When in the cloister again they learned that the discipline of the canons was no less severe than their own. Still sitting near the chapel door, the prior was interrogating a white-faced young fellow charged with separating from a companion when in Beverley.

" You are aware that you broke a statute? " the prior said. " Answer."

" Yes, My Lord," the culprit muttered.

" What is the purport of that statute? "

" So that we may watch over the other's conduct, My Lord," the young canon said wretchedly.

The prior raised his hand. Four hardbitten-seeming seniors came forward to march the defaulter to the chapter house, their stern superior in the rear. In time, the punishment did not take long, but must have been remarkably efficacious, for when the victim re-appeared he looked as though half the life had been flogged out of him.

In the chapel, to which they had gone afterwards, Brother Aubrey came to a decision.

" I have all I need and I shall not ask further about the other side," he said, shuddering. " Nor shall I continue with my epic poem until I am on the way home. It is futile to dream of conjuring up fine sentiments in an atmosphere filled with nonsensical suspicion."

" I think you are wise, my brother," Ughtred said. " In its place, why not start the chronicle? " His eyes twinkled at Brother Aubrey's expression. " The chronicle Brother Robert asked for."

Brother Aubrey flushed with annoyance. " You fall in my

regard, Brother Ughtred, if you imagine I would lend myself to paltry purveying."

But he soon recovered his good humour, and began to speak about the Lady Philippa, a sensitive female who would have been tenderly sympathetic about his poem had she known of it.

Ughtred was also thinking about the Lady Philippa, wondering how she could take him round her convent when, at the canons' side, the slightest inquiry about the nunnery raised the most profound antagonism.

The answer was obtained the next morning, during which he did not so much as glimpse a fleeting flash of the habit of a dedicated lady. At every passage entrance, or open doorway, a lay sister stood on guard; but he did hear sounds occasionally, as if a flock of the holy brides was being ushered from his path.

That tour with the Lady Philippa was an eye-opener to Ughtred, for never could the two halves of a convent have provided a more striking contrast, the one ugly, the other near to beautiful, though perhaps lacking colour. In the chapter house nothing could have surpassed the perfection of a figure of the Blessed Virgin on a pedestal, with an angel on each side; and the reader's pulpit in the refectory, made of blue marble, would have been a considerable acquisition even to Rievaulx.

The church, on the nuns' side, was glorious, with a profusion of crosses and reliquaries blazing with precious stones; the High Altar, with a magnificent canopy, stood out superbly against a fine screen; and the array of sacred vessels, gold chalices, censers and cups, could not have been more impressive, especially as many were jewelled. Silver candlesticks were in abundance, some six or seven feet in height; and the effigy of the Virgin Mary and the Infant Christ, near the door, was breathtaking in its lines.

Here, the Lady Philippa was principally interested in a stretch of wall from the cloister doorway to the corner of the north transept. For this, from Ughtred's drawings sent to her by Abbot Hugh, she had chosen: *An Angel Laying Hold of the Dragon which is Satan.*

Ughtred jerked himself out of his reverie, which was about the canons' bitterness. He thought they had substance for complaint.

" My Lady," he said, " there I would be working in a different medium, and the warmth of summer is the only time for it."

" Nonsense."

" It is so, My Lady," Ughtred said firmly.

" Have I not told you that you are talking nonsense," the prioress snapped. " Let me hear no more."

" My Lady," Ughtred resumed doggedly, " the winter is not yet over, and many nights of frost may still be anticipated."

Dame Philippa turned to him, but her veil was too thick for him to see her expression and, uneasily, he wondered how she was taking his opposition.

" You are a very stubborn young fellow," she remarked.

" No, My Lady," Ughtred said earnestly, " but I would not have the start of the picture crumble before I had finished its end."

" My son," the Lady Philippa said patiently, " have you never heard of charcoal burners? They will be kept burning day and night. Does that stifle your objections? Speak out."

" Yes, My Lady," Ughtred said. " But . . . but . . ."

The prioress sighed as she flicked a speck from her cloak. The garment was made from a soft stuff, of bishop's purple to match her head-dress, and, fastened only by a large, diamond-studded brooch at her throat, gaped below to reveal a habit in malachite green.

" What is it now, my son? " she asked.

" How . . . how may I work, My Lady? " Ughtred said. " When frequently throughout the hours of daylight——"

" That reminds me, my son," the Lady Philippa interposed. " You will attend Prime with the brethren of the other side, but after that you are excused all observance until Compline. Nor will you rise during the night for Matins and Lauds."

" My Lady," Ughtred said tentatively, " that may not please My Lord the prior, the more so as when my brothers depart for home I am to leave the guest house for a cell in the canons' dormitory."

" In that case we would have to move you into the dormitory over here."

" My Lady! " Ughtred gasped.

The Lady Philippa's silvery laughter rang out very clearly, but when she spoke her voice had become steely.

" If there are objections," she said, " you may be sure I shall dispose of them. Now what was it you were trying to tell me about your work? "

" My Lady," said Ughtred, " how can I work in here when the holy maidens will be constantly present for the prescribed Hours? "

" That is quite simple, my son," the Lady Philippa said. " You will wear a thick veil."

" A . . . a veil, a thick veil," Ughtred stuttered. " But if I have a thick veil——"

My Lord's blood cousin laughed again, immoderately, and while Ughtred was thinking that Friar Jerome was not the only one hard to understand, at least at the beginning, she told him that carpenters would erect tight screens to hide him from sight.

" All will be ready for you within a few days," she ended.

" Yes, My Lady," Ughtred said.

The Lady Philippa signed to a lay-sister standing near the entrance to the prison cells below the oratory in the west walk.

" That is all, my son," she said.

Ughtred bowed before following his conductor into the silent cloister, and along an entry as far as a postern guarded by My Lady's own yard porter. From there he crossed to a small door, so coming into the narrow passage he had been through before. At the extreme end there was another door to be unlocked, when once again he was at the canons' side, in the west end of their church.

When walking slowly round the building towards the pentise and approach to the cloister, Ughtred thought of Sister Lazelle, so near and yet so far. On the ride down he had told himself sternly that there was no hope of their meeting, but in his heart had never accepted it. Now, complete and crushing, he realised there was no possible prospect of seeing her even for a few stolen moments.

" It is sinful of me to repine about it," he told himself, repining none the less. " I have vowed myself to God for the span of my mortal life, and she no less. O God, forgive me, and in your bountiful mercy extend to me your pardon for forgetting this thing."

Sighing deeply, he increased his stride and went to discover how Brother Martin was faring with the clock. Soon his companions would be starting for home, which for him would be the beginning of a strange and lonely existence.

Brother Martin, who did succeed with the Lady Philippa's clock, left for Rievaulx with the others two days before the Purification, a feast marked at Watton by a dinner of pheasant and spiced wild boar, and on the afternoon of the day following the celebration Ughtred was able to start work, busying himself to begin with on the preliminary lay-out of the immense wall-painting in the church. As day succeeded day he became more absorbed in what he was doing, a form of compensation for which he sent up many a prayer of thanksgiving.

Despite this concentration, however, there were often times when a sense of the queerness of his situation in the nuns' quire flooded him. It was odd to know that when he heard footsteps Sister Lazelle's must surely be amongst those making them; tantalising to feel that often, within arm's length, she would be passing by. And during the singing and chanting of the Offices, when the deeper voices of the more distant canons regular were muted by the dividing wall and open arcade, and the nuns', though higher, seemed so much stronger, he strained in vain to pick out Sister Lazelle's.

Ughtred had several callers, some surprising, from time to time. The first, a grey-striped cat which crawled in beneath the cloth screen; the second to arrive—half-way through the *Magna Missa*, a dog of the like he had never seen before, woolly-haired and truly a toy of a dog; and third, a kestrel hawk, which surveyed him unblinkingly for the best part of an hour.

" It could not be, could it," he muttered incredulously, " that the holy brides bring them into the church? But what else could they be other than pets, and if so why were they not safely secured beforehand? "

His fourth visitor, a few days later, made his heart beat joyously, for no one except Sister Lazelle would be at such pains to steal on him silently, for his sake and hers. Just then, when he heard a quiet drawing aside where two of the screening sheets met, he was on the floor, trying to re-touch the hem of the angel's drapery more to his liking. Fearful that he might cry his delight too loudly, he was remaining where he was, striving to compose himself, when a lingering hand on his shoulder caused him to glance round.

Ughtred saw a bear, a large and nearly full-grown bear.

" Jesus! " he gasped, springing up.

From a very short distance, his legs beginning to tremble, he stared into a pair of small eyes, and, sweat pouring down his forehead, remained rooted where he was. So they looked at each other, the lumbering animal and a very frightened man.

Ughtred's lips moved as he noticed the cruel claws and the powerful, furry forelegs. His lips moved.

" May the Lord have mercy on me," he whispered.

The bear had grown weary. With a light cuff he sent Ughtred sprawling, with another sent a jar on a bench flying; and, sniffing in a bucket, emerged with nose and whiskers dripping blue. Then, grunting to himself, he dropped on all fours and shambled away, his passage through the overfold in the screen promising to take everything with him, cloth sheeting and timber supports.

Ughtred knuckled the moisture out of his eyes. " Never in a few short months can any man have experienced what I have, no, not even a secular man," he muttered. " And I thank you, O Lord, for your mercy in safeguarding me, my Shepherd, my God."

It was not until later that he fell to puzzling. It seemed impossible to credit that holy brides would be allowed to have pets, which would distract them from their devotions; and even more fantastic was it to suppose that a bear would ever be present at any one of the seven daily Offices. One thing did seem clear, though—this convent of Watton was a queer place indeed.

# 6

It was High Mass on the first Sunday in Lent. The salt and water had been blessed, mixed and the sisterhood sprinkled. Magnificent new pastoral staff in hand, the prioress was on the point of leaving the church, with a party of four, to make a round of the domestic apartments and offices.

Daydreaming, Sister Lazelle might have played havoc with the orderliness of the proceedings if Sister Hilda had not given her a healthy push towards the gold ewer she was to carry in the train of Dame Philippa. The incident was not noticed, and thereafter all was well. While the majority remained in the nuns' quire chanting, the prioress did her duty as laid down: sprinkling each chamber she went into and saying an appropriate prayer, beginning by entering the chapter house through a beautiful doorway, coloured and picked out in gold. In this manner the dormitory, refectory and kitchen were also blessed, as were ailing sisters in the infirmary.

As soon as the small company returned to the church the remainder of the community formed in behind, in pairs, and a far extending procession did two complete circuits of the four walks of the cloister before a final round of the church, where a lengthy, screened off portion was passed in which, had it not been a day of reverence, a strange monk would have been working on a painting about which all were agog.

In due course, the bell rang for dinner: a piece of cheese and a small portion of bread, with a drink either of ale or milk, little enough to stave off the hunger of those who, earlier, groaned at the sight of the *mixtum*, a pittance which, during Lent, served as breakfast. In addition to this food the servers had laid at each place a dish containing half a pound of ginger and a pound each of raisins and dates, an annual Lenten bequest to the nuns of Watton willed by a long-dead draper of Great Driffield. Inevitably, each year, his kindly foresight caused a dilemma for many of those benefited.

" For myself," said Sister Maud, while appearing to be listening intently to the reader at the desk, " I hold off as long as I am able, and then I devour the lot."

Speaking was forbidden in the refectory, but Sister Maud enjoyed a unique gift. While masticating freely, for all to see, she could also speak extremely softly.

By signs, which took time, Sister Sibilla indicated, with some superiority, that she spread out the bounty evenly through Lent. She was a most prim person, but had a tongue capable of causing mischief.

" Do you grasp that, Sister Lazelle?" Sister Maud said as caustically as her mode of speech allowed. " Who would believe that only yesterday she was telling us each in turn, *confidentially*, that Sister Beatrice must have a most *unusual* reason for so often petitioning to have the prior receive her at the church for confession."

While Sister Sibilla was shaking her head in shocked repudiation, Sister Lazelle managed to convey a message to Sister Katherine, whose Puchin had managed to work his head out of the neck of her habit, at the back. The monkey was hastily dragged out of sight as soon as the message was understood.

When addressed, Sister Lazelle edged her napkin to the floor and, while groping for it, kept her eyes fixed on the sub-prioress, who was sitting at the high table.

" I think we should tell Sister Beatrice how Sister Sibilla worries about her," she whispered mischievously. " I'm sure Sister Beatrice would soon persuade her there was nothing to fret about."

Sister Edith joined in: " If Sister Beatrice couldn't, her Brussie might take a hand," she said from her mouth corner. " He doesn't like people who don't like Sister Beatrice."

Still stooping, Sister Lazelle was not entirely successful in biting off a laugh, partly because of the bear being drawn into this matter, and partly because of Sister Sibilla's extraordinary contortions as she tried soundlessly to demonstrate how wrong they were about her.

By then the Reverend Sister Melania, sitting at a table opposite, had begun to watch suspiciously, but fortunately the ringing of the bell signalled the end of the meal, and a second bell sent the community into church for grace.

As the remaining Sundays, Wednesdays and Fridays of Lent were to be, this was a day of endless processions, and before Vespers the sisters had done many barefooted circuits of the cloister and other penitential exercises, with a short respite only in the afternoon when the Reverend Sister Naomi, opening the book aumbry, distributed reading matter appropriate for the period.

Monday, following Quadragesima, was much easier, all the Offices so much conforming to the normal that, during Lady Mass, Lazelle was able to recite almost mechanically while her glance stayed more or less constantly on the screen behind which Brother Ughtred must be working. On that side the stalls had been taken out, and as Lazelle was in the rear rank of the double row now set up at the other, she had no fear of arousing suspicion in the minds of the Reverend Sister Melania and others of the four mistresses, and still less was troubled about My Lady and the various underprioresses and obedientiaries who were much higher up the church, towards the Holy Sanctuary.

Subsequently, in the chapter house, both during the reading of the Daily Chapter and when the affairs of the house were under discussion, Lazelle had to *seem* more attentive. Nevertheless, between the fourth prioress complaining that latterly the chanting had become too quick, and Sister Paula vehemently objecting to a girl from Stamford Bridge—her own neighbourhood—being considered for admission as a novice, on the grounds of not being from a good enough family, Lazelle decided she must before long make a supreme effort to have a talk with Brother Ughtred. From this it was only a short step for her to fix that afternoon for the attempt.

" Yes, I shall try," she said to herself, excitement rising. " It will be easier while Brother Ughtred is working in the church than when he is painting elsewhere. Yes, this afternoon I shall try."

Meantime, various matters of business were being deliberated. Two merchants, Manent Francisci of Florence and Bartholemew Grimbaldi of Chieri, had submitted contracts for the season's clip, but the prioress was of the opinion that the prices were not good enough.

" Two-thirds of our revenue comes from wool, which makes it all the more necessary for us to obtain the very best return possible, my daughters," the Lady Philippa pointed out. " Unhappily costs are ever rising—the hospitality and alms we gladly give to travellers and the needy is year by year becoming more of a burden, and always it is incumbent on us to continue to clothe our beloved house, and all matters appertaining to it, to the greater glory of the Lord."

" That is so, My Lady," said the third prioress. " But still, My Lady, tender roe in the pie is more toothsome than a fish in the sea, and the offers of Messrs. Francisci and Grimbaldi are not to be despised."

The Lady Philippa laughed. " Far from it, my daughter," she said. " All I propose is that we keep them in suspense while using them as a lever with the Flemings."

" Whom we used as a lever to persuade Messrs. Francisci and Grimbaldi to think again," the Reverend Sister Naomi said with a smile. " But we are weak defenceless women, My Lady, and so must use our wiles as best we may."

" Exactly, my dear daughter," said Dame Philippa. " *Exactly*."

The next item concerned the moneylender Antony Richi of London, who was threatening, in default of immediate payment of five hundred pounds, to levy on the convent's lands and chattels.

" The insolence," the sub-prioress said angrily.

Deeply worried, the third prioress rose. " But, My Lady," she asked, bowing, " what shall we do? Many weeks must pass before we can draw against our wool."

The Lady Philippa was able to reassure her. She had had, she said, several conversations with the noble-spirited clerk, Geoffrey Bewsley, whom they all knew visited Watton several times each year. He had most willingly promised a loan of a thousand pounds for two years; it was to be without interest during the first year, but ten per cent would be added for the second.

" A thousand pounds, My Lady? " the Reverend Sister Joanna gasped.

" I had thought it prudent to have a little extra in hand, my daughter," the Lady Philippa explained.

The Reverend Sister Blanche, who dealt with accounts, observed that it was most desirable. There were, she added, a number of tradesmen, including jewellers, who were importuning to a deplorable extent.

" It is good, My Lady, that thanks to God we have such a powerful and influential friend," she ended.

"And wealthy also," the Lady Philippa said. " Yes, he is a good and true friend, my daughter."

" I have always known he was that, My Lady, though I have never spoken to him," said the Reverend Sister Melania. " Ever since he presented the convent with a magnificent bed for your chamber in your lodging, My Lady."

The sub-prioress closed her eyes ecstatically. " Never have I seen so roomy a bed, My Lady. As for elegance, it is more superb than that my respected father bequeathed to my second brother in his will."

" Of such wonderful beauty and comfort, my daughters," the Lady Philippa said solemnly, " that often before I sink into slumber I send up a prayer for the safety and well-being of our most generous benefactor."

" No less could be expected," the Reverend Sister Naomi murmured.

The prioress nodded. " What have we next? " she asked briskly.

To many, these exchanges had been most boring, but everyone woke up when the Reverend Sisters Blanche and Joanna, sent to the prison cells beneath the oratory in the west walk of the cloister, brought back a nun who was under sentence of being transferred to the Gilbertine priory at Sempringham for punishment.

With the two mistresses at each side of her, the culprit, a heavy-faced young woman, was placed so that she was standing mid-way between the end stalls, looking towards the prioress's chair.

" Have you repented, my daughter? " the Lady Philippa asked sternly.

" I ask God's mercy and yours," Sister Amiccia said stubbornly. " But I have nothing to repent about, My Lady."

" My daughter," said the Lady Philippa, " you will know that I never allow anyone to cast a slur on this beloved foundation of ours. That is why, swearing before the Almighty, you must withdraw the monstrous charge you have made."

Sister Amiccia shook her head decidedly. " Before the Lord

Jesus, I cannot, or I would imperish my immortal soul, My Lady, and I repeat, My Lady, that Sister Hilda has been consorting with little Canon Alfie."

There was a flurry of activity farther down the chapter house, as a buxom young woman jumped up impetuously.

"My Lady," she cried resentfully, "must we have more of this? I have explained, My Lady——"

The Lady Philippa waved her down before turning her attention to Amiccia again.

"My daughter," she said, hard put to keep her temper, "have I not assured you that your sister-in-God Hilda is no more familiar with Canon Alfred than you are yourself?"

Sister Amiccia crowed triumphantly. "Then why, My Lady, does she speak of our brother in the Lord as being *little*, and why has she told of his brown eyes?"

Sighing deeply, the prioress glanced despairingly at her under-prioresses and the four mistresses.

"My daughter," she said, "how many more times must I tell you that Sister Hilda, when a young girl, knew our brother Alfred when he was only a boy. There is no more to it than that."

Convinced to the contrary, Sister Amiccia released what she most obviously considered to be a devasting shaft.

"She speaks of him as Alfie, My Lady," she said slyly.

The Lady Philippa lost patience. "Take her away," she snapped. "And, my daughter Melania, make arrangements for her to go down to Lincolnshire as soon as possible. We have had enough of her foolishness."

While the reverend sister was making a note on her tablet, the prioress inquired if there was anything else.

"With humility, yes," the Reverend Sister Naomi said, after prostrating herself. "This afternoon, about an hour before Vespers, the body of our esteemed benefactor, the Lady Anne Camin, is expected. I am to remind you, My Lady, that Vespers are to be shortened so that there may be a solemn Mass for the blessed departed's soul."

"Thank you, Sister Naomi," the Lady Philippa said. "You have assigned those who will pray over the mortal remains of the Lady Anne during the night hours?"

"Yes, My Lady, their names have been written on the main *tabula* in the cloister," the reverend sister said. "To those names, My Lady, I have added that of Sister Lazelle."

"Why is this?"

"The most revered mother, the sub-prioress, reported her to us, to the four mistresses that is, My Lady, as being absent-minded about her devotions," Sister Naomi said regretfully. "Since then we have all watched her carefully, and it is so, My Lady."

All heads turned towards the nun Lazelle. "Let it be so," the Lady Philippa said.

Although to Lazelle it was a shock to discover she had betrayed herself to the extent she had, this in no manner altered her determination to slip into church as soon as possible after grace had been said as thanksgiving for a very meagre meal. She knew how imprudent it would be, however, to make the venture too soon, and so, when the period for work and recreation arrived, she went with Sister Katherine, and Katherine's long-tailed monkey, Puchin, to the kitchen door at the junction of the north and west walks.

Others were also making the same journey: Sister Alice, her kestrel Lively on her shoulder; Sister Constance and her Maltese dog Gozi; the Lady Petronilla with Warwick, her cat; and, given a wide berth by everyone, Sister Beatrice and Brussie, a bear whom many were asserting was growing much too large to be kept.

Dishes of all sizes for the pets, from a very small one to Brussie's tub, were stored near the kitchen door, and it was there that food of a miscellaneous nature, to cover the respective requirements, was handed out by the larderer and the cook.

The Lady Petronilla, an expression of joyous hopefulness in her faded eyes, began to talk to Lazelle as soon as she had satisfied herself that Warwick's platter of fish, which would be followed by creamy ewe's milk, was to his liking. She was not a nun, but had lived at Watton for forty years, since being ten years old, when her betrothed had been killed at Poitiers. From then, almost every day had been the day when she expected him to return to her from the French wars.

"I have news of my dear one," she said, her breath catching. "It is not to-day nor to-morrow that he will be here, but ere another week has passed we shall be together once more."

"Small wonder you look gay," Lazelle said gently. "But please don't raise your hopes too high, for it is a long journey and the seas in the Channel can impose many a weary delay."

"Oh! I know that, my dear," Lady Petronilla said proudly. "I am of a family of warriors and before I was betrothed I knew full well the heartaches and waitings I would have to endure. Indeed . . ."

Warwick, muttering angrily and with mouth open, was flipping the side of his jaw with a paw. His mistress, forcing rheumaticky limbs into action, joined him on the floor where, her cries a mixture of tenderness and alarm, she helped him to search for a bone caught between his teeth.

"Poor old thing," Sister Katherine said to Lazelle as they strolled back. "How tragic it is for her, even though she seldom shows it."

"I think it is more sad for us who know the truth than it is for her, so don't worry," Lazelle said. "She isn't unhappy, praise be."

"Perhaps it is so, for you talk to her far more than I can bear."

"I am sure of it," said Lazelle.

Quite cheered, Sister Katherine surprisingly began to talk about an aspect of the business discussion after the Daily Chapter which had impressed her enormously.

"Such wonderful names," she said.

"Names!"

Sister Katherine nodded. "Bartholemew Grimbaldi of Chieri and Manent Francisci of Florence," she said dreamily. "Don't they conjure up wonderful pictures of blue skies and dazzling sun? And of our noble crusaders and the dauntless Duke Richard of Aquitaine, the lion-hearted, sailing far away and beyond to the hot sands of the Holy Land."

Lazelle smiled. "I never knew you were so romantically inclined," she teased her. "But I doubt whether Messrs. Grimbaldi and Francisci would spend as freely of their own monies and others' in a cause which could never have brought a profit to our never-to-be forgotten poet-soldier and sovereign."

"He was a most perfect knight of a truth, wasn't he?" Sister Katherine said wistfully. "Would that I had lived in those days and could have seen him."

"Had you been a cloistered nun you would not have seen him even then," Lazelle said. "But supposing you could have chosen in those days . . . where would you have been—inside these walls or away in the world outside them?"

Sister Katherine started off impulsively: "To set my eyes on the lord lion-heart——" she said, but with this broke off abruptly and glanced about quickly before resuming, when her tone was very different. "There could be no question about my course. What might we do more glorious than we are doing—giving ourselves body and soul to our Lord Jesus, and serving Him here until our dying day?"

Lazelle sighed. "I wonder," she murmured.

Her companion was so much shocked by this that she did not at once notice that Sister Paula was standing at the end of the walk. When she did she was in the middle of an aghast: "Sister Lazelle, you *can't* doubt that in becoming a widow of Our Lord on His earth below——" This was when she saw who was lying in wait. "Look, there's Sister Paula," she hissed, "and though I hope Our Blessed Saviour will forgive my wickedness I always *hate* to have her near me. She is always touching me . . . and . . ."

"I will stay with you," Lazelle said consolingly.

Near to panic, Sister Katherine snatched up Puchin. "She would still try to hold my hand under the folds of my habit," she gasped. "Only yesterday she came into my cubicle in the dorm, for why I know not even now, but——"

Fortunately another of the sisterhood chanced to be passing and, with a sound excuse, she seized her as a drowning man grasps a straw.

"Sister Maud, could I come with you?" she asked. "I . . . I so much enjoyed myself the last time."

A good-natured creature, Sister Maud had no objection and, though as always professing scorn about pets, paused long enough to scratch Puchin's head, in a place he evidently appreciated. Devoted wholeheartedly to sport, she had her own hounds and hawks, housing them with My Lady's in the kennels and mews adjoining the yard of the prioress's lodging, which she never failed to visit every afternoon.

Whether or not Sister Paula guessed the reason for Katherine's flight Lazelle could not be sure, but she was certainly very tart.

" I suppose Sister Maud has taken little Katherine off to the kennels again," she said. " I like it not."

" You . . . you like it not! " Lazelle exclaimed. " Why not? "

Sister Paula drew nearer. " I am much older than you," she said, lowering her voice, " so my words must be picked with care. But I tell you this—that Katherine should not be alone with Sister Maud far away beyond My Lady's lodging."

Against blood-drained cheeks her burning eyes contrasted strangely. Bewildered, Lazelle stared at her.

" What hurt could there be in it? " she asked. " Katherine will come to no harm there, for Sister Maud has always had the whip-hand of all the mastiffs and hounds, even those most fierce."

" She could be soiled," Sister Paula said passionately.

Lazelle was beginning to wonder whether Sister Paula were ill. " Soiled! " she said. " I know not what you mean."

Her perplexity was very obvious. " Perhaps soiled is not the proper word," Sister Paula said hurriedly. " All the same," she went on, sharpness creeping into her tone, " it may not be too inept when one considers that Sister Maud so much resembles a groom that some of the coarseness of the stable-yard must have rubbed off on to her."

" Coarse! " Lazelle said indignantly. " Sister Maud is not the least coarse and it is wrong of you to say she is."

It seemed as if Sister Paula might burst into tears. " The Lord Jesus bids us be charitable to all," she said painfully. " But . . . but in my concern for dear little Katherine, which is no excuse whatsoever, I have failed Him whose shining example never . . . never . . ."

" Don't, Sister Paula," Lazelle said. " It is not as serious as all that."

Sister Paula sniffed. " It is grievously so."

Lazelle shook her head. " Surely you are beating your breast unnecessarily," she insisted. " As our Divine Maker would speedily tell you, and more sharply, if you could speak to Him."

" That is what I shall now try to do," Sister Paula said brokenly, " and without delay. On my knees at the steps of the sanctuary I——"

" It is forbidden to enter the church," Lazelle intervened hastily, " save with the full community for the holy Offices. Have you forgotten that the monk of Rievaulx is working there? "

Tears trickling, Sister Paula nodded blindly. " I had so forgotten," she said. " But I can confess to my evils before the crucifix in the chapter house, and . . . and to there I will now go."

Habit flapping, she scurried away, leaving Lazelle staring after her until she disappeared into the chapter house.

Although Lazelle was both troubled and baffled by Sister Paula's queer behaviour she had a single, dominating purpose that afternoon, and soon, thinking how best to accomplish this purpose, she was continuing along the walk, towards the stone staircase to the refectory and the lavatory beyond it, where a sister of about her own age, who had brought a small wooden tub and hot water from the kitchen, was washing handkerchiefs, a wimple, two undershifts, and many pieces of ribbon. The laundering was done by lay-sisters in the wash-house, which officially allowed a change of linen three times in each two months, but for Sister Deborah, as with Lazelle and others, this was by no means enough.

" You look most intent," Deborah remarked while busily rinsing. " If it is that you are worrying about Sister Naomi reporting you, I would not any more. My Lady didn't seem really very cross."

Lazelle started out of her reverie. " No, I don't believe she did."

Sister Deborah sighed deeply when pointing to a neat darn in a wimple. She was fashionably inclined and, largely by ingenuity, did her utmost to keep level with the prioress in the fancies of attire.

" What can one do on our trivial pocket money, Lazelle? " she remarked scornfully. " When we have provided ourselves each year with a new white woollen tunic, a scapular, a veil and a linen wimple, what is left out of six and eightpence? I ask you."

Lazelle smiled. " Very little, dear Deborah," she agreed. " But nevertheless, you seem to manage to create a handsome sensation every now and then. Those cunning little tucks in your cap . . . on the afternoon of the Eve of Saint Agnes——"

" You liked them? " Deborah asked eagerly.

" They were wondrous, and I told you so then," said Lazelle, her eyes starting to dance. " But Sister Matilda nearly swooned when she saw you, though it was with surprise and not for anything nasty."

Deborah wrinkled her nose. " She's nice, but no dress sense."

" She makes glorious tapestries," Lazelle pointed out.

" Yes . . . yes, so she does," said Deborah, apparently surprised. " That is strange when you think of it, isn't it? "

" It is as God shared out our talents," said Lazelle.

Sister Deborah nodded, but was more concerned with a secret she confided. This was that, the matter arranged through several channels, the gardener had promised her a supply of moss from which a most delicate green dye could be brewed. Her ambition was a wimple of this shade.

" But not a word to a soul, Lazelle," she said, her bright eyes anxious. " Promise that you will ask the Lord to cleft you in two should you reveal what I have told."

" Gladly," said Lazelle, half-laughing, " if you will promise to let me know in advance when you will be wearing the green wimple. I want to make sure of being close to the fourth prioress."

Her sister-in-God wavered between indignation and giggling. " Imagine *her* criticising anyone," she said. " She, who always looks like a pack of wool waddling along, and as dingy."

Just then, Lazelle had to step aside to permit the passage of a nun who aroused even more comment than Sister Deborah. Barefooted voluntarily, Sister Isabella was walking slowly, with head downcast. In this manner, unless she deviated from her usual custom, she would continue to perambulate the four walks of the cloister until a bell summoned the community.

Both Lazelle and her companion watched her, and both, when she had gone, shook their heads at each other before nearly bursting into laughter—and that, if unrestrained, would have cost them dear. Doubtless each was thinking of what, some time before, Dame Eleanor had been heard to say to Dame Jean de Warke. The widow had remarked crisply that Sister Isabella, with all her stagy displays of piety, was in her wrong element—she should have been in a company of players; and Dame Jean's comments had been even more devastating. Their observations had never been forgotten, and still were repeated as joyously as when they spread through the convent on the first day.

Taking leave of Sister Deborah, Lazelle wandered on, but as the distance from the church door decreased her legs became progressively more wobbly. This was no state in which to undertake a daring excursion and so, to compose herself, she went into the warming house, where she sat on a stone seat with her back against one of the octagonal central pillars.

While there, she chatted for a few moments with Sister Ealdgyth, a brawny and energetic young woman who could never bear to be still. She was hanging her washing on a line to dry, and after that intended to give her cubicle in the dormitory a thorough turn-out.

When Sister Ealdgyth strode off, Lazelle, her chin determined, decided that it must be now or never, but was twice delayed in her plan, first when some novices, Elizabeth, Margaret and Mercy, came in and begged her to explain to them the earlier part of the seventeenth chapter of Revelations, a hopeless undertaking.

Next, near the prison cells at the south end of the west walk, there was the chaplain, Sir William, a pleasant old gentleman whom all the younger nuns, or at least those mischievously inclined, could twist round their little fingers. Lazelle talked to him for a few minutes before curtseying and slipping away.

When near the church door she feigned to pay attention to the notices on the *tabula,* meantime surreptitiously glancing along the south and west walks, where many of the sisterhood were diverting themselves with needlework, drawing, brushing and combing pets, and so on.

At last, taking a deep breath, Lazelle entered the church, forcing herself to walk leisurely up the steps and beyond, as far as the effigy of the Blessed Virgin and the Infant Child, to whom she bowed deeply. By then her limbs were trembling afresh, and they shook still more when she turned to look at the screen-enclosed south wall of the nave, behind which she could hear sounds as though some thick liquid was being stirred in a bucket.

" He is there," she whispered to herself. " Brother Ughtred! "

She was nerving herself for a vastly greater disobedience when her name was called, severely, from behind. A small gasp of fright escaping her, she spun round and saw one of the four mistresses.

"What are you doing here, my daughter?" the Reverend Sister Melania demanded as she came from the western, galilee end of the church with a silver reliquary in one hand and cleaning cloth in the other. "You are surely aware that outside the holy Hours only obedientiaries are allowed in the church for the present?"

"Yes, Reverend Sister."

A tiny smile of satisfaction appeared on Sister Melania's not unkindly face. "I know you know, too," she said. "Because when I was passing through the cloister a little earlier I heard you warning one of your sisters. Is that not so?"

Lazelle bowed. "It is so," she admitted.

The senior mistress carefully placed the reliquary on the pedestal of the Blessed Virgin and Child.

"If I leave it there I shall see it and so remember," she murmured before turning again to Lazelle. "You are doing a great deal of day-dreaming lately, my daughter. Is that not so also?"

"I . . . I fear I am," Lazelle stammered.

Sister Melania nodded, as if to herself. "Winter, with its restrictions, takes more toll on the youthful, my daughter," she said. "But spring is not far away and then you will quickly feel much different. You love spring, my daughter?"

Lazelle smiled. "It is a wondrous time."

"I loved it, too," Sister Melania said with a sigh. "With my dear brothers—I had seven of them and as the sole girl-child they tended to spoil me, and often . . . H'mmm, I think you must have a draught to tone you up. The bowels are the seat of all trouble; so over to the infirmary where you shall have a potion to remove your vapours."

Lazelle clasped her hands imploringly. "Please, with duty and respect, please not," she said.

Sister Melania's eyes twinkled. "They are monstrous strong, aren't they? H'mmm . . . yes, perhaps a dose of one of the milder mixtures Sister Alice makes will suffice."

"Reverend Sister," Lazelle said anxiously, "Sister Alice's are just as searching, and I have no need of any."

"Come along, my daughter."

"Oh! Reverend Sister," Lazelle pleaded.

The senior mistress used her authority. " That is enough, my daughter," she declared firmly. " You will follow me."

After a rosily confused glance of despair at the screen, Lazelle reluctantly tagged behind until they reached a carrel in the north walk where Sister Alice, the kestrel snoozing close to her, was working on an altar cloth. Lively's mistress was as skilled in embroidery as in physic, but preferred the second, and therefore got up with alacrity as soon as she knew what was expected of her. Within ten minutes, sternly watched over, Lazelle had gulped down to the last drop a dose of a bitter and most obnoxious medicine.

" You will soon feel very different, my daughter," Sister Melania said encouragingly.

Entirely convinced about that, Lazelle nodded. " I think it is very possible, Reverend Sister," she said ruefully.

" Unfailing in its action," Sister Alice said with a very professional air. " Never leaves room for any doubt."

The Reverend Sister Melania began to make inquiries about Lazelle's present duty-task, which was to make deer-skin gloves for outdoor servants engaged in ditching and hedging.

" Very well, my daughter," she said. " You will return to the cloister and try to make up for arrears. And remember, my daughter, no more aimlessly wandering about. You understand?"

" Yes, Reverend Sister," Lazelle said.

Miserably she went to the north walk where, with little spirit, she rummaged in her sewing box for thread, specially stout needle and thimble, and the parts of a glove she had cut out more than a fortnight before.

" I . . . I nerve myself to visit Brother Ughtred," she told herself, lips quivering. " And what happens—I have to drain an enormous drench to cleanse my stomach and bowels, as . . . as it will forsooth. What . . . what an ignominious end to thrilling adventure! "

Sniffling as she sought for her handkerchief, she might have sunk into a worse apathy had she not heard the conversation of Dame Jean de Warke and Dame Eleanor, who were sitting near.

" This young monk must be a wonderful artist," Dame Eleanor said. " Lady Philippa told me only this morning that she had heard from her cousin the lord abbot of Rievaulx, in which he said the

Madonna picture looked magnificent now that it was in its appointed position in his church."

Dame Jean demonstrated that she was on equally confidential terms with the prioress.

" That is why I am all agog to see the vast creation that is being done here, in the nave," she said. " Lady Philippa, when I insisted, was good enough to promise me that we should all see it as soon as it is finished."

" Oh! she said that to me as well," Dame Eleanor said with a smile. " A small matter I had not thought to mention to you."

Indifferent to the condition of her eyes, which were now brimming, Lazelle sprang up and, hastening by the nearest way, ran up the steps to the refectory, through which she passed to her cubicle in the dormitory, where she sank to her knees by the side of the canopied bed.

" Lord Saviour," she beseeched, " now that Brother Ughtred's great picture is in its place on the wall of his church for all to behold, please never again let My Lady visit her cousin the lord abbot of the abbey of Rievaulx in Ryedale. For if My Lady ever did Brother Ughtred would be sorely in trouble. O Lord God, grant me this precious boon lest . . ."

Darkness had fallen when she rose, summoned by the mourning bell to receive with the combined communities the hide-wrapped, salt-pickled body of the Lady Anne Camin, which rested in an ornately carved and decorated coffin carried in a lumbering hearse drawn by six powerful horses, each funereally plumed and with long-hanging black cloths. At each side of the hearse eight bearers held bright, sizzling torches, and when the cortège had passed through the main gateway the brothers and the more closely hooded sisters fell in with them, to march slowly across the outer court and then by the road circling the east end of the precincts, where the men's quarters were. Throughout, a solemn dirge was sung, until the moment when the hearse, a pinnacled shrine on wheels, came to a standstill at the south door of the church. There the canons regular, as they were daily accustomed, entered their quire, and the nuns, leaving unfamiliar territory behind, proceeded through the processional doorway to their side, the remains of the Lady Anne borne in with them.

That night, with others, Lazelle prayed for the soul of the Lady Anne Camin, for whom in due course, over the months, a thousand Masses were to be said. The coffin, with twenty-four large candles burning on it, lay on a bier placed in the sanctuary towards the High Altar, and around it Lazelle, with seven more, sent up their pleas to Heaven.

For these eight, lacking sleep, there was further strain when, the next day, the Master of Sempringham, the Superior of the Gilbertine Double Order, arrived at Watton and was received with the ceremonial appropriate. And still more strain the day after that, the day of the funeral, to which the Master had come to lend his authority and presence.

It made a change, as Sister Ealdgyth remarked between yawns. " I always prefer to be kept busy," she added, an observation which, heard by the sub-prioress, earned her seven days on bread and water. Unluckily for her, her next cheerful comment: " Thank heaven I can't feel any emptier than I do already, and I trust Our Lord Saviour will forgive me for declaring that I devoutly wish Lent were over," though sotto-voice, was not missed either by the sub-prioress, who had very sharp ears. The seven days were changed to a fortnight.

The convent then settled into its normal routine, until a night exactly a month to the day following the Lady Anne's impressive funeral, when a strange incident occurred shortly after the second retirement of the night, before all had gone to sleep. Somewhere, not so far away, there was shouting, hammering, and an occasional drum of hoofs, and within little over a minute every bed in the long dormitory had been vacated. All, from the third prioress to the newest accepted novice, congregated in the broad corridor outside the cubicles, some plainly very frightened and others stimulated by excitement.

It was a clear night, with the moon a day before full, but the annoying thing to the bolder spirits was that not a single window faced towards the outer court, which was plainly the neighbourhood of the disturbance.

" But if I climb on to the roof," Sister Hilda said excitedly, " Sister Lazelle, if you could hold me when I was standing out on the sill reaching for the gutter . . ."

" Whatever it is, Brussie would make everybody run if I could let him out," said Sister Beatrice eagerly. " Reverend Sister Blanche, have I your permission to . . ."

" No, it needs someone stronger, Sister Lazelle," Sister Hilda said, screening her mouth to shout: " Sister Ealdgyth, here . . . quickly."

At this point Sister Eva went into hysterics. Between shrill screams, she announced that it was the Scots, bloodthirsty assassins who considered a day had been ill-spent if a few throats had not been slashed.

" Jesus Our Lord, fold your embracing arm about us," Sister Constance begged. " O Lord, shield my dear Gozi from danger."

With others, Sisters Alice and Matilda had sunk to their knees before the silver crucifix. As each tried to outcry the remainder in their pleas for divine assistance, the noise in the dormitory became even more deafening. But Sister Eva's voice had a piercing quality which could rise above any challenge. She had changed her mind to some extent—*they* were now raiders, moss troopers from the Border who, after putting all the men to the sword, would ravish the women before collecting together the plunder.

" They don't ravish all the women," Sister Katherine tried to tell Lazelle. " They carry off the more comely, and, if the Lord will forgive my conceit, I think we two, and . . ."

The third and fourth prioresses, supported by the mistresses, the Reverend Sisters Melania, Naomi, Blanche and Joanna, were making valiant efforts to restore order, by clapping hands and exhortations. Of them the Reverend Sister Joanna, much the toughest, was outstandingly the most successful, soon bringing the tumult to an end. In the ensuing silence it became very evident, as everyone listened carefully, that all was peace and quietness outside, as so, for another quarter of an hour, during which tension largely diminished, it continued to be.

" Yes," said the third prioress, sighing with relief. " All to your chambers at once. Swiftly."

" Most Revered Mother," Sister Constance said faintly, " how can we sleep unless——"

" The canons regular will have heard also and be on guard, won't they? " the Reverend Sister Naomi pointed out.

" Moreover, the Reverend Sisters Blanche and Joanna will stay up, and until the rising for Prime will sit at the top of the stairs from the cloister," the third prioress said. " That," she wound up emphatically, " should be enough for all save those who waver in their faith in the Almighty's sure shield. To your beds, my daughters."

" It might be something and nothing, Most Reverend Mother," Sister Katherine wheedled. " If we could only learn that——"

" You must wait until to-morrow," the Reverend Sister Joanna said sternly. " We shall hear then."

As it proved. After the Daily Chapter the prioress informed the community that, in consequence of a well-planned raid, the convent had suffered serious losses, enumerating the stock stolen: oxen, cows, asses and sheep. Seven quarters of wheat had also been removed, and the fishpond had been maliciously damaged. There was evidence to support the belief that the robbers might be followers of Roger de Birthorpe, an arrant thief himself.

" I have consulted with the lord prior," the Lady Philippa went on grimly. " Within the hour, to recover our property we must trust, he is riding into Holderness at the head of every able-bodied brother and servant as can be mustered."

" We must pray for a successful outcome, My Lady," the Reverend Sister Blanche said anxiously. " Our monies are most delicately balanced at the moment, and there is much that is pressing."

Lady Philippa frowned. " We will cross our bridges when we come to them, my daughter," she said.

Sister Blanche looked even more worried. " Bridges, My Lady," she said. " There is much complaint about the state of our bridge in the forest near Aike, and clamour that we have taken tolls without using the receipts for what they were intended."

She was reassured. The Lady Philippa reminded her hearers that, as far back as the Festival of the Body of Christ the previous year, she had written to the king regarding a number of grave financial matters. A reply to that letter had now been received.

" As to our problems concerning the bridges we possess, my daughters," the Lady Philippa resumed, " it is pleasing for me to be able to inform you that our sovereign lord has come to our aid nobly. For seven years from now we are licensed to employ three professional beggars to collect for their repair, with no hindrance as to where they may go within the royal realms. That should provide a most useful income for the purposes we all have dearly at heart."

From time to time both the fourth prioress and the Reverend Sister Naomi had been heard to mutter strange innuendoes about their prioress, but this information so overwhelmed them that they were able to join in the congratulations she was given.

" No, no, my daughters," the Lady Philippa said modestly. " It is not I whom you should praise, but my friends and your friends, friends of our loved house. And, thanks to the Almighty's inscrutable ways, many of these friends of ours are at our sovereign's illustrious court."

" Thank Heaven! " the Reverend Sister Blanche said fervently.

Everyone laughed, and the Lady Philippa, not a hint of scolding about her, laughed too.

A letter from the Bishop, next spoken about, was responsible for a tremendous commotion. In it he proposed himself for a visit on the fourth day after the Feast of St. Mark.

" When Lent is over," Sister Edith whispered to Lazelle out of the side of her mouth. " So that there can be a banquet. The Lord Bishop is a piggish glutton."

In the letter there was a reference to a Papal Bull concerning fashions in the cloister, His Holiness forbidding personal adornment. The Lord Bishop was tactfulness itself in his allusions to this, as he had sound reason to be, for whereas the majority of the nunneries were under diocesan authority the Gilbertine foundations answered to the Master of Sempringham alone.

" The insolence," the sub-prioress said furiously.

Sister Katherine rose indignantly. " My Lady," she said, " two Christmases ago it was the Lord Bishop who tried to prevent us playing the game we have always played at the time of the Holy Birth, when the youngest of the novices takes your place, My Lady. If you are gracious enough to permit it, My Lady, why should he object? "

" My Lady," said Sister Deborah, " what has he to do with how we attire ourselves? It is intolerable for him to interfere."

"He has no right to interfere," said Sister Maud, who cared nothing about dress. "And if he does come, and if you don't refuse me, My Lady, I shall try to wear something extravagant."

"It is trickery, My Lady, and I beg that if you do agree to receive him the understanding shall be that it is out of politeness and nothing more," the third prioress said. "He writes of a visit, My Lady, but this could be the thin end of the wedge, for it is a small cry from a visit to an official visitation."

The Lady Philippa held up her hand. "I have listened most carefully, my daughters, and with your views I am entirely in accord," she pronounced. "It would be discourteous to refuse My Lord Bishop, but I shall eschew the word visit when I respond to his request. Now what else, if anything?"

Scarlet-cheeked, Sister Beatrice stood up to complain that frequently when she had occasion to go to the necessary Richard the plumber was hovering in the vicinity—or rather Richard the plumber's apprentice lad.

"It is an affront to my modesty, My Lady," she went on doggedly. "Surely it cannot be that the pipe should always require attention when I have need to go there."

"Mmmm," the prioress murmured. "Have others the same experience?"

Heads were being shaken when Lazelle sought permission to speak, which was granted.

"My Lady," she said, "twice when I have been in the dormitory and Sister Beatrice has gone by to the nessy I have seen Richard the plumber's boy afterwards, over at the other side."

"Have you, my daughter?" the Lady Philippa said ominously. "Yes, God's wrath, the most salutary action shall be taken about this."

Lazelle bowed. "With respect, My Lady, but Sister Edith once said something to me that comes to mind, which used differently would affright Richard the plumber's apprenticed youth very much indeed."

She leaned across her neighbour to whisper to Sister Edith, who had blushed painfully at being publicly singled out. What passed between them no one heard with the exception of Deborah, who barely stifled a giggle. For her part Sister Edith listened, shook her head violently, and ultimately gasped: " No, you tell, Sister Lazelle."

" Come, my daughters," the Lady Philippa said indulgently. She was lying out for foxes that night, in the moonlight, and the pleasure of anticipation overweighed her anger about the raid. " Speak, my daughter Lazelle, if your sister Edith is too shy."

" My Lady," said Lazelle, " I had thought that if Sister Beatrice cautiously secreted her Brussie in the nessy and then later pretended to be going there herself——"

Seldom had the Lady Philippa laughed more heartily, not even when jesting with her cousin the lord abbot of Rievaulx and other coarsely-inclined gentlemen.

" I fear I begin to regard you as a maid of many parts, my daughter Lazelle," she said, her voice throaty with exhaustion. " As to your cunning plan, I can have no connection with such duplicity, but should it happen I shall eternally regret I was not present."

" Oh! we understand that, My Lady," the sub-prioress called out, her face still wreathed with delight.

What with this prospect, the thrills of the night, and the news their prioress next gave them, that they were to see the big picture in the nave during the afternoon, it was the most exciting day many of them had known, so there was scant debating about the last business brought before the chapter, the application by a nobleman and his wife for their daughter, a deaf and dumb girl, to be entered as a novice on probation. This was summarily rejected.

Very little work was done subsequently. Needles, whether for sewing, or at the tapestry frames, were not plied very seriously; drawings were not greatly advanced, nor many pages of books turned to the next; wool was combed haphazardly and spinning wheels revolved only spasmodically.

Shortly before one o'clock in the afternoon the Lady Philippa appeared at the church door, where she rang a silver-gilt bell. At this signal, and as one body, the aged and the youthful abandoned their tasks and eagerly following her, trooped into the nave, where the stalls on the north side had been replaced in their positions. Above them, viewed from the aisle, a far extending picture could be seen in its vividly colourful glory.

A mass gasp of amazement ascended towards the roof, prelude to cries of wonder as details, from small to large, were picked out for comment: the droppings of blood from the Evil thing, and the realistic finger-nails of the Good; the awful fear in Satan's expression on sensing defeat, and the calm confidence of the triumphing Angel.

" Oh! My Lady," Lazelle said, nearly weeping with joy, " never could there be anything to compare, and would that Brother Ughtred could remain here for long to come."

" Brother Ughtred! " the Lady Philippa said sharply, but her brow cleared as she remembered. " Yes, I recall it was he who saved you, my daughter, so you would know his name."

" Yes, My Lady," Lazelle said. " I . . . I was thinking how much more he could do were he to remain."

" He will be staying here for awhile yet, my daughter," the Lady Philippa said briskly. " I have coaxed the lord abbot Hugh into consenting to his being with us until the rise of the leaf in the spring."

" That is good, My Lady," Lazelle said, her eyes glowing. " In that time, though it is not so long, he may paint several pictures if they are not too big."

Dame Philippa nodded, but was more interested in Sister Maud who, although the strictest of ceremonial was not being demanded, had sunk to her knees before her.

" Yes, my daughter? " the prioress said inquiringly.

Sister Maud had a line to the stables in the outer court through a chain of friendly intermediaries and always knew in advance what was afoot on the sporting side.

" My Lady, I ask and beseech God's mercy and yours," she said.

" What is it, my daughter? "

" My Lady," Sister Maud said, looking up imploringly, " might I accompany you when you lie out for foxes this night?"

" Bless my sinful body and wretched soul," said the Lady Philippa, " hasn't there been enough stirring for you since those godless marauders aroused us in the small hours? I am sure your sisters in the Lord have had a-plenty."

If this were so, there was nevertheless more in store for them, for a second night in succession. The alarm was given midway between the start of the Great Silence and what should have been the time of rising for Matins a few minutes short of midnight—by Sister Alice who, troubled about Lively's moult and trying to decide whether he would be healthier with more or with less live mice daily, had not slept at all well. When turning over again restlessly, she smelled burning.

"Fire!" she gasped, jumping out of bed to fumble for her night boots. "Fire!" she repeated much more loudly as she hurried along the dormitory, banging doors. "Fire!" she was screeching long before completing one side.

. It was not an auspicious example, but the rot was really started by Sister Eva, who set up a sustained and ear-piercing scream. Demoralised by this and billowing smoke, there was a mass rush down to the cloister, where the sub-prioress's sense of leadership disastrously failed her. Wringing her hands in the middle of the moonlit garth, all she could do, between spasms of coughing caused by ever-increasing smoke, was to wail interminably: "And with My Lady away chasing foxes, and the brothers away chasing a ruffianly robber band."

The Reverend Sister Melania was of slightly sterner metal, but even she, at the inception, omitted to realise it might be of advantage to locate the source of the fire, though she did detach a party to collect as many leather firebuckets as possible.

"There are still a few canons at the other side who are vigorous, if not suited to hard riding, and they must be informed of our perilous situation, which is theirs also if the conflagation spreads," she rambled on. "Assuredly, if this side is razed . . ."

"Reverend Sister, Reverend Sister," said Lazelle. "What have we to do, please?"

"Oh! yes," said Sister Melania, holding her forehead. "Yes, of course."

Sisters Hilda and Isabella were despatched—by way of the prioress's yard, the processional door in the church, and the night-stairs in the canon's chapel—to the end of the "other side's" dormitory, where they were to shout until they made themselves heard; and Sisters Ealdgyth and Lazelle were sent to the turnover house in the west adit—there they were to open the small, shuttered window, through which they were to scream their heads off, also until heard, a much more hopeless quest.

" Come on, Sister Lazelle," said Sister Ealdgyth. " And, please God, make our feet fleet."

Luckily the moon created ample illumination, even in the adit, lighted from brilliant squares high up. Here difficulties were encountered, for there was an iron grille in the " talking " opening and another shutter on the east side. As frantic pushing and beating with fists on the first of these obstacles was soon shown to be futile, Lazelle had to race back along the adit and down the stairs to the warming place, where she groped about in the smoke to find the poker. However, once this hefty weapon was being wielded by Sister Ealdgyth's muscular arms, the life of both grille and shutter quickly ended. Then, in turn, they began to shout through the small opening in the thick wall, until both were croaking.

" It is useless, Sister Lazelle," Sister Ealdgyth said hoarsely. " The east adit is lengthy and they would not hear even in their garth, and still less in the dormitory at the far side."

" The others who went through the church will have roused the brothers long ago," said Lazelle. " By now they could have walked nearly to Beverley, so let us return, Sister Ealdgyth."

" Yes, to where we can do *something*, Sister Lazelle," Sister Ealdgyth grunted. " It is wrong to criticise our superiors but it cannot be denied that the Reverend Sister Melania has sent us on a senseless mission. So let's away, back."

The pets had been released and in the cloister garth Sister Constance's Maltese dog Gozi was furiously pursuing the Lady Petronilla's Warwick, with respites mutually agreed for a breather, when there was offensive snarling and spitting. Otherwise there was far more orderliness; the sisters who had fainted were now in the church, watched over by those who had carried them there, and elsewhere, extended between the kitchen well and the source of the fire in the ground-level undercroft below the refectory, others had formed a long line.

Lazelle joined the bucket chain, taking her place with Sister Deborah on one hand and Sister Sibilla on the other. The outlook, she heard, was far more promising than had been feared; by some mishap the covering of straw and rushes on the stone floor had become ignited, but as it was damp there was smouldering rather than fierce flame, and if those who laboured inside for short spells could rake out the glowing portions before drier stretches were reached all would be well, the damage superficial.

Almost sure that Brother Ughtred would be there, and convinced that if he were he would be in the forefront, Lazelle tried to pick him out from the shadowy creatures who, emerging from the undercroft, coughed and coughed with their hands on their knees, bent double, before re-entering the doorway again. It was a tantalising business; sometimes the grey gloom was impenetrable, sometimes the curling eddies of smoke, lighted by the moon, made a picture which, though of weird beauty, was deceptively hard for streaming eyes to see through.

Sister Sibilla, reduced to sorry straits, was gasping that she could not continue much longer when Lazelle fleetingly perceived the light-grey habit of a Cistercian. Fortunately, before the ordeal became too much for Sister Sibilla to endure further, and before Lazelle's thumping heart could choke her, as she felt it would, the word was passed that no more water was required.

Smoke there still was in abundance, from a vast heap in the garth which spurted tiny flames from time to time, and through it Lazelle edged, that thumping heart resolute, towards the angle between the kitchen quarters and the western range, a two-storied building with the lay-sisters' sleeping chamber at the top and, below, a storage basement and a broad area, with a porch behind, which led to the nunnery's guest house.

Standing in the doorway, Lazelle waited, too taut even to smile when, smoke momentarily drifting away, she saw a very diminutive canon regular collide with Sister Hilda who, rock-like and unshaken, looked down and recognised him.

" It is, isn't it? " Sister Hilda screeched, bending as if inclined to lift him. " It's Little Alfie, Little Alfie."

Canon Alfred's grin extended from ear to ear. " Hilda, Hilda, after all these years," he shouted.

" But I've heard about you all the time, Alfie," Sister Hilda gabbled. " Whenever my dear and holy mother visits me . . ."

" It's the same with me, Hilda," Canon Alfred chattered away. " I know about the law dispute your honoured father is involved in concerning his boundary line at High Top, and of your sister Ruth's

new girl-child after such an interval that it must have been
supposed . . ."

As they were enveloped again, someone brushed swiftly past
Lazelle, but she had no idea who it was.

" O dear God," she whispered, " let me see him . . . for the most
revered mother the sub-prioress will not countenance any mingling,
and she will ensure they are all shepherded to the other side as soon
as it is expedient."

God was good to her, so benign that when they met He arranged
they should be hidden by a curtain of smoke.

" Sister Lazelle," Ughtred said joyously. " I have been searching for you, for I felt certain you would be here."

Swiftly, taking his arm, she drew him into the dark area, and
from there led him to the porch where, the moon lighting up their
grimy faces, they looked at each other for some moments without
speaking.

" Oh! Brother Ughtred," Lazelle whispered. " I am so glad for
this."

Ughtred nodded. " The Lord is being amazingly kind to us,
Sister Lazelle, and I shall thank Him before I lay my head down to
rest."

" As I," said Lazelle.

The wonder of it quietened them again, but then Lazelle told
him she had seen his great picture in the nave: how beautiful it was,
how marvellous they all deemed it to be.

" As to how I did it, it was my best, Sister Lazelle," said
Ughtred. " But the subject did not appeal to me. Few of them do,
that My Lord and your Lady go into raptures about."

" I like it, loved it, Brother Ughtred," Lazelle said stoutly.

Ughtred smiled. " Then I am content, Sister Lazelle," he said.

Wondering whether he already was aware of it, Lazelle told
him that his Madonna painting was in position in his church at
home.

" It is, Sister Lazelle? " Ughtred said eagerly.

" I heard Dame Eleanor talking to Dame Jean about it," said
Lazelle. " She said that your lord abbot had written to My Lady
saying it looked superb. They both were certain you were a very
great artist, Brother Ughtred."

Ughtred's smile was checked when he noticed how grave and anxious she seemed to have suddenly become.

"Sister Lazelle," he said, his voice charged with authority, "you are not to worry. You understand?"

Lips slightly parted and eyes widened, Sister Lazelle stared at him. "Oh!" she murmured.

"I shan't repeat the reasons whereby I have tried to allay your fears beforehand," Ughtred went on firmly. "But if it should be that I am exposed I shall tell My Lord that as a painter I have the right to paint the face I please."

Again, perhaps unaware that she was slightly shaking her head, she stared at him, resolutely checking a tendency to sigh.

"If you must, you must, Brother Ughtred," she said, striving to sound gay. "But if you have to, will you promise me to speak in a different tone?"

"A different tone?" said Ughtred.

"Never mind, Brother Ughtred," she said gently.

Both were conscious that at the most they would have no more than a few minutes together, and trivial matters were quickly disposed of. It was inevitable that soon they would come to the serious issues discussed between themselves before.

"I have thought often of the unfortunate Lollard, Brother Ughtred," Lazelle said a little later. "He was an honest man, but even honest men can be misguided in their beliefs. Nevertheless I am certain that, as I have often confided to Our Lord Jesus since then . . . that in many matters he was more truly a Christian than those who sent him to the stake, and I wish now that I had thrown the curtains of the cart apart and cried out my protest."

Frightened for her, realising that if she had her time to go over again she had the spunk to carry out her threat, Ughtred shivered.

"It could have meant your own death," he said urgently. "Besides, what good would it have done, what chance has a lone voice crying in the wilderness?"

"To what would the world sink if never a lone voice was raised in protest against cruelty, and inhumanity and want, Brother Ughtred?" Lazelle said very quietly.

Ughtred bowed his head. "It is so, Sister Lazelle," he said humbly. "I am in error, and I thank you for pointing it out to me."

Surprisingly, to him, Lazelle smiled. " I prefer your other mood, Brother Ughtred," she said. " It sits on you better."

Perplexed, Ughtred eyed her. " I don't understand."

" Let it rest," she said sweetly. " For after all, Brother Ughtred, I do not think you are so much in error. You are not without a distaste for cruelty and you have a regard for the poor and needy."

" I have more than a distaste," Ughtred growled. " I think it damnable that Holy Church's prelates should consign a man to a hideous end, and I am sure both Holy Church and the monasteries would be applauded by the Almighty if they shed some of their riches to the advantage of those less well endowed."

Lazelle again smiled. " There! " she murmured.

Bewildered by her changeability, Ughtred had turned to her when a bell started to ring. Outside, in a dark corner near the church door, the novice Mercy had at last found the bell. She had taken it to the sub-prioress, who was now swinging it energetically.

" I must leave you, Brother Ughtred," said Lazelle.

" Wait! " Ughtred said hurriedly. " I have a present for——"

He dried up, confronted by a fearsome dilemma. To reach the oval locket he had to unloose his girdle, hoist his scapular above his waist and, standing revealed in his drawers, detach it from a piece of cord circling his waist.

" Sister Lazelle, will you turn round? " he asked desperately, beginning to sweat. " And keep looking to your front."

" Yes, Brother Ughtred," she said.

Bashfulness, fumbling fingers, and haste, did not make Ughtred's task any easier, but he was to have his reward.

" Oh! Brother Ughtred," Lazelle gasped as she held the little picture of Our Lord so that the light fell on it. " It . . . it is exquisite . . . and His face . . . never in so small have I . . ."

" Sister Lazelle, I must be quick," Ughtred said anxiously, " for the locket fastens to the box containing the relic you wear, and if you would let me have it . . ."

Still gazing at the miniature, Lazelle felt for the chain round her neck, and she was still lost in the beauty of the gift as, very close to her, he began the joining. In that light it was not too easy, harder because he was so aware of her proximity.

" Oh! Brother Ughtred," she said softly.

In the garth, on the eve of leaving, the old canons regular began to chant the ninety-fifth Psalm, and a woman's voice was raised as if she were gathering together her flock.

" Sister Lazelle, you must leave or questions will be asked of you," Ughtred said, becoming terrified for her. " This stout gold thread—if later you gave it two more turns and then knot, it would be safe."

Her forehead touched his cheek as she looked. " I can finish it, Brother Ughtred, so care no more about it."

" You must hurry, Sister Lazelle," said Ughtred. " No, no, go into the garth leisurely, for there may be less smoke now."

" Let us peer carefully," said Lazelle. " For you have to leave also, and although my brothers-in-the-Lord still sing it cannot be long before they depart."

Half a dozen steps revealed only a few wisps of smoke rising from the charred heap, and that the moon's silvery light was shining on two sides of the cloister, none of which was really dark.

Lazelle's breath caught. " If the canons regular depart without you, Brother Ughtred, the processional door in the church will be locked behind them and you will be trapped at this side."

" I will manage somehow, Sister Lazelle," said Ughtred. " So long as I know you have rejoined your sisters I shall——"

She caught his hand and, half pulling him with her, ran up a curving stairway which ascended from the area. On the floor above, no word spoken, they raced along a broad corridor to a small oratory at the end, with a spy-hole window, and then into the larger chapel next to it. This had a broad but rather narrow window, facing the nuns' side of the church.

" If you could squeeze through and drop to the floor, but pray take care for it is high," Lazelle gasped. " Then if you hid in the gloom behind the effigy of the Blessed Virgin and the Infant Christ you might——"

" I'll slink in with the brothers, Sister Lazelle," Ughtred said confidently. " Have no fear."

" I hear them, Brother Ughtred, but do be careful," Lazelle said. " And God be with you, Brother Ughtred, now and for always."

" And with you, Sister Lazelle, as I shall always hope and pray,"

Ughtred said huskily. " But I beg you to speedily join your sisters, for already you may have been missed."

" I shall hurry, and all will be well, Brother Ughtred," Lazelle whispered before he fell in the darkness.

But she stayed, until the dimly-seen shapes of the old canons could be perceived below, a slowly-moving line which advanced towards the quire and presbytery before turning sharply to the dividing wall and the processional doorway; leaving only when the wards of a lock clicked noisily, by then satisfied that, in a shaft of moonlight, she had seen a hooded cowl of alien cut and hue.

Despite anticipating the worst, Lazelle had the easiest of passages on entering the cloister, where her sisters were at the lavatory washing away the dirt they had gathered. She slipped amongst them without a comment being made and, when clean though chilled, was able to thank the Reverend Sister Joanna quite naturally and freely when receiving a towel.

Later, when the third prioress had seen that all were properly in bed, Lazelle got up cautiously and went to the window, where for long she gazed in enchantment at the appendage to her precious little box. Even when at last she put it away she could not resist another look and, holding her clothing from her, peeped down at the locket resting between her breasts.

" Dear Brother Ughtred," she murmured, " My very dear Brother Ughtred, God bless him ever . . . dear Ughtred."

Ughtred's name was on her lips as she fell asleep.

\*　　　\*　　　\*　　　\*

On the following afternoon, driving the stolen stock before them, the canons regular of Watton rode in, an auspicious event for the first day of spring. Subsequently a *Te Deum* of Thanksgiving was sung, for the recovery of so much of the convent's property and for its saving from destruction by fire. The Feast of the Annunciation came four days after that, when the almoner and his assistants washed the feet of the poor and gave them Maundy money, and the refectorian laid clean cloths on the tables and provided all with an extra glass of wine.

Good Friday was given to penitential exercises and processions, one by the joint community twice round the four walks of the canons' cloister, throughout which, in the middle, screens had been erected so that sisters and brothers could walk together while neither could perceive the other. That day there was one meal only, of red herrings, eggs and figs.

Baths were taken by everyone on the afternoon of Easter Eve, the Vigil of which ended at midnight, when the bells pealed the glad tidings of the Resurrection. This was the day when the almoner scattered bay leaves, herb bennet and hedge avens on the floors of the dormitory and cloister, and the salter made vertsauce to serve with the lamb. Dinner, after so many weeks of fasting, was almost unbelievable: with such delicacies as fresh salmon and turbot, chicken, capon and tender veal.

On the Monday tenants arrived to pay their rents, which added a note of jollification, but it was the day also from which no more fires would be permitted in the warming house. Happily the weather was sunny, and the breeze warm, the conditions so pleasant that a few ewes and their offspring were shepherded into the nuns' garden for an hour or thereabouts, so that the sisters could be delighted by the gambolling of the lambs.

This pleasure could not be repeated the next day, as it started to rain when the community was filing into the chapter house for the Daily Chapter, and although the sharp shower was soon over it was enough thoroughly to wet the grass.

That morning, the Lady Philippa had several items of interest: superior offers had been received for the season's wool crop, which caused the Reverend Sister Melania to bustle off for the convent's seal, so that the contracts could be stamped; and a salted deer had been presented to the convent by the forester-in-fee at Pickering, a gentleman whose acquaintance the prioress had made when staying at Rosedale Abbey—an announcement which caused both the fourth prioress and the Reverend Sister Naomi stealthily to seek the other's eye. There was also another small matter: a party of servants, sent out to cut the green growth of hazel and thorn for smoking herrings, had been caught red-handed on another's property and an action for trespass and damage was likely to ensue.

At this point, Lazelle, arm down to the full, let her breviary slide gently to the floor. At the east end the chapter house had been boarded off, and My Lady's fine chair brought to the front; behind the barrier she supposed Brother Ughtred would be working. When the period for recreation came she intended to retrieve the breviary, and the thought was thrilling her until she saw Sister Eva staring. That was a nasty jolt, until a closer look told her that in all probability Sister Eva was moving towards one of the frenzies that frequently affected her.

"And now, my daughters, I must dwell upon a most serious issue," the Lady Philippa said gravely. "As you all know, the Rogation Days will be with us in shortly over a month's time, when as usual I shall be at Sempringham for the Annual Chapter of our Order. I have, my daughters," her voice sank, "reason to believe that the lord prior here, who will be there also, is aiming to wrest some part of the financial control of this convent from our hands."

"He cannot, My Lady," the sub-prioress said indignantly. "We follow what the Blessed Saint Gilbert laid down, and it has always been so, as in all the double foundations."

"And that is how it will remain, my daughter," said the Lady Philippa, "beyond any doubt or question. But I thought it my duty to acquaint you about the sly and cunning scheming that is afoot, and as a reminder to you all to be ever on your guard about concessions to the other side."

"Never an inch, never a stiver, My Lady," the Reverend Sister Blanche said dourly. "I have enough difficulties as it is, and I would have many more if we yielded even a tithe of our revenue to them."

The Lady Philippa nodded. "Precisely, my daughter. What powers our Beloved Saint Gilbert ordained for us weak women, through the Lord God, them shall we hold, for ever."

More trivially domestic matters followed. Sister Ealdgyth was accused of falling asleep during Lauds, so fast over that when the Reverend Sister Joanna, who brought the charge, held a lamp close to her face, she did not waken. And Sister Matilda, to whom petty maliciousness had been imputed not many days before, demanded that Sister Constance should be severely admonished and ordered to apologise, for careful watch had proved that it was Sister Constance's own Gozi who had made off with his mistress' spinning bobbins and secreted them.

In both cases the Lady Philippa adjudicated fairly and not too harshly.

Lazelle's presentiment about Sister Eva was justified, for she ruined the solemn Office of High Mass. Recently, the receiving of the Blood and Body of Christ had translated this afflicted sister to the Holy Manger at the time of the Birth, when she had held the Child and shown it to the Wise Men. In a high-pitched ecstasy, Sister Eva now revealed her participation to the community, none failing to hear, at both sides. She was coaxed from the church to her cubicle in the dormitory, where Sister Alice forced a few drops of a herbal tincture into her mouth, and they laid her out stiff for over twenty-four hours.

Throughout all this, and forward to the moment of the start of the recreation period, Lazelle was becoming more worked up about the venture planned to the chapter house. It would be to invite questioning, however, if she looked excited, and so, trying to compose herself, she sat on a bench in the west walk and, opening her sewing box, took out a partially-made glove.

The Lady Petronilla went past, cajolling Warwick along with her. She was trying to shame him with the threat that, if he were not more soldierly and obedient, she would report him immediately to the noble Black Prince, her betrothed's comrade-in-arms.

Nearby, a group of novices were arguing about inspecting an enormous pike which the larderer at the other side had delivered to the kitchen porter. Within hearing of them was Sister Paula— and Sister Sibilla, too, never one not to seize a favourable opportunity. Sweetly she asked Sister Paula if she had seen the monster and, on receiving an impatient shake of the head, went on to suggest, even more sweetly, that Sister Paula should search for Sister Katherine so that they could visit the buttery together. For a fleeting interval, until Sister Paula turned away, it seemed there might at least be hair-pulling.

Lazelle sighed as she recalled that Brother Ughtred's Friar Jerome believed that those who sought to serve the Lord might be best fitted to accomplish His design if they lived in the outside world, away from the cloister.

" Oh! I so often have strange and forbidden thoughts," she told herself. " I . . . I wish I could have talked with Brother Ughtred longer, but perhaps I may soon, even this day."

To her surprise, for it was a surprise at that hour, she saw My Lady bending over the big tapestry frame, at which Sister Matilda was working on one of a series of historical pictures which, when completed, were to be given to the lord abbot Hugh of Rievaulx, for further beautifying his great convent.

Forewarned, Lazelle was on her knees, with many others, as the Lady Philippa swept majestically by, to her chair near the church door. When seated, My Lady nodded to Sister Matilda, who ran off on an errand, and beckoned to Lazelle, who hurriedly rose, crossed the walk, and dropped to her knees again.

" My daughter," the prioress said severely, " you are not in my favour. Well, use your tongue."

" I am sorry, My Lady," Lazelle faltered.

" What ails you? "

" Nothing, My Lady."

" I am told that you are always woolgathering," the prioress went on sternly. " Moreover, and much more practically," she stamped the ferrule of her staff on the stone flag, " I am informed that you are backward in your work by as much as four pairs of gloves and a left hand."

" I . . . I will try to make up, My Lady."

" I shall provide you with the chance, my daughter," the Lady Philippa said harshly. " I had intended to take you with me to the priory of Sempringham, but now you shall stay at home as a punishment. And if, my daughter, your work is not up to date on my return I shall punish you again, by having you whipped before your sisters. Now go away."

" Yes, My Lady."

Lazelle's cheeks flamed scarlet when, on regaining her bench, she noticed how many pairs of eyes had witnessed her ignominy. Hardly ever had she seen so many of the lesser ranks of the community at that end of the walk, and, in addition, the sub-prioress, both assistant prioresses, and the four mistresses were gathered round My Lady. She could not imagine why, and guiltily wished she had looked at the *tabula* that morning.

Dame Euphemia Middleton, another lady of position who found

it convenient to live in the nunnery, was talking volubly to a quartette of novices to whom shortly she was to give a lesson in making confectionery. She was exceedingly proficient in all housewifely matters but, considering where she now dwelled, it was unfortunate that she always seemed to condescend to those who had not been married.

The Lady Philippa thumped her staff on the floor. " Dame Euphemia," she called out brusquely, " would you be so kind as to shift yourself to one side? As it is, you are obstructing the walk, and anyhow I much prefer a clear view of the staircase leading down from the dormitory."

Rapidly becoming puce-coloured, Lady Euphemia gasped. " I . . . I have never been so wantonly insulted in my life."

Lady Philippa laughed. " I beg to differ, my lady."

Lady Euphemia drew herself up haughtily. " I do not know what you mean, Lady Philippa," she said. " But if my dear husband were here——"

" It would be by mistake and instantly he would be off hell for leather, nor would the fleetest beast I have catch him," the prioress remarked acidly. " And more to the side, closer to the wall."

" You shall answer for this," Lady Euphemia cried, her bosom heaving. " *Never* have I been spoken to thus."

The Lady Philippa, lips curved cruelly, stared at her. " No? " she murmured. " Not even when your dear husband cast you from beneath his roof? "

The Lady Euphemia wilted. Stricken, she looked round and saw the sea of faces and, her cheeks soon bloodless, would have fallen had she not been assisted to a bench.

" Dear God, as if I wouldn't have known everything about her," the Lady Philippa commented. " A fool of a woman, but she shall be bundled out before nightfall."

The Reverend Sister Melania sighed with relief, before admitting she would rejoice at such an outcome. Pressed to explain, she pointed out that young wenches were impressionable, and could soon acquire silly ideas. It would be a tragic misfortune if any of the novices came to think there would be more merit in wedding a sinful man than in becoming a bride of the snow-white Lord Jesus.

The Lady Philippa's voice quivered with rage. " If this was in your mind why did you not come to me long ago? " she demanded.

The Reverend Sister Melania began to tremble. "I . . . I could not be sure, My Lady, that the Lady Euphemia's influence would have such a result. It was only once or twice that it occurred to me."

" You shallow-pated dullard," the Lady Philippa said balefully, " who as from now will be the fourth of the mistresses instead of the first, who as from now shall daily pay forfeit by——"

A howl of fear, and a frantic patter of feet, stayed her. Enthralled, too startled even to hide their faces with their hands, the sisters of Watton stared as if mesmerised at what was taking place—at the youth fleeing for his life down the dormitory staircase, too terrified for himself to consider what he would suffer for his intrusion into the private quarters of the holy maidens; and at a brown bear which, through over-eagerness, cart-wheeled behind him down the stone steps, bumped heavily into the cloister arcade and, bouncing off, shook his head before resuming the chase. On three sides of the cloister the pursuit continued: along the west walk towards Lady Philippa and a spell-bound community, where the lad, tripping over the bottom step to the church doorway, fell and slithered on his face; along the south walk, where Brussie, roaring loudly enough to set the roof reverberating, would have caught up had not his flank touched against a broad loom, so sending him rolling over; and down the east walk towards the exit at the porter's lodge, where Warwick did a standing jump that finished a fifth of the way into the chapter house, and Gozi, a late starter, skidded nose-on into the closing kitchen-lobby door.

The Lady Philippa laughed until tears streaked her cheeks, and was still laughing, though less freely, when Sister Beatrice came down the dormitory staircase.

" It was well done, my daughter, and he'll never pry near the necessary again," she said, her voice feeble with mirth. " But go to the porter's shutter and there ascertain what has happened to the lout."

When Sister Beatrice returned she reported that Richard the plumber's apprentice, after jumping into the fish stew, where he was followed by the bear, had now sought refuge on the top of a short, ornamental column in the outer court. Of these there were

several, each with a circle of stone seating. Brussie was now patrol-
ling round the base, although occasionally, when on his hindlegs, he
had succeeded in getting a paw within a few inches of the youth's
boots.

The Lady Philippa chuckled as she rose. " My daughter," she
said, " your Brussie's next few meals shall be eaten out there, so
you will hood yourself closely and take his victuals to him."

" Yes, My Lady," Sister Beatrice said.

All sank to the floor as the prioress left. After that what a
chattering there was, during which Lazelle debated with herself
which would be the more advantageous: to slip off to the chapter
house there and then, or wait until the others dispersed to their
various affairs. She had just decided it would be preferable to carry
out her design when there was more movement in the walks, but
in the outcome, as she prepared to saunter off nonchalantly, her
hopes were dashed when she saw her breviary, in a sister's hand,
held out to her.

" It must have come loose from your girdle," Sister Beatrice
said. " I noticed it near your stall, but wasn't able to return it to
you because My Lady took me off to her lodging. You know now
for what," she ended laughingly.

" Yes," said Lazelle, making a valiant attempt to smile. " And
thank you very much."

" Wasn't it a do? " Sister Beatrice said delightedly. " I
think the Lord God, knowing how nastily I have been pestered,
made sure that not a thing went wrong."

Lazelle's face wrinkled with distaste. " He deserved all he got,"
she said. " Horrible to spy on you when you were *there*."

That caused Sister Beatrice to become very solemn. " Of a truth
it was, Sister Lazelle, and often I have been so upset that I put off,
and sometimes I haven't felt at all well because of it."

" I'm not surprised," Lazelle said sympathetically. " Still, it
will be finished for always now."

Sister Beatrice was claimed by Sisters Ealdgyth and Deborah,
who wanted every detail of the famous trapping repeated, and so
Lazelle, feeling desolate, wandered off by herself. But soon, as
determined as ever, she was fast recovering from her disappoint-
ment.

"There is still another day," she told herself fiercely. "And more days after that."

This was very true, but unhappily for her, though to the good fortune of others who enjoyed sun, warmth and blue skies, for nearly three weeks the weather was wonderful. The whole of the community spent every minute outdoors in the garden, trooping out as soon as permissible and returning only at the last minute. To be an exception posed tremendous difficulties, and invited curiosity.

On an afternoon a few days before the Feast of Saint Mark, during which harmony was destroyed by two most unpleasant quarrels, Lazelle learned to her distress that any further efforts towards seeing Brother Ughtred would be in vain. Until then, she had believed he was still working in the refectory, which was more easy to gain stealthily than the chapter house, where he had completed a painting of *Josiah ordering the repair of the Temple*.

Play-time in the garden was following its customary peaceful routine. Sister Alice, sitting in the shade of a clump of trees near the lake, was making an altar cloth and simultaneously keeping an eye on her kestrel, Lively, who was taking some interest in a family party of swimmers, a duck and her fluffy little offspring. Sisters Hilda, Maud and Lazelle herself, were trying to persuade one of the peacocks to spread his tail; and Sister Isabella, in a newly-discovered and somewhat exaggerated attitude of humility, was walking to and fro across the grass. Elsewhere sisters were reading, sewing, or busying themselves either at the goat-house or in the sundry cultivated gardens: for simples, pot-herbs and vegetables. It was all most relaxing, and the only disturbing note—so far, and but a mild one— was when the Reverend Sister Blanche, scowling at figures that refused to balance, reproved the novices Elizabeth and Mercy.

"You are here, my daughters, to acquire piety, obedience and humility," she said sharply. "Not to behave like uncouth hoydens."

Shortly after that Dame Eleanor smacked Dame de Warke's face, prelude to a terrible row which did not end until they were forcibly separated, when, both crying and each supporting the other, they went back to the convent, with Sir William the chaplain, also in tears, hovering near them.

"I shall mortify myself for this," the third prioress said dismally. "They are both touchy and desperately unhappy on the day they lost their dear ones, and this is the anniversary of the dread day when Lady Eleanor, in one fell swoop, had her husband and two sons killed by the Scottish rebels. I should have remembered, and made an excuse to keep them apart."

"But the Lord de Warke was not even fighting in the same battle, Reverend Mother," said Sister Naomi.

The third prioress sighed. "No, it is just that they were on different sides," she said. "And he could have been."

Defeated by the obstinacy of a bird who refused to perform, Sisters Maud, Hilda and Lazelle were sitting close by.

"It is very sad, Reverend Mother," said Sister Hilda. "But it happened last year, and they were good friends afterwards."

"So long as they can share their grief all is well with them, my daughter," said the third prioress. "Trouble rises only when, as on this day, one attributes to the other some responsibility for her loss."

"Dear Lord God, console them," the Reverend Sister Naomi murmured.

From then the conversation of the two superiors dwelled exclusively on gossipy affairs to do with the convent, of not much interest to those junior. Indeed Lazelle, lulled by the warmth, had slipped into a reverie that was half thrilling and half melancholy when she heard a remark that did not at first fully penetrate her consciousness.

"I had thought, Most Revered Mother," Sister Hilda said, "that the monk of Rievaulx would have remained to do more than the one picture in the refectory. It needs many to make it pretty."

"He has been here for close on four months, my daughter," the sub-prioress was replying when Lazelle sat up. "The lord abbot Hugh has been most magnanimous in sparing him so long when there is much for him to do at home."

Desperately Lazelle hoped that she was not showing any of the desolation she felt.

"Perhaps the lord abbot might one day send him again, Most Revered Mother," she said.

"It may be so, my daughter," said the sub-prioress. "The lord abbot Hugh is My Lady's blood cousin, and has a most tender regard for the priory over which she rules."

Even small details would have helped to numb the ache in

Lazelle's heart, and if moon-faced Sister Isabella had not come and, bowing, asked permission to sit with them, she would have asked if Brother Ughtred had ridden out by himself, or whether one of the canons regular or a post-messenger was accompanying him part way.

"You have finished your perambulations, my daughter?" the sub-prioress dryly asked Sister Isabella.

"Yes, Most Revered Mother," Sister Isabella replied in a little girl voice, "and now I am at peace."

The sub-prioress was staring at her when Sister Katherine, cheeks hotly flushed, and walking very quickly, joined the group. Sister Paula, dark eyes frantic, was not far behind.

"Sister Maud," Sister Katherine said jerkily, after a hurried and quite inadequate bow to the sub-prioress, "you said you might clean out the hawk mews this afternoon, and if it should please you I would enjoy helping very much."

Sister Maud laughed jovially as she scrambled up. "That's an offer I would never refuse, but find an old habit to put on."

"I have warned you, Sister Katherine," Sister Paula said, her deep, man-like voice strained. "As the Lord is above, little Katherine, haven't I tried to warn you about consorting with Sister Maud?"

"Warned her!" Sister Maud spluttered. "Warned her about what?"

"And I have warned you, Sister Paula, to cease your queer pestering of me," Katherine said hysterically.

Both the sub-prioress and the Reverend Sister Naomi spoke together, their words different but the stern instruction the same— they would not countenance quarrelling.

"If I do not speak now, before Sister Maud has led her away, I shall speak after the Daily Chapter to-morrow, Most Revered Mother," Sister Paula shouted. "And when I speak then I shall accuse Sister Katherine and Sister Maud of being too friendly."

The sub-prioress gasped. "As God is above, you must be out of your head. How can sisters-in-the-Lord be too friendly?"

"They can be, Most Revered Mother," Sister Paula said frantically. "That is why Sister Maud takes her to the kennels and into My Lady's stables, so that she can fondle her."

Sister Maud's mouth opened. " I . . . I fondle her? " she said, dazed.

Her face a tight mask, the sub-prioress pointed towards the convent. " My daughters Katherine, Paula and Maud, you will go to my chamber," she said. " This matter shall be thrashed out before the bell rings for Vespers."

When alone, Lazelle also left the garden, for it did not matter now whether anyone asked the why and wherefore. Her listless steps took her to the church where, kneeling below the steps of the presbytery, she prayed for Brother Ughtred's well-being and safety, and for herself and for her sisters.

" O Dear Lord," she whispered, " I think it may be wrong that some whom you have created should dwell in narrow precincts, for the weak-minded tend to become weaker, and many of the stronger all too bitter. And if, in thinking thus, I am sinfully offending against all the tenets of the Order in which from baby days I have been trained, then give me the fortitude to bear the pains I should suffer if these thoughts of mine were ever discovered. Grant me this, O My Saviour."

When, at last, she left the church and went into the cloister, she found that many had left the garden and, in hushed tones, were speculating about the reason why the sub-prioress had marched three of their sisters indoors.

In ' narrow precincts ' sensations do not die quickly, but talk about the present one was petering out when Sister Paula was publicly whipped for the last time on the seventh day. After that there was mounting excitement concerning the Lord Bishop's visit which, if odd whispers and giggles occasionally were any omen, promised to have results which would have astounded that prelate. However regrettable this might have been it was also regrettable that My Lady was somewhat unguarded in her speech, dropping several remarks which were decidedly inciting.

The Lord Bishop, arriving with a sumptuous retinue of fourteen, paid a cursory call upon the prior, who kept a poor table, before entering the other side by way of the gateway to the prioress's lodging, his escort and personal chaplain remaining for the time being in the outer court.

Inside, in the yard, the Lady Philippa and her daughters were drawn up to receive him and, as soon as suitable courtesies had been exchanged, a move was made to the church. After prayers, the whole assembly repaired to the chapter house, where a finely carved chair had been placed alongside My Lady's at the east end.

The Lord Bishop, at Lady Philippa's request, spoke to the community, but there was nothing very arresting about his homily until, not without craftiness, he brought himself to disclose that at a nunnery within his jurisdiction, unnamed, he had learnt to his horror that rabbits and other pets were taken into the holy Offices.

" With the deepest respect, My Lord," Sister Constance said with determination, " is not a rabbit one of God's creatures? "

Sisters Beatrice, Alice and Katherine rose together, and of them, by the shortest of margins, Alice got her question in first.

" My Lord Bishop," she said reproachfully, " surely you have not forgotten how our Lord spoke of the sparrows in the field."

Considering how frequently there were heated complaints about pets, it was surprising how many supported the kingdom of animals and birds, and as all spoke at once the babel became of such proportions that the Lady Philippa had to hammer her staff to restore order.

" My daughters," she said gently, " you must hear out the Lord Bishop more patiently. I am sure that when he has finished he will be happy to clear up any doubts. Is that not so, My Lord? "

The Lord Bishop nodded not too happily. " It will be my pleasure, My Lady," he muttered.

The tumult of a few moments before was nothing to the tumult that followed, when the Lord Bishop, unrolling a Papal Bull for all to see, read out His Holiness's strictures upon personal adornment in the cloister. To this he added his own condemnation, which so moved the fourth prioress that she left her stall and, a dumpy and drab figure not unlike a stuffed sack, waddled up the aisle towards him, an example enthusiastically followed.

" My Lord," the fourth prioress cried, " why is it sinful for us to make ourselves pleasing in the sight of the Lord who looks down on us? "

" My Lord," Sister Matilda demanded passionately, " is it vanity for us to try to be becoming for Him to whom we are espoused? "

The Lady Philippa's veil hid the twinkle in her eyes as she glanced at Sister Matilda, who could not have been more indifferent to clothes; but she closed those eyes in sheer horror on perceiving the wimple of a much more youthful daughter, Deborah, which was of a bilious shade of green.

Tall and brawny Sister Ealdgyth bent down to the Lord Bishop. "Would My Lord have Our Blessed Saviour Jesus ashamed of those who are his ever-devoted wives?" she asked.

She had to shout to make herself heard, and the Lord Bishop had to shout to make sure that the Lady Philippa heard him. And the Lady Philippa had to bang very hard indeed to restore order.

"My daughters," she chided them, "why all this unseemly noise? The Lord Bishop is merely confiding in us what he would wish in the nunneries which *are* under his episcopal authority. It is only the act of a dear friend who would spurn the notion of interference in the affairs of a house whose ways have always been different, and always will be different, from those which are privileged to be under his beneficent control." She turned to him gravely. "Is that not so, My Lord?"

The Lord Bishop looked hard at her. "Yes," he said, his nostrils tight. "Yes, it is so, My Lady."

This triumph went to the heads of the sisters, and the proceedings, far from settling down, were soon moving from bad to worse. Used to orderliness and deference, the Lord Bishop found himself hemmed in by a horde of yelling women, his ear-drums assailed to bursting by the shrill din. In an effort to assert his presence, he rose from his chair and, impressive in rich vestments and glittering mitre despite his rotundity, held up his be-ringed hand for silence. That was as little successful as when Canutus demonstrated to his flatterers how impossible it was to hold back the flood tide.

"My Lord Bishop," Sister Beatrice screeched, "would you deny that many of the great beasts have more cleverness than some humans? Answer that, My Lord Bishop, if you please."

"Yes, answer that," a chorus yelled.

The Reverend Sister Blanche had seized the red-sealed, Papal Bull. She brandished it at My Lord.

"My Lord Bishop, if we manage to pay our way decently in days when there are so many calls on our revenues, do you consider it an evil in God's sight if we squeeze out a few pennies towards prettifying ourselves for Him?" she cried to the heavens. " Tell us that, My Lord."

The chorus fired again. " Yes, tell us that, My Lord Bishop."

A combination of two things was the Lord Bishop's undoing, the first when Sister Eva went into hysterics, her scream so eerily high that if it had been a trifle higher only a dog would have heard it; the second when, as his bulbous-eyed glance roved over those so close to him, he had a fleeting hallucination that, between two of the faces pressing him was another face, a howling monkey's.

The Lord Bishop lost the remnants of his nerve, giving vent to a far from saintly observation as to what should be his fate if ever he were lunatic enough to venture again beneath the roof of a woman with the reputation of the prioress of Watton. In the uproar this remark was not heard, but his break from cover was evident to all. Whooping joyously, the pack set off in pursuit, and My Lord, with the community at his heels, was chased out of the chapter house, half round the cloister to the entry at the far side, along the passage to the gateway to the prioress's lodging, and across the yard to the door, which he slammed behind him, though not quickly enough to prevent the Reverend Sister Blanche from throwing His Holiness's Bull inside.

The sisterhood were weak with laughter when the Lady Philippa, staff in hand and bearing herself with great dignity, walked into the yard.

" My daughters," she said, " I find it deplorable that you are convulsed at the Lord Bishop's expense, and if I were not of a kindly nature I should cancel your outing to the country to-morrow when I have departed for Sempringham. Moreover, if I did my duty, there would be no May Day revels for you on the following day."

Sister Deborah, bubbling with mirth, bowed very low. " My Lady," she said daringly, " I ask God's mercy and yours, and with respect suggest you should inform My Lord that you have sharply censured us."

The Lady Philippa eyed her. " I think that beyond my daughter Lazelle I have others of more than one part," she said. " For that, my daughter, is precisely what I propose doing."

Needless to say, the community had their two consecutive days of pleasuring. As soon as My Lady's closed cart, with Old John at the reins, started out from the prioress's yard for Lincolnshire, ranks were broken and the more youthful sisters raced off to the dormitory. When changing tunics, whose various parts were supposed to represent the six wings of the cherubim—two in the hood, two in the sleeves, and two in the body—prayers could be heard as usual in the cubicles, but though the snatches were much too gay not a single superior uttered a word of reproof. This was a time when discipline was relaxed.

The excursion was to the farm of one of the priory's tenants, and every cart, each carefully covered in, was drawn into service, and even then some of them were packed to suffocation for the short trip. At the place where the hogs were to be washed the canons regular of the escort withdrew, and the sisters descended to the springy turf, many giggling because they had peeped out occasionally. All, young and old, very happy.

It was delicious fun watching the year-old sheep being washed by the old farmer and an equally old shepherd, who took turns. Whichever of them it was who stood thigh-deep had often to struggle hard before a reluctant victim could be hauled from the pen at the side of the stream, which had been dammed; then the hog was thoroughly ducked thrice, an operation so strenuously resisted that often it seemed that both man and animal would end by being immersed, a prospect naughtily hoped for by the onlookers; and, finally, it was amusing when, its ordeal over, the poor creature leapt up the bank and ran off as if pursued by the devil, only to stop suddenly as if restrained by an invisible rope, when it started peacefully to browse.

Eating, too, was different, without any observance excepting a *Gloria* beforehand and Grace afterwards—no reader at a desk, either, and no prohibition on chattering to heart's content. The platters were arranged on clean white cloths spread on the ground, and there was plenty on them: meats, creamy cheese, butter, and a tremendous assortment of pastries and cakes, though nothing of the lusciousness of Dame Euphemia's confections had she still been with them. The wine was perfection also, and could not have been sweeter.

" Oh! I *am* enjoying myself," said Sister Beatrice. " I shall offer special thanks to our Saviour before I lay my head to rest this night."

Lazelle was staring into the distance. " It is wondrous not to have walls, to be able to gaze across the fields to the fringe of the forest without hindrance," she murmured.

One of the novices touched her breast. " I am Mercy of Thixendale," she said with a comic air, " and from where I came there is a hill nearby from which I have seen miles and miles. This is nothing, dear Sister Lazelle."

All attention now switched to Sister Ealdgyth who, with Sister Constance's Gozi tearing along with her, was once more chasing a hare. All laughed when Sister Ealdgyth, hopelessly outdistanced, gave a pantomime representing exhaustion.

" Hares," said Sister Alice. " A delight to watch on the run, but . . ." She shook her head.

" But what, Sister Alice? " Sister Matilda asked.

An authority in ailments and their treatment, Sister Alice's expression was grave. " Too much eating of the flesh promotes melancholy. The instances I have seen . . . you would never *credit* them."

Young Sister Katherine was more concerned with the morrow. " Oh! I do trust it will be fine, Lazelle. The monk Godwin of the abbey of Rievaulx predicts it will be dry until the Feast of the Ascension, but George of Pontefract, of the abbey of Kirkstall in Airedale, differs considerably. The Reverend Sister Naomi styled it on the east walk *tabula* after the post-messenger called. What do you think? "

Lazelle, who was throwing tit-bits to Puchin, looked at the sky. " The monk of Rievaulx, Katherine," she murmured. " My favour is with him always."

" Of a certainty," Katherine said wisely, " he has been most reliable for many months now. Yes, I shall put my trust in him, and——" She broke off to admonish Puchin, who was chattering too noisily.

Brother Godwin would have been very amused could he have known how a junior nun of the priory of Watton was depending on his skill from that moment; and would undoubtedly have been gratified by the praise Katherine heaped on him the next morning.

May Day was lovely, with hardly a cloud. Games were played in the garden, and both Sister Beatrice and her lumbering pet, whom she had been rehearsing secretly, were wildly applauded when, facing each other, they did a dance together. An enthralled audience would have watched for hours, but unhappily it was too hot for Brussie's comfort, and he spent much of his time in the lake.

"Just once again, Beatrice," Sister Hilda begged when the bear, after another cool off, was coaxed out of the water for the fifth time. "Brussie loves it, too," she added, which was dubious.

So, once again, Brussie stood on his hind legs and, with hairy fore-paws dangling, swayed and took tiny steps this way and that, his mistress and partner opposite responding faithfully to his movements. And Sister Hilda held out her hand to Lazelle, and Lazelle grasped Deborah's, and Deborah, wildly waving, summoned Katherine to hasten, so that very soon fourteen or fifteen of the sisterhood, joined in a ring, were whirling at a dizzy rate round the two stars, smilingly watched by some of the mistresses.

Sharp-eyed, it was the Reverend Sister Joanna who saw a small object fall, and she hurried forward to save it from being trodden on by flying feet.

"It is a locket, with a beautiful little picture of the Lord Jesus in it," she said.

Puzzled already, the Reverend Sister Melania, who had been most subdued latterly, examined the painting more closely.

"I have never seen it before," she said. "As I should have, for it is I who check what they have."

"It is not old, either," Sister Joanna said.

Worried that she might be in further trouble for negligence, Sister Melania shook her head. "And we have had no merchants or hucksters calling so far this year," she said despondently.

The dancing had ended. Brussie, sitting down resolutely, was being fussed over, which did not please him, for he was surrounded by the sisters, and it was airless, and that made him hotter. Then, as the lord bishop had done, he burst through the barrier of over-talkative females and ambled towards the lake.

The Reverend Sister Naomi, who had taken charge, held up the locket. "Who does this belong to?" she asked.

Lazelle's hand instinctively flew to her bosom. " It is mine, Reverend Sister," she said.

" Where did you obtain it? "

The flush from exertion had passed from Lazelle's face. She was deathly pale. " With the utmost respect, does that matter, Reverend Sister? " she said, a small quaver in her voice. " There could not be a more holy picture to carry on my chain."

" I asked you where you got it," Sister Naomi said sternly. " Where and from whom? "

Lazelle's chin went up. " I cannot tell you, Reverend Sister."

Two friends made a bid to help her. Deborah explained that she had not been well recently, and this Katherine attributed to too much praying, over and above the amount laid down. Both were silenced.

Eyes hard, Sister Naomi turned again to Lazelle. " I shall ask this once and no more. Where did the locket come from? "

" I shall not say, Reverend Sister," Lazelle replied quietly.

" You will accompany us," Sister Naomi said thinly.

Now senior to Sister Melania, she beckoned to her, and with Lazelle between them the two obedientiaries marched off, gapingly watched. The walk ended at the dormitory, in Lazelle's cubicle.

" Except for the holy Offices, to which you will go when the bell rings and from which you will return immediately at the conclusion, you will stay here until it is decided differently," said Sister Naomi. " Such pittances of food as may be permitted to you, will be brought by one of the lay-sisters. Is that clear? Answer."

Lazelle bowed. " Yes, Reverend Sister," she said.

" I shall report your conduct to the sub-prioress," Sister Naomi continued bleakly. " Perhaps she may speak to you before the Great Silence, but I think she may well allow some considerable time to pass so that you can reflect on your sinful disobedience."

" Yes, Reverend Sister."

The Reverend Sister Naomi's surmise was accurate. On Rogation Sunday, when the almoner distributed boxwood sticks to the aged and infirm, Lazelle was still confined to the dormitory; and on the next day, when a great cleaning-up began throughout the convent in preparation for the Feast of the Ascension, she remained there until half an hour before Compline, when the Reverend

Sisters Blanche and Naomi came to take her to the sub-prioress, which entailed a humiliating walk during which at least two score of the sisters and lay-sisters saw her.

At first the sub-prioress assumed that the punishment Lazelle had already undergone would have been sufficient to chasten her, but nevertheless related how a nun she had once known, for an offence no more grave, had been deprived of communion for seven years and sent to another convent with a name for rigorous discipline.

" Now where did you get the locket, my daughter?" she wound up.

" With respect, Most Revered Mother, I cannot tell you," said Lazelle.

The sub-prioress flushed with anger. " Are you out of your mind? " she demanded.

" I trust not, Most Revered Mother," said Lazelle. " But my mind was given to me by God, and I do not think He would condemn me for wearing a little picture which is holy and exquisite, and painted with reverence."

" Cease your quibbling," the sub-prioress said sternly. " Have I to remind you that by the Rule absolute obedience to your superiors is insisted upon? "

Lazelle, tears starting, tried to appeal to her. " Most Revered Mother, humbly I ask you this—if the Lord gave me a mind, did He not also give me the right to think for myself? "

" Not if your thoughts run counter to the orders of those He set over you," the sub-prioress stormed. " When My Lady speaks to us she is speaking as God's chosen deputy below, and when I stand in her place, as now, my voice is also God's voice."

Screwing up her courage, Lazelle shook her head. " Only God himself can speak to me," she said. " No one between can take His place, however illustrious, Most Revered Mother."

The mistresses, Blanche and Naomi, gasped; and for the moment the sub-prioress was so taken aback that her mouth opened and closed like that of an expiring fish, until her lips closed tightly, though briefly.

" This is your last chance," she shouted. " How do you come to have a locket picture? "

" I will not say, Most Revered Mother," Lazelle said.

Confronted by a defiance she had never met before, the sub-prioress turned to the sisters.

" If I did not know it to be impossible," she stuttered, " I would conclude that she has been standing in a market place absorbing the evil doctrines of those wicked preachers who boldly proclaim the foul assertions of the perverted John Wycliffe."

" It is so, Most Revered Mother," said Sister Maud.

Agitated and yet seething with rage, the sub-prioress paced the chamber until coming to a decision. Then she extended her arm towards Lazelle, pointing a shaky finger.

" Your sinful behaviour, my daughter, will be made known to My Lady as soon as she returns home. Until then, for your obduracy and stupidity, you will suffer solitary confinement and a diet of bread and water."

Lazelle was taken to the west walk, where she was locked into a cheerless cell furnished with nothing more than a wood bench and a pot. By the third morning of her imprisonment, which was the eve of the great feast celebrating Christ's ascent to Heaven forty days after the Resurrection, she was becoming ill with worry lest she missed participating in one of the four greatest occasions of the year. She prayed and prayed that it might not be so.

Her desperate petition was granted and on the day of the Ascension she was escorted to a tiny oratory on the floor above, where there were two small slits in the shape of a cross through which she could see into the church, and hear the Office. Thus she was present at the awesome moment after the Gospel at High Mass when, symbolising the Lord Christ's parting from His disciples, the paschal candle was extinguished.

That night it was the Reverend Sister Melania who came with the lay sister, whom she signed to leave when a pitcher of water and a small loaf had been put down.

" There is news that My Lady will not be home as early as expected," she said austerely. "The lord abbot of Crowland, who has a deep regard for her, is arranging some sport and she will be remaining in the Fens for a period of wild-fowling."

To Lazelle it seemed to make little difference. " Yes, Reverend Sister," she said dutifully.

Cautiously Sister Melania glanced at the doorway. " My dear," she turned to whisper, " the day of My Lady's return being so uncertain, I think the Revered Mother would deal with you herself if you submitted yourself penitently to her, and acquainted her with what you have so wrongfully refused to disclose. She would punish you harshly, but my counsel to you is to grasp the nettle now. For many reasons it would be better for you."

Lazelle tiredly shook her head. " It is sweetly kind of you to think of me, Reverend Sister," she said, deeply touched. " But . . . but I cannot change my mind."

For a few moments, the momentary softness of her expression vanished, the Reverend Sister Melania stared at her.

" So be it then," she snapped before leaving the cell. " So be it on your own head."

Without appetite, Lazelle ate a small piece of crusty bread and drank a little water before seeking the consolation of her breviary. But after a short while she slipped from the bench to her knees and, with hands together, began to pray.

" O Jesus Christ my Saviour, make me staunch so that never will I betray Brother Ughtred. It is not a question of the beautiful gift he made for me, though for doing so I know he would be fearsomely scourged. But one thing may lead to another, Almighty Lord, and if ever it became plain that my face is the face on Brother Ughtred's Madonna painting, of which the lord abbot Hugh is so proud, cruelties would be inflicted on him nigh as terrible as those to be endured in the bottomless pit. So, O Lord God, Jesus my Saviour and the Blessed Virgin Mary who bore Him, stiffen me in my weakness, ensure that I shall never falter whatsoever befalls."

Weary and sick at heart, consumed with anxiety, she rose and, dragging the bench nearer the small, barred window, opened her breviary. Soon it was darker inside and, swathing herself with the solitary blanket, she sank against the cold wall, trying to rest.

# 7

On the afternoon of the day following the Feast of Pentecost, Ughtred was leaving the church, feeling very cheerful about progress, for another few hours would complete the fresco he had abominated since starting it. As usual, on reaching The Holy Three, he paused to stare at the brilliantly-colourful Madonna on the wall of the north transept, a piece of vanity he had not yet succeeded in curing himself of.

" Yes, I am satisfied," he murmured. " It is the Madonna I had hoped for, and it stands out nobly. And it is Sister Lazelle."

Reflecting contentedly that the guest master had told him that never since the picture had been placed in position had it failed to hold spellbound every visitor on reaching the crossing from the west end, Ughtred went along to the nearer lavatory, where he was washing his hands behind the arcade when, shaken some distance away, he heard the infirmary clapper. As the sound came closer Ughtred hurried to dry himself, and the brethren in the cloister walks made haste to close their books and return them to the aumbry, so that by the time the infirmarian appeared at the end of the Passage the community was in readiness to fall in behind him as he returned to the infirmary, where a brother was either dead or expiring.

Wondering which of the wisemen it was, Brother Luke or Brother Godfrey, Ughtred soon found it was his old friend, to whom the prior was giving extreme unction and the last sacrament. When the community had gathered round the bed the plea was sung to Him who renewed the face of the earth: *Emittes spiritum et creabuntur; et renovabis faciem terrae.*

As the passing bell started to toll, Ughtred, with Brothers Henry, Edgar and Ranulf, carried the dying old man to the misericord, where ashes were being spread on the floor in front of the magnificent new crucifix. Over the ashes a blanket was placed, and on to this the bearers' burden was gently lowered; then Brother Pagan de Bolebec closed Brother Godfrey's feet together, and Ughtred and Brother Martin opened out his arms, so that he was lying in the form of the cross on which the Lord Jesus died.

The wiseman's eyes were clouded, but recognition came into them when he saw Ughtred. He smiled and tried to speak.

" Yes, Revered Father," Ughtred said forlornly, bending lower.

Brother Godfrey called on his few resources for another effort. " My son Ughtred," he said almost inaudibly, " be valiant, my dear son. Better . . . better the short and heroic journey to Heaven . . . than mine, so unduly delayed. I have not . . . I have no great news for Saint Peter."

Blinded by tears, Ughtred nodded. " I understand, Most Revered Father," he muttered. " It is what I am beginning to think myself."

" I . . . I should have thought of it . . . long ago . . . long, long ago, my son," Brother Godfrey said wistfully.

After another struggle, the old wiseman asked his brothers in God to chant the *Dies Irae* with him. He had said the last response: " Save me, O Lord," when his gentle soul fled.

His body was then taken to the stone slab in the infirmary chapel, where it was washed before being laid before the cross, on a bier. From then onwards, Ughtred and old Brother Basil kept vigil at his feet.

On the next morning the remains were rested awhile in the chapter house, and again in church, for Requiem Mass. From there, with solemn dirge, Brother Godfrey was borne in the sunshine to the cemetery. As was customary, he was buried in the habit and sandals he had worn in life, with rosary and crucifix at his side, and sheet of lead on breast.

Saddened by the loss of the sole person from whom he had received any affection throughout his years in the abbey, Ughtred walked slowly to the workshops. Gazing unseeingly at the light green of birch, ash and alder beyond the wall, he almost stumbled into a litter on which the auditor, home at last after his terrible accident near Newminster, was being carried.

Hurriedly Ughtred bowed. "Praise be to the Lord!" he exclaimed. "It is good to see you again, Brother Roger."

Implacably the older monk stared at him. "So it is you," he hissed. "Away from me, breaker of God's ordinances and foul fornicator."

Ughtred was so nonplussed that he was unable to find a word. Later, he came to the conclusion that the blow Brother Roger had sustained when pitched from his horse on to his head, which was believed responsible for the paralysis of his limbs, had also affected him mentally.

Ughtred knew better than this the next morning, after the Daily Chapter, when the auditor, who had been brought from the infirmary, charged him with carnal association with a nun.

If with little knowledge of the world, all religious knew what this meant, and every eye was on Ughtred when, ignoring procedure, he jumped to his feet, white with rage.

"It is a lie, My Lord," he shouted.

"Sit down," Abbot Hugh said sternly, "or I will have you whipped for your impertinence before we proceed further." He turned to Brother Roger. "Continue, my son, and establish the accusation."

The auditor described how, when but a few miles out from Rievaulx on his mission to Newminster, he had lingered behind his companions to watch the chase, at a point on the highway from which there was a view of the grange at Riggs, where he had seen Ughtred of Monkseaton with one of the brides of Christ who was presumably in attendance on the prioress of Watton.

"With my own eyes, My Lord," he went on, "I watched them ascend to the dormitory, and although I waited many minutes they did not appear again. I would remind My Lord that there is still a bed in the dormitory, as is shown in the inventory."

Abbot Hugh nodded grimly. "It seems sufficient, my son, but, owing to the wisdom of those who drew up our Rule, it is now my duty to lend an impartial ear to the other side." He signalled to Ughtred.

Despite this judicially fair statement, it was very evident which way My Lord was leaning, and excitement in the chapter house was attaining a feverish pitch about the outcome if the terrible accusation was deemed proven. Moreover, in a few moments the monk Ughtred had become one apart from themselves. He was suspected of intercourse with a woman.

" My Lord," Ughtred said, hard pressed to control his anger, " if this monstrous allegation were true I would deserve to be struck down by the Almighty's bolt as I speak. But it is not so."

He told his simple story: how, when the hunt moved away, he had ridden down to Riggs out of curiosity, and when there had met the nun whom he had been able to aid when nearing home on returning to England from the abbey of Citeaux.

Ughtred paused, and then addressed the prior: " Most Revered Father, do you recall my explaining to you that that was the reason I did not come back until a few hours after Brother Roger? "

A harsh man, but an honest man, the prior confirmed this. " It is so, My Lord," he said.

Abbot Hugh fingered his chin. " H'mm . . . yes, I remember that I was also informed about the incident."

From then it was as if a blown-up pig's bladder had been pricked with a needle, before being slashed with a knife.

" My Lord," Ughtred resumed, " this was not the encounter of a monk and a nun strangers to each other. I had been of service to her, for which her Lady, the Dame Philippa, was gracious enough to reward me, with your permission. I freely admit, My Lord, that I should not have stayed talking to her, but I was inquisitive about the grange and so was she . . . and we went everywhere, including the dormitory where Brother Roger alleges we sinned."

" There is a bed there, is it not so? " Brother Roger snapped.

" Yes, there is that, my son," the lord abbot said suavely. " You can personally testify, under God, that forbidden relations ensued? "

" How could I, *Domine*? " the auditor protested. " I was on the highway."

" True, it would be difficult," Abbot Hugh agreed.

" My Lord, she is a widow of Christ, and pure," Ughtred said furiously. " It is sacrilege to imagine she would consent to evil doing."

" Nature will out with some, My Lord," Brother Roger said obstinately. " They had the opportunity, there was the bed, and they made the time."

" My cousin the Lady Philippa, prioress of Watton, with a strumpet serving her," the abbot mused. " Would that she were here, so that you could thus inform her. I think it might be most amusing."

With a surprising change of tone he reminded the auditor of that part of the Rule whereby an accuser who fails to make his case good receives the same punishment the accused would have suffered had the offence been pinned to him.

" I shall spare you now for your insult to the Lady Philippa," he said harshly. " But should you ever recover from your sickness, as I trust you will, the penalty is to be paid."

He gestured impatiently. Brother Roger was carried to the vestibule, where servants were waiting to bear him back to the infirmary.

" As for you, my son," the lord abbot said severely to Ughtred, " you should have withdrawn immediately, and for your indiscretion you also must pay. From now until the Martyrdom of Saints Peter and Paul you will eat alone, at a table placed in the middle of the refectory floor, where your brothers may witness your shame."

Ughtred bowed. " Yes, My Lord," he said thankfully.

The next business was a discussion about the form of the document notifying Brother Godfrey's death which the brief bearer would deliver at the abbeys of the Order.

Brother Roger's attack had other consequences, and for some time afterwards Ughtred was nagged by Brother Robert, who had already begun a stirring writing headed:

*Heroic Rescue by a monk of Rievaulx of a Holy Nun of the Priory of Watton in the wapentake of Harthill and their subsequent meeting in a Lonely Place.*

The chronicler's importuning petered out before the Feast of Corpus Christi, when it became the aim of both Ughtred and Brother Robert, and the majority of the community, to avoid Brother Edmund, who delighted to air his knowledge of the historians whenever, as now, he considered it fitting. To hear Brother Edmund expound on the doctrine of transubstantiation as defined by the Lateran Council of A.D. 1215 might be stimulating on the first occasion, but repetitions were tedious.

At the end of the month there was a sensation about Brother

Ralph, the expert in precious stones, whose pot-belly had always been difficult to reconcile with the many fastings he was permitted to reduce his weight. The rumour was that Brother Ralph, always a baby about his aches and pains, had consulted the infirmarian—a suspicious-minded individual—in regard to a severe stomach upset, and on admission to the infirmary had been tricked into believing he was on his deathbed. Faced by the prospect of eternal damnation unless he made amends, Brother Ralph had confessed that, by means the most sly and wicked, he had always managed to eat heartily even when supposed to be fasting. Many were the grim suggestions as to the penalties he would incur for his unholy conduct.

On the same afternoon, the lord abbot's secretary came to the church to tell Ughtred that My Lord required him at once. Ordinarily, with a single exception, Ughtred had always found him a pleasantly talkative fellow, but on this occasion he acted as if he were dumb during the walk to the abbot's lodging, in the reception room, and the ante-room. In fact, he spoke once only, on coming out of the dining-hall, where he paused at the side of the doorway.

"My Lord will now receive you, Brother Ughtred," he said.

On entering the long apartment, Ughtred had a devastating shock when he found that the prioress of Watton was with My Lord. Before sinking to his knees he noticed that both looked extremely angry.

The Lady Philippa thrust out her hand at him. In her palm was the picture in little of the Lord Christ he had painted, and his own chain and relic box.

"That comes from your brush, probably made with the Italian coffer of paints I gave you," she said sharply. "And that is your chain and holy relic."

Ughtred thought faster than ever before in his life. Intuitively he felt that she was seeking confirmation, and at the same time he was convinced that if Sister Lazelle were in trouble it would be better for a minor offence than a major.

"They are all mine, which I lost when I was favoured with the hospitality of the canons regular of your convent, My Lady," he said gladly. "Where were they found, My Lady? I searched everywhere——"

He was allowed breathing space when the chaplain ushered in the sub-prior, the cantor, sacrist, infirmarian, and the guardians of the cloister.

" My sons," the lord abbot snapped at them, " have any of you ever heard the monk Ughtred make a remark or comment which could be considered noxious? "

The obedientiaries gave thought to the question, deep thought.

" He was solicitous about the monk of Jervaulx, when on the roof with him, My Lord," said the sub-prior.

Prostrated, Ughtred leaned slightly more forward to hide his actions. Cautiously he worked his hand inside his habit until he sprung the catch of the chain round his neck; then, bringing the relic down his body, he wrapped the chain about the linen belt holding his drawers. Meantime the investigation proceeded.

" My Lord," said the cantor, " it comes to my mind that after returning from the Annual Chapter in Burgundy he evinced an interest in the writings of the blasphemous John Wycliffe."

" In his last days, My Lord," the infirmarian said eagerly, " the wiseman Godfrey developed strange questionings, snatches of which were overheard. He and the monk Ughtred often talked together."

" We may obtain what we seek in another fashion," said the Lady Philippa. " My son Ughtred, you will have missed your locket and relic? "

" Its absence has troubled me immeasurably, My Lady," Ughtred said sorrowfully.

Savagely, she tore open the front of his habit. " No, he has nothing about his neck," she snapped. " But as I have told you, my cousin Hugh, the girl no longer has the relic she was known to have, and it must be somewhere."

" As God is above," the lord abbot said grimly, " it will be found if it is here."

Peremptorily he ordered the sub-prior, the third prior, and the infirmarian to institute a thorough search: of Ughtred's cubicle, the workshop, the *locutorium*, and even the box in which Brother Godfrey had kept the possessions allowed in old age.

When the party of three left, the Lord Hugh and the Dame Philippa went on talking as if the cantor, the sacrist, the fourth prior, and Ughtred were not present.

My Lord said violently: " It would seem that the auditor Roger was right—that he did lie with her at our grange of Riggs."

" They may have come together more than that," said the Lady Philippa. " There is every presumption that they also met at Watton when the fools ran amok, imagining a great fire. But none of that is of any import."

" *Not* of import? " said the lord abbot.

" There are deeper affairs than this," Lady Philippa said shortly.

My Lord shrugged. " You have always dealt effectively with the prior before now."

The Lady Philippa banged her fist on the long table. " He scents he has me in a cleft-stick," she said in a rage. " If I deliver her for trial I bring notice and public shame to my house, which I would abhor; while if I harbour her until I break her stubborn spirit he will only let me be if I consent to a different arrangement of the monies between the two sides, to which I shall never agree."

" At the worst you should relinquish her," the lord abbot commented. " These are dangerous days in such matters, and if you were thought to be lax you are the one of whom questions would be asked."

The Lady Philippa's mouth was ugly. " I have time yet," she said. " If she could conceive what is still before her . . ."

The lord abbot put his hand under her elbow, and they went into the parlour, closing the door; and did not reappear until after the secretary advised them that the three superiors had returned.

" What have you to report? " My Lord said as he entered.

" We have discovered nothing, save a few sketches and a miniature painting of the face in the Madonna picture which because of its different nature we think you should see, My Lord," the sub-prior said. " It was, My Lord, hidden away most cunningly."

Abbot Hugh held out his hand. " Yes," he grunted, after scrutinising Ughtred's second most cherished possession. " Small wonder he secreted this, for it is a painting of our Madonna in the guise of a secular maid."

One brief glance at the little picture was sufficient for the Lady

Philippa who, watched with amazement by the obedientiaries, laughed until she was exhausted, finishing up bent over the table, supporting herself with her hands.

" What is all this mirth about? " the lord abbot asked suspiciously.

In a voice roughed with the after-effects, the Lady Philippa told him, in stages.

" O my dear cousin, of a truth it is side-splitting indeed, though I fear it may not thus appeal to you. To think that here, in this austere male convent, you have a picture about which you have boasted to the skies, a picture which, though I have not seen it as yet, most assuredly displays . . . but I must not make play at the expense of the Lord Abbot Hugh of the famed abbey of Rievaulx, a proud man forsooth."

The lord abbot was much too familiar with her not to apprehend that a most unpleasant blow was in store for him, but it was worse than he could have surmised.

" She is the nun whom you are here about? " he exclaimed. " The nun you call Lazelle? "

For the next few minutes, the veins in his neck and temple swelling, he behaved as if he had lost his reason. His words thickened with rage, he commanded a withdrawal to the church, and when there continued to rave, his passion such that even those of his inferiors who had nothing to fear were white with fright.

" I shall be mocked by the world when it becomes widely known that I have bragged about a Madonna whose face is that of a whorish nun painted by one of my own monks," he bellowed. " My son," he went on, half-choking as he addressed the sacrist, " you will fetch the *custos fabricae* with all speed, so that this accursed blemish may be ripped from the wall and destroyed."

The Lady Philippa, who had been changing positions to view the picture, first on the side of the two chapels and then the other, turned quickly to him.

" No, My Lord," she said determinedly. " Whatsoever its origins the painting is superb, and I will have it myself if that is your mood."

The lord abbot reacted violently. " It reflects abominably on me. Being so, do you expect me to allow it to exist? "

The Lady Philippa spoke soothingly: " We both have the same haughty blood, my dear coz. If you will trust me there shall be no stain."

" I prefer to have it consumed by fire," Abbot Hugh said sullenly.

The prioress was again staring towards the wall of the transept, but her profile could be clearly seen through a thin veil.

" My Lord will please himself," she said distinctly. " But in the future I shall be very cold with my dear cousin if he does not accede to my desire."

The lord abbot eyed her, bit his full, lower lip, and then snarled: " By the blood of Christ, have it your own way if you must."

She smiled at him. " I am deeply grateful, my dear cousin," she said meltingly.

My Lord was not mollified and immediately vented his fury on Ughtred who, at the sub-prior's whip-like order, had been kneeling throughout on the tiles.

" Why did you paint the nun's face? " he shouted.

" My Lord," Ughtred pleaded, " she is of God's creation, and in painting the most pure and lovely face I have ever seen I was but glorifying God."

" With the face of a harlot? "

Ughtred's expression changed. " She is not that, My Lord."

" Do you contradict me? " the lord abbot thundered.

" With respect, as to that, My Lord, I do," Ughtred replied quietly.

It was difficult to guess which shocked the group of obedientiaries most, this reply or his rising without permission.

Abbot Hugh was concerned only with the greater sin. " You contradict me, your superior, set over you by the Almighty," he yelled.

Pale but indomitable, Ughtred burned his bridges. " You were set over me, My Lord, by the vote of the community in Chapter, who then submitted your name for approval to His Holiness the Pope."

The lord abbot had difficulty in breathing. " Never will there have been such a scourging as shall be your lot shortly," he gasped.

" You have the power, My Lord," Ughtred said levelly. " The

power to inflict fearsome cruelties upon whomever within these precincts as may suit you, but it is not the Lord God you claim set you over me who wishes for those cruelties. It is yourself, My Lord."

"For this," the abbot said, dark eyes glittering, "you shall suffer to the point of death."

"Because your pride has been pricked, My Lord," Ughtred said.

Momentarily Abbot Hugh was nearly beyond speech. "You . . . you, a monk of less than ten years profession, have the temerity to rebuke me . . . *me*, your intercessor with God."

"I could, My Lord," Ughtred said, "condemn your vanity also, a vanity which compels you most of all to consider the figure of magnificence you cut in the world—a world in which the vast amounts you fritter away could do so much for the starving and the distressed, as Christ would wish it to do."

"So now," the abbot roared, "you bring in the Lord Christ on your side?"

Ughtred smiled faintly. "I would be satisfied enough if the Blessed Saint Bernard could descend on us, My Lord. From what I have read of him he would drive you forth with scant ceremony, after he had stripped you of your pretensions."

The Lady Philippa had sauntered as far as the doorway of the pulpitum, but her comment carried clearly from the crossing.

"It is plain, my dear cousin, from whom my erring daughter Lazelle acquired her poisonous Lollardist ideas," she remarked tartly.

Abbot Hugh pointed a shaky finger at Ughtred. "Take him to the chapter house," he said thickly. "He will withdraw all he has so evilly said, however many weeks and months it may require to reduce him to abject submission. I have no prior breathing down *my* neck."

Whatever appearance of dignity the lord abbot believed he displayed in the world, dignity was conspicuously absent in him during the next few minutes, after he led the way tempestuously from the church to the east walk, where Ughtred was thrust through the doorway of the chapter house. Brother Eustace, mourning for his sins under the shrine of St. William, received a savage kick in the ribs—which left him terrified until, scrambling out, he learnt what it was all about from My Lord's harangue to those kneeling in the walk. Then he licked his lips, anticipatorily and hopefully.

In the meantime, when alone for a brief interval, Ughtred acted purposefully. In the corner on entering the chapter house proper, beyond the vestibule, there was a seldom used silver wall-basin. Delving beneath his clothes, he unloosed the chain and tiny relic container, Lazelle's gift to him, and dropped them down the drain, where there was scant likelihood of them ever being found until the day came, if ever, when the building was pulled down to its foundations. He was tidy again when the brethren surged to their stalls, from which they rose to bow when the lord abbot, last of all, came to take his seat in the high-backed chair at the apse end.

Ughtred was stripped to the waist, and his outstretched arms and legs were manacled to the Greek cross. The execution of the sentence: eighty stripes, was entrusted to Brother Eustace and another brother who managed to breathe a few vengeful and triumphant words:

" Did I not tell you the fate of favourites, Brother Ughtred? " Brother Left-handed Thomas said. " And the Lord giving me strength you shall know it before the eightieth falls."

There were to be more than eighty, however. At the end, as was his duty, the infirmarian made an examination. By then Ughtred was little more than hanging in his chains, but through a haze of agony he saw a gleam in the eyes of a superior who had a long memory.

The infirmarian turned towards the chair. " My Lord," he said, bowing, " he is amply well enough to sustain more, if that should please you."

" I have infinite respect for your judgment, my son," the lord abbot replied approvingly. " Another thirty."

Again the searing leather thongs of the *flagellum* began to fall. Ughtred was dimly aware of the first respite, when Brother Eustace took over, but after that remembered no more.

When Ughtred became fully conscious again he found he was fettered differently, at the wrists and ankles. A grey light filtered into the chamber, where he was lying on the stone floor, and he could perceive a stone pillar in the centre supporting the arched ribs of a roof. A flight of steps led up to one corner, beyond which was a small annexe with a square flagstone above it. That was when he knew where he was—in the vault gained by a short alleyway off the Passage, where the monk of Jervaulx had been imprisoned.

A groan startled him and, turning so quickly that he moaned himself, he saw who was with him.

" Brother Ralph! " he exclaimed. " You here."

" Since yesterday," the portly brother said painfully. " I had fifty stripes, and they are not to end the matter."

" How long have I been? " Ughtred asked. " If you know."

" Three days, Brother Ughtred," Brother Ralph said faintly.

Bread and a pitcher of water each was brought down every forenoon, and on the second afternoon after this they cleansed each other's backs, an anguishing ordeal when clothing and skin were matted together and the water chilly; and awkward, with hands that were closely joined, and two handkerchiefs only between them. This eased them and, with the passing of two more nights, the tendency to slide into the sleep of exhaustion lessened, so that they talked more. The next morning Brother Ralph was taken away, and did not return.

From then, finding a sharp-cornered fragment of stone, Ughtred marked off the days with scratches on the floor. He had also other indications of the passage of time. Smelling mint and fennel, he knew that the refectorian and sacrist were throwing down flowers, as was always done at the beginning of summer; and he heard the tramp of feet at the Feast of the Nativity of John the Baptist, and on the day of the anniversary of Saint Peter's crucifixion and Saint Paul's beheading.

On the thirty-second day of imprisonment the third and fourth priors, with Brothers Hubert and Bernard, came to take him to the lord abbot in the parlour. It was not a long walk: up the steps, a few yards along the Passage, and then round the corner into the east walk, where only a few paces remained. But the scabs on Ughtred's back prevented him straightening, his legs were too weak to hold him, and so he had to be supported on both sides, on Brother Hubert's most tenderly.

Ughtred, when in the parlour, made no attempt to kneel, but gripped a knob in the carving of the wainscot.

" I await your withdrawal of every heinous statement you have uttered, my evil and wicked son," the Lord Hugh said brusquely.

"That I am unable to do, My Lord," Ughtred said quietly.

The lord abbot's brow beetled. "My son," he said grimly, "I shall crush you as the mills grind the grain, even should it take me a year, which I consider doubtful. Your fate shall not be that of the abandoned creature with whom you have sinfully consorted."

Ughtred swayed. "What is that, My Lord?" he asked.

He was told that unless Sister Lazelle confessed to her errors she would be brought before a court of her superiors for trial as a heretic. If convicted, as was certain, she would then be handed over to the temporal authority for burning at the stake.

"She has not long to wait," the lord abbot added. "Unless she totally recants by then, the Lady Philippa has fixed the day after the Feast of the Apostles to institute the necessary action, and the Lady Philippa is not one to be stayed when once decided on a course."

"My Lord," Ughtred begged, "the nun Lazelle is but youthful, and if she could be treated gently— —"

"Treated how she is I know not," said the lord abbot. "But I can assure you, my son, that unless your paramour becomes penitent and submissive the end of the month will see her on the first miles of a journey to the flames. But, by all the saints, that is not to be your route and so enough of it. Do you admit to your evil folly?"

"No, My Lord," Ughtred said, without defiance.

His dark eyes smouldering, Abbot Hugh tried another threat. "There are worse pains than the *flagellum* and its aftermath, my son."

Ughtred nodded. "I think that may be true, My Lord. The devil's own implements used on the monk of Jervaulx would be more excruciating. I saw his hands, My Lord."

Furiously the lord abbot rang a bell. "By all the holy relics . . . the blood of Saint Stephen, the hair of Saint William, the teeth of Apollonius, and the bones of Remigius, if I do not tame you——"

The third and fourth priors hastily entered from the cloister. "Remove him," he roared.

"Yes, My Lord." The guardians bowed.

The abbot held up his hand. "Wait, for I have a notion about a more suitable place for his confinement. Yes, I think *that* would cool his tempers." He smiled wolfishly. " Take him away and stuff him into No Ease. It has never been used in my day, but the archives I have studied insist its medicine does not linger in the belly. So away with him, speedily."

Half-carried, Ughtred passed through the east walk, up the day-stairs to the end of the dormitory passage-way, and from there into the corridor, as if proceeding towards the night-stairs and the south transept and clock house.

No Ease was about mid-way along, and there was a considerable delay until the key of the low, iron-barred entrance could be found and brought, when he was manhandled inside. Almost at once the lock clicked, and the sound of feet soon died in the distance.

For the moment, with his knees near his chin and the back of his head, bowed forward, touching the stone roof, Ughtred was not too uncomfortable, apart from pain where the lower part of his back was pressed against the wall.

" From now," he muttered, " until the Feast of the Apostles it is . . . twenty-six . . . twenty-seven days. Then they will take Sister Lazelle away."

He shifted, twisting on to his left rump so that he could flex his right leg. For a minute or so he was eased.

" If I could escape, and reach Watton, and throw myself on the Lady Philippa's mercy, and plead with her . . . my plight could be no worse, and Sister Lazelle's might be improved."

After a struggle, he turned himself the other way, so that he faced the corridor. The change was bliss to his constricted left leg.

" My Lord and his cousin may share some of the same blood, and I think there is the same savagery in them," he thought. " But the Lady Philippa is different in that she is unpredictable, and has wit . . . to tease My Lord, she might even . . ."

The cramp in his calf was increasing, and he felt sick. " O Lord God," he whispered, " give me the courage to endure, so that I may *think*."

After several attempts he found a new position in the box-like cell, gaining extra length by squeezing the front of his boot between two bars.

" But even if I got away from here I am too weak to walk far, if I can walk by myself at all," he muttered. " Even with hours of start I would have walked and crawled not much farther than the Rievaulx cross out on the road."

His condition was deteriorating, and once, in a frenzy, he screamed feebly, sweated, and beat his fists against the wall; and once, spent, he whimpered, kissed his crucifix, and cried. Later, in a period of acuteness, he heard the soft scuffle of night boots, but did not know whether the brethren were going to bed in the Great Silence, descending to the church for Matins, or returning from Lauds for the second slumber.

In the morning, when the corridor was bright with the rising sun, he came wholly to his senses for a short spell, lucid-minded, at peace, his pains gone.

" If she must burn I shall strive to be with her to the end, as Friar Jerome is with the Lollard preachers," he told himself. " That is, if I am not at another stake close to her, which I would prefer . . . so that we may die together."

Then, quite suddenly, he furiously rebelled, discarding much in which he had been rigorously trained, repudiating tenets that less than a year before he would have been horrified at questioning.

" No, it is morbid to have such notions, and the holy Saint Bernard was wrong in instructing us to regard death as a loved companion always walking at our side, whose taking of us should be welcomed with open arms. O dear Lord, surely we were brought into life to live more fully."

Ughtred began to think about a man who had made a deep impression on him from the day they had met.

" Friar Jerome said that one blessed day I might see the light, and I think this is the day . . . the day when, as if I am detached from my body, I can look down on myself and the things around me as from a great distance . . . perceiving the frailties and fripperies, the self-indulgence and inhumanity of man towards man . . . to which, unwittingly, I have lent myself."

The pains were beginning again and, wriggling, he tried to arrange his limbs differently.

" From now, God helping, I shall do my utmost to fight," he muttered. " If ever I can get out of this place."

The torments were increasing and by the time the bell rang for

Lady Mass he was terrified he might be losing his reason. But, merciful in the outcome, the combination of a meagre diet and some weeks of unsalubrious imprisonment, on top of a whipping which Brother Robert had already recorded in the chronicles as being ' the most severe since the brothers Odo and Oswald were surprised in the act of sodomy one hundred and seventy-three years ago, and may they still be writhing together in Gehenna '—but, mercifully, he was soon in a coma.

Ughtred was saved by Brother Martin, and an unwritten law which deprecated the death of a prisoner either in No Ease or the vault.

Brother Martin's part was this—he was anxious about Ughtred and, on the pretext of adjusting the clock, took his tool-bag to the south transept at the beginning of the period for work and recreation. After carefully glancing about the church, and on receiving a nod from Brother Theobald, who was carving the chapel screens, he daringly went up the night-stairs and tip-toed along the corridor. At No Ease, he dropped on one knee and looked inside.

" No, he sleeps deeply, and I am glad," he murmured to Brother Theobald later. " It would have been wicked to have disturbed him."

Long after that, when walking in file to bed after Compline, Brother Martin again glanced into the tiny cell; and did the same at midnight, as the brethren went to church for Matins. Alarmed by now, he saw that Ughtred was in exactly the same spider-like position. And so, between the conclusion of Matins and the beginning of Lauds, he reported his fears to the sub-prior, who reported to the prior, who reported to the lord abbot. Shortly after one o'clock of the morning, in consequence, No Ease was opened and its occupant was carried to a small chamber off the main hall of the infirmary.

When Ughtred awoke he could hear the shouts of novices playing ball, which told him the hour; through the doorway he could see a line of beds, which told him where he was.

" I do not know how this has come to be," he thought, tears of weakness in his eyes, "but I thank you, O Lord and Saviour, for bringing it about."

Some few minutes afterwards an infirmary servant looked in on him. In due course, held up in bed, a cup of broth was spooned into his mouth. That, and the ecstasy of stretching his legs, invigorated him. Clear-headed, jaw determined, he declared himself to his Maker.

" O Lord," he cried passionately without speaking, " I cannot expect your forgiveness for what I shall now confide in you, but I humbly ask for a tithe of clemency and understanding. For from this moment, Redeemer and Saviour, I shall be as cunning as the fox, and I shall lie and cheat without compunction if these sins serve my ends. And those ends, O Lord, are to leave here and betake myself to the priory of Watton, where I had proposed throwing myself at the feet of the Lady Philippa. That I shall not now do if I am able to escape, for it contains a risk I cannot face. This is what I have in mind—to penetrate the holy nuns' side and so reach Sister Lazelle . . . and then, if she be there and if it is within my ingenuity, to carry her away, far away, to my dear mother and father in our beloved Northumberland."

Ughtred of Monkseaton's career of duplicity started with the visit of the infirmarian shortly after the bells in the tower rang for Vespers. His feebleness was not assumed, but he could have raised his voice higher than he did, and his eyelids need not have drooped so wearily. On the other hand the obedientiary's tone cut as sharply as a knife.

" I cannot hear you, my son," he said, stooping.

Ughtred, moistening his lips, made another attempt. " I think I may be at the end of my earthly journey, Reverend Father, and I fret sorely," he said.

" You have cause, my son," the infirmarian said harshly. " For nothing but the fires of Hell await you."

" If only I could regain a little strength, Reverend Father," Ughtred said pitifully. " Enough to totter to My Lord, so that I could lay myself flat on my face before him."

Without question, it could not have been a more astute move. Ever since Ughtred's unconcealed defiance the lord abbot's temper had been sultry, and all ranks of the community had trod in terror. It would assuage My Lord's savage humour to hear the culprit was to beg for pardon, and there would be a mark of approval for the one who could assure him that the offender might be fattened up for further penalties.

" My son," the infirmarian said comfortingly, " have no qualms. I shall place you on a diet that will soon restore you, Our Lord God willing."

This promise was carried out lavishly. Ughtred began with eggs beaten up in milk, and from that to tasty dishes of ling and turbot, chicken and veal. He had plenty of fruit, an abundance of the best blood-building wine, and between the main repasts many cups of the most savoury beef essences. By the end of four days he felt himself a new person, but still rang a bell when requiring to be assisted to the necessary where, pleading looseness of the bowels, he remained by himself for as long as possible exercising his limbs.

About then he discovered the strangeness of his appearance. Once, while being helped back to bed, he paused for breath and chanced to see himself in a bright metal mirror. A man unknown looked back at him, an older man with sunken eyes, colourless cheeks, pate covered with a tangled growth of hair, and bearded from ear to ear.

" It is better," he thought exultantly.

On the fifth day he came to the conclusion that his pretence might be suspected if he dallied much longer, and he decided to leave the abbey the next night. Before then, until the moment of slipping out of bed to start the great adventure, he planned every detail.

On the night of escape, thanks to God, there was a gusty, noisy wind. Leaving the infirmary by the cook's quarters, Ughtred, stepping cautiously, crossed the inner court to the workshops, where he provided himself with an iron bar; and while the bell sounded for Matins, he used the bar to force the door of the chequer, where small sums were often kept until sufficient was amassed to be locked more safely in the treasury. His enterprise was rewarded with a handful of silver pennies and half-groats in a draw-string pouch.

In the kitchen he had the good fortune to stumble on a large leather bag, with a looped strap. This made an excellent carrier for food purloined in the larder and buttery: three loaves, a piece of beef, a whole chicken, and a quantity of raisins. Accidentally knocking over a flagon was a reminder of another useful requirement, and he went through a narrow doorway and down a few steps into the cellarage below the refectory where, in the darkness, spilling plenty, he drew wine.

The brethren were still in church, and so next, leaving the bag in the kitchen porter's familiar lobby, he tip-toed along the south walk to the day-stairs, and crept up to his cell in the dormitory. Fumbling, he eventually put his hand on the Florentine box entrusted to him by the Lady Philippa.

"Maybe with these paints and little brushes," he murmured, " I could earn sufficient for victuals to support us on our walk to my lady mother, *if* I can bring Sister Lazelle out. O God! grant that this be."

On the way back he rummaged in Brother Robert's carrel for vellum and parchment—warily, for the west walk ran along the wall of the church. When done, he listened carefully, his heart thumping when he was sure the Psalms were ending, which meant that the officials who had other duties would be leaving the quire.

Silently he returned to the kitchen exit, but had an afterthought before picking up the bag. Slipping into the side scullery, he took a mantle and a hat from the rack, clothing kept there for the convenience of anyone who might have to cross to outbuildings in rain; of dark grey and in lay style, the wearer would never strike an observer as a Cistercian.

Ughtred heard a noise and, turning sharply to stare across the garth, saw the brethren coming out of church, either to promenade round the four walks of the cloister or otherwise occupy themselves until the bell rang for Lauds. Bending low, and remaining so, he grabbed the baggage and crept towards the door of the kitchen lobby.

When outside, steering wide of the kennels, he headed for the fish-ponds and the crenellated wall beyond. Climbing this obstacle exhausted him more than he would have believed, and after fording the river he realised it would be inviting disaster to begin the long walk to Watton before he had more vigour.

"My Lord will have riders searching for me to-morrow, and I would be caught before I had even attained the region of the castle," he muttered. "And as yet there is enough time."

And so, for two days, he hid in a thickly-wooded ravine within sight of Rievaulx, and there ate and drank and slept in the sweet air, slept so soundly that on the first morning he did not wake when the clamorous peal of the abbey's bells rang out a message that had nothing to do with a summons to an Office. That day and on the next parties of horsemen rode out; but by that second evening he was feeling stronger and, as the moon rose, began the journey.

In the earlier stages, during which he only used the highway cautiously, to reach the next side-track or bridle path, Ughtred avoided villages and habitations, but on the fourth evening out, confidence increasing with the renewing of energy, he was sufficiently bold, on glimpsing a timber-and-clay, thatched cottage, to seek a night's lodging. Hospitably he was invited into a smoky, barely-furnished room, and given a stool, a wooden dish and spoon, and a generous helping of a rabbit and vegetable stew from a pot over the fire. Later, when the woman and the children had retired into an inner chamber, he slept with the labourer on the earth floor. Next morning, refreshed, he put away a large breakfast, of rye bread, pork and ale. On leaving, he bought loaves and a lump of cold bacon, and for these things and the service laid out money, the first time in his life he had ever paid for anything of that kind.

Ughtred had one immense advantage, in that he had been to Watton before, and so it was impossible for him to go astray if he kept close to the tracks along which he had ridden. But once he had a fright as he was striding on an uncultivated strip separating two fields, one fallow and the other in corn, when he almost blundered into villagers driving their cattle through a midsummer bonfire to ward off disease.

Twelve days before the Feast of the Apostles, Ughtred sighted the priory of Watton. Doing his utmost to subdue a mixture of cold fear and excitement, he took to the woods and made a circuitous approach to a point on the road not far from the main gateway, where he found a spy-place in a clump of brambles. He had not been long there, hardly enough to capture old memories, when he heard the sound of horses' hooves, the tramp of feet, and laughter and chatter. Drawing back, he waited and watched, until a large and miscellaneous company passed by: merchants with pack-horses, hawkers with corded bundles, others whom he guessed were strolling players, and a small party carrying balls of wick-threads and frames of a pattern he recognised.

"They are candle-makers," he murmured. "Here for the

annual candle-making, while the others will be showing their wares."

Without giving further consideration to an idea that had flashed into his mind, he snatched up the leather bag and, when sure he was unobserved, stepped into the road and started after the tail-end of the procession.

At the gateway the delay was slight, which was fortunate as one or two stared at him in surprise, and might have asked questions; and there was none at all in the outer court, where all proceeded as if familiar with their route, the candle-makers turning to the left, towards the canons' side, the others in the direction of the gate leading into the prioress's yard, where the merchants dismounted. Soon, the lively-behaved players in the van, the traders were heading for the side-door of the Lady Phillppa's lodging.

Ughtred was not with them. Bending as if the buckle on his shoe was loose, he had opened a narrow postern and peeped beyond, into the holy nuns' garden, where the sole living thing he could see was a peacock. Hastening through, he paused at the other side to get his bearings, and then, noticing thick bushes at the west end of the church, sought their cover.

It had been his intention to hide until darkness before climbing into the canon regulars' enclosure, but as he worked his way round the north-west corner of the church, where the growth of shrubbery was most dense, progress was unexpectedly barred by massive masonry.

"A buttress," he muttered, peering through the tangle of branches and leaves over his head. "And beyond it will be a niche in which I can secret myself until ready."

Ughtred was crawling forward when he made an astonishing discovery, that of a minute doorway in the face of the buttress. The door was not locked, but stiff to open. Inside, a wheel staircase ascended into darkness.

"It will be to gain access to the leads," he thought. "And there must be at least one other, for this has not been used for years."

Bent on exploring, he mounted the stone steps, so many of them that he began to wonder when the climb would end, and he was, in fact, pawing for another riser which was not there when he found that he was in a shoulders'-width passage extending a long way

eastwards. Small apertures in the outer wall let in a faint light, but
for some moments he did not realise that in front of him, at right-
angles to the other, was another passage. It was in total darkness,
but he felt his way across until, certain he was then over the nuns'
side of the church, he came to another passage. This, running the
length of the church, corresponded with the first, and he had
complete surety that somewhere along it would be a means of
descending to the nuns' quarters.

The first obstacle had been overcome and he was filled with
joyousness as he returned to the head of the staircase, where the
baggage had been left. Then he had a meal from the abundance he
had brought, before stretching out for a sound sleep in preparation
for the night. But he was much too tense even to doze.

" Would that it were winter," he sighed, " so that I could start
out sooner."

Ughtred had no difficulty about estimating the passing of the
hours, for he could hear the bells—the sweet-tinkling one which he
assumed was the hand-bell in the holy sister's cloister, the deeper
toned bell used at the church door, and the thunderous bells in the
nearby tower.

About eleven o'clock at night, palms damp already, he started
out on the foray, reaching ground level by a spiral staircase which
brought him into an alley between the north transept of the church
and the chapter house, where he had worked. Fortunately, the
Gilbertines had copied the Cistercians in the arrangement of their
convents, which helped him to locate himself; and, as fortunately,
the moon was obscured by cloud, though its influence was enough to
prevent him making errors which would have caused a noise.

It was a nerve-racking affair, this creeping silently about the
precincts of a nunnery, but Ughtred kept stubbornly at it, always
with his mind on what he might need within the next few days,
whether this were rope or a tool.

His present quest ended two hours after midnight, when he
began a second, with such success that before dawn he had established himself, and everything he had brought with him, in the
underdrawing of an extension to the refectory. From there, through
a small gap where a tile had slipped, he could view three of the walks
of the cloister.

Sister Lazelle had once told him, to his astonishment, that at Watton there were prison cells for unruly sisters, and that was where she must be, if still there. As yet he was not certain where the cells were, although he had an idea, but the cloister was the heart of all convents and in one way or another, if he could keep the three walks under constant observation in daylight, he would learn much. It might be that he would see food carried from kitchen or refectory to another place; or possibly in womanish communities there were leniences unknown to monkish Orders, and it could be that Sister Lazelle was allowed exercise in the garth, when he would watch to where she was returned.

As the light in the east strengthened, Ughtred of Monkseaton secured a length of rope to two rafters, so that it hung down in the shape of a loop. With spare clothing cushioning the bight, it would make a convenient seat from which he could maintain his vigil.

\*　　　\*　　　\*　　　\*

On and on the tirade continued, the drone of the Master of Sempringham's voice and the short, fierce interventions of the Lady Philippa. Over and over again the nun Lazelle's sins were reiterated: her rebellious answers to the superior the Lord God had placed over her; the yielding of her body to the monk of Rievaulx of which she, a wife on earth of Our Saviour Jesus Christ, had been guilty; her breaking of the Rule to which she was sworn to obey. And, again and again, with horrific detail, she was reminded of what, unless she became pliant, she would soon endure when flames began to consume her soft flesh.

Kneeling in the little cell, drooping with weariness, Lazelle was no longer listening to them. Benumbed, worn out with weeks of relentless assault, she had one desire only, that they would go away.

The Superior of All, brought in two days before, was becoming tired also. He was, after all, as he complained to himself, not as young as he had been and, as more than once before, wished that his daughter-in-God, Philippa, were less demanding, less dominating.

Irascibly, he shook Lazelle's shoulder. " My daughter," he snapped, " crushed beneath a burden of infamy as you must know you are, will you not submit? I ask you this, my daughter, in the name of Him above whom you still profess to adore."

Slowly, Lazelle raised her head. " How can I confess to evil doings I have not fallen into, My Lord? " she asked. " It is true that I have disobeyed the Rule, but it is a Rule much of which the Almighty would strike out if it were shown to Him."

The Master of Sempringham, remembering thankfully that the days were now long, wondered what would be the best excuse for not staying another night.

" My daughter," he said sadly to the Lady Philippa, " I can do no more. She has the devil in her and will not be moved."

If the Lady Philippa had white powder on her cheeks, the angry blood beneath was too strong for it.

" We will leave her, My Lord," she said thickly. " She is aware of what I have promised, and she knows that if she fails to abjure by then events must take their dread course."

The Master of Sempringham left the cell first, but the prioress did not follow. She signed to the Reverend Sisters Melania and Naomi, who were waiting outside, to escort him to her lodging. That done, she closed the door.

" I shall not come to you again, my daughter," she said harshly. " I have demeaned myself twice before in efforts to bring you to your senses, and by all that is holy it shall not be again."

" No, My Lady," Lazelle said tiredly.

The Lady Philippa did not speak for a few moments. When she did her manner was more considerate.

" My daughter, I cannot tell whether you have noticed what a grievous effect your obduracy has had on the Lord Superior of All," she said. " But he is aged, and for all your waywardness I do not think you would like to have it on your conscience that you have occasioned him so much distress. He is, my daughter, most gravely ill, and if he departs from here with the knowledge that the Order he has cherished throughout his life is to be brought into disrepute I doubt if he would ever reach his house at Sempringham."

" I should be sorry about that, My Lady," Lazelle said.

The Lady Philippa seemed emotionally affected. " He would be wondrously joyed if I could tell him, my daughter, that I had sound reason for believing you would acknowledge your errors . . .

and if that were so, my daughter, I would be so gladdened for his sake that your punishment hereafter would not bear on you so hardly."

Lazelle's lips quivered, but there was nothing of irresolution about her when, lifting her head, she looked at her superior.

" I have a belief also, My Lady," she said. " The Lord knows, as I most humbly do, that I am far from perfection, far indeed . . . but He also knows that I have not sinned with Brother Ughtred of Rievaulx . . . and in the other matters on which I am charged I believe He will be on my side."

Viciously the Lady Philippa struck twice before leaving, the bolt of the lock snapping into position when she was at the other side of the door.

Dizzy with the blows, Lazelle felt her cheek, and then, sinking towards the stone bench, rested her forehead on her folded arms, where she stayed until trembling ceased.

She was not disturbed before supper-time, when the turn-table in the wall creakingly revolved until a shelf came into view. On it was a beaker of milk, a piece of bread, and a few figs. It was not possible to see who was at the other side, but she waited for the inevitable warning, when she would recognise the voice.

" Sister Lazelle, here is your pittance, for which, if you are not as ungodly as is feared, you will thank the Lord."

It was the third prioress. " Yes, Reverend Mother," Lazelle said.

The third prioress cleared her throat. " Another dawn will soon be here," she said sepulchrally. " But as yet it is still five days from the Feast of the Apostles, after which, if you do not humbly repent, you will be brought without further ado for trial as a heretic. Do you hear me, Sister Lazelle? "

" I hear you, Reverend Mother," said Lazelle, nodding to herself as if she had made up her mind. " But can you hear *me*? "

This departure from routine took the third prioress aback, for she did not reply for a few moments.

" Yes, I can hear you, Sister Lazelle," she said. " What is it you wish to say to me? "

" This is what I have to say, Reverend Mother," Lazelle said firmly. " That for many days I have been denied from taking the

327

holy water, receiving the *pax*, and being communicated. And as I must have my soul relieved before the day fades I beg of you to make the necessary arrangements, Reverend Mother."

The third prioress sounded outraged. " Before God, you are as pert as if—I shall do no such thing."

" If you do not, Reverend Mother," Lazelle said, speaking slowly, " and if it should be that I die during the coming night, for who knows when the hour cometh, I will haunt you for as many days as you may have left on earth. I——" she heard a gasp, " I, in whom you contend an evil spirit lurks, promise that, Reverend Mother."

There was a long silence. " I . . . I will inquire," the third prioress said eventually, and shakily.

Lazelle remained hopeful until, through the bars in the high window, she saw the sky darkening, when she knew sadly how vain those hopes had been. Then she prayed.

" Dear God, I had so wanted once again to be a part of thee, but it is not to be, and for that I am to blame . . . because I have not been honest, wholly honest . . . because part of that wanting is to leave for a while these walls which confine me so tightly, which press on me more nearly with every day that passes . . . until I feel that I must choke or dash myself against them . . . O dear Lord, forgive me, forgive me."

They came, after all, past one o'clock in the morning, when the sub-prioress and the Reverend Sister Melania woke her from fitful sleep. She was taken to the church where, surprisingly, the whole of the sisterhood were in their places. But, instead of leading her to the turn-table in the inner wall, by which a priest on the canon regulars' side could pass a wafer and the sacred chalice, she was steered to the confessional, a finger breadth's slot beyond the processional doorway, through which questions and answers could be heard.

Lazelle made no protest, though realising that once more she was being subjected to pressure, this time before the entire community.

The Lady Philippa, from the right-hand stall nearest to the presbytery, spoke to her.

" Your father confessor awaits you, my daughter."

Lazelle turned towards the quire. " I am not to have the blood and body of Christ, My Lady? " she said.

The church was not well lighted, but the waving flame of the candle on the prioress's book-desk illuminated her face.

" My daughter," she said sorrowfully, " I have told you that your confessor is there. For the sake of your sisters-in-God, who are stricken by your behaviour, you must address yourself to him."

Lazelle bowed. " Yes, My Lady," she said.

The interior wall was thick and the aperture through it angled and narrow, designed to prevent priest and suppliant from each seeing the other, the construction of the hole robbing voices of their strength, so that they acquired a disembodied quality.

" My daughter, at whose feet yawns the flaming pit of damnation," Lazelle heard. " Before it is too late, before you may participate in the holy——"

After that, all she heard was on her own side of the church. In sequence the noises were a lusty scream, shouting, and finally the Lady Philippa's exasperated cry to the effect that she would not tolerate her imbecile daughter Eva's presence in the priory more than a few days longer.

Sister Eva had been maligned. The screamer, of all people, was the Reverend Sister Blanche, who normally was as well balanced as the figures she kept; and the shouter was Sister Maud whose nerves, as the Lady Philippa knew from the many sporting occasions on which they had been together, were of iron. Both had left their seats and, terrified, were advancing up the aisle.

" What is the matter? " the Lady Philippa asked furiously. " You are in the house of the Lord, and——"

" So is John the Baptist, and I have just seen him, My Lady," the Reverend Sister Blanche blubbered. " And *with* his head on, not as the monk of Rievaulx painted it for the refectory, on a dish."

" It would seem you have more imagination than sense," Lady Philippa said angrily. " Just because this morning we spoke of the Blessed John's martyrdom, and looked at the picture——"

Sister Maud's teeth were chattering. " I s-s-saw him as well, My Lady," she said, adding with some incongruity: " And if it wasn't the Blessed John with his tangled beard it was Beelzebub himself."

The Lady Philippa became less strident. " Where was this? "

" B-b-behind the effigy of Our Virgin and the Infant Christ, M-M-My Lady," Sister Maud said.

Sister Blanche differed. " Nearer to the cloister door, My Lady. He was there and . . . and then sank into the darkness."

Uneasily the Lady Philippa glanced towards the unlighted end of the church, a movement made simultaneously by everyone present. This should have been the moment for Sister Eva to throw back her head, but it was heavily-built Sister Ealdgyth who touched off panic by springing up frantically. This example was followed, so much so that candles were knocked off desks in what became a mass rush towards the prioress. The result was that the church was even gloomier than it had been.

" Why this disorderliness? " the Lady Philippa shouted, voice pitched higher than usual. " Answer me, answer me at once."

Sister Ealdgyth was willing enough. " My Lady," she gasped, " I saw evil eyes peering from the oratory. They were red and gleaming——"

" There! " Sister Beatrice screeched.

Gibbering, she pointed at the projecting stair-turret in the south-corner of the nave, where a small door was moving—as it often did in a draught. But before she had managed coherently to explain that she had seen a face resembling Sister Katherine's Puchin, only twenty times larger, at least three other sisters were declaring feverishly that they had sighted demons at widely-separated places: leaning from the triforium, hanging upside down from the roof, and long neck stretched round the marble capital of a column.

It was enough; as a horde in shrill flight the community streamed towards the steps in the north transept. This left Lazelle, the sub-prioress, and the Reverend Sister Melania.

" My Lady . . . My Lady may have gone to ensure they . . . they are safely abed," the sub-prioress panted. " But I think it is also so that . . . that she may avoid leaving by the cloister door . . . where it was first noticed."

The Reverend Sister Melania swallowed. " I fear to do so also,

Most Revered Mother. Far better if we go round the whole range, and may the Lord God protect us all from the fiends that are abroad."

" Come, my daughter," the sub-prioress said tremulously to Lazelle. " If it had not been for your wickedness . . . yes, indeed, Sister Melania, we must rely on His shield to guard us this fearsome night."

In the dormitory, where every lamp had been lighted and would be allowed to burn until dawn, the sisters were doubling-up in the cubicles, and the Lady Philippa, who looked as if she also was under considerable strain, made no protest against this breaking of one of the most stringent regulations.

In due course a small party left the dormitory, each of the seven members, including Lazelle, holding a candle. This small company, frightened glances darting this way and that, remained one story above ground level, proceeding through the refectory and the western range of buildings to the stairs descending to the entry at the south-west corner of the cloister, where it split into two parts without ceremony: Sisters Constance, Matilda and Alice, all praying audibly, left with the prioress to escort her to the door of her lodging, while the sub-prioress and the Reverend Sister Melania hastened Lazelle to the prison quarters, where she was locked into her cell with as much despatch as trembling hands permitted.

Lazelle was quivering also, so shaky that she was glad to seat herself on the stone bench. Her agitation did not subside quickly, for it was impossible not to think again and again about the position of the cell, which was remote from the dormitory across the garth, and an appreciable distance from the lay sisters at the extreme end of the range. In this highly-strung mood she could not sleep, and so, her hands tightly clasped, she continued to sit, jumpy even about the shadows made on the walls by the candle, which the obedientiaries in their hurry had forgotten to take from her.

Some time later she was terrified by a series of small and varying sounds, neither close nor very far away. For the first few moments she was rigid, but then sprang up to listen intently both at the turn-table opening and the door. The noises: scratching, squeaking and twice a low grunt, did not last long, and then there was silence.

Lazelle stumbled from the door to the bench. " O dear Lord," she whispered, "surely I have enough of horror without this."

She did not fall asleep until the morning sun's rays shaded the bars in the window, but then her slumber was so deep that she never heard the summons for dinner. But she was wide-awake when, as evening approached, the Reverend Sister Joanna brought a frugal supper.

"Sister Lazelle," she called.

"Yes, Reverend Sister."

"It is but four days to the Feast of the Apostles, Sister Lazelle," the Reverend Sister said mechanically. "After which, if you do not humbly repent, you will be given over without further ado for trial as a heretic."

"Let the days pass swiftly," Lazelle said wearily.

Angrily Sister Joanna responded: "It is well that to-night you are to be excluded from God."

Lazelle fingered her brow. She could not think very clearly.

"Excluded from God?" she said.

"This day, by prayer and invocation, in procession and at observance, we have exorcized the evil spirit that was in this place," the Reverend Sister Joanna said triumphantly. "This coming night, in full assembly," she continued savagely, "we shall also drive forth the one remaining evil which for the present is beneath this hallowed roof . . . the evil that is in your bosom, Sister Lazelle. For to-night, Sister Lazelle, you are to be excommunicated."

"I am to . . . to be excommunicated?" Lazelle faltered.

"This night," said the Reverend Sister Joanna.

And so, during the dark hours, by bell, book and candle, Lazelle was expelled from the society of Christ with every terrifying manifestation that Holy Church could devise. During an ordeal from which the stoutest of heart would have shrunk, lighted candles were hurled to the floor at her feet, each a sign that the spirit of God had been extinguished in her, that her flesh had been delivered to Satan. Maledictions were called down on her head, so virulent that others beside herself quailed: Sisters Katherine and Deborah wept for her, and both Sister Beatrice and Sir William, the curate, were palpably distressed. With many it was the opposite, and as hysteria in the church grew these pressed vixenishly on Lazelle, two of them spitting in her face.

At two o'clock in the morning she was taken back to her cell, and secured in it by those nearly in as sore straits as herself.

An outlaw in the eyes of every Christian, she sank to the bench, trembling uncontrollably. Shocked and wretched, tears streamed as she cried helplessly.

" O dear Saviour," she murmured brokenly, " why should this be, when so soon I may have to feel earthly flames . . . when I shall need what courage I have? "

About three-quarters of an hour later, when the streak marks on her cheeks had dried and she was beginning to hope that shortly she would be mistress of herself, she heard a sound, a recognisable sound. At the other side of the cell, unseen in the darkness, the turn-table window was moving. Petrified, sure that soon she would faint, she waited. Then she heard her name whispered, but could not believe what she heard.

" It could not be," she said inaudibly. " I am distraught even to imagine . . ."

" Sister Lazelle," Ughtred said a trifle more loudly.

Strength and power miraculously regained, Lazelle ran to the turn-table.

" Brother Ughtred! " she gasped. " I had thought I was unhinged."

" Shhhh . . ." Ughtred hushed her. " Sister Lazelle, I have much to do before the light breaks, which is soon. God helping, to-morrow night you shall escape from here. But now I must test a key I have been altering, so stay where you are and I shall quickly be back."

Lifting the eternal lamp, borrowed from the sacristy, Ughtred tried the key, one from a rusty bunch found in an outhouse, which he had been working on for many nights, using a file stolen from a workshop in the outer court. To his delight he discovered that with another hour or so's effort the key could be made to engage effectively.

" Sister Lazelle," he said elatedly on returning to the revolving structure, " all will be well, of that I am now certain. Before this time to-morrow you will have the Lord's heavens above you."

" Oh! Brother Ughtred," Lazelle said unsteadily " I . . . I . . ."

" Have they treated you brutally? " Ughtred asked grimly.

Lazelle pulled herself together. " It could have been much worse, Brother Ughtred," she said.

" I wonder," Ughtred muttered.

" Brother Ughtred, I won't ask how you come to be here, for I am sure it will be an amazing story, and . . . and I would rather hear it afterwards . . . when I am free," Lazelle said. " But have you been to the prison quarters before this? "

" Many times," said Ughtred. " On the first I had the good fortune to find that the locks of the cells were alike, and after that, when I came, I tested on the lock of the outer one so that I could see two walks of the cloister and hear if any were abroad. Had there been I could have crept away, whereas here, at the innermost, I might have been trapped."

" Oh! Brother Ughtred," Lazelle sighed. " Would I had been aware."

" I did not dare to make myself known to you, Sister Lazelle," Ughtred said regretfully. " And, until very recently, I would have been frightened of raising your hopes, for there was so much metal to be cut away that gradually I nigh wore the file down, and though I searched there was not another of the proper size."

Realisation of what this meant flooding her, Lazelle was too choked with joyousness to speak, but as he was painstakingly describing incomprehensible things it did not matter.

" Brother Ughtred," she asked when his explanation of mysteries peculiar to locksmiths ended, " were you in the church two nights ago, in many places? For there was great fright—some declaring we had the Blessed John the Baptist with us, others vowing it was the devil . . ."

Ughtred smiled about the beard. " No, but I was close-by the cloister entrance, where I hid when surprised by your community of sisters, whom I had not expected at that hour from the spying I had done before. But I had the tangled hair, Sister Lazelle, and of a truth I am so filthy and unkempt that I must alarm anyone."

For a little while they talked quietly of this, each striving to be a trifle gay, neither giving expression to what was uppermost in their minds: that a whole day and part of a night had still to pass before escape could be attempted, many hours during which the most carefully planned scheme could come undone.

"Now I must leave you, Sister Lazelle," said Ughtred. "I have to light my candles, I have to restore the eternal lamp to its place, and I have to climb to my hidey-hole beneath the roof of the church, where I can work without caring about noise until shortly before the bell rings for Prime."

Lazelle gasped. "You are in the roof of——but no, Brother Ughtred, that also can wait until . . . until we are away and at peace."

"We have much to tell each other, Sister Lazelle," Ughtred said. "It will be wondrous so to do."

"Oh! Brother Ughtred, may the Lord have mercy so to grant."

"May He be so moved," Ughtred said devoutly.

"God be with you, Brother Ughtred," Lazelle whispered.

"As with you, Sister Lazelle," said Ughtred. "And sleep well, for there is much before us that will be arduous."

"I shall sleep well, Brother Ughtred," said Lazelle, her voice catching, "for so much is changed."

The yellow light which had showed through the gap at the foot of the door vanished, but she never heard a sound and decided that Brother Ughtred must be walking in his hose. Then, more tired than ever in her captivity, she sat on the bench. But though she tried to be obedient she could not sleep; and had not slept at all by mid-morning, when the Reverend Sister Melania sent through the turn-table a dish of beans, a cup of milk, and the twice-daily message.

"Sister Lazelle, it is but three days to the Feast of the Apostles, after which, if you do not humbly repent, you will be given over without further ado for trial as a heretic. Have you heard me, Sister Lazelle?"

"I hear you, Reverend Sister," said Lazelle.

For the sole time since entering the cell, she scraped a dish to the bottom, not because she had an appetite but because, if stronger, she would not be a handicap to Brother Ughtred. From then she waited for bells—the bells for Vespers, and the bell for the Collation; and after the Reverend Sister Naomi had brought the supper, which she forced down as she had done the earlier meal, she listened for the bells for Compline.

When the Great Silence came, as her sisters were ascending to

335

the dormitory, her head was craned as she watched the changing colour of the sky—the last shafts of the sun and the rosy afterglow, the deepening of blue until it became grey, the appearance of the first twinkling star. After that she was seldom still, pacing the narrow confines of the cell far more than resting.

It seemed as if a lifetime had passed before she heard a faint rasp in the keyhole, and even then there was an agonising delay before the heavy door could be opened.

" Thank God, Brother Ughtred," she breathed. " I have loosened my shoes and will take them off, as I am sure you do."

" Yes," Ughtred whispered. " Sister Lazelle, give me your hand."

They stole along the cell corridor, across the dark south walk, and down the east walk almost as far as the chapter house, where a turn was made into an alleyway passing beneath the dormitory. Beyond, at the far side of a court, was a tall wall which ran without break from the west adit to the north-east corner of the church.

As Ughtred helped Lazelle over the wall he realised how weak she was, and he decided there and then that, as he had done when leaving Rievaulx, they must lie-up as soon as possible, until she had recovered a little. He knew the place—a dell about six miles from Watton, with a stream winding through it.

Lazelle had found that, though still within the precincts of the priory, she was in strange territory indeed. Involuntarily she started on brushing against a gravestone.

" The canon regulars' cemetery," Ughtred whispered. " We have to climb two more walls, one to reach the canons' garden, and the other the outer wall. From now, Sister Lazelle, we must be very cautious."

In all, the distance was not excessive, but it was eerie in the graveyard, and near the bowling square were shingly paths where footsteps had to be light and progress slow; while at the east end of the priory, where the two-storied canons' dormitory loomed above them, they had to walk on tip-toe. From this point everything steadily became easier, and there was small danger of being heard when mounting the outer wall.

" There! " Ughtred said as he picked up two heavily-laden bags. " Now we must head for a forest track I know."

Lazelle had been bending. " You carried those here beforehand, Brother Ughtred? "

" Sister Lazelle, I have been extremely busy in many fashions," Ughtred said with a touch of grimness. " Notably at stealing goods belonging both to your chapter and that of the canons regular."

" What did you steal, Brother Ughtred? "

" Food, and a-plenty of it," Ughtred said succinctly. " And drinking vessels, wine, blankets, towels, a razor, linen, and a lay sister's outer attire into which you must change in due course."

Awed, Lazelle hardly knew what to say. " Brother Ughtred," she began, " I can hardly believe that since being grown up you have lived a life of seclusion in the cloister."

" Sister Lazelle, I thought you knew I had travelled widely," Ughtred said with dignity. " Moreover, I come from a fighting strain."

" Oh," Lazelle murmured, but soon thought of a more fitting reply. " I knew you were changing, Brother Ughtred."

" It is a remark you have made before, Sister Lazelle," Ughtred said. " But I vouch I am the same as I have always been."

She did not argue, but smiled, which he could not see. " Brother Ughtred," she said instead, " if it pleases you I would like to carry one of the bags, so that I felt I had a share in the thievery."

Ughtred stopped. " Sister Lazelle, if you will carry yourself to where we shall rest during the day I shall be more than satisfied. You are very weary."

" I could quite easily carry a bag, Brother Ughtred," Lazelle protested.

" Sister Lazelle," Ughtred said gently, " we cannot have two captains."

Lazelle was longer in responding. " No, Brother Ughtred, it is wiser not," she whispered. " And I am more than happy it is so."

Dawn was breaking when they came to the dell where, while Lazelle washed herself, Ughtred opened a bag and took out a bakemeat, bread, pastries, cups and a flagon of wine. After they had eaten, he spread a blanket and rolled a mantle to pillow her head.

When he left her to wriggle up the bank, Lazelle's eyes filmed with moisture as she watched him, but there was nothing of sadness

337

in her expression as he disappeared from sight, and her sigh, before slipping into sleep, was one of pure contentment.

Ughtred's vantage point gave him a view of a stretch of highway not much more than half a bowshot's distance away, and so he had no difficulty in identifying a small company of Gilbertine canons who, dressed in summer-weight black habits, cantered past when the sun showed it was not far from noon. They returned, their horses then walking, in the late evening.

His present vigilance ended, Ughtred slid down to the dell, where Lazelle was deep in her second sleep of the day. Tenderly he looked at her.

" This will restore her," he murmured, " as it restored me, and soon, please God, she will have her vigour back."

From one of the bags he took out a small box with flint and tinder, the property of the priory of Watton, but was too preoccupied with the sleeping maid to inspect it very closely.

# 8

Bantering one another, exchanging quips, roaring with laughter frequently, and always carefree, the tatterdemalion company marching along the shady forest track was a mixed one, composed of players, tricksters, old soldiers, and professional pilgrims who enjoyed the irresponsibility of a vagrant life, whose only problem daily was to reach the next religious house by evening, where generous hospitality could be obtained as a matter of course.

The trees were thinning, and to one side were glimpses of a great lord's park, with next a coneyry, where a halt was called and purposeful, quiet activity began. Five of the party faded into the greenery, scouts were posted, and a fire started. Astonishingly soon a savoury smell of roast rabbit filled the air.

As she ate with relish, and wiped grease from her chin and sucked fingers to clean them, Lazelle listened wide-eyed to an account of the battle of Crécy, told to her by an incredibly ancient but still robust man.

" No, no, mistress," he objected at one point, " it was not that our aim was better—though it was—rather it came about because— see, I will show you." He stood up and, watched with interest by all, held his arms and hands as though he had a bow in them. " Regards, as the Frenchies say . . . I lean forward, my left arm stiff, not depending so much on the draw with the right, thereby using my weight for the effort. It was by such means, mistress, that the battle turned in our favour almost before it started, when we riddled the fanciful Genoese cross-bowmen, they who bragged in their cups that they were the best warriors in Europe. The best! " He spat contemptuously.

Lazelle smiled at him. " It was not so proven, Sir Bowman," she said admiringly. " How proud you must be for bearing arms there."

Just as enthralled, Ughtred resumed a conversation with a pilgrim who, in his turn, was as disdainful of ordinary pilgrims who led a vagabond life moving from shrine to shrine. This gentleman worked on commission, and was as airy about a journey to Rome as he was about a mere outing from London to Glastonbury. It was all in the way of business, a business in which he served those requiring prayers to be offered at distant shrines, by proxy, and for suitable recompense. He had, he confided, excellent connections with the attorneys—and his frock was certainly of superior material to any about him.

It was involved, and Ughtred was becoming muddled. " So, if by his last will and testament, a——"

The pilgrim interrupted. " No,no,no,no,no," he said. "My clients are not necessarily deceased. For example, young fellow, it may be that a wealthy merchant wishes to square his conscience about a transaction in which he feels that . . . er . . . he has adroitly taken rather *too* much advantage. So he delegates me, on his behalf, to beg forgiveness at the shrine he favours. That is why I am often in Italy, on missions for merchant-bankers hailing from the states of that region who reside in London."

Ughtred fingered his beard, now in better shape since Lazelle trimmed it with a razor, an operation during which, for all the tugging and minor pain, they had laughed themselves silly.

" Sir Pilgrim," he said, " would it not be better if the merchant restored the position with those he has duped? "

The pilgrim was outraged. " Apart from ruining my profession, decidedly not," he said austerely. " It would be most unkind, for no man would like it to be shown that he has acted with folly. That would rankle with him, so it is wisdom to be silent."

" I see, Sir Pilgrim," Ughtred murmured.

His attention was soon elsewhere, when the players and jugglers treated their comrades-in-travel to a free entertainment. There was also a mock fight between a pigmy of a man and a towering giant, in which the latter was disastrously worsted. It was uproariously funny, and Ughtred quickly was grinning from ear to ear, while Lazelle clapped until her palms were sore.

Both would have been only too happy to continue in this style much farther, but their friends' route was through towns and villages and so, when a hamlet came into view, a path forking to the right was taken.

During the next two or three miles Ughtred and Lazelle paused several times: to pick bilberries, to sit on the parapet of a bridge to watch trout below, and to buy food at a lonely farm-house.

That night they slept in the forest, sweet-scented buckler ferns around them and, where the ground hollowed, bog mosses in glorious shades from bright green to deep crimson. Close to them, in a low rock face, chives were growing.

" Brother Henry, of whom I have spoken, is interested in botany as well as geology, Sister Lazelle, and once told me," Ughtred rolled on his elbow to point, " that wherever the Romans went they planted chives."

" It is interesting to think, Brother Ughtred," Lazelle remarked politely, " that a legion may have had a camp about here."

" Or an outpost," Ughtred said, hiding a smile.

" Or an outpost," Lazelle agreed. " Yes, interesting indeed."

Ughtred shook with laughter. " To return," he said between chuckles, " to my dear sister Ada and her twin daughters, my nieces, in whom also you have been expressing an interest."

" Is it not to be expected that I am interested in your family, whom soon, God favouring us, I shall be meeting?" Lazelle said hotly.

" It is most natural," Ughtred admitted, much too gravely.

He was eyed with the deepest suspicion. " I trust not your tone, Brother Ughtred," Lazelle said distantly, but struggled with a dimple.

That dimple was also in evidence the next morning when they came to a ford, summer-dry shallow and with stepping-stones which, if green, did not seem at all slippery. Despite her protests, Ughtred took the baggage over first and then, making more of the difficulties of crossing than appeared necessary, splashed back to carry her.

That was the second time Ughtred of Monkseaton, formerly a monk of Rievaulx, held in his arms the nun Lazelle, late of the priory of Watton. The intimacy of that contact kept both quiet for some time, until they stumbled on a pool fringed by junipers, where they sat to eat dinner.

" Oh! Brother Ughtred, it is so different," Lazelle said dreamily. " I . . . I feel so free."

Ughtred was watching a dragonfly soaring above the limpid surface of the water.

" You remember my speaking to you about Brother Giles, who ran away," he murmured. " He once shocked us all by declaring that the cloister was death-in-life, and that it was always bells, bells, bells."

" So it is," said Lazelle. " And harsh punishments and the most foolish of penances. Thus for one, Brother Ughtred," her lovely eyes widened as she emphasised, " we had to labour at trying to move a monster boulder in the garden to another place. A hundred men could not have budged it, for it must have weighed as much as a thousand packs of wool, or more."

Ughtred sighed as he thought of old Brother Godfrey compelled senselessly to water a stick.

" We had similar stupid tasks, and I do not know what good ends they served," he said.

" But there is to be no more for us, Brother Ughtred," Lazelle said joyously. " It is now three . . . no, four, four days past the Feast of the Apostles, and we are far away."

Ughtred reminded her that to avoid dangers as they appeared, frequent traverses had been made to east and to west, and consequently their northern progress was not as handsome as she imagined.

She was not dismayed. " In that we are doing exactly as you thought we should at the beginning. A little that is safe each day, howsoever long it may take."

Ughtred, who had risen, held out his hand to help her up.

" Last night, Sister Lazelle," he said, " when we knelt together we thanked Our Lord and Saviour for His loving kindness, and so far this day we have nothing to complain to Him about either, and I am very happy."

" Oh! Brother Ughtred, so am I," Lazelle murmured blissfully.

The walk was continued without another real stop until Vespers, when beneath a leafy, wide-spreading sycamore they paused for a *Pater* and *Gloria*, and a snack of bread and wine, before resuming. As always, they were alert for anyone approaching on the winding

forest track, ever ready to flee into the sunless spaces to each side
if needs be.

Since the previous morning it had become evident that Lazelle,
as she boasted then, was much stronger, and so Ughtred did not
argue when she pleaded later for them to put another mile or so
behind them. But, just as the glades grew wider and more frequent,
and the timber correspondingly less, when both were on the watch
for a promising indication of a secluded retreat for the night, Lazelle
sighted a village and Ughtred a number of tethered horses.

" Sister Lazelle," he whispered, grabbing her arm and drawing
her deep into a stand of fir, " there are some uncommonly strange
horsemen about. Stay here while I have a spy."

" You will be careful, Brother Ughtred? " Lazelle said anxiously.

Ughtred nodded reassuringly before making his way back to the
rough road. From there, taking advantage of the cover of every
blade and branch, he crawled through the undergrowth until
within close range of the beasts, who were feeding. They were
shaggy nags, and hanging on the flank of one he perceived a silver
censer and a small, silver image of the Blessed Virgin, fair evidence
that a church had been plundered. If this were not sufficient proof
he had it after edging a few more yards, when he was able to listen
to the talk of a group of men. Their speech would not have been
understood by those of the immediate neighbourhood, but to
Ughtred, reared in Northumberland, whose northern boundary lay
against Scotland, it was soon plain what cruel design was in train.
Cautiously retreating, he rejoined Lazelle.

" They are moss troopers or the like, bent on pillaging the
village after nightfall," he told her. " We must warn them so that
they will not be surprised and murdered in their beds."

The village was larger than he had supposed, and at the door of
a hay-house built on the end of one of the most prosperous-looking
dwellings a thick-set man was sharpening a reaping hook. He turned
quickly on hearing footsteps.

" Good sir," Ughtred began, " a band of cut-throat robbers are
resting not far from here, I reckon about fifteen in all. I have seen
them at close quarters—and their swords and head-pieces, and
breasts of rusty steel-jack, which is not ordinary travellers' wear.
I glimpsed them first when with my middle sister here—we are

footing it to the shelter of our eldest brother's homestead in the western lakes, since both our dear parents have died, within the week of each other . . . and as we came out of the thick of the forest . . ."

Within half an hour an empty barn showed signs of becoming an armoury within which every able-bodied man in the vicinity, and every youth of sufficient age, made his chosen weapon ready: long knives, short daggers and swords were whetted; ancient battle axes and bills were sharpened; long bows and cross-bows, though mostly in trim, checked carefully.

" You will be striking alongside us, good friend? " the blacksmith asked Ughtred, after a practice swing with a heavy sledge hammer.

" I am no fighting man, Sir Smith," Ughtred replied.

" You have a comely sister," the blacksmith grunted. " Still, all to one's own taste, and you have done well enough for us without. For myself, I have only the one cow that could be lifted, but I have a wife and fair daughters and before they shall be ravished they will have to stretch me out dead before them."

When preparations were completed, the farmer to whom Ughtred had first spoken took him to his house, where a substantial meal of meat, eggs, peas, bread and ale awaited them. After eating, Ughtred told Lazelle he thought it would be safer to remain where they were for the night.

" The light will soon start to fail, and though we could steer clear of the band we know of, there may be others, and as we sought for a place to sleep we might blunder into them, which would be the end, Sister Lazelle," he said. " Here we are amongst friends, who are resolute and well armed, and have the advantage of being prepared."

Lazelle and the baby she was holding, the one making endearing but silly noises and the other gurgling delightedly, seemed to be very happy with each other, but Lazelle's smile faded as she turned to Ughtred.

" Brother Ughtred," she said, " will you be . . . be . . ."

Ughtred laughed. " What skill think you I have in wielding an axe or a blade? " he asked. " Have no fear, Sister Lazelle, I shall come to no harm."

When the shadows were lengthening, the goodwife and her large and lively brood, Lazelle with them, climbed the ladder to the upper room; the trapdoor was dropped, and they bolted themselves in. Then the menfolk agreed on final dispositions against the raiders, and Ughtred retrieved the cudgel he had borrowed earlier. It was a most ugly weapon, whose balance and weight he had been very particular about when making a choice.

The moss troopers, though this made no difference, arrived sooner than had been anticipated, a village lad with a gift of mimicry sending out the warning signal, the hoot of an owl, shortly before midnight. For seven or eight minutes after that, and for no more, the air resounded: with thuds, curses, the clash of iron, the vicious twang of bow strings, choking calls, and a single, slowly-diminishing scream. From then the rapid movement of shadowy figures ceased and, surprised at the onset, out-manœuvred and out-numbered, the robbers fled, leaving two of their comrades dead and two wounded. The living were hanged from the branch of an ash at dawn.

If Ughtred and Lazelle had drunk all the mead offered them they would have been incapable of leaving for many days; and the cheese, cold bacon, meat and bread pressed eagerly on them would have foundered a pack-horse. Nevertheless, mindful of the many long miles still before them, they managed to get away in good time, waved off by every man, woman and child in the place.

It was not until almost two hours later that they discovered it was Sunday, when they watched the inhabitants of another village, in best doublets and mantles, respond to the call to Mass rung from the low tower of a grey Norman church.

" Brother Ughtred," Lazelle said wistfully, " do you think it would be too risky if we went, too? It would make me very happy to sing the *Gloria in Excelsis* and to repeat the *Credo*."

Deeply touched, Ughtred looked at her. " It should be quite safe, Sister Lazelle," he said, for some reason troubled by a lump in his throat. " We are neither vagabondish nor of superior quality in these clothes we wear, and the sole interest we shall arouse will be because we are strangers."

So, kneeling closely together near a recess containing an effigy of a knight in mail, they attended the Holy Office. The service was

345

not uplifting: the clerk's delivery was monotonous, and he was so ignorant of the Latin he mouthed that it was a fair assumption he was standing, cheaply, in a well-to-do and absent rector's place. The singing was hearty, however, and the walls were brightly aglow with frescoes which Ughtred, afterwards, remained to study.

A small crowd of worshippers was still outside the church door when they left, amongst them a shrewd-looking gentleman in a long gown and plain hood who bade them " Good day," and showed every sign of a desire for conversation. But Ughtred would have none of that—he bowed, replied courteously, retrieved the bags, and took Lazelle away.

That night they slept much less comfortably than previously, and so their journey was resumed unusually early the next morning. Within the first hour there were two incidents which thoroughly upset Lazelle: three gamekeepers viciously belabouring a poacher, and a farmer and his sons netting thrushes. It was not the happiest of starts, but utter disaster was soon to follow.

Shortly before noon Ughtred and Lazelle were caught.

At the time they were pausing at a well, where a brass dish was chained to a stout post for the benefit of thirsty travellers.

Hearing the clip-clop of hooves, Lazelle looked over her shoulder. On sighting the oncoming riders, six in all, she speedily lost the colour she had acquired since escaping from Watton.

" Brother Ughtred," she whispered, her voice trembling, " there are canons regular approaching us. Six of them."

Ughtred continued to sip leisurely. " Be of good courage, Sister Lazelle," he said quietly. " As we are attired they cannot conceive we are religious, and up here they will not be from Watton."

" No," Lazelle murmured, bracing herself. " But please God do not allow them even to have a suspicion."

Strangely, and ominously, the riders dismounted on reaching them. Their leader was a middle-aged, beaky-nosed man with sharp eyes.

" What is your name, young mistress? " he asked Lazelle " And where are you going? "

" Is that the business of Gilbertine canons? " Lazelle said haughtily.

Both the canon regular and Ughtred spoke to her, together, and neither pleasantly. The religious was quick to repeat his question.

"How is it you know us as being of the Order of Saint Gilbert?"

Before Lazelle could reply, Ughtred was scolding her. "Our dear mother is in Heaven now," he snapped, "but how often before she left us did she instruct you to guard your shrewish tongue? What need was there to speak to the holy father so uncouthly?" Ruffled, he turned to the canon. "I humbly ask your pardon, Reverend Sir, but she has always been a mutinous maid. As to your question—our home was in the fens of Lincolnshire, and often we have seen the canons of Sempringham riding abroad on their errands of godliness and mercy, so the habit is familiar enough."

"You hail from Lincolnshire?"

"Of a truth," Ughtred said, scowling. "And would that we were there now instead of walking to our brother's house in the lakes below the turbulent Scottish Border."

The canon nodded as if satisfied. "Then we must not detain you further, so allowing you to resume your way." He bowed. "*Pax vobiscum.*"

Ughtred bowed in response. "*Deo volente,*" he said gladly.

The canon made a quick sign, and Lazelle was seized. With an enraged cry Ughtred leapt forward, but was overborne after a violent struggle.

"H'mmm," the canon regular murmured, staring hard at him. "So you are a man of some education, which stimulates my thoughts, for though we have been searching for a nun of our sister priory of Watton I seem to recall a strange rumour to the effect that she was linked in some manner with a monk of the abbey of Rievaulx, who is also missing from his home. Great foundations hug their more loathesome secrets closely, and whether there was a sinful relationship between——"

White with anger, Ughtred lessened the distance between himself and the superior, dragging along those trying to hold him.

"You will answer for this unless you unloose us," he said tightly. "Even the religious cannot with impunity seize innocent wayfarers."

"I shall answer if and when I am called on to do so," the canon regular said dryly. " Meantime your hands will be tied and you will accompany us."

By late afternoon Ughtred and Lazelle were lodged in prison cells at the priory of Malton, from which messengers rode out not very long afterwards, one bound to the north-west and the other south-eastwards.

On the day but one following, the sub-prior and the lord abbot's secretary arrived from Rievaulx, and the third prioress and the Reverend Sister Joanna, in a covered cart, came in from Watton.

When the identity of the captives had been established they were ceaselessly interrogated for eight days, until the eve of the anniversary of the ascent into Heaven of the Mother of Jesus.

On the fourth day after the Feast of the Assumption of the Blessed Virgin Mary the prisoners were brought from their cells for trial, which took place in the long hall of the guest house.

While waiting, Ughtred held Lazelle's hand. " Brother Ughtred," she whispered, " you must not fret for me. I am not for myself."

" That is because you have the courage I lack," Ughtred said heavily.

Lazelle shook her head. " If you shiver, Brother Ughtred, you are shivering because of me. And you must not . . . for I have seen the light as your Friar Jerome believed you might one day, and I would be on no path than that on which I stand."

" O Sister Lazelle," Ughtred muttered.

The judges were entering, three Cistercians and three Gilbertines, each of " wise counsel " as the statute laid down. They were all vestmented, but not gorgeously—these were proceedings from which the public was barred, an exclusion also ensuring the minimum of cant and ranting.

Ughtred knew four of the judges, the lord abbots of Kirkstall, Fountains, Rievaulx, and the prior of Watton; and Lazelle the latter and also the fifth, the Master of Sempringham. The sixth was strange to them, but in all probability, as a gesture of courtesy, he would be the prior of Malton.

Lazelle had been close to the lord abbot of Rievaulx before this, but had never really seen him properly.

" So that is the face of My Lady's blood-cousin," she said fiercely. " He who is responsible for the weals on your back, Brother Ughtred, for flesh that has been so cruelly used that it no longer seems flesh."

From then, unless directly concerned, and even so not always then, she never took her eyes off Abbot Hugh. That kind of thing, an unwavering stare, can induce the most odd fancies in the superstitious, and appreciably before the verdict was reached My Lord of Rievaulx was wondering uneasily whether his cousin, the Lady Philippa, had had a witch amongst her daughters.

Throughout the trial there were only the most trivial references to offences which could so easily have been elaborated to telling proportions: the flouting of authority, stealing, the violation of a nunnery, and falsehoods; and there was merely the slightest allusion to the prisoners' lying together lustfully which, though no crime in common law, was an act beyond redemption when the dedicated religious were involved.

In the event, an admission by each of the accused, obtained during interrogation, was considered sufficient to condemn them. The clerk-of-the-court read Lazelle's first:

" ' With all my heart and soul '," she had said, " ' I believe it is inhuman to send people to agonising death by burning at the stake, whatsoever they may have said or done, and I believe that the mighty prelates who send them thus must be cruel and inhuman and ungodly in themselves for so doing '. "

" Do you deny those were your words, my daughter? " the Master of Sempringham asked a little sadly. " And if they are, will you abjure? "

" No, My Lord," Lazelle replied. " It is ' no ' to both."

" Those wicked words represent your belief," the abbot of Fountains said.

" I have already said so, My Lord," Lazelle said.

My Lord of Fountains leaned forward. " If that is your belief, it is a belief you share with the accursed Lollards."

" I know little of the Lollards," said Lazelle. " But it is my belief, My Lord."

The lord abbot of Fountains spread his hands eloquently. " If you have the same belief, then you must be a Lollard yourself. Have you an answer to that? "

" None, My Lord, save those I have given, and they should be ample if you were fair-minded," Lazelle said. " But you are not, My Lord, and so perforce I am left to answer to my own conscience, which does not displease me."

" I think your final answer may be different," said the prior of Watton. " When it is too late and your flesh is being seared by flames."

" My Lords," Ughtred cried angrily, " does he not show himself prejudiced in advance? What chance has she when there is this bias amongst you? "

" What chance do you think she should have? " the unknown prior asked.

Ughtred spoke very quietly. " Every chance, My Lord, for she has lived a life of seclusion in the cloister from being a babe, and that is why, My Lords, I beg you to give her a chance. She is not as I, for I have travelled vastly and seen many things and talked to many people, people good and people ill. I have talked to Sister Lazelle also, injudiciously as I am now aware, and from that talking she has picked up something of what I have said, and has prattled later as a child will prattle, not realising the meaning. For that reason, if there is guilt, I am the one who should bear the brunt alone."

" You accept full responsibility? " the abbot of Fountains said. " I must remind you that we have not heard evidence against you as yet, but this acknowledgment in itself would be enough to condemn you, so weigh your words carefully."

Ughtred shook his head. " There is nothing to weigh, My Lord," he said, placing his hand on his chest. " *Mea culpa, mea culpa*, My Lord. If there is sin it is mine, and mine the blame."

" It shall be noted that you are a self-confessed heretic."

" My Lord of Fountains," said Ughtred, " who shall decide which is a heretic and who is not? "

The lord abbot of Kirkstall laughed. " You can answer that yourself," he said. " Tell us this—do you believe in the Real Presence at the Lord's Supper? "

" I don't know, My Lord," Ughtred said wearily.

My Lord of Kirkstall turned with a broad smile to his colleagues. "Here we have another Abelard," he remarked with a chuckle. "He neither accepts nor rejects, but rationally inquires."

The lord abbot of Fountains, who to the annoyance of Abbot Hugh had taken charge, at the opening, of a silver-gilt bell on the table, nodded to the clerk.

"It becomes only a matter of formality now," he said, "but to proceed in an orderly fashion . . . read the pertinent portion of the second indictment."

The clerk-of-the-court cleared his throat. " ' It is my profound conviction', " he said, repeating Ughtred's words, " ' that Holy Church and Monasticism, instead of wasting immense sums on pomp and senseless self-gratification, should use the major part of their great revenues, and the talents and skills of many among them, towards improving the sorry lot of the poor, the sick and the aged, and that in not doing so the lord bishops and lord abbots are failing lamentably to act as the Lord Christ has taught us to do."

"That is enough," the abbot of Fountains said crisply.

"More than enough," the prior of Malton growled.

As the judges talked together, Ughtred stared at a distemper painting in black, white and red, of a saint, with bright aureole about the head, draped in a prelate's garments. Then he turned to Lazelle, and was surprised to find her gazing fixedly towards the dais. She was so intent that he looked the same way and, again surprised, saw My Lord Hugh crossing himself furtively.

"What is amiss, Sister Lazelle?" he asked.

She smiled at him. "Nothing, Brother Ughtred," she said.

"Nothing!" Ughtred said desolately. "Nothing . . . and I have brought you to this sorry pass."

"Which you have been doing your utmost to save me from," Lazelle said tenderly. "But it will be of no avail, and never could."

"A foregone conclusion before this mockery ever started," Ughtred said.

The judges, even for appearance sake, before a handful of monks and canons regular, did not prolong their deliberations. After a lengthy preamble, the material part of the sentence was delivered by the lord abbot of Fountains within a few moments.

". . . after just trial, that the accused, Ughtred of Monkseaton and the woman Lazelle of birthplace unknown, being convicted of heresy, shall be handed into the custody of the sheriff of York who, under the act *De Heretico Comburendo*, will take the necessary steps for their purification by fire, which arrangement shall bring about the death of each. We, the undersigned, in the name of the Lord Jesus Christ, do herewith, by our hands . . .''

Eleven days later, Ughtred and Lazelle, each with wrists fettered and mounted together on one horse, rode through Malton. The town was packed with farmers, journeymen and labourers, with wives and families; everywhere crowds listened to ballad singers and musicians, or were amused by the patter of hawkers and cheap Jacks trying to trade. Hardware, woollens, earthenware and cooperage were on show, and there were refreshment tents with banners and streamers, stalls with finery, sweet confections and gingerbread, and plenty of customers for them.

As the small cavalcade, with Ughtred and Lazelle in its middle, forced a path through the throng, the chatter and the laughter died, and many were the women who called out a blessing, and men of all ranks who doffed their hats. It was a strange and unexpected passing-by, and there was another queer incident on the outskirts, when a mother and her small daughter, noticing the sheriff's men and whom they had in custody, hastily gathered blue and white harebells, fastening them together with round grass, a joint effort. The posy was presented to Lazelle by the child, who was lifted by the mother.

" God be with you both, my dears," the woman said. " Always."

Long after they had thanked her and the child, Lazelle said over her shoulder: " It must be that they all have known what lies before us, Brother Ughtred, and they are sorry."

" I think it is more than that, Sister Lazelle," Ughtred said. " When I witnessed—no, what I mean is this, that the temper of the people is rising against insensate persecution, and many of them are expressing that feeling."

" Brother Ughtred," said Lazelle, " you were striving to shield me from what we are to meet, by not naming it, but you need not, for I am not afraid."

" Before God," Ughtred said with disgust, " if I had not been witless we would not be here. Even a man who can read a few verses of the Psalter is regarded at once as a clerk, but to answer the canon regular in Latin as I did . . . Bah! "

" It would have made no difference, Brother Ughtred," Lazelle said firmly. " He was suspicious, and I am certain he was pretending when he told us we were free to go our way."

" He was setting a trap," Ughtred said bitterly. " And the Lord above must be sighing about the fool He has made."

Lazelle turned again, twisting shoulders and neck so that she could look into his face. She spoke very decidedly.

" Brother Ughtred, I will not have you make me miserable. It is true this is a wretched business, but our hands are clean and I refuse to sniff and snuffle."

Ughtred was not the only one to marvel about her on that ride, and certainly for most of the journey an escort nearby was guilty of doing what she declined to do, sniffling and snuffling. Throughout, until the spires of York were sighted, and beyond, she was gay. When passing the archery butts outside the wall, where men of all ages were practising, she joked about her own skill in the garden at Watton; and near Goodramgate Bar made faces about the smell from pack-horses bringing in fish from the coast.

Within the city, where the narrow streets were crowded, progress was slower, at a snail's pace in the Shambles, dark as always with the overhang of buildings. Then into Pavement and over Ouse Bridge, the journey ending in a high-walled courtyard behind St. William's Chapel.

Only then, as Lazelle was parted from Ughtred, did she reflect the strain she was under.

" For once we can be sure of meeting again, Brother Ughtred," she said, the smallest tremor in her voice.

" And never, if it has to be, could I have a more staunch comrade, Sister Lazelle," Ughtred said, his heart aching.

She held her fettered hands towards him and, for a few precious seconds, before the last separation of all, they clung together.

Ughtred was lodged in a cell with a view of the river, and when the gaoler had brought him food and drink he spent the hours until darkness at the barred window, staring at ships and wishing again and again that he could have taken Lazelle to his home, where he could have shown her the sea. From there also he saw that the tower on the Minster had not grown much since he was last in the city.

The next day one of the sheriff's officers came to tell him they would be burned three days later. He added to this:

" Out on the Knavesmire, at a place named Tyburn."

" Appropriately so-called," Ughtred murmured. " I know it."

" You will not be permitted to address the throng."

That aroused Ughtred who, between beseeching God to ensure that Lazelle speedily lost her senses, and wondering if Friar Jerome were still in the city, had been composing a scorching speech—not one of piety and acquiescence—in which he would demand that his hearers should hasten the long-overdue day of reformation.

" Why not, Sir Captain? " he asked. " It is usual."

At first, the officer seemed disinclined to answer, but relented. " Latterly there has been too much of incitement in them," he muttered. " And often too much mischief afterwards."

Ughtred was aware of the futility of remonstrating, but his lips were compressed as he decided that he would be cut down before they should force him to desist—that is, until he realised in so doing he would be leaving Lazelle alone.

The chaplain appointed to the prison visited him before bed-time, a tall and heavily-built man with a florid complexion.

" I am here, as is my duty," he said, " to help you make your peace with the Lord."

" For your trouble you have my gratitude," Ughtred said civilly. " And if I tell you, as I do, that I have no need of your services I trust you will not charge me with offensiveness, for that is not my intent."

" You have no need of my services? "

" No, Sir Clerk, but I thank you."

The cleric's face had become a sneering mask. " *You* . . . you, who ere long will be consumed by fire, have the monstrous presumption to spurn the charity which through God's grace I offer you . . . you, a renegade monk who for infamous conduct . . ."

Ughtred's despair and frustration crystallised into a white-hot element of fury.

" Out! " he growled.

"Out!" thundered the chaplain. "You, spawned by the devil, dare to give orders to a priest of Holy Church."

"I shall dare to do more to a priest of Holy Church if you are not gone," Ughtred said with a repressed quietness that might have appeared alarming. "Soon, as you reminded me so gently, I am to die, but I think you will agree, Sir Clerk, that I shall die no less horribly if I cut another notch in my bow beforehand."

"You . . . you threaten my life?" the chaplain stuttered.

Eyes burning in pale face, Ughtred advanced on him.

"Out!" he shouted. "Out!"

With a squeal of fear, the clerk-in-orders darted to the door.

Shakily, ashamed of himself, Ughtred walked across the cell, which was more commodious than those to which he had been used, and for a little while paced about, before sinking to his knees in prayer. Afterwards he went to the window again, standing there lost in thought until his attention was arrested by a distant sound, a queer roar which repeatedly rose and faded.

This odd sound was resumed during the forenoon of the following day, in greater volume, and when the gaoler, the guard remaining outside, carried in dinner, Ughtred had an eye squeezed between the window bars trying to locate its direction, which seemed up-river.

"What is that strange tumult, good fellow?" Ughtred asked.

"Rioting, Sir Monk," the gaoler replied. "Two mobs and, by my truth, not all scallywags either. The city fathers have been trying to quell them from what we hear, but were shouted down. What a to-do!"

Ughtred broke a piece of bread and dropped it into the broth. "What are they rioting about, and where?" he asked indifferently.

"In the Minster garth and outside the gatehouse of St. Mary's, hundreds and hundreds, they say."

Ughtred stopped chewing. "In the shadow of St. Peter's and at the abbey? But why?"

The gaoler looked curiously at him, and then glanced at the door. "There's some, Sir Monk," he said darkly, his voice lowered, "who aren't all that fond of the clerics being able to order certain deeds on their own, as if they were above the laws of the land."

THE FACE OF A MADONNA

" Oh! " Ughtred said, understanding. " It has got abroad that there is to be a burning? "

The gaoler nodded. " But," he said with gruff kindliness, " don't raise your hopes because you'll only have 'em dashed, for a burning there will be. This old place has seen a-plenty of savage unruliness in its day, and so the sheriff always has a rare number of men, and in extreme can call out the garrison from the castle."

Ughtred sighed. " Yes, I suppose so, good gaoler."

For the remainder of the day, the faraway racket hardly ever lessening, he could never keep still for long, alternating between abject despair and wild visions of a multitude breaking open Lazelle's and his prison, and releasing them.

Later, as the bell of St. Michael's in Spurriergate sent out its homing toll towards travellers in the forest, the sheriff's officer came with the news that the execution of the sentence had been postponed.

" Postponed! " Ughtred exclaimed, his legs suddenly jelly-like. " Why is that, Sir Captain? "

The officer was not talkative. " I know not," he said as he left.

The uproar in the vicinity of the Benedictine abbey and the great minister continued the next day, until shortly before the bells of the city's churches began to ring for Vespers, when it ended. Seven hours later, when Ughtred, restless beneath a blanket, was trying to solve the problem of the deferment of the burning, the sheriff's officer entered the cell again, with two guards carrying lanterns. He unrolled a sheet of red-sealed parchment containing an intimation that the sentence had been changed.

" Changed! " Ughtred said. " What is it to be now, Sir Captain? "

The guard who was holding a light aloft brought it nearer to his officer, who began to read, mumbling through the early portions until reaching the vital lines:

" ' In lieu the aforesaid Ughtred of Monkseaton and the woman Lazelle, of birthplace unknown, shall be conveyed to the grange named Riggs and there immured for their heresies, as is appropriate elsewise, it being the place in which they sinned together carnally, thereby so offending spiritually as to be beyond even the Lord Christ's power of redeeming.' "

" Immured," Ughtred murmured.

The sheriff's officer shivered. " It is being walled-up when alive," he said.

Ughtred nodded. " I have the Latin and so I understand, and would that it were not so, for we might not have been here," he said sadly. " When do we depart, Sir Captain? "

" It is the Sabbath to-morrow, and you both will ride out with me early on Monday," the officer replied unhappily. " Towards the other end we are to be met by a guide, for I understand that we go to a wild and remote place."

" It is so," said Ughtred.

The sheriff's officer swallowed. He was perhaps five or six years older than Ughtred and, under different circumstances, would probably have been a most pleasant companion.

" I have other business now, for I have to rouse the maid to acquaint her with the tidings," he muttered. " As for yourself, if on waking you have need of anything . . . extra victuals, parchment, writing implements——"

" I thank you, Sir Captain, though I have no such requirements," Ughtred said. " But if you will be so considerate as to tell the maid that she is always in my thoughts I would be grateful to you for the remainder of my span. Not that that," he added ironically, " is a very lengthy inducement, I fear."

" It shall be done," the sheriff's officer said hurriedly.

When alone in the darkness, Ughtred sat to think. In the main he tried to evaluate—which would be the easier of two cruel deaths for Lazelle: short searing agony, or a long, drawn-out passing which would have its phases of pain, not physically only.

The next morning, as hundreds of bells were calling the faithful to High Mass, Ughtred was standing at the window when the door of the cell was unlocked. The guard ushered in a tall, barefooted, gaunt-faced man in a shabby, brown Franciscan habit.

Idly Ughtred turned, but quickly ran forward. " Friar Jerome!" he cried gladly. " Praise in abundance to the Lord for this mercy. I had hoped to see you, but my expectations have been dwindling."

After they had embraced Friar Jerome explained that he had been away from the city until the previous evening, at Selby, attending on a brother who had been gravely sick, now fortunately much improved.

" On my return," he went on as they seated themselves on the bench, " I heard about crowds demonstrating fiercely, and how, almost at the beginning, the archbishop and the lord abbot, annoyed themselves and in no wise concerned, and also under pressure from the aldermen, sent messengers post-haste to various abbeys and priories. That was when I had a glimmering of suspicion that you might be involved, Brother Ughtred, which was confirmed when I saw the maid Lazelle an hour ago."

" You have been with Sister Lazelle? " Ughtred said eagerly.

The friar nodded. " I am entrusted to deliver to you her fondest greetings." He reflected for some moments. " You will not have to tell me again, as you once did, Brother Ughtred, that she is both a sweet and a very pure maid. To look into the depths of her eyes is to know that she is guiltless of evil in thought and deed."

" It is so," Ughtred said huskily.

Friar Jerome, in his conversation with Lazelle, had learnt a great deal beyond the fact that the sentence had been changed. He knew about her meetings with Ughtred: here in York, at the little monastery of Riggs, and after the fire at Watton; she had described the night passed together in a small cave near the bank of a river—which he had heard of before, from Ughtred—and he was now aware how Ughtred, following merciless punishment, had broken out of the abbey of Rievaulx to come to her succour.

" Yes," said Ughtred, when the friar had briefly mentioned these things. " But she has not told you why she refused to reveal that it was I who gave her my relic and a picture in little of the Lord Christ. She feared if our connection became known it might lead to a discovery for which I would suffer excruciatingly— because in the abbey church of Rievaulx is a picture of a Madonna I have painted, and the face is hers."

For a minute or more Friar Jerome had been intensely scrutinising Ughtred, but now a smile transfigured his face.

" Of a truth, Brother Ughtred," he said as he rose, " I come to the conclusion that you and the maid are at your most loquacious when parading the merits of the other. Now turn round a little so that I can examine this back of yours."

Pulling Ughtred's doublet away, he probed gently with fingertips. When finished, his eyes had darkened with anger.

" It is healthy enough, my brother," he said.

" The scourging alone has not caused me to see the light, Brother Jerome," Ughtred said slowly. " For I *have* seen the light, as you once said I might some blessed day."

While Ughtred continued to talk, Friar Jerome opened a leather satchel he had placed on a stool when entering. Within it were many phials, small boxes, rolls of clean linen, a beaker, and various strange-looking tools. There was a jug of water in the cell, and after pouring a small amount into the beaker he counted drops from one of the little vessels, and added twice as many from another.

" This will fortify you, my brother," he said when rummaging for a spoon. " The maid Lazelle has already had the same concoction."

Ughtred had picked up and was looking at a small bottle containing a thick, greenish liquid.

" What is this, Brother Jerome, a deadly poison or a miraculous cure distilled from flowers or herbs? " he asked. " Whatever it may be the hue is one I could have used to profit had it been paint."

The Franciscan glanced up. " My honoured master at the university of Ravenna, from whom I acquired much that is unknown to the ordinary practitioner, used to remark jestingly when he compounded it that it would raise the dead. But, more seriously, Brother Ughtred, it has in my hands revived the apparently drowned, and also men, seemingly lifeless, cut down from the gallows."

Ughtred's thoughts were racing and when the medicine was handed to him he walked to the window. Raising the beaker, he drank the draught, but did not return at once, remaining to stare fixedly at two lads with crude fishing rods, who probably were playing truant from church. When he turned his manner was different, grim and determined.

" Brother Jerome," he said, " when we are immured, unless no air enters at all, we shall die by inches only, and for long we shall know the pangs of starvation . . . and while we remain clear-headed we shall know that nothing but death is before us. In God's name, Brother Jerome, would it not be better, and I speak about Sister Lazelle only, if at the start of our prisoning she could sink into an unconsciousness from which she would never wake? "

Friar Jerome's deep-set eyes were on him. " If it could be, it would be better, Brother Ughtred," he said guardedly.

" It could be," Ughtred said, pointing to the satchel. " For there you must have powders and essences which could be rolled into a pill big enough to have that effect."

" I have, my brother, but they are poison in quantity."

" What of it? " Ughtred demanded. " What is wrong in making an end to what has already ended? "

" It is murder nevertheless," the friar said sternly.

" It is kindness," said Ughtred.

" It is deliberately taking life," said Friar Jerome.

" I repeat," Ughtred said insistently, " what of it? "

Friar Jerome came nearer to him. " My brother," he said compassionately, " how can I, and how can you ask? "

For some long moments, in silence, they faced each other, the friar's expression unvarying, Ughtred's gradually changing: acceptance slowly replacing hot resentment, grief more swiftly displacing acceptance, until he sunk strickenly to the bench, where he buried his head in his hands. When more composed, he looked up.

" I have erred flagrantly, Brother Jerome," he said, his lips still tremulous. " In my selfishness I forgot that our Saviour Christ bore his cross to the end, as so we must. For this, Brother Jerome, I shall find it hard to forgive myself, even if He will."

The friar clapped him on the shoulder. " If you wish to lacerate yourself you must, my brother, but it seems unnecessary as the Lord will have excused you already," he said cheerfully. " But now I must be away."

Disappointed and shocked by the abrupt termination, Ughtred jumped up. He had been cherishing the notion that he would have company for some time, in the circumstances.

" You go so soon? " he asked.

Friar Jerome smiled. " If I am to find my way by to-morrow evening to this outlandish place styled Riggs, which is my purpose, I must not dally here in the city." He held his leg up to show a leathery foot. " These have to get me there, Brother Jerome, not the broad back of an amiable mare."

Ughtred's eyes shone with relief. " You will be with us, Brother Jerome? "

The friar was hammering on the door for the guard to let him out. " I shall be with you and the maid Lazelle, never fear," he said when leaving. " And may the Lord God be with you now and forever, my friend."

" As with you," said Ughtred. " Our very dear friend."

Feeling much brighter, he sat down. As he thought about his visitor he hoped that Brother Jerome's presence had comforted Lazelle as much as he had been comforted himself, though as he reflected upon this more objectively he wondered just what had occurred to comfort him. Then he let his mind dwell upon Sister Lazelle, whom he would be with again in a few hours.

Next morning, fettered as before at the wrists but separately mounted, he and Lazelle left York by Bootham Gate. It was drizzling slightly, but the early sun increasingly made its power felt from behind thin clouds, and shortly it became fair, with a refreshing breeze.

Allowed to ride together, to begin with they talked exclusively about Friar Jerome, but later about such things as interested them along the road: the neat manner in which a line of labourers in a golden field, sickles flashing in unison, cut corn with their right arms and gathered the stalks in the left; or a scene at the wayside in which a group of sceptical-looking foresters completely encircled a man who, an enormous pike at his feet, was indignantly declaiming to the heavens.

This was becoming a familiar route to Ughtred, and constantly he pointed to this side and that as the forest thinned. At the edge of the plain he knew a glade through which he showed Lazelle a glimpse of the hills ahead of them, and when a halt was ordered for dinner, close to a waterfall tumbling over lichen-covered boulders, he was able to tell her roughly how far they had gone on their journey.

The sheriff's officer in command of the company had been very gentle with them. When nicely clear of the city, on their solemn promise not to take advantage, he had ordered the fetters to be removed; now, he added to his kindness by permitting them to eat their meal a little apart.

More than once during that pause the glances of the sheriff's men-at-arms strayed to the couple, a couple plainly more absorbed in each other than their situation, and more than one head was slowly shaken, in wonder.

*     *     *     *

Overhead, shrill-voiced peewees capered in flight, while from near the hoofs of the leading horse a blackcock shot up with an alarmed squawk to wing towards purple, heather-clad slopes. The great castle to which the sub-prior of Rievaulx had ridden to borrow grotesquely-shaped irons was some distance behind, and just in front there was a gap in the trees through which the abbey could be perceived.

"It is there," Ughtred said. "The place I called home for nigh on ten years."

For a reason entirely feminine Lazelle had acquired a loathing for the abbey of Rievaulx and everything concerning it, from the lord abbot Hugh downwards. In consequence, although she turned towards a woods-surrounded, green valley, and a low-towered church and grey monastic buildings within a castellated wall, her interest was but cursory.

"Even the devil himself could not have discovered a place more remote for imposing cruelties," she said, and would look no more.

When conditions were convenient they rode with their beasts near together, but as the track, dipping occasionally but on the whole ascending, wound over the moors, this was not always possible, and they did not come close very frequently until a fork and a stone cross were reached. From that point, leaving the poor highway, they were able to talk again during the descent to Riggs.

On sighting the bridge the man-at-arms riding at the head of the little column expressed vivid doubts about its stability, and was sent forward to reconnoitre. As a result the whole party dismounted to cross on foot, and were compelled to tread cautiously on the crown of the hump-back, where there was a large hole through which the stream could be seen flowing below.

"As the horses now, the Gilbertine holy ladies' hooded carts will also have to stay back on the morrow," the sheriff's officer remarked to one of his men. "Nuns of a special Order or no, they will have to reach this side of the water as we have if it is meant for them to pass on, as an example to absent sisters as well, a description of what they have witnessed."

Ughtred, in the meantime, had taken Lazelle's arm, tentatively and then more firmly. Linked so, they had walked through the doorway of the gate-house, across the weedy courtyard, and round the south wall of the church to the open end of the chapter house. In the garth there was some delay while the sheriff's officer made an inspection of the premises with one of the senior servants of the abbey of Rievaulx who, with various others under him, had been making certain arrangements while awaiting the party's arrival. As could be expected, those who knew Ughtred, by sight or otherwise, had difficulty in keeping their eyes off the couple, but none of them approached him.

On returning, the officer pointed to the outer staircase to the dormitory, but held out his other arm to stay Ughtred.

" If you would wish to wash, Mistress," he said to Lazelle. " Er . . . towels have been brought, and are up there."

" Thank you, Sir Captain," she said gratefully.

Similarly, later, Ughtred was sent off for the same purpose. From the top of the steps he passed through the dormitory to the necessary, which had been provided with a fresh boxful of sweet hay. There was also a lavatory close at hand, and in both that and the necessary water still flowed as efficiently as when a monkish engineer, a specialist in sanitation, had nodded with satisfaction at practical proof that the levelling and figuring on his plan had been accurate.

While Ughtred was drying his hands he heard heavy thudding. Looking into the garth, he saw a mason knocking bars out of a window in the western range. The man was standing on a heap of newly-squared stones.

" So it is to be there," he murmured to himself.

Lazelle had also noticed this activity, but did not mention it to him until they had eaten what they could of the food provided, which was both ample and good. She said precisely what he had said to himself.

" So it is to be there, Brother Ughtred? "

" I would think so, Sister Lazelle. As I recall it, the end cell is larger than the others."

Her face lighted up. " Then we shall be together, Brother Ughtred. I had wondered, for I did not want to be . . . be by myself."

" Nor I, Sister Lazelle. But I would almost vouch that it is a surety, and I am glad."

They were smiling at each other when a sheriff's man came to tell them they must now leave the refectory. With two other guards falling in, they were escorted across the derelict cloister garth to the old west walk, on to which the doorways and windows of the punishment range directly abutted. They were lodged in adjoining cells, but although they could not see each other speech between them was easy, when both stood at the windows. But they did not talk freely until the men, who had to improvise fastenings to the doors since the locks were rusted solidly, went back to the refectory.

Friar Jerome arrived when they were beginning to speculate about him. They saw his tall figure in the chapter house opposite, and watched him striding along the east walk as far as its junction with the southern side of the cloister, where he went inside to the sheriff's party. What happened then Lazelle and Ughtred could not know, but there were several roars of amusement before the friar, a broadly-grinning fellow at his side, walked over to them.

Their visitor went into Lazelle first. He was not very long with her and, on entering Ughtred's cell, announced he would not be long with him either.

" Howsoever, I shall be with you both again before the light fails, Brother Ughtred," he said while opening his leather satchel. " In the meantime, thanks be to Our Lord's loving kindness, the generosity of the officer yonder, and the aptitude of a mendicant friar in begging, I am to have good ale, bread and meat. After that, I shall stroll beyond the gatehouse, to cool my feet in the river."

" They must need it," said Ughtred. " You have had a lengthy and arduous walk."

Friar Jerome, who was stirring the contents of a beaker, paused to shake his head.

" It does not compare, Brother Ughtred, with a walk I once did across the Apennines to Florence, where it was believed that shortly the populace would be dying in their hundreds daily. The heat! Never have I endured such a stifling."

"That would make it much more serious, Brother Jerome," Ughtred said. "I have read that such conditions are breeders of pestilence."

"The manifestations had much in common with the two major forms of plague, which caused so much alarm that the wealthier of the citizens were fleeing with their families in droves," the friar murmured. "But despite the similarity of the symptoms it proved to be a sickness fatal only to a few of the very weakly, and others were able to throw it off speedily."

"God be praised," Ughtred said.

"Of absorbing interest," the friar said absentmindedly.

Ughtred stared at him. "What was, Brother Jerome?"

Friar Jerome brought himself into the present. He smiled as he handed Ughtred the beaker.

"Subsequently, with my master of Ravenna, I worked for many weeks on that strangely-deceiving visitation," he said. "It was the most fascinating piece of research in which I have ever been engaged."

Ughtred became aware that he had drunk a most nauseous draught. "This is different from what you gave me before," he said, grimacing.

"Very different, my brother, as will be the next when I come again to you and the maid," Friar Jerome said gravely. "As I plodded here I turned things over in my mind, and although I cannot, if I believe in the Lord, lend myself to what you asked for in the city——"

"It was wrong of me, and I bitterly regret that——"

The friar, waving Ughtred into silence, told him that he had no desire to harp about a matter on which contrition had been expressed.

"But if I am not able to aid you thus, Brother Ughtred," he continued, "I can at least endeavour to ease your passage."

"You would have my blessing if you would but try," Ughtred said slowly. "It is all very well to be brave beforehand, but as the minutes decrease before the hour . . . fright tends to elbow out courage. That is why I keep thanking Our Saviour for ensuring that we are not entirely alone, that we have a friend nearby."

"You have a friend, my brother," said Friar Jerome.

Ughtred looked at him, with eyes strained and tired. " I do not know what you are giving us, nor do I ask, but if it numbs the senses a trifle I shall be grateful . . . especially for Sister Lazelle, because everything concerning her makes me think she has a passionate love of life. Sometimes, since we were captured, I have wished she did not bear up so proudly . . . that she might have relief if she would let herself weep."

" I understand, my brother," Friar Jerome said gently. " As to the specifics—I have confidence they will do far more than take off the sharp edge of your distress."

" Is it cowardly to desire that? " Ughtred asked wistfully.

Friar Jerome shook his head. " The coward thinks of nothing but his own skin, my brother, but in what you seek you are not moved by thoughts of self, and if I were to tell you that it might be in the best interests of the maid if she alone had the physics, then that would be the course you would insist on."

" Would it? " Ughtred asked sharply.

" There! " The friar laughed. " No, my brother, it must be both or none."

Ughtred smiled faintly. " You have me again, as you nearly always do," he said ruefully. " So it shall be both, and right gladly do we entrust ourselves into your hands."

Friar Jerome's voice deepened with conviction. " You and the maid are in the hands of God, my brother. I am not without knowledge; perhaps during my wanderings I have acquired strange knowledges, but howsoever I may strive to help it is He who will decide the outcome. Always remember that, Brother Ughtred."

" I shall remember," Ughtred said.

When the friar had gone to his repast, Ughtred and Lazelle, at their windows, talked quietly to each other: about inconsequential incidents and amusing happenings which had occurred before and after their stolen meetings—always of what had passed, and never of what was in front. They spoke, too, of Friar Jerome, when they saw him leaving the cloister by way of the chapter house.

" I have been with him very little, Brother Ughtred," Lazelle said, " but somehow I *know*, something deep inside tells me, that he is a godly and noble man, ever caring for others and nothing for himself."

"And yet there was a time at the beginning," Ughtred marvelled, "on first meeting him, when he so angered me that I was in grievous danger of forgetting that my duty was to turn the other cheek."

The sun had gone down, and twilight was not far away, when the friar came again to them. As previously, he visited Lazelle before Ughtred, to whom he also gave a dose of a yellowish liquid to which a finely-crushed green powder was added. In neither cell did he stay longer than was needed to prepare the medicine, but afterwards hunted about outside until he found an old stool which, used cautiously, would bear him. He placed this in the west walk, between the windows of the habited cells, and began to talk about his travels in the Holy Land and Egypt.

Friar Jerome had the gift of vivid narration, and his stories of adventure momentarily helped his hearers to forget their troubles, until the greyness of night started to close in, when their attention wavered.

Rising and picking up the stool, Friar Jerome stepped closer to a window, when he saw that the maid Lazelle's fingers were tightly clasping a bar, and that her eyelids were drooping.

"That must be enough of my tales for now," he said. "Soon the physic should be having an effect, my brother and sister."

Lazelle made an effort. "It . . . it has already, as I live, dear Brother Jerome. I am so . . . so heavy."

"Then the ingredients of my tincture were not stale," the friar remarked cheerfully. "But I must not keep you chattering, for of a surety this is the time you must lay your head down, my sister."

"Dear Lord, I think I must," she said, her words slurred. "Brother Ughtred, we will talk . . . talk again."

Ughtred heard her as he had heard Brother Jerome, as if she were far away. Struggling, he raised himself a little from the dark whirlpool into which he was sinking.

"Rest yourself, Sister Lazelle," he muttered. "Rest yourself as our brother wishes you to do."

His expression agonised, the friar watched through one window as she stumbled to the bench, and then he looked at the next, where Ughtred, head sunk on breast, was clinging to hold himself upright.

Friar Jerome's lips moved but no sound emerged as, standing

very still, the stool dangling from his hand, he poured out entreaties to the Lord for whom, every day of his life, he was spending himself. In time, his devotions were short, but his forehead was beaded when he had done.

" Brother Ughtred," he said, repeating himself when there was no reply. " Brother Ughtred, do you hear me? "

" I . . . hear you," Ughtred mumbled. " I . . ."

" Brother Ughtred, you must now stretch yourself out," Friar Jerome said, enunciating clearly and with quiet forcefulness. " You must follow Sister Lazelle's example."

Dizzy with fever, using the wall for support, Ughtred staggered to the bench, on which he collapsed rather than arranged himself. His body burned and his eyes were pools of pain; his throat was constricted and his mouth dry, and hammers pounded in his head; he had cramps that tightened his chest, during which he fought for breath, and he often felt close to suffocation.

It was a nightmare of illness and wretchedness which, when at long last displaced, was exchanged for a frenzy less intimately personal and of wider scope. Unknown faces loomed immensely over him, and as he was plucked upwards the faces rose with him. The light changed, becoming piercingly bright, hurting his eyes. Vision blurred and distorted, he moved without making an effort, passing along far-extending ranks of black-and-white clad Gilbertine nuns formidably drawn up in battle array; he encountered their bedizened standard bearer, the Lady Philippa, with whom were canons regular he had met near a well, men she favoured in some queer way; and, as he encountered a vast army of monks of a scandalous Order to which in another life he had belonged, he shrank from a personage magnificent in mitre, lavishly-embroidered vestments, and with a glittering staff, who was kind enough to commend him to God and to tell him he might go in peace, though that was only a cunning trap. Friar Jerome was there somewhere, and he, as could be expected, was gentleness itself, as were rough-voiced strangers who supported him considerately and helped carry his heavy cross along the hard way of grief to Calvary.

It grew gloomier, and with the change he fleetingly saw Lazelle, but knew she was an illusion. Joining the buzzing in his ears was a new but familiar sound, of voices raised in the Office of the

Dead—and he heard the mournful toll of the passing bell, and with a pang of anguish knew it rang for her who was gone.

The darkness increased, and with that he was aware of being returned once again to a dank, underground vault; head swimming, he stared at a flight of steps descending from the Passage, quivering at the thought that soon they would come to take him to the Greek cross in the chapter house, where the *flagellum* hung on the wall; and he shuddered uncontrollably when he saw Brother Eustace lick his full lips, and Brother Left-handed Thomas' sly smile. Terrified, he began to sweat, and in sweating slipped into oblivion.

Sick, clay-cold, but clear-headed, Ughtred of Monkseaton opened his eyes. For a while he did not move, his gaze staying fixed on a narrow slit of light.

Lazelle, kneeling behind him, remained as motionless, a pitcher of water in one hand and a handkerchief with which she had been wiping his brow in the other.

" O dear Lord and Saviour," she murmured brokenly. " Never shall I be able to thank you enough for your mercy and goodness."

Ughtred twisted his head. " Sister Lazelle! " he gasped feebly. " You! With me! How do we come to be together? "

She was weeping quietly. " I cannot tell, Brother Ughtred. All I know is that I wakened . . . it must be two hours ago . . . and found myself here, in a different place . . . and with you. Since then, as I watched over you, you breathed so softly that I have been affrighted your eyes might forever remain shut."

Rolling himself on to his face, Ughtred crawled to the bench, where he levered himself up. In the quarter-light he saw two chairs, and a table with a candlestick in which a candle had burnt to its end, so that wax lay thick round the base.

" Cry no more, Sister Lazelle," he said tenderly. " For I can see now, and we are together, and we can talk."

Her voice trembled as she pointed towards the top of the doorway. " Under God, I hardly dare say what I have been thinking, but . . . but it may be that we can do more than talk, Brother Ughtred."

For a second or so, dumbfounded by his own stupidity, Ughtred stared at that bright gap. Then he jumped up, but sat down as suddenly.

" Don't try just yet, for you will soon be different," Lazelle said. " I felt fearsome when I came to my senses, but the worst of the weakness quickly began to pass."

" I may be able to see, but I am still dim-witted," Ughtred said. " Howsoever else could I have gazed as I did without wondering why we are not walled in solidly. True, it is inexplicable, but if the slit could be increased in width, and so long as no one is outside . . ."

" I have heard no sound save the call of the curlew," Lazelle said. " As to making it wider . . . when you are able, you will see for yourself, Brother Ughtred."

Nothing could have stopped Ughtred after that, and though his legs were very shaky he managed to make his way to the doorway which, to the height of his head, was as massively blocked as the window. Above that, however, the stones of two courses had been laid in a most unworkmanlike manner, and the mortaring was careless.

" It should be possible, Sister Lazelle," Ughtred muttered.

Standing on the table, which they had carried to the doorway, he removed a few of the stones on the cell side, handing them to Lazelle to put down quietly. This enabled him to thrust his head farther into the interior of the thick wall to listen. He heard nothing, but the great test came when he pushed a large stone the other way—it fell with a crash into the walk beyond, but no one came.

Excitement renewing their strength, they began in earnest and, oblivious to cuts and abrasions, were no longer than half an hour in opening out a hole as wide and deep as could be made without tools. Ughtred made the first attempt to escape—the early stages of wriggling through were more awkward than hard, but later it was different, when his head was hanging down towards the cloister walk while the lower part of his limbs and feet were to some degree still jammed in the hole. Eventually he fell, so nearly knocking himself out that, to recover, he stayed for two or three minutes where he had sprawled.

For Lazelle it was easier, with Ughtred outside stretching up to hold her shoulders, though at that, at the end, he was not strong enough to support her full weight, and the consequence was that they tumbled together.

" I am not hurt, Brother Ughtred," she gasped.

It was a sunny day and Ughtred was now able to see her properly. Horror-stricken, he stared at her. Her skin was discoloured, and from throat to brow there were livid eruptions; her eyes, so lovely always, were more fiercely red than he had ever seen eyes, and her neck was very swollen.

Lazelle nodded to him. " You are the same, Brother Ughtred. I think it is some grievous sickness we have had, and I . . . I have wondered whether Friar Jerome, in his affection for you and to save us both misery, gave us a death potion . . . which perhaps was not as potent as he supposed."

Ughtred shook his head decidedly. " He would not have done that, for I asked him and he refused."

" You asked him, Brother Ughtred? "

" I asked him," said Ughtred. " It was sinful of me and he very properly rebuked me."

" I thank Our Saviour that he refused," Lazelle said fervently. " For we are alive, Brother Ughtred, and while we are alive we may still cherish hope."

An onrush of emotion so affected Ughtred that he gave the closest attention to the hole at the top of the cell doorway. As composedly as possible, he expressed the opinion that the masons, left to themselves to complete their task without anyone of authority over them, had scamped the job, not troubling too much because of a conviction that the prisoners were on the point of death.

" It could be so, Brother Ughtred," Lazelle agreed.

He helped her up, and together they walked to the end of the west walk and along the south walk as far as the open doorway of the refectory, where they turned in.

Lazelle halted abruptly when only a step beyond the threshold. " Brother Ughtred! " she exclaimed. " How comes this? "

Ultimately Ughtred found tongue, after gaping at a long table set for a meal. On it were bakemeats of various kinds, dishes of salted fish, loaves, tarts, pastries, fruits, and flagons of wine. On a side-table was a cask of ale, and on settles, as if tossed there, were riding mantles and cloaks.

" Here is great mystery, Sister Lazelle," he said. " And I know not what to make of it."

" It is as if a spread had been prepared, and those for whom it was prepared never came . . . or," Lazelle glanced at the clothing, " or never returned."

Ughtred made up his mind. " Sister Lazelle," he said, " I am going to spy round these precincts."

Swiftly she turned to him. " Brother Ughtred, I am frighted to be alone," she confessed. " Could I not come with you? "

Hating to refuse her, but convinced he was right, Ughtred shook his head.

" Sister Lazelle, it is better if I am alone, for single it is easier to withdraw unnoticed or to hide. And I promise I will never be beyond earshot if you cry loudly for me."

She put a good face on it, so that he left her cheerfully to make an inspection of the buildings flanking the cloister and the court-yard as far as the gatehouse. He had not intended a lengthy absence, but was delayed by several most extraordinary discoveries, which increased his bewilderment vastly.

Lazelle, who had bathed her face in cold water during his absence, looked much better when he next saw her.

" You must go up to do the same, Brother Ughtred," she said. " It has soothed me wondrously."

" I will, shortly," said Ughtred, " but first I have something for you to puzzle over."

He took her to a small apartment off the east walk, where a number of ornamental phials and small, silver-lidded coffers were arranged on a beautifully embroidered cloth. Marvelling, she identified them as belonging to the Lady Philippa.

In another chamber Ughtred showed her clothing which a gentleman of great rank might wear when riding out on a sporting occasion. It was not unreasonable to assume it belonged to the Lady Philippa's cousin, or that the room had been used for changing into different attire.

" I think they were both here, and that there may have been some form of ceremonial gathering to witness our immurement, Sister Lazelle," Ughtred said. " We were senseless and knew nothing either of that or of the sheriff's men placing us in a cell together, as they surely must have."

" It may be so, Brother Ughtred, but it still leaves us in dark mystery," Lazelle said. " Why did My Lady and your Lord leave their possessions, and how is it there are many cloaks in the refectory and an untouched repast waiting on the table."

" Yes," Ughtred said, " and why isn't there a cross at the other side of the bridge, where the land is rising? "

" There was a cross when we came, I remember," said Lazelle. " No, *two* crosses, Brother Ughtred, and they were alike."

" One, at least, has gone now, Sister Lazelle," Ughtred muttered.

Some elusive memory was nagging at him, in which he vaguely felt that Brother Robert, the chronicler, was involved, but he could not pin it down.

" Of a surety it is not the wind," he wound up. " For it is much too heavy to be blown over."

As they walked back to the refectory, Lazelle dwelt on more practical considerations.

" Brother Ughtred," she said, " I think we should try to eat."

" Eat! " Ughtred considered. " Yes, I think I could eat a little, Sister Lazelle . . . yes, forsooth, I am sure I could."

" I also," said Lazelle. " And I am certain the food is good and without taint."

While Ughtred was at the offices on the floor above, she washed dishes and cups, drying them on a towel brought down from the lavatory. This work she did in the kitchen, where water flowed plentifully through a leaden channel, and off which she found a small store with victuals in it: beans, flour, and dried fruits. But when Ughtred came down he told her that this was nothing to wonder about, as the grange was always stocked to a small degree towards the end of summer, for the use of messengers, shepherds and others during severe winter storms.

They ate at the end of a long refectory table, and to begin with had scant appetite; but the bakemeats, which Ughtred thought came from the kitchen at Rievaulx, were very tasty with the sauces Lazelle had found beneath a napkin, so that very shortly they were eating, and drinking an excellent ale, with much more zest.

It was the first time they had sat at a table together, and both were restrained, not speaking at all freely until the meal ended, and Grace had been said.

"Brother Ughtred, what time do you think it is now?" Lazelle asked as she began to collect the dirty platters. "About the hour of Vespers?"

Ughtred stepped out of the door, to glance at the sky. "If not beyond, Sister Lazelle," he said.

"Was it last night we talked to Brother Jerome?"

"I fancy," said Ughtred, as he followed her into the kitchen, "that it must have been the night before, otherwise the mortar in the window and door would not be so bone hard."

"So we have stayed unknowing so long?"

She was busy at the stone sink and, his heart filled with tenderness, Ughtred looked at her. He was sure she was recovering from her ordeal, for her eyes were less inflamed and the fire in the blotches and eruptions was beginning to fade.

"So long, I think," he said. "And now, if you will give me leave, I had thought to walk as far as the stone cross which I cannot see, so that I can carefully spy out the land. While I am away will you not rest until my return, when we can talk about our plans, for it will be as well if we leave before daylight?"

This sensible suggestion had most revealing repercussions, for he learnt that she was in a state of strain far graver than he had supposed, and from then onwards he knew that for the next few days he must guard her to the utmost of his power.

"No, Brother Ughtred," she implored. "Please take me with you . . . the . . . the fresh air will do me good."

"So it shall be," Ughtred told her gently.

When the refectory had been tidied to her liking, they left the cloister by the chapter house, Ughtred holding her arm as they crossed the courtyard to the gatehouse. Beyond that, when walking to the bridge, there was another surprise, for farther up the river, clothing, and much of it, seemed to be scattered about. As it proved to be: men's clothing both secular and religious, from ordinary outer garments to snowy-white albs, from plain habits to underdrawers and hose; there were also a few purses with money in them, and a gorgeous vestment, with saints embroidered on it, which Ughtred recognised beyond any doubt as belonging to the lord abbot Hugh.

"It is out of my understanding, Brother Ughtred," Lazelle said

374

when returning along the bank. " A charade I cannot even guess at."

" Nor I," said Ughtred. " But I shall go there again, for I saw silver pennies and some groats and they will be of value to us on our journey northwards."

In the middle of the bridge he held her firmly as they edged past a yawning hole, and on the winding track which climbed to join the lonely moorland highway he assisted her along as much as possible. During the final rise to the cross he put his arm about her waist.

" The cross, it is there after all, Brother Ughtred," Lazelle cried out. " It has but fallen across the path."

Ughtred stared from the cross to the liquid in the square sump of a massive block of stone. He bent and, smelling ale, saw a few coins at the bottom. That was when he recollected.

" I have it now, Sister Lazelle," he said, snapping finger and thumb together after he had straightened sharply. " It comes back to me," he went on, awed astonishment in his expression. " The cross has been placed thus deliberately, and the other is also a sign to ward travellers away from a place in which there has been the Black Death. I saw it used in France, to turn wayfarers from a village."

Lazelle's lips parted. " We have had that ill pestilence, Brother Ughtred? And recovered? "

Glancing first round the moors, and still with his arm about her, Ughtred assisted her down the hill, back to the little monastery below, which the low rays of the evening sun was now shadowing.

" If we have had The Death, Sister Lazelle," he said, " it started soon after the last dose of medicine Friar Jerome gave us."

" Brother Jerome is your dear friend, and as God looks on us now I am certain he would never——" Lazelle began indignantly, but halted abruptly to turn a startled face to Ughtred. " Oh! " she gasped, as if a light had dawned.

" It could explain why they fled," Ughtred murmured. " We were to be purified by burning, but there is another purification acceptable to Holy Church—by water. It is another matter whether the learned doctors of physic believe water to be efficacious in cleansing those who have been in contact with the plague-stricken . . .

but Brother Jerome has an uncommon presence, and could so have persuaded."

" There is no denying they must have been in great terror," said Lazelle. " For how otherwise would they have taken off all their clothes, as they——" Her words died, as an incredible picture flashed into her mind, that of My Lady abroad when stark naked.

About then Ughtred sighted more clothing strewn about the bank of the river, beyond a bend higher up the stream than they had previously been. When the bridge had been crossed again, Lazelle, despite his entreaties, insisted upon accompanying him to them. This time the garments were exclusively women's, and amongst the shifts was a saffron-coloured wimple.

" It is My Lady's," Lazelle said. " And if it were not it would be dear Deborah's, who . . ." she smiled, " who loves clothes and fashion." Her eyes widened. " But what would Sister Deborah and so many other of my sisters, *and* My Lady, do when . . . when they had nothing on? "

" What would they all do, Sister Lazelle? " Ughtred said hurriedly. " For by my reckoning there must have been a goodly company in all."

Talking about this, but avoiding anything embarrassing, they sauntered up to the gate-house, and from there to the refectory, where Lazelle said they would be wise to eat again soon, if only a little.

" While you take stock of what we shall have, Sister Lazelle," Ughtred said, reluctantly releasing her, " I will strip the bed in the dormitory, and then fetch mantles as covers and for you to rest on snugly."

He had been joyously thinking that, in spite of her fatigue, she was rapidly improving and would soon look her sweet self. But now he had a shock, for she worsened before his eyes.

" Brother Ughtred," she said tremulously, " the dormitory could hold a score or more of beds, and I would be frightened to sleep in such an apartment by myself."

" But I cannot sleep there with you, Sister Lazelle," Ughtred blurted. " It would be sinful."

" Was it sinful on past nights when we were together? " Lazelle asked.

"That was different, Sister Lazelle," Ughtred urged. "We were under God's sky."

Lazelle shook her head. "What difference does a roof make, Brother Ughtred?" she said, continuing piteously: "Oh! I am craven, I know, but could we not remain in here, and make ourselves cosy on those benches?"

Ughtred tried to be well-balanced in his argument. "Sister Lazelle, you have undergone much, and that makes it all the more essential for you to have a sound night's sleep, against what is before us to-morrow. You would be in no case to start out after the discomfort of hours on a narrow bench."

Woebegone, Lazelle looked at him. "I would be in no case to start out after lying awake all night in that vast chamber," she said, shivering. "There . . . there may be evil spectres."

Neither of them spoke for several minutes, until Ughtred, the silence too oppressive for him, decided to gather kindling for a fire.

"I had thought, Sister Lazelle," he told her, his voice not wholly under control, "that I might mull some ale in the kitchen when the light has sufficiently failed for smoke not to be seen by any chance traveller."

"It is a good restorative, Brother Ughtred," Lazelle said in a whisper.

Ughtred not only collected kindling but, finding an axe, split a fair quantity of wood. He also made two trips to the river bank, returning with bundles large enough for all needs.

On re-entering the cloister, he found Lazelle busying herself between the kitchen and the refectory. Her mood had strikingly altered and she smiled at him in greeting, though was soon most serious.

"Brother Ughtred," she said, "I have been thinking that we are behaving as ordinary people who go to church only on feast days and the Sabbath. As yet we have never thanked the Lord for our deliverance."

"It was on my mind, too, as I came back the second time," Ughtred said. "So let us repair to the little church, and kneel together as we did once before at the altar."

Lazelle wiped her hands and, after pulling the hood of her mantle over her head, went with him along the east walk to the arched

377

entrance to the church. The door was stiff, jammed on a stick, as Ughtred found on using his shoulder, but the delay was trivial and within a few moments they were inside, walking towards the east end. A few paces from the simple stone steps leading to the sanctuary, both stopped simultaneously to stare at a small, circular wooden box standing on the High Altar. Near it were two wax tablets.

"Why are they there?" Lazelle said wonderingly. "It is sacrilege to use such a place for other than the sacred vessels, or ornaments and candlesticks which are suited. And though disused, I know from what My Lady once said that this is still holy ground."

"It is a day of strange happenings," Ughtred murmured. "By all the blessed saints, an extra riddle is of minor consequence."

He bowed thrice before treading in the sanctum, and then mounted the steps and crossed to the altar, where he picked up one of the tablets. There was writing on it.

Ughtred read a few words, made a muffled exclamation, and glanced at the end before turning an astonished face towards Lazelle.

"It is from Brother Jerome," he gasped. "He has written to us."

The tablets were not large, and the writing, of which there was much, of necessity minute. They pored over it together, against a window of the nave for better light.

"*If God has granted my prayer for your survival, and the maid's, dear Brother Ughtred, your own natures will bring you to this hallowed place long before a few suns can blur this message,*" the friar had scratched with his style. "*And if this is so the risk I have taken will not be a crime I must explain on the Day of Judgment.*

"*On this I shall dwell no more, save to tell you that I did not deem it prudent to arouse curiosity by remaining behind. Moreover, if you were dying, I could do nothing, whereas if you lived your recovery would be so swift that it would not be beyond you to break out of the cell, from whose closed entry I have furtively removed a course of stone.*

"*Think no more of this. Neither you nor Sister Lazelle should*

378

*pester your brains for an explanation, but accept with gladness and
humility that you have been spared.*

"*Three pills each every day. There are berries in the garden-
waste and apples of a sort in the orchard. Eat as much fruit as you
can, and drink to your fill of water.*

"*Remain here until strength is with you again. Be not alarmed
about molestation, for the fear of where The Death has lurked strikes
deep into every man, and for months none will dare approach this
grange.*

"*May the blessing of our Lord Jesus Christ be with you both
always, and if He, in His goodness and mercy, has granted me that
first prayer, then perhaps He will also look with kindness on a second,
that some day we shall meet again.*

"*To this I subscribe myself, your loving friend, the friar
Jerome.*"

Ughtred was blinking as he repeated the closing lines for Lazelle,
whose reading was not as quick as his own.

"How could anyone have a more loving friend, Sister Lazelle?"
he said.

Lazelle's eyes had filled with tears. "Dear Brother Jerome,"
she murmured. "How wondrous he has been to us."

"I . . . I know not why it should be, Sister Lazelle," Ughtred
said slowly, "but I truly believe we shall meet him again, be the
day distant or near."

Lazelle was trembling. "We!" she whispered. "You speak,
Brother Ughtred, as if we shall always be together."

Ughtred looked at her wonderingly. "So I did," he muttered.
"Never can it have been consciously in my thoughts, but ever since
we left the priory of Watton it must have been in my heart that
I could wish for no greater heaven on earth than to have you always
at my side."

Lazelle's lips quivered. "O Brother Ughtred," she said.

"But for that, we would have to be married . . . if that would
please you, Sister Lazelle?" Ughtred said gravely.

Blindly, she nodded. "It would please me, Brother Ughtred.
It . . . it would be bliss, the sweetest bliss."

Ughtred fingered his beard. "But no clerk in Holy Orders

would dare join two heretics, Sister Lazelle, for he would be excommunicated himself—and even if we hid that it were so from my honoured father and beloved mother——"

Lazelle made a tiny gesture of dissent. " I would not care to start our life together with a lie," she said.

" Nor I," said Ughtred.

He took her arm and, thinking about their problem, they walked up and down the church. At the third turn, Lazelle restrained him.

" Brother Ughtred," she said, her breath catching, " could we not ourselves wed each other in the sight of the Lord, kneeling at the altar before Him? He would understand."

Within a few moments Ughtred let out a great shout, and there would have been a second if she had not put her hand over his mouth.

" Brother Ughtred! " she exclaimed, far from scoldingly. " More of that and they would hear at your pestilential abbey of Rievaulx."

" It shall be so, and within the hour, Sister Lazelle," Ughtred roared joyously. " And far better it be than by one of those snivelling clerics it has been my sorry lot to come against and to hear since I was back from Burgundy. And listen, Sister Lazelle."

" Yes," Lazelle said radiantly.

" I have much to do before we plight ourselves before the Lord," Ughtred said, rubbing his hands. " I have the altar to clean and other important matters to attend to, so you must be gracious enough to excuse me."

" I also have affairs, Brother Ughtred," Lazelle said gaily. " For when we come out of church there must be a feast for us on the table, when we shall have call for your mulled ale."

" Let us to our separate concerns," Ughtred said excitedly.

From then he had a hectic period, beginning by tearing a garment into pieces to use for cloths to remove dust and dirt from the sanctuary and its approach. Next, rummaging in the store-place off the kitchen, he found a few candles and, with tinder and flint, returned to the church and lighted up the altar. Then he laid a fire in the kitchen, and later spent several minutes cogitating in a room adjoining. As a result of these deliberations he went up to the

dormitory, where he dragged the palliasse off the bed; one outcome was that Lazelle, hearing a terrific crash, subsequently ran out
in alarm. She found the bed at the foot of the outside staircase,
and Ughtred picking himself up from the ground.

He was winded. " While we are here, Sister Lazelle, which
may well be for some days in the circumstances," he wheezed,
" we are to have a house of our own. There is a chamber next to
the kitchen, and . . ."

Lazelle blushed vividly. " It will be . . . be much nicer than . . .
than that monstrous dormitory," she said, almost inaudibly.

Furious with himself, Ughtred wished he had been less clumsy.
" I ask your forgiveness, Sister Lazelle," he said humbly. " I
should have talked with you first."

To him, it was remarkably unexpected that she smiled at him, if
shyly.

" More than once, Brother Ughtred, I have told you that I
thought you were changing," she said. " And when I have done
so I have also told you I liked it much."

Ughtred stared. " I don't understand, Sister Lazelle."

Her smile persisted. " Perhaps it may be that some day I will
explain, Brother Ughtred," she said.

Although Ughtred had not troubled with the canopy, the bed
was as stupid about entering its new quarters as it had been
obstinate about removal from the dormitory, and so when at last
he left the chamber, the bed by then more happily reconciled,
Lazelle was no longer in the kitchen. As he went outside into the
cloister she was descending the stairs from the dormitory above.
Her head was covered with the saffron-coloured wimple he had
brought back from the river bank and, tongue-tied, he thought how
sweet she was.

" I am ready, Brother Ughtred," she said.

" I must wash myself also, Sister Lazelle," he said confusedly.

Ughtred raced up the outer steps and ran through the dormitory
to the lavatory, which proved by his shortness of breath that he was
still weak. Then he stripped and washed himself as well as he could
in clear-flowing, chill water. His drying was more perfunctory
than thorough, and as soon as he was dressed he hurried down again.
Lazelle was sitting in the refectory, and he held out his hand to her.

" Come, Sister Lazelle," he said, choked by emotion.

" Yes, Brother Ughtred," she said softly.

Together, hand in hand and hearts thumping, they walked round the cloister, each speaking once only—when Ughtred said that from the morrow they must not use either the west or the south walks, which could be seen for a short distance along the moorland highway, she replying that she would remember. But Lazelle turned shining eyes to him as they entered the church, when she saw candles burning on the altar.

They knelt at the foot of the sanctuary steps, on cloaks Ughtred had arranged. Then they looked at each other.

" You start, Brother Ughtred," Lazelle whispered.

Ughtred nodded and, putting his hands together in prayer, began to speak to his Maker.

" Lord Jesus Christ and Saviour, before I come to the second business that brings us here, I want to thank you for your loving kindness to myself and the maid Lazelle, who is beside me. Had it not been for your protecting arms, O Lord, we would have perished at the stake in great pain; and if we had not had your sure shield guarding us, we would have been dead or have been dying by now, of suffocation or starvation, in this place. For granting us our lives, Almighty God, we humbly thank you."

" We thank you also, Blessed Redeemer, for sheltering us in our travels," said Lazelle. " And we offer our homage to you in all ways, O Lord and King."

She glanced at Ughtred, who again nodded to her.

" O Lord God, Ruler of all mankind," he began, " we are here, the maid Lazelle and I, to join ourselves in the bond of holy matrimony, and for that reason, as matrimony is a solemn ceremony of Holy Church, I must strive to present ourselves fittingly and properly, though all I shall say will be well known to you, O Lord. I shall now start, Lord and Master.

" I, Ughtred of Monkseaton, do herewith declare before you, O My Lord, that I now take the maid Lazelle as my wedded wife, and I do swear by all that is holy that I will cherish her preciously to the end of my days on earth. And, O Saviour, as evidence before you that she has now become my wife, I take her hand into my own. Bless us, we plead, and——"

Lazelle leaned towards him, and he leaned towards her. A few words passed between them, and once more Ughtred nodded, before looking to his front again.

" O Lord," he continued, " I had forgot that there must be two sides to make a contract, and so the maid Lazelle, who is not as yet a wife, will now pledge herself to me for all the years ahead."

This time it was Lazelle's turn to give a little nod, when he turned to her.

" O Blessed Redeemer," she began, very clearly, " Ughtred of Monkseaton now having taken the hand which I so gladly entrusted to him, I, the maid Lazelle, of birthplace unknown, here vow before you that I accept him as my honoured husband, whom I will love and obey until the earthly light in my eyes shall be dimmed forever. So bless us, O Saviour, and let the light of your countenance, the eternal light which shall never dim, shine on us always."

" So let it, O Lord," Ughtred said fervently.

For several minutes longer, with heads bowed, they remained on their knees before the altar, pouring out their prayers of thanksgiving.

After rising, Ughtred blew out his breath. " I would not care to be wedded every day, Sister Lazelle," he said.

Lazelle laughed. " *Wife* Lazelle," she said.

" Wife! *My* wife," Ughtred muttered.

Both dazed by the wonder of it all, they puffed out the candles on the holy table before leaving the church for the north walk. The day was coming to an end; the starkly-cut high line of the hills was showing against a darkening sky, and soon it would be twilight.

Near the chapter house, Ughtred paused, and Lazelle, in whose pretty face the blemishes were fast disappearing, glanced inquiringly at him, a young man with a worn and sensitive face.

" What is it, dear Ughtred? " she asked fondly.

Ughtred spoke as if speaking of a miracle: " Yes, I am your husband, and you are my beloved wife," he said.

For several seconds, beyond speech, they stared solemnly at each other, before instinctively drawing together. Then, their expressions joyous, they turned towards the refectory, to eat their wedding feast.